MANDI MAY

Minnie Maple

C. Edward Press llc

First published by C. Edward Press LLC 2023

Copyright © 2023 by Mandi May

All rights reserved. No part of this publication may be reproduced, stored or transmitted in any form or by any means, electronic, mechanical, photocopying, recording, scanning, or otherwise without written permission from the publisher. It is illegal to copy this book, post it to a website, or distribute it by any other means without permission.

This novel is entirely a work of fiction. The names, characters and incidents portrayed in it are the work of the author's imagination. Any resemblance to actual persons, living or dead, events or localities is entirely coincidental.

First edition

ISBN: 979-8-9885776-1-4

This book was professionally typeset on Reedsy. Find out more at reedsy.com

To everyone who feels like they need a pen name

Contents

Chapter 1	1
Chapter 2	13
Chapter 3	19
Chapter 4	25
Chapter 5	31
Chapter 6	43
Chapter 7	47
Chapter 8	55
Chapter 9	60
Chapter 10	74
Chapter 11	79
Chapter 12	83
Chapter 13	92
Chapter 14	97
Chapter 15	102
Chapter 16	109
Chapter 17	114
Chapter 18	121
Chapter 19	128
Chapter 20	134
Chapter 21	140
Chapter 22	145
Chapter 23	153
Chapter 24	162

Chapter 25	166
Chapter 26	172
Chapter 27	177
Chapter 28	185
Chapter 29	192
Chapter 30	203
Chapter 31	212
Chapter 32	219
Chapter 33	226
Chapter 34	237
Chapter 35	247
Chapter 36	253
Chapter 37	260
Chapter 38	271
Chapter 39	278
Chapter 40	289
Chapter 41	296
Chapter 42	302
Chapter 43	314
Chapter 44	322
Chapter 45	327
Chapter 46	331
Chapter 47	337
Chapter 48	341
Chapter 49	351
Epilogue	360

Chapter 1

Mary-Beth Caroline Abernathy
Sinner

I, Mary-Beth Caroline Abernathy, am a sinner.

Now, don't get me wrong, I'm not *that* type of sinner. I'm actually a very good person...most of the time.

I always go to church, and although I'm not the most faithful believer, I've read the entire Good Book, *including* the Old Testament. I graduated from a Christian college and got a job teaching kindergarten in the town I grew up in. Good old Daisy Bluff, Indiana, the last town before you hit Kentucky. I live on my own, but I still make it to family dinner every Sunday night and to visit my grandmother in the nursing home once a month.

I've been known to have a drink occasionally, though I've rarely been drunk. Hardly ever *drunk* drunk. I'm generous and kind—I even gave a homeless man my sandwich once, and I always drop at least a paper bill into the plate and not coins. And although I'm well versed in what the bases are, I've been standing squarely on second base ever since Sutton Heard, my high school boyfriend, put one hand under my bra and another down my pants senior year.

But sometimes...I have urges, usually involving Drew Coyne. And those urges need to be released.

The worn blanket is scratchy against my skin as I readjust my weight on the desk chair, tucking one foot under me. I'm surprised I can't see my breath with how cold it is in my drab one-bedroom apartment, but I turned down the heat to lower my gas bill. At least the heat in my house still works; it's completely broken in my poor little Kia. Along with the air conditioner, the suspension, the radiator, and a myriad of other things.

I stuff a handful of peanut butter M&Ms in my mouth, crack my knuckles, and squint at the bright screen. After seven straight hours, it's hard not to let the words blur. I take a deep breath, listening to the rain pattering outside, then let my fingers and imagination take over.

He slid his hand under her dress, pausing at the apex of her thighs, I type, smiling as I bite my lower lip. *She moaned and leaned into him, dragging her lips against his jaw. He skimmed her wet lace undergarments, growling in approval.*

There's a knock at the front door, and my body tenses all the way from my feet to my typing fingers. I accidentally slam my pinky finger inside when I snap my laptop closed.

"Mary-Beth, are you home?"

I relax a little when I hear my best friend Harper's voice, sighing as I slump into my chair. I grab another handful of peanut butter M&Ms and quickly shove my laptop under a stack of papers.

"Coming!" I holler through my chewing, running to the front door. Catching sight of my reflection, I pause to fix my hair and wipe the guilty look off my face.

Harper catapults herself into my arms as soon as I turn the knob, collapsing into a sobbing heap of limbs.

"Hey, Harp." I pat her hair. "What's wrong?"

"I tried calling," she manages to get out amongst her blubbering. She looks up at me through mascara-blurred eyes. "Why didn't you

CHAPTER 1

answer?"

Guilt crashes into me next.

I didn't answer because I put my phone away whenever I write. Along with locking all the doors, pulling all the blinds, and covering all the pictures of my mama, Nana, and Jesus. Oh, and let's not forget my daddy, Pastor Clark Abernathy.

I stretch my arms above my head, pretending to suddenly be tired. "Oh, sorry," I say through a fake yawn. "I was, uh, in bed."

"At seven o'clock?" Harper's tears pause long enough for her forehead to wrinkle.

"Yeah, uh, up super late last night." I rub my eyes. "Uh, grading papers."

"Kindergarten papers? On a Friday night? During Christmas break?"

"Yeah, uh, their handwriting can be super hard to read." I shake my head. "But hey, what's wrong?"

"Jake Ursley dumped me!" Harper bursts into tears again.

"Jake? Jake *Ursley*?" My nose crinkles, and Harper nods timidly. "You've been seeing Jake Ursley, like used to play dungeons and dragons in the back of the cafeteria, Jake Ursley?"

"Not my finest moment," she admits with a sniffle. "Drown my sorrows with me?" She sticks out her bottom lip and unveils a large bottle of vodka sticking out of her purse.

Harper Elizabeth Watkins is also a sinner, but in more of the traditional sense. She hasn't gone to church since her dad left when she was five, and I don't think she's ever made it past Genesis. Her grandma sent her to a Christian school in an attempt to save her, but I think it somehow had the opposite effect. She is an amazing hair stylist specializing in icy blonds and prom updos, but really just loves to spill the town's best tea. When it comes to baseball, she's hit more home runs than I can keep track of, and when it comes to her family, she'd rather pretend they don't exist.

Her rainbow hair and voluptuous curves are the ultimate contrast to my straight brown hair and even straighter body. And her candor perfectly complements my meekness. We've been best friends since she told Tomas O'Reilly to eat worms on the kindergarten playground after he pushed me down and I skinned my knee.

Every single time I've gotten *drunk* drunk it's been because Harper convinced me to just do *one* shot. Every time I've worn a skirt too short or a shirt too low and ended up with questionable company trying to take me home, it was because I was borrowing something of hers. Every time I've watched a movie too raunchy or said a word too four-lettered or told a lie any color other than white, I was with Harper.

She also kicked Sutton Heard in the groin for dumping me when I wouldn't put out. And stayed up crying with me all night when my cat, Minnie, got hit by a car. She does my hair for free because I can't afford her otherwise and will drop everything when I need her.

She's the Shawn Hunter to my Cory Matthews. The Ferris Buller to my Cameron Frye. The Rizzo to my Sandy. I think every good girl needs a rebellious best friend they can live vicariously through. And I couldn't love mine more.

"Oh, Harp." I pull her into a tight hug and lead her into my tiny apartment. "Of course. But you're going to have to mix that into something if you want me to drink it."

Harper wipes away the black mascara spiderwebs crawling down her cheeks and gives me a weak smile.

"Oh, don't worry, MB. I brought some cranberry juice just for you." She steps inside my little apartment and shivers, rubbing her arms. "Good lord, Mary-Beth, turn on the heat. It's just as cold in here as outside."

I begrudgingly raise the thermostat three degrees on my way to the kitchen. I grab a half-eaten gallon of ice cream and two spoons, while Harper pours two large glasses of cranberry juice. Into mine, she puts

CHAPTER 1

a splash of vodka, and into hers, well...more.

"So, tell me—" I take a small sip and the fiery liquid forces a choke from the back of my throat. I think that splash was actually more wave. I swallow hard and try again. "What happened?"

Harper chugs a few gulps of her drink, her mouth only puckering slightly. She pushes her long rainbow hair out of her eyes with the back of her hand. "Well, I didn't want to tell you because, well, *Jake Ursley*, but at first things were really great..."

Harper proceeds to dive into the details of her and Jake Ursley's whirlwind romance. How they ran into each other at a bar two towns over. How he seemed so much cooler than he did in high school. How his new beard hid his acne scars. How he sent flowers to the salon the day after their first date. How the sex was fascinating, but not in a bad way—her words, not mine. How after two weeks of being loosely exclusive—again, her words—she saw him out with another girl at a Chili's Christmas happy hour. How she'd thrown a drink at them and caused a scene in the middle of a little kid's birthday party.

Which led us here, curled up on my couch, two very strong Bay Breeze's, half a bottle of red wine Harper found in the back of my pantry, and a gallon of Blue Bell later, watching our favorite Hallmark movie.

"Lord, why can't every guy be like Drew Coyne?" Harper asks, staring dreamily at the screen and taking a swig of wine.

"Because this isn't heaven."

Unlike the rest of humanity, Drew Coyne isn't a sinner. In fact, save Jesus Himself, I'm sure there's never been a more perfect man. He's tall and dark with a jaw that could tame a wild horse, eyes so blue they could seduce a mermaid, and skin so brown and smooth, you'd want to run your hands across it like a fine leather-bound book.

He's a mixture of boy next door, meets misunderstood bad boy, meets lumberjack, meets prince in disguise, meets city boy moves to the country, meets struggling bar owner, meets washed up football star, meets small town weatherman. Which is only a fraction of the roles he's played.

In tonight's made-for-TV of choice, *A Royal Duet*, he's a pianist with a past, hired by the queen of some tiny country to teach her unruly daughter how to play the piano for some royal duty. It's our favorite because there's nothing like watching that man tickle the ivories. I think he actually plays, but Harper isn't convinced.

Off-screen, he's just as kind, talented, humble, and personable. Always posting shirtless workout videos, but in a tasteful way, not a sleezy way. Always talking graciously about his female costars and making sure they get equal pay in his movies. Always promoting his environmentally-conscious brand of hammocks and hiking boots. Always snuggling with his equally adorable rescue dog, Maggie. Always seen putting away his own grocery cart—really! I read that in a magazine. Always answering his fans' tweets. He even liked one of Harper's tweets once.

I'm pretty sure the reason I'm still single is because of my obsession with Drew Coyne. Well, that and my aforementioned virginity. He's my celebrity crush. My dream man. My infatuation. My muse. No matter how many dates I go on, no one compares to him.

Harper snores loudly next to me, the wine bottle drooping in the crook of her elbow, about to spill.

"Okay, Harp." I untangle myself and carefully place the wine on the end table. "Time for bed."

Harper mutters something before standing and stumbling down the hallway to my room. Even eighty-five percent asleep, she still manages to grab the wine.

After finishing my fifteen-step nighttime skin routine and brushing my teeth, I make my way down the hall to my room, looking forward to sleep. I can already feel tomorrow's hangover.

CHAPTER 1

"Mary-Beth Caroline Abernathy, what in the world is *this*?" Harper is standing in the doorway, my laptop in hand, looking suddenly very awake and very interested in my very embarrassing, very incriminating, very *secret* hobby.

I put a horrified hand to my mouth, leaping across the room as I reach for the computer. "I thought I closed that!"

"Oh, I can assure you it was very much open and very much about to fall off your desk," Harper says, stepping out of reach. "*He dropped his trousers, and his arousal sprung free,*" she reads, and now I nearly fall over myself trying to wrangle the computer away. She pounces to the back of the room, and keeps reading, her delighted smile growing wider. "*And I could no longer control the sounds coming from the back of my throat. Yearning and physical attraction took over from there, the pulse between my legs too urgent to ignore.*"

I go for another snatch at the laptop, but Harper escapes again, jumping onto my bed. Bouncing, she keeps reading: "*His shaking fingers found their way into my corset, untying it slowly. When my undergarments fell to the floor, I clung to his broad shoulders, feeling the warmth growing against my skin.*"

Hearing my writing out loud makes ants crawl across my picnic-blanket skin. If I don't get that computer away from her soon, start digging, because I'm going to die of embarrassment. Tears prick as I make one final attempt to make this torture stop, jumping onto the bed with her.

Harper finally stops and slumps to her knees. I scramble over and grab my computer just before it topples out of her arms, slamming it shut. I turn away from her, hiding the laptop and my tears in shame.

"MB, did you write that?" Her voice is noticeably softer.

"Uh, well... You see..." I panic, not wanting to admit, but not knowing what else to do.

I stand and trip over the corner of my bed. The fact that I'm one swallow away from *drunk* drunk probably isn't helping this situation.

"Mary-Beth, this is really good." Harper comes to stand next to me, wrapping a supportive arm around my shoulders. "Why didn't you tell me you were a writer?"

I shudder at the word *writer*. "Because I'm not. I just...um... I do it for fun."

"Uh, as someone who loves to read smut as much as the next girl" – Harper raises her right hand as if she's making some sort of oath – "I can tell you without any hesitation that, girl, you most certainly are a writer. And a damn good one at that."

My face convulses. "Really?"

Harper grabs the laptop from me, opening it up to the most recent Word document. It takes every single ounce of control I have not to swat her hand and scream for her to stop. Scrolling slowly, Harper's mouth falls more and more open. I can barely look at her, focusing instead on the bottle of wine on my bedside table, contemplating guzzling the rest.

"Uh, Mary-Beth, this looks like an enemies-to-lovers, holy grail of book boyfriends, playful banter, heaving bosoms, steamy goodness, Regency-era bodice-ripper to me." Her eyes dart up to mine, and I swallow nervously. "Where did you learn this? Soaked cradle of femininity? Quivering manhood? Undulating? Sheathing? I didn't know you knew half of this!"

"Well, I have been best friends with you for almost twenty years." I huff, carefully taking the laptop back. I shove it under my bed as far as it will go. "But it's just for fun. Just when I like...am feeling creative."

"When you're feeling *something*." Harper shimmies. She leads me to the bed and places her hand on mine. "MB, you should publish this. You could make some extra cash. I just read that some lady makes like over a hundred thousand dollars a month self-publishing romance novels. It's like a billion-dollar industry. You could fix your piece-of-

CHAPTER 1

shit car, turn the heat up to fifty-five degrees, and start living above the poverty line."

"My car isn't that bad," I mutter, but Harper's eyebrows rise. I sigh and look away. "Okay, it's bad."

"Women lose their shit for these kinds of books, MB," Harper says encouragingly. "For when their man isn't cutting it in the bedroom. Or when there's no man at all." She winks, then recognition dawns. "Oh my gosh, is *that* why you've been writing these?"

"No!" I cry out, shocked she would ever assume that about *me*.

"I mean, women have needs. If you want, I can teach you—"

"I think I'm good, thanks."

"True. I mean, clearly you know enough." Harper laughs, nodding at the computer under my bed. It feels like a monster that might reach out and accost me at any moment.

I shake my head. "There's no way." I frown. "What would my mother say? Or my dad? And the people at church... I could never."

"Pen names are a thing for a reason, MB."

Harper hops off the bed and wiggles on her belly until she finds my laptop. She sits, patting the comforter to invite me to listen to a dirty bedtime story, and I hesitantly climb in. The screen glows against her blotchy, tear-stained face and rainbow hair like she's some sort of mad scientist.

Now, I do grab the wine and take two deep swallows. Here comes *drunk* drunk. I'm gonna need it.

"Holy cow, woman, how many books have you written?" Harper asks, scrolling through my long list of Word documents.

"Just, like, a few...series," I say sheepishly.

"A few *series*?" Harper looks up from the screen, and her ponytail whacks me in the face. I lick at the pink and purple strands, trying to get them out of my mouth. Harper readjusts so we're sitting face to face and blinks one time, hard. "You're telling me you've written a few *series*? As in, like, multiple books?"

"Just like... maybe three series," I say under my breath. I pick at the worn threads on my oversized pajama pants, the ones with the hole in the thigh. "With five books each."

Now Harper's eyes look like they might actually pop out of her head. "*What?* You've written *fourteen* books?"

I laugh. "That's fifteen, Harp."

"*Fifteen* books?"

"It's my...outlet." I take another pull of the wine. "It's my hobby. Some people knit. Some people paint or like play an instrument. I like to write."

A deadpan expression settles on Harper's face like a dead slug. "Nobody knits, MB."

"Some people do," I insist, my eyes pleading. "They like, you know, sell stuff on Etsy."

"Well, it's time you sold your shit on Etsy. Or Amazon, or Barnes and Noble, or wherever the hell people sell books." Harper turns to me with a girl-on-a-mission-look. "So, Mary-Beth, which book is your favorite?"

"The *Swallow Manor* series, for sure," I say, finally cracking a smile. That series was my first, the one I've spent the most time on, edited for years. The one I could probably recite in my sleep.

"Shit, Mary-Beth! You wrote a Regency romance with the word *swallow* in the title? This is gold!"

"It's a *bird*, Harp."

Harper's eyes grow into little slits as she nods and pats my hand. "Sure, it is, MB. Sure, it is."

🐦🐦🐦

What comes after *drunk* drunk? Because I'm there.

"Okay, okay, key words," Harper says as we both squint over the computer screen. I've joined the mad scientist club, and I'm not

CHAPTER 1

mad about it. I don't know why I never considered publishing before. Amazon makes it so easy.

"Uh, what did you say earlier?" I close my eyes, willing my brain to work. "Enemies to lovers?"

"Oh, yes, yes. And I think I said something like *steamy goodness*. And *heaving bosoms*."

"Ooh, yeah. That's really good. Put that."

"And *holy grail of book boyfriends*. And gotta put *sexy* in there, of course."

"Put fine piece of a—"

"Oh shit, MB? Where you just about to cuss?"

"I mean, it's really the only way to describe Captain Ambrose Archibald Fitzwillliam IV. I mean, for accuracy purposes, we need to put it."

"That name is freaking poetry, woman. I love it."

I smile over at Harper, barely seeing her through my squinty eyes. "It's good, right?"

"A work of art."

"He's basically just Drew Coyne, but like, in the 1700s. He needed a name just as glorious."

"Dream Coyne. Let's put him as a key word."

"*Dream* Coyne?" I giggle.

"Drew. I meant Drew."

"Dream works too."

When the keywords section won't let us type anymore words, we move on.

"Okay, it's asking for your author name."

"Something as far away from Mary-Beth Caroline Abernathy as possible." I grab Harper's face and bring my forehead to hers. I need her to understand this. Her puckered lips and squished cheeks look at me with urgency. "This can never ever ever ever never"—I pause and blink—"*ever* be traced back to me. Never."

"Girl, it never will." Harper squeezes my hand supportively. "I would never let that happen to you."

I throw my hands around Harper's neck. "I know," I say into her shirt. "You're the best. When I'm rich, I'm taking you to the Red Lobster."

"Girl, you know how much I love endless shrimp!"

"All the shrimp!" I put my hands in the air. "Just for you. Like, they're going to need to bring in a whole new truck of them, we're gonna eat so much."

"Shrimp for everyone!" Harper shouts, and I giggle. Then, she raises her eyebrows. "But like, you still need a name."

"Jane Smith," I say flatly. Harper rolls her eyes. "There's got to be so many of them, they'll never find me."

"No, no, no, no!" She punches the pillow next to her. "This is a *romance* novel, dammit! You need a romantic sounding name. What about... What's your stripper name?"

"Geez, Harp. I write romance novels. I don't strip!"

"Ugh, you know, it's like the combination of your first pet and the street you grew up on. Didn't you ever take that quiz on the internet?"

"Oh. Well..." My eyes turn downcast. "You remember my cat, Minnie."

"May she rest in peace." Harper does the sign of the cross, but I'm pretty sure she does it in the wrong order.

"And, uh, you know I grew up on Maple Avenue. So, I guess it would be Minnie Maple."

Harper raises a triumphant fist.

"Now there's a pen name for a romance author!"

Chapter 2

4 Months Later

Mary-Beth Caroline Abernathy
Itchy

It was a very warm winter. Well, at least for me. I kept that thermostat set at a gluttonous seventy-two degrees and didn't bat an eyelash.

However, such indulgence comes with consequences.

I have a big problem. A sublime, petrifying, shameful, *very big* problem. At first, I was in denial. But the morning I woke up and had made five thousand dollars on *Swallow Manor* overnight, I couldn't dispute the evidence any longer.

I have a wonderful, horrible problem.

And so...I've taken up knitting.

Every scandal needs a front business, right?

Unfortunately, this new "hobby" has created two additional very big problems. First, I suck at knitting. And now my mother and all her friends are expecting scarves and hats come October. Scarfs and hats I will most certainly be pretending to knit and then buying from an actual knitter on Etsy. And second, I've learned I'm allergic to wool. And that devil's yarn has been making every orifice of my body itchy.

I tried to switch to synthetic yarn, but the wool fibers are hardy and still cling to every surface of my apartment.

Harper keeps telling me I should just move. Into someplace bigger. Better. Fancier. One of those apartment complexes with a swimming pool and gate. Or heck, even buy a house. I could pay for a pretty decent house in *cash*.

Yes, cash.

Because, as if visited by the independent publishing fairy godmother herself, I've turned into the woman who makes six figures a month selling romance novels to sexually despondent – or maybe it's *dynamic?* – women. Like, for reals.

But I can't buy a house. Because no one makes that much money knitting.

I still can't figure out exactly how this all happened. I published those books while I was intoxicated past the point of *drunk* drunk, in the middle of the night, with covers that Harper and I made on Kindle Select with stock photos, a blurb that reads like a drunken text message, and key words that might as well have been alphabet soup.

I'm a disgrace to actual writers, truly. Some people work their entire lives and don't have this level of success. They eat and sleep and sweat words. Poetry drips from their fingertips. They edit and market and post Instagram pictures and perform TikTok dances and would literally do anything for someone to buy their book for ninety-nine cents, read it, love it, and maybe even write a review. They'd take four stars and say, "Thank you, ma'am. Can I have another?"

And here I am, someone who can't physically utter the words, "I am an author," who has accidentally been gifted the honor of best-seller and can't even say I'm all that happy about it.

Well, I take that back.

Mary-Beth Caroline Abernathy is a sinner and a kindergarten teacher who still drives a broken-down Kia and is currently scratching a rash she got from pretending to knit.

Minnie Maple is a bestselling author.

"Yeah, we are gonna start with the shrimp scampi and the popcorn shrimp." Harper hands the baby-faced server, Keaton, her menu. "But you can just like, keep them coming, if you know what I mean." She winks and takes a sip of her wine.

Waiting until he's out of earshot, I lean forward, taking a bite of my cheddar bay biscuit. "Harper, he's too young for you."

She sighs, stuffing a piece of biscuit into her cheek. "Probably. But it would be fun, don't you think? To sleep with a barely legal teenager?"

"Didn't you sleep with enough teenagers when you *were* a teenager?"

"True. But I think it would be different now that I'm more experienced. I could teach them, instead of the blind leading the blind like it was when we were in high school. Hey...maybe you could write about that in your next book!"

Harper's voice lowers an octave, and she sticks out her ample chest. "A rich, sexually mature widow takes a young, strapping squire under her wing and helps him become a man." She swallows her biscuit and immediately takes another bite, waving the half-eaten bread at me. "I'd read that."

"The series I'm coming out with next month has a secondary storyline kind of like that in the last book, actually."

"You're finally gonna publish the next series?" Harper's eyes light up. "Mary-Beth, that's fantastic! The world *needs* more from Minnie Maple."

"Don't say that so loud." My eyes dart around the outdated, nautical-themed restaurant, mostly empty on a Wednesday afternoon.

Harper rolls her eyes and downs another biscuit.

"But yes." I fold my arms across the table. "This time I'm hiring a professional cover designer and having it properly edited. The editor I chose only had one slot open for the next six months, and I snagged it. The books still need some work, but luckily, I don't have to give them the final draft for another four weeks. If I'm going to publish again, I want it to at least be a representation of the best I can do. I've already sold my soul to the devil; I might as well go all in."

"I still can't believe those books went viral. I think people were, like, 'Wow, that book looks like such a dumpster fire, I can't *not* read it.' But then, you, like, blow their knickers off because it's so damn good. Did you see the new TikTok video about Ambrose that's trending today?"

"Harper, you know I don't have TikTok. The closest thing I have to TikTok is ClassDojo so I can send videos of my kindergartners to their parents." I toe the worn carpet underneath the table.

"You know Dream Coyne has TikTok, right?" she says in a sing-song voice.

"Drew has TikTok?" I sit up in my chair. "Since when does Drew have TikTok?"

"It's new." She smiles.

And suddenly, I've become very interested in getting TikTok.

The first round of shrimp arrives. Harper grabs a tiny popcorn shrimp in between her index finger and thumb and gestures for me to do the same. Then she whacks her shrimp against mine like it's some sort of tiny teacup.

"To *Swallow Manor*!"

I mutter, "To *Swallow Manor*," under my breath and begrudgingly tap my shrimp against hers before popping it into my mouth.

"Hey, my mom loves those books!" Keaton says, and I immediately start choking on the miniature crustacean and reach for my water.

I chug, shooting daggers at Harper.

"We love them too," she says sweetly, smiling up at Keaton. "Some of our favorite books."

"My mom is really hoping they turn it into a movie. Something

CHAPTER 2

about wanting to see Ambrose on the big screen."

"That would be amazing." Harper turns to me. "Mary-Beth, wouldn't that be amazing?"

"Amazing," I rasp with a heavy dose of eye roll.

"Can I get you ladies anything else?"

"Yes, let's do the teriyaki shrimp skewers and the shrimp alfredo next, thanks."

"Sure thing."

"And more biscuits," I add, reaching for the last one. Since the shrimp are trying to assassinate me, I'll drown my anxiety in shortening, flour, and cheese instead.

"I'm on it."

"See? Everyone loves your books, MB," Harper says when Keaton and his mother's literary tastes are gone. "Doesn't that make you feel good?"

"Not really. It mostly just makes me feel anxious."

"Well, there's less of a chance someone will find out if you just play it cool instead of freaking out every time someone mentions it."

"You're righ—"

"Not that anyone is going to find out. You're literally the last person on earth anyone would suspect. I think someone could broadcast it and still no one would believe it."

"Okay, got it."

"Like, you shouldn't worry at all. I could shout, 'This girl wrote that book' right now and—"

"Okay, Harp, *I got it*!" I reach over the table to try and pinch Harper's mouth closed.

She laughs and puts her hands up innocently. "Sorry, MB. I just don't want you to worry."

"That's okay." I sigh and cautiously pick up a shrimp. "So...you said there was a dance on TikTok about it?"

"Oh, yeah, let me show you."

Harper pulls out her bedazzled phone case and opens the app. Typing the hashtag #OAmbroseMyAmbrose brings up a seemingly infinite number of videos.

Teenage girls dancing with my books. Grandmas with silver hair. Men wearing captains' hats. At schools. On beaches. In bedrooms and classrooms. There's even a video of a dozen nurses and doctors dancing down a hospital hallway.

I scroll. And scroll. And scroll. And the longer I scroll, the more my heart lurches against my rib cage. It's pressing so hard, I might need surgery to repair the damage.

"Oh, no..." I groan.

This is the same feeling as the day I woke up to that five-thousand-dollar surprise. Like this is a runaway train that can't be stopped.

I shove the phone back at Harper like it's a bomb about to explode. "Put it away." I fan myself with my napkin. "I can't bear to look anymore."

"Oh, Mary-Beth, calm down. Like I said, I could literally go around telling people you're the auth—"

"Shrimp teriyaki, shrimp alfredo, and more biscuits." Keaton sets the new dishes onto our already full table.

I put my bread plate on top of my empty entrée and salad plates to make room, glaring over top the dish tower at Harper. She smiles sheepishly back at me.

When Keaton leaves again, Harper grabs one of the teriyaki skewers and whispers, "I promise, Mary-Beth, no one will find out." She pretends to lock her lips and throw away the key, then fishes one of the glazed shrimps off the stick with her teeth. "You're going viral! Enjoy it!"

Chapter 3

Andrew Edward Coyne
Lighthouse Keeper

"A lighthouse keeper who falls for his grandmother's caretaker?" I throw the script onto the table, looking out the window of my Los Angeles apartment. "What is this shit they keep sending me?"

I fist the nearest tumbler, quickly fill it three-quarters with ice and then whiskey and take a long sip. Then another. Looking at Will, my agent and best friend, I accusatorily wave the glass at him. "I don't pay you to send me this."

"No..." Will adjusts his glasses, trying his best to sort the shuffled papers. I put the glass down and help him. "But you do pay me to make you famous, and I think I've done a pretty bang-up job of that."

"You have. Thank you. But now I'm a fucking slave to the Hallmark brand. How many movies did we do last year? Three, or was it four?" I rub my already pounding head and grab my glass. I try to take another sip but only find ice. I chew on a piece, crunching loudly.

"Three, but you started filming *Second Chance Romance* in December."

"And now I can't book any other gigs. It's like, I'll just make these movies until the day I die. I'll never escape."

"You say that like it's a bad thing."

"It *is* a bad thing." I stride across the wide living room, motioning to no one and nothing in particular. "I want to do something different, something edgy. Something sexy and raw, and not rated PG. I'm twenty-eight years old, dammit, it's time for a challenge, you know? There's a void in my life, and these Hallmark movies aren't fucking filling it."

I pour Will a glass, and he lets out a long sigh before cautiously taking a sip. "You know I've tried to find you edgier work, Drew. But no one is willing to take the risk. They don't want to be the one responsible for robbing America of its sweetheart."

"Fuck America's sweetheart. I want a movie that doesn't even have a sweetheart. Or a happy ending. I want to take risks, dammit. I'm sick of *safe*. I'm sick of the same old fucking thing all the time."

"Drew," a voice croons from my bedroom down the hall, and I nearly drop my glass.

A split second later, high heels click in our direction.

"Oh, hey," I sputter. I kind of forgot – *oh shit*, what's her name? I forgot she's still here. It *is* almost noon. "Sorry, did we wake you?"

A woman with long legs and tousled blond bedhead comes strolling around the corner, wearing her silver mini dress and leftover makeup from last night. I can't help it as I stare at her tits, bouncing across the living room until she's standing right next to me.

"No, I was just getting dressed." She kisses me on the cheek and pats my chest before nodding politely at Will. He grins comedically big back at her. *Jackass.* "This time next week?" she whispers, her lips grazing my ear lobe.

"Yeah, sure." *Andrea? Abigail? Audrey?* I feel like it starts with an A.

She sashays past the wall of windows and out of my apartment, giving me a finger wave and biting her bottom lip before beginning the walk of shame to her Uber.

CHAPTER 3

"Amanda?" I raise an eyebrow at Will. "Alexis?"

"Britta."

"Wow, I was way off."

"Isn't this the third time you've slept with her?" Will asks. "You should probably learn her name."

I pour myself another glass and shake my head. "I think this was the last time. Three is my max as you know. She was fun, but not memorable." I purse my lips and swallow. "Clearly."

"How could anyone be at this point?"

I raise my glass to that sentiment. My secret identity isn't Los Angeles's biggest playboy for nothing. Women in this town know I'm not looking for a relationship, and I'd like to keep it that way.

"If only America could see this side of you." Will takes a sip of his first drink. "You'd have no problem getting sexier roles. Hell, they might even cast you in their next porno."

"William!" I slam my glass on the table and raise my hands in triumph. "That's it! We've got to show America who I really am. What I'm really capable of."

"Nailing a different girl every night?"

"No, not that," I say, though he's not wrong. "If the execs won't send me any good scripts, I'll take matters into my own hands. I'll produce a movie myself. I've always wanted to go into production someday. Maybe not a porno, but something porno-adjacent. And I could star in it too. If I'm the executive producer, I can do things my way. Make choices I want—"

"Drew, are you sure –"

"And when the movie is a huge success, they'll never be scared to cast me in anything again. Or maybe I could switch over to production altogether."

I stride over to my large, leather chair and slump into its buttery softness. This is such a great idea, I'm shocked I've never thought of it before. I pull out my phone and open the Google app. All that's missing now is the perfect movie pitch.

"Where exactly do you find scripts these days, Will?"

I type **movie scripts**, then shake my head and try again. I edit it to say **movie scripts for sale.**

"Not like that." Will snatches my phone out of my hand. "Not if you want it to be good, anyway."

"Oh, it'll be good, all right." I'm getting more excited about this idea by the second. "Sexy leading man, obviously. Danger. Suspense. And a sad-ass ending. Maybe I could even die at the end. Find me that."

"You could try buying the movie rights for a book that isn't already claimed. Then you'd have a built-in fan base when you adapt it."

"You know, that's not a bad idea." I try to think if I've read any movie-worthy books lately. I shake my head; I haven't had time to read in forever. Taking my phone back, I pull up Amazon instead of Google and type in **popular books**.

"Too bad *Harry Potter* is taken, am I right?" I joke, scrolling through the colorful book covers. "I would have made one hell of a Snape."

"Indeed." Will pulls up a chair next to me, leaning over my phone. "You're a regular Alan Rickman."

"You say that like it's not true." I laugh. The different covers begin to blur with the staggering number of options, and I slump into my chair as my eyes dart to Will's. "We need to narrow this search."

"Okay. Well...what are some things you want to have in this movie?"

"Hmm..." I pause, sincerely considering his question. When I dropped out of college six years ago and started auditioning for films, I would literally take any gig, and I've been stuck in that rut ever since. It's a novelty to be picky. And by *novelty*, I mean *overwhelming*. "Why don't we just put my name? And see what comes up."

"I thought you wanted do something different."

CHAPTER 3

"Well..." I rub the back of my neck. "We have to start somewhere."

Will takes the phone and types **Drew Coyne Books** into the Kindle Store.

"Oh, and add *sexy* too. I mean, not that that's not already understood, because it is."

Will laughs. "For good measure."

"And steamy. And daring."

Drew Coyne Books sexy steamy daring

Click.

The first title that comes up is ranked number six in all of the Kindle Store and the best-seller in Romance Fiction, Victorian Historical Romance Fiction, Women's Romance Fiction, Regency Romance Fiction, and Holiday Romance Fiction.

My forehead creases. The cover looks like an eight-year-old got her hands on a digital library of old Fabio pictures and went crazy in the 1999 edition of Microsoft Paint. The description isn't much better.

By all accounts, Captain Ambrose Archibald Fitzwillliam IV is a man of high status. A decorated war vet, handsome to boot, a man about town, good in the boudoir, and quick with his wit...and his tongue. Born into a life of extreme privilege, he's never known want. That is, until he meets the vivacious and mysterious Susan Adamson.

She is the eldest daughter of a prestigious London family, and the lady of famed Swallow Manor, and yet she has no interest in getting married, but instead dreams of traveling the world and becoming a writer. Unfortunately, her father has other plans, hatching a devious scheme with the captain to woo his daughter in exchange for clearing his father's good name. When Ambrose and Susan meet, she'll be writing more than just stories about love. She'll be experiencing it firsthand. That is, if she can overlook the captain's abrasive nature and sharp sarcasm.

Luckily, banter—and love— is a dance best done by two.

I look up from the phone. "This has to be a joke."

"I mean, it has over fifty thousand five-star reviews. And it's only been out four months. I'm guessing no one has the rights yet."

My face contorts into a disbelieving smirk. I scroll to the bottom of the Amazon page, clicking on the first review.

Okay, so I know this book looks like it would be horrible, but if you can get past the terrible cover and sketchy synopsis, you will NOT be disappointed. I've just got four words for you: O Ambrose, my Ambrose!

"Seems like people like the male lead," I mumble. I scroll further down. The next review I click on is from someone called booklovr2482.

Oh my heart, Ambrose and Susan sizzle off the page. 5 stars/3.5 peppers. I read all five books in the series within 48 hours. I couldn't sleep, I couldn't eat. I just needed more more more!! Please tell me someone is turning this into a movie!

So...there's a movie demand. I rub my jaw and scroll further down.

I've never read a story like this. The writing is clean and smart. The author is a genius. She knows how to write a sex scene, that's for sure. Ambrose is the perfect leading man. Edgy and sexy and not at all like you'd expect. He's my new favorite book boyfriend.

The review has then been edited to add: *I'm still crying about this book two weeks later. Please tell me this author is publishing more?????*

Review after review gush about the writing and in particular, Ambrose. It's enough to make me download the book. We also find a few more *conventional* options of thrillers and action novels and buy those too.

After Will leaves, I settle into my chair, resting my feet on the mahogany coffee table. I open my Kindle and pull up *Swallow Manor: Book One* by Minnie Maple.

Lord, even the author's name is over the top. Who is this lady, a Regency-era stripper?

Chapter 4

Andrew Edward Coyne
Ambrose
something something something
IV

It's not hard to see why these books are such a massive success. I'm with booklovr2482. I couldn't put them down, reading all five in the series within two days. I told Will to start working on securing the rights halfway through the first.

As an avid and very discerning reader, I was expecting these books to be a massive shitshow. I've dipped my toe into the romance genre a time or two, and never cared for the cliché story lines or ridiculous tropes. God knows I have enough of that in my professional life. And don't even get me started on the corny sex scenes. I like my sex hard and impersonal. Both in books and in real life. Consensual? Always. Protected? Of course. Passionate? Hell yes. But I'm not trying to fall in love. Give me a thriller where the main character fucks an undercover prostitute over lovemaking any day.

But this book, while on the surface appeared to be more of the same, can't be more different. I'm not saying it's going to win a Pulitzer Prize or anything, but it's the best book I've read in years. The characters are flawed and brilliantly written. The main character,

Ambrose something something something IV is a badass, while still being real and damaged, edgy and multi-faceted like I need him to be. Like *I* am. I've already started thinking about choices I would make in portraying him. For the first time in a long, long time (ever?), the prospect has me excited about acting again.

The storylines are deep and tangle together so masterfully, I didn't even realize I was ensnared in their grasp before it was too late. And the sex, while a little too sentimental for my liking, is fucking hot. Although the author is probably a middle-aged spinster with too much time on her hands, and not the sex goddess I'm imagining, I can't stop thinking about meeting her.

Which makes Will's news so upsetting.

"What do you mean, you can't find the author?" I take off my sweaty gym shirt and throw it onto the kitchen island's marble countertop.

Will has gotten even less sleep than I have the past forty-eight hours, though less from reading panty-melting novels and more from playing detective.

"I mean"—Will waves me over to the couch, turning the laptop so I can see the screen—"she doesn't have a website, an author page on Amazon, any social media accounts, or any contact information listed. Whoever she is, she doesn't want to be found."

"You okay, man?" I look at Will, his eyes sunken deep into their sockets. "You look like shit if I'm being honest."

"Just up with Chloe last night. She had a nightmare about unicorns turning into green monsters and trying to kidnap her."

"Want me to watch her tomorrow? You can take the day off. I really appreciate you, man. Sorry this has turned into such a fucking wild goose chase."

Will's eyes dart up. "Are you sure, Drew? We need to get this deal done."

"I'm sure. We'll find her." *We have to.*

CHAPTER 4

I clap Will on the shoulder, and my sweaty back sticks to the leather as I sit.

"What if she knew the type of money we were willing to pay?" I ask, rubbing the back of my neck. "I'm sure there's a way to make our intentions known. The public doesn't need to know who she is. Can't you have our people call her people, or however that works?"

"She doesn't have any people." Will's eyebrows dart up and then fall. "She's not even a real person. Minnie Maple is a pen name. I mean, for all we know, *she* might not even be a *she*."

I hadn't considered the possibility of Minnie Maple being a dude. I'm not sure why that prospect is so upsetting. I guess as long as he's a dude willing to let me make his book into a movie, it shouldn't matter. But for some reason, here it is, mattering.

"This book is *the book*," I reiterate, waving my hands around for emphasis. "So, whatever we need to do to make it happen, I'm willing to do." I stare at a plant in the corner before meeting Will's eyes again. "What information *do* we have?"

"The book is dedicated to someone with the initials H.E.W. And in the acknowledgments, she, or, um, he – uh, let's just go with *they*. They thank God and wine. I also tried to hack into the bank account where they get paid royalties. All I got is the last four digits of their bank account number: 3442."

"Fuc—" The curse word is drowned out by my daily Facetime call from my social media manager and sister, Darcy.

I pick up the phone, not even waiting for her to say hello before I jump into my request. "Darcy, how do you find someone who doesn't want to be found?"

"Um, hi to you too." Her dark brown eyes scowl into the camera.

"Sorry, hey. So, how do you do it? I need to find a woman. At least, I think she's a woman, and I have no contact information for her."

"Oh, no, Drew, who did you sleep with now?" She rubs her forehead.

"Do you have the Twitter handle, at least? I can work on blocking them."

"Jesus, why do you assume this has something to do with sex?"

"Umm...have you already forgotten about the two women you had me block last month?"

"And I really appreciate that, Darc. You know why I can't..." I shake my head and start again. "Anyway... This isn't like that. This is for a new project I'm working on. I need to find the author of *Swallow Manor*."

"Really?" Excitement momentarily replaces the annoyance in Darcy's voice. "I love those books."

"I want to make them into a movie, but I can't find the author. She wrote it under a pen name."

"Ask Will." Darcy brings her shoulders to her ears and shakes her head. It makes her black curls bounce. "That is not my expertise."

"Will can't find her. We've tried everything. We need you to work your social media magic."

"Yeah, hi, Darcy." Will leans into view. "I've got nothing."

Darcy sighs, her face growing blank. But then, her eyes flicker with an idea. "I mean..." She pauses, chewing on a long, manicured fingernail before continuing, "I guess you could try and have her come to you. You have gained ten thousand new followers on Instagram in the past month with the release of *Second Chance Romance*, taking you up to three hundred thirty-eight thousand. I know that's still slightly below where we wanted to be mid-year, but I think the place we can make up that ground is on TikTok. You've made a few TikTok videos here and there. Mostly gym videos..." She purses her lips.

"You say that like it's a bad thing." I laugh. She must have seen my video from an hour ago.

"No judgment here." Darcy throws her arms up in surrender. "Like I always say, your life, your content."

"Except with the environmental shit," I point out, chuckling. "And all the ads. And Will's dog. That brilliance is all you."

"It helps with your likability score. Plus, it's good income. Anyway, I think"—she clears her throat, her voice squarely back to annoyed—"we have an opportunity for you to capitalize on your recent Instagram growth and grow your followship on TikTok. And maybe this is the way to do that."

"Darcy, enough with the numbers and shit. I always trust you on that front." I put my feet on the coffee table, staring out at the Los Angeles skyline. "What's your idea?"

"TikTok is all about content engagement. Creator and follower relationships. Giving your followers something they can not only like, but use to help build their own brand. A little nugget they can take for themselves. Like a new dance or a new sound or a new trend. In this case, it could be a cause. Let TikTok help you find Minnie Maple."

"Help me?" I unstick my back from the couch as I sit up.

"Post a video detailing your intentions of buying the movie rights. Tell them you need their help. This book has been all over BookTok lately. With a celebrity on board, this could really take off."

"But since Minnie Maple clearly doesn't want to be found" —I roll my eyes— "then why would having more people looking for her help? If she's so dead set on staying anonymous, wouldn't she want *less* people talking about her?"

"Because the more people who see it, the more likely *she* is to see it." Darcy's eyes twinkle wickedly. "You'd be the face of the cause, giving her the information of where to find someone who wants to buy the rights. She comes to you, you promise to keep her identity a secret, you get the movie rights. She, I'm assuming, makes a shit ton of money."

"Oh, yeah, definitely a shit ton," Will chimes in.

I catch his eye, cocking my head to the side. "Well, boss? What do you think?"

"I mean...if you posted this and got people on board, you'd have to be committed to following through. Hallmark darling Drew Coyne would officially be dead."

My smile widens, and I turn back to Darcy. "Get it set up. Let's make a movie. Or a reel, or whatever the hell it is you call it."

Chapter 5

Mary-Beth Caroline Abernathy
Concussed
(Possibly)

Growing up, I never wanted to be an author, but I *always* wanted to be a teacher. The way their little eyes light up when they learn something new. How their gravelly, squeaky voices don't quite know what they're saying until it's already out. How they love you regardless of age, gender, race, sexual orientation, or *book genre* of choice.

Because I might never have kids of my own, teacher is a good alternative.

"Ms. Abernathy, Ms. Abernathy, come look at mine!" my sweet little student, Emilia, croons, waving me over to her table. The students are working on gluing cotton balls to their Easter bunny crafts, and hers looks especially fluffy.

"Oh, Emilia, this looks beautiful. I love how soft it is." I turn my sights to her neighbor, Colin. "Oh, dear," I mutter before I can stop myself. Colin's Easter bunny is swimming in a pool of Elmer's. "I think, uh, no more cotton balls needed for you, Emilia, and no more glue for Colin." I quickly grab the craft supplies and move to the next table.

Before I know it, I'm hugging each student goodbye and wishing them a happy Easter and a lovely spring break. I'll see them in two weeks and, thank goodness, because I have a book series to finish.

I pull the blinds and stroll around the classroom, putting away stray books and pencils and picking up abandoned art supplies. There's one forlorn cotton ball under the table in the corner I have to crawl on my hands and knees to retrieve. Pausing, I stuff it in my pocket and cautiously take out my phone.

Glancing one last time at the closed door across the room, I eagerly open my Kindle dashboard. When I woke up this morning, I was at one hundred and twelve e-book sales and just over twenty-five thousand Kindle Unlimited pages. A slow morning for me, honestly. One of the slowest since #OhAmbroseMyAmbrose went viral.

I click on today's sales, and my mouth turns as dry as the cotton ball in my pocket. Over five thousand new e-book downloads and two hundred thousand pages. Just for book one. Just since this morning.

Sweat forms along my neck as my shaking fingers click on each tab, digging deeper into the statistics. While I've been here gluing cotton balls onto bunnies with five-year-olds, I've made over twenty-five thousand dollars. That's close to my *annual* salary.

What the hell?

I can't help but laugh. This feels like some sort of demented dream. Like something from an alternate reality. An alternate reality where I can be who I want, and people accept me. Where I can buy a new car or a new house and no one wonders how. Where I wake up excited to tell my loved ones about my work. Where twenty-five thousand isn't the amount of money I make in a year, but in a day. Where—

"Beth, darling, are you under the table? What's so funny?"

My mother's unexpected entrance startles me, and I jump. I whack my head on the metal framework of the ancient desk so hard, I might be concussed. Cursing under my breath, I jam my phone away like

CHAPTER 5

I'm a fifteen-year-old getting caught sending nudes and begin army-crawling out of my chewing-gum-riddled sanctuary.

"Mama!" I hop to my feet and plaster on a guilty-as-charged grin.

The clicks of Mama's kitten heels make their way past the ABC rug and onto the linoleum, her short brown hair bouncing ever so slightly. When she reaches me, it feels like she's towering over me, though she's only two inches taller than I am. I cower like a child about to be reprimanded.

"What are you doing here?" I squawk.

Twenty-five thousand dollars. Twenty-five thousand dollars. Twenty-five thousand dollars.

I can practically see the number floating in the air behind my mother's perfectly coiffed hair.

"I thought we could go to an early dinner. Celebrate the start of spring break. Is everything all right, darling?" She pulls me into a gentle hug, and I breathe in her perfume. The scent usually comforts me, but right now it's nauseating. "What was so funny under the table?"

"Oh, uh, just, like, something that kid wrote. You know how silly those kindergartners can be." The lie doesn't sound believable, even to me. I should be grateful I didn't blurt out *twenty-five thousand dollars!* instead. I take a step back, laughing awkwardly. "Dinner sounds great. Thanks, Mama."

Mama narrows her hazel eyes, like she knows I'm lying and is trying to decide what to do. It reminds me of the time she caught me trying to sneak out of my window to meet Harper at Jason Foley's after-prom party junior year. And while I'm not exactly stuck halfway in a window and dressed in pink tulle, I still brace myself. My mind whirls, trying to come up with what exactly said kindergartner who can't write, especially not upside-down and underneath a table, wrote.

Fortunately, she decides not to go there. She shakes her head, sighing as she looks around the room. "Are you all finished up here? Your dad is leaving straight from church to meet us there."

I release a breath and blink a few times, not realizing she's expecting me to answer.

"Beth?"

"Yeah, um…" I cough and shake my head. "Let me clean up these, uh—" *Twenty-five thousand dollarsssss. No, Mary-Beth, no!* "These, uh—" I pull out the lost cotton ball from my pocket. "These cotton balls. Then, I'll be ready to go."

🐑🐑🐑

We arrive at the country club before my father. My parents have never been wealthy, but they joined the club when my dad got promoted from youth pastor to head pastor at the church. He believes it is important to be out amongst his parishioners, and this is one of the only things the old people in town do for fun.

"For Miss Mary-Beth," my favorite waitress, Mariah, says, setting my usual Shirley Temple down in the corner of my place setting. I've been ordering it since I was eleven, and yes, I'm still ordering it.

"And for you, Mrs. Abernathy." Mariah places a steaming cup of coffee in front of my mother and another in front of my dad's still-vacant chair. I've never understood how they can drink coffee at night. They drink so much of it, sometimes I think their pee must come out hot instead of warm.

"Thank you, Mariah," my mother says graciously. She opens a packet of sugar and dumps it into her mug, followed by a miniature cup of cream. I watch her swirl the brown liquid until it turns to tan, my heart racing, though I'm not sure why.

It's been a half-hour since I checked my sales. At the rate it was surging before, what would the royalties be now? Twenty-six thousand dollars? Thirty thousand? I'm dying to check again but fight the impulse, determined to have a normal dinner with my parents.

CHAPTER 5

Still...

Thirty-five thousand?

Fifty?

"So, Beth, how's work been going? Is that a new purse?"

My eyes shoot up to hers, and I uncross my legs, bumping the table. It makes our drinks slosh, and my mother steadies her coffee. She takes a small sip, her eyes never leaving mine over the cup.

"Work?" I ask nervously, before realizing she's talking about my kindergartners. "Oh, work. You know, it's fine. I love those kids." I clutch my new Kate Spade purse defensively. "And, uh, yeah. Just bought it a couple days ago. It was on sale at Nordstrom Rack."

Not one hundred percent a lie. It *was* technically for sale. At Nordstrom. Though certainly not the Rack.

"You know I'm friends with your vice-principal, Charity Greene." Mama readjusts her napkin. "She and I are in the same bunco group. She said the kids all adore you."

"Well, they're a really great bunch." I smile. That's not a lie.

"There's my two favorite girls!" My dad rushes to the table, and my mother stands to greet him. Wrapping his arm around her waist, he kisses her cheek. "Sorry, I'm late." He reaches over and ruffles my hair as he sits down. "How are you, Bethie? Oh, coffee. Thanks, honey."

After pleasantries are exchanged, the conversation focuses on me.

My dad, with his light brown hair, gray at the temples, and bright blue eyes, beams across the table. "What are your plans for spring break, Bethie? Gonna do anything fun with all that knitting money? Maybe go to the beach for a day?"

Oh, if only they knew how much "knitting money" I had. I could take us all to go live at the beach indefinitely.

"Um, maybe." I study the swirling grenadine in my Sprite. "Maybe I'll see what Harper's up to."

"How is Harper these days?" My dad's smile and crinkled forehead tell me he's genuinely interested. He tried so hard to save her when she was a teenager. I think she's the one who taught him not everyone *wants* to be saved. Or needs to be.

"She's good. Busy at the salon."

"I saw her mother stumbling out of Jack Harvey's a few mornings ago on my way to yoga," my mother says out of the corner of her mouth. She has never quite been as invested in helping Harper as she has in judging her alcoholic mother. "I thought she was back in rehab."

"I don't know," I say honestly. "Harper doesn't talk about her mom much."

"She's lucky to have you." My dad pats my hand. "You've always been a good influence on her."

I try to hold back my laugh. Have I been a good influence? Or has she been a bad one? Or should we let the twenty-five thousand dollars I made today answer that question?

As if she could hear us talking about her, my phone buzzes with a text from Harper. I check it as inconspicuously as possible on my new Apple watch.

Harper: Holy shit holy shit HOLY SHITTTT!!!

I quickly put my hand under the table.

Harper: MB did you seeeeeee Drew's TikTok from today???????

Harper: You know what... I'm just gonna call you.

Before I even have a chance to text her back, my phone rings. I immediately send it to voicemail, trying to play it cool across the white linen-clad table. Before I can exhale, it rings again.

I continue trying for small talk with my parents, but the onslaught continues. One message right after the other after the other. It's so many that I finally excuse myself to go to the bathroom.

"You know what, darling, I'll join you." My mother smiles, pushing

CHAPTER 5

away from the table.

Shit. I mean, *crap.*

No, I mean *shit.*

I keep my head down, clutching my phone and darting through the maze of tables. Behind me, my mother waltzes slowly, waving at friends enjoying dinner, occasionally stopping to make small talk. Finally, we make it to the bathroom, and I dash into the closest stall.

Mary-Beth: What the heck is going on? I'm at dinner with my parents.

Harper: To recap my 50 text messages and ten voicemails: Drew Coyne posted on TikTok that he wants to buy the movie rights to *Swallow Manor* and is calling for all of BookTok to help him find Minnie Maple. And it's gone viral. Like wayyy more than before. It's all anyone is talking about.

Harper: Dream Coyne is looking for you MB!!! YOUUUUU

It's a good thing I'm not actually going to the bathroom, because I nearly black out. I catch myself just before I hit the toilet paper-covered floor, my wobbly legs struggling to support my gelatinous body.

My first reaction: euphoria. My second: panic.

I scroll through Harper's previous messages until I find the link to the video. Triple checking that the volume is all the way down, I click on it.

Drew's angelic face stares up at me from the screen, and I instantly relax, sucked like a vortex into his brown skin and icy blue eyes. I catch myself smiling as I follow along with the closed captions.

"Hey there, BookTok!" Drew smiles at the camera. "I recently read a book series that I cannot get out of my mind. I think you know the one. That's right—the *Swallow Manor* series."

I sigh, watching his face as he speaks. The way his eyes crinkle at the corner when he smiles. The way his plump lips move across his perfectly white, straight teeth. How he occasionally licks said lips. How the spit makes his lips shiny for just an instant.

The tantalizing combination makes my mouth water. I pause the video to wipe the drool puddling at the corner of my mouth, then greedily press play again.

"I've been searching for a new project for a while. A project that will stretch me as an actor and help me make my mark on the entertainment industry. Something that can help define my career moving forward. Something smart. Something edgy. Something sexy."

I nearly drop dead when he says the word *sexy*. *Drew Coyne thinks my writing is sexy.*

"And I've finally found it. I'd like to announce my plans to buy the movies rights to the *Swallow Manor* series and to produce and star in all five films. That's right! You're looking at Captain Ambrose Archibald Fitzwillliam IV."

Pounding on the stall door makes me jump and drop my phone. It bounces off the seat and clatters to the floor, video still playing. I fumble to pick it up, grateful it landed face-down.

"Beth, sweetie, are you okay in there?"

Mama. I totally forgot she's here.

"Yeah, I'm fine." I need to think of a reason to be in here long enough to watch the rest of the video. "I just, uh, ate some bad sushi at lunch. Gave me really bad diarrhea."

Dear Lord. I'm spewing something, but it's not diarrhea. How has this one lie turned into a life of dishonesty? So much for a normal night out with my parents.

"Oh, uh, okay. Take your time, honey," my mother says awkwardly, and I hear running water. She's washing her hands. Again. "I'm gonna head back to the table."

"Okay. Thanks, Mama."

CHAPTER 5

Once I'm positive I'm alone, I start the video over, turning up the volume just one click. Good Lord Jesus, it's even better now that I can actually hear him.

"But there's just one problem." Drew looks straight at the camera like he's speaking to just me. I guess, in a way, he is. *Gulp.* "Minnie Maple is a pen name. The author's true identity remains a mystery."

The edge of my vision begins to blur, and I clench my butt cheeks to stay on the toilet.

"This is where you come in, BookTok!" Drew rubs his hands together, breaking into a huge smile, one that seems to take up half his face. I can't help it when I beam back, but flinch when he claps and points at the screen. "Help me find Minnie Maple! Send her my way! Ms. Maple, I guarantee your identity will remain anonymous, but let's get this deal done. BookTok, help me spread the word. Let's find her!"

"I'm Sorry Miss Jackson" by OutKast starts playing in the background, and Drew does a quick and adorable dance, which ends in him falling off screen. Then the hashtag #ImSorryMsMapleButIAmForReal appears.

I'm frozen on the toilet with a perma-smile watching the video on repeat for God knows how long. Long enough that Mama returns.

"Beth, darling." Her voice oozes with that motherly love vibrato. "Are you sure you're all right? Do you need help?"

I flush my imaginary excrement and glue on a grimace before exiting the stall.

"Are you okay, dear? You're as white as a ghost."

Apparently, gobsmacked and food-poisoned look eerily similar.

"Yeah. But I think I should probably head home." I offer her a pitiful laugh, careful not to stand up too straight. "Don't want to spend all night in the bathroom."

Mama gently places the back of her hand on my forehead, holding it there until she's satisfied I don't have a fever. Her eyes soften as she carefully swipes a strand of hair from my eyes. "Of course, darling. Feel better soon."

🐑🐑🐑

I park my car at my house and make Harper come pick me up, just in case my parents drive by to ensure I made it home okay. I'm not used to lying to them, and I don't like it. At all.

We kneel on Harper's soft, blush-colored rug, using her coffee-table as a countertop while Drew's movie, Love in Snowflake Valley, plays in the background. Harper is already dipping into her wine of choice for the night, but I opt for Chick-Fil-A. I'm starving after not actually eating dinner at the country club.

"So, like, what do I do?" My deer-in-headlights eyes reflect off Harper's wine glass.

"You go to him. Obviously."

"Go to him?" I wrinkle my forehead and take a huge bite of my chicken sandwich, swallowing without really chewing. "What do you mean, *go to him?*"

"MB, Drew Coyne wants to meet you." She says the words like she's trying to explain the concept to my kindergartners. "How could you not?"

"You mean, like, *physically* go to him? Like my body to his body?"

"Ooh, Mary-Beth, skipping ahead. I like that." Harper gives me a coy smile.

I groan and roll my eyes, stuffing a waffle fry into my mouth. "No, I mean, like, he's probably thinking someone is going to slide into his DMs and claim the books. But you think I should go to California and meet him in person?"

"If you're really worried about being found out, then don't leave a paper trail. DMs mean receipts and screenshots. It's hackable. A secret meeting wouldn't be like that. It's spring break the next two weeks. Go to California and tell him in person. No one would be able to trace it back to you, and..." She lets a huge smile spread across her face, cocking her head toward the TV. "You'd get to meet Drew handsome-as-the-day-is-long Coyne. The man of your dreams. And I'd get to meet him too, of course."

I soften my brow and grab her hands. "You'd come with me?"

"No shit, I'm coming with you. You really think I'm going to let you meet Dream Coyne without me?" She laughs and takes a sip of her wine.

"I don't know, Harp. Maybe this is all a big joke. Maybe he thinks the books are horrible and doesn't actually want to buy the rights."

"Why on God's green earth would he go through all this for a *joke*? Do you really think a celebrity that you've never met is trying to play you? A small-town virgin he doesn't know exists?"

"Do you have to describe me like that?"

"You don't like it when I use *bestselling romance author* either."

I wince. "You're right, I don't."

Harper comes onto her knees, bumping the table and spilling my fries. "Mary-Beth, this is your chance! He's going to pay big freaking money. And you'd get to see your stories on the big screen." She waves her arms at the movie. "Played by your favorite actor. And he's offering you the chance to do it all anonymously. If that's not the dream, I don't know what is."

"But I have to finish my next series." I eat a fry from the carpet, and the lint makes me cough.

"You've got three weeks before your deadline. Take a week to go to California and finish it after. You'll still have a whole week off work. That's plenty of time."

"And then there's Persimmon Festival. And parent-teacher conferences. And your birthday. Your party..." I count off the events on my fingers.

Harper clamps her hand over mine. "MB, we'll be back for all of that.

Stop making excuses."

I slump against the foot of the couch.

"But how would I find him?" I point at the TV and Drew smiles back at us. "He's a celebrity, Harp; he's not just gonna be, like, sitting around waiting for me."

"MB, you've been stalking this man's Instagram for years. I'm sure we could figure out where he'll be."

Chapter 6

Andrew Edward Coyne
Ass

Darcy wasn't kidding when she said this would go viral. She asked for a raise mere hours after we posted the video, pursing her lips with that told-you-so smirk she does. She's never been shy to pat herself on the back. Of course, I gave it to her.

My initial video already has thirty-five million views and thousands of stitches and duets (whatever those are). And while that's all fine and dandy, it's created a completely different problem. It's not going viral in the way we wanted. Thousands of DMs have flooded in since we posted the TikTok two days ago, but none of them are the actual Minnie Maple. Not even close.

Poor Darcy and I are spending every waking moment sifting through varying degrees of X-rated videos and messages with no luck. For the first time, it seems my playboy alter-ego is a hindrance.

Even if the real author did message me, the chances of actually seeing it are slim to none at this point. I officially feel like Prince Charming stuffing a glass slipper on the nasty-ass feet of a sea of ugly stepsisters on my quest to find Cinderella. A Cinderella that definitely doesn't want to be found, and I increasingly believe I'll never meet.

There are a bunch of batshit crazy girls out there, ready for their five minutes of fame. Believe me, if flashing their double D's and screaming how badly they want it was all it took, there would be a long line of Drew Coyne-made celebrities already.

Sorry, ladies, you can't sign over movie rights to a book you don't own. Not even if you show me your tits.

"Uncle Drew, my daddy says you're in a pickle."

I'm at my weekly dinner with Will and his daughter, Chloe. It's supposed to be our time to talk about non-work-related things, but let's not kid ourselves, that never happens.

Chloe's big brown eyes and chubby cheeks stare up from the red, vinyl-covered booth across from me.

"Your daddy's not wrong." I frown down at the little girl. "I *am* in a pickle."

"I'm afraid probably more than you realize." Will rubs his temple. "I just talked to the network today."

"Oh, no. Hallmark?"

Will nods, helping Chloe unwrap her crayons. I'm not picky by any means, but typically, I try to avoid eating in restaurants that have the option of crayons with your dinner. God knows I ate enough shit as a kid. Yet here I am at this crappy diner week after week because I'd do anything for that little girl. And she loves to color.

"Don't sugarcoat it. Tell it to me straight." I take a few bolstering swallows of my beer.

"They aren't happy with our little PR stunt. They said if you don't sign on to do *Love's Lighthouse*, you're done."

"Why are they acting like they own me?" I growl through clenched teeth. "I'm leaving *them*, not the other way around."

"But if we can't find Minnie Maple, there might not be another option for you. We've kind of put all our eggs in one basket. Hallmark is the only network offering you a script right now, and if we don't take it, there might not be others."

CHAPTER 6

"I'm not filming the lighthouse movie. I'm done with fu—" Chloe's sweet little face looks up at me from her drawing. "With *freaking* Hallmark," I censor. "We're gonna find the author. We have to."

"We better. Your career is kind of counting on it."

"That's the pickle!" Chloe chimes in, raising her hands up to emphasize her point.

I watch as Chloe's crayons roll onto the floor, Will stooping under the shiny, silver table to retrieve them like the doting father he is. How old is Chloe now? I know she's starting kindergarten in the fall, so she must be five. Shit. *Five years.* Five years since Julia.

"That *is* the pickle, darlin'," I agree, ruffling her chestnut hair.

From the corner of my eye, I see a woman with a low-cut shirt and an eager look in her eye making a beeline for our table. I shift my chair to block Chloe from her ambush.

"Oh my gosh, Drew Coyne!" she screams when she's still at least ten feet away. "I know where you can find Minnie Maple!"

I roll my eyes as Will puts a protective arm around Chloe. Her confused eyes dart from me to her dad and back again. Will crouches down to whisper something to her, and she nuzzles her face into his shirt.

"Can't you see that I'm trying to have dinner with my friend and his daughter?" I say, my voice gruff. I like the way it sounds, menacing and annoyed with a hint of *I don't give a shit* thrown in. I lower it another octave as the woman continues her approach. "This isn't the time."

"But I want to help you find her." She slides a phone number across the table. "I promise I'll make it worth your while."

I wish I could say this is the first time this has happened this week, but to be honest, she's not even in the first fifty. And while I typically enjoy women throwing themselves at me, it's getting really old.

"Listen, unless you can make the real Minnie fucking Maple appear right now, with proof and a pen, I'm not interested in whatever shit it is you've got. Understand?" I hiss under my breath, quiet enough that Chloe can't hear.

The woman takes a step back, the lust in her eyes replaced with vitriol. "Wow, who knew you were such an ass?" she spits, before turning on her heel and marching away.

When she's officially gone, Chloe lifts her gaze to Will's. "Daddy, what's an ass?"

Will laughs, both of us stumbling as we try to cover the woman's tracks.

"It's a donkey."

"It's a not-nice name for your bottom."

"It's something you should never call someone."

"She's someone who just had a bad day."

But what I really want to say is, she's right—it's me. I'm the ass. I'm the ass, but not because I told that woman to leave me and my family alone. I'm the ass because I bet on a woman that's probably a dude and although they write amazing sex scenes, is most likely going to fuck me over instead, and she doesn't even know it.

Chapter 7

Mary-Beth Caroline Abernathy
Prostitute

I'm not entirely sure how Harper got me on this airplane. I don't even have alcohol to blame this time, just the unhealthy love of a man I've never met and an abundance of Chick-Fil-A sauce. And yet, here we are, first thing Monday morning, on an airplane above an unknown flyover state, en route to Los Angeles and Drew Coyne's beckoning of Minnie Maple.

Because my mother dropped me off at the airport, in my carry-on, I have knitting supplies for fictitious scarves and a barf bag in case my imaginary sushi-induced illness returns. The only thing I don't have packed is a plan. Luckily, Harper seems to have that covered.

"So...you've been following Drew for years?" She scrolls through Drew's Instagram. "Where does he hang?"

"I follow the man online; I don't actually stalk him," I say defensively.

"Okay, well, what does he usually post? Maybe we can figure out where he'll be from that."

"Well, every day he posts a story from his morning workout, along with the ads of the day. Then—"

"Wait, did you say he posts a gym selfie every day?"

"Yeah, along with the ads from his new granola endorsement and the hiking boots. Oh, and the new skincare one—"

"No, Mary-Beth, don't you see?" Harper shifts in her seat so she's facing me, running her fingers through her tangled rainbow hair with an excited look in her eyes. "If he goes to the gym every day, we'll just figure out which one and go there."

"Is it that easy?"

Harper is already pulling up photos of posh Los Angeles gyms frequented by celebrities on her phone. She turns the screen to me.

"Any of these look familiar?"

"Are we *sure* this is a good idea?"

I tug on the designer crop top and leggings I've somehow found myself in. Yesterday, after we'd checked into our bougie hotel, Harper convinced me to go to Rodeo Drive and buy an entire new wardrobe. We stormed through the palatial lobby with armfuls of bags, just like Julia Roberts in *Pretty Woman*.

I have to admit, it almost feels like I'm actually in the movie. Except, I'm buying my own stuff, and I'm not a prostitute. At least not a prostitute of my body. I'm more of a prostitute of words, I guess.

"This gym is very exclusive, so you need to look rich." Harper puts her hands on my shoulders and clinches, forcing me to stand up straighter. "Which you are, by the way. You've got to start acting like it."

"How do rich people act?" I ask, knowing I'm probably not doing it right..*What do rich people do with their hands?*

"One, they don't give a sh—" Harper cocks her head to the side to finish her sentence. "Two, they expect to get what they want at all times. It's like that Ariana Grande song. You want it, you got it."

"Ariana Grande," I mumble, trying to picture how she would walk into a gym she's not a member of, in a city she's never visited, approach

CHAPTER 7

a God-like man she doesn't know, and divulge a secret she doesn't want to tell.

I think I need better hair for this; my ponytail isn't nearly high enough.

The hotel doormen open the double doors, and we step outside to wait for our Uber. Uber Lux, of course. Ariana Grande would never ride-share. I close my eyes, letting the Los Angeles morning sunshine warm my face, "Seven Rings" playing in my mind on repeat.

The Uber arrives, and the driver opens the door to his Tesla, offering us two bottles of Evian. The inside smells like leather and lavender, and the windows are tinted beyond what I assume is legal. Harper doesn't bat an eyelash as she casually confirms the address, slinking into the butter-soft seat next to me.

I try not to act like a dog, tongue flapping in the wind, but can't help but press my forehead against the glass. Through the darkened windows, skyscrapers and palm trees rush by, and I even catch a glimpse of the famous Hollywood sign. I hope we get a chance to do some sightseeing amidst all our scheming.

Before the driver announces we've arrived, I recognize the five-story glass building from Drew's Instagram stories. My heart nosedives into my new Nike sneakers as I check my watch. 10:04. If Harper's calculations are correct, he should be inside.

And if my calculations are correct, I should have brought my barf bag.

Inside the lobby, I spy the juice bar Drew always raves about. My legs take on a life of their own as I rush over.

"I'll have a kiwi-blueberry smoothie with turmeric and pumpkin seeds added," I spit out to the bewildered-looking employee. "Please."

She raises her eyebrows. "Tumeric? You sure?"

I nod enthusiastically. "I've heard it's supposed to help with anxiety."

The woman turns to hide her smirk. "All right..."

Last month, Drew posted about this exact smoothie, saying it helps calm his climate-change-induced anxiety. And if anyone needs an anxiety-taming elixir, it's me. I actually tried to buy pumpkin seeds weeks ago, but our dinky grocery store didn't carry them in February.

I pay the woman and grab the brown, lumpy concoction, waving the cup at Harper. "Drew's smoothie order!" I mouth, before wrapping my lips around the straw and sucking hard.

What happens next certainly doesn't ease my anxiety.

One of the pumpkin seed pieces gets stuck in my throat and that, combined with the God-awful taste of the blueberry and turmeric, makes me convulse so violently, I'm lucky I make it to the trash can. I knew I should have brought my barf bag.

Harper guides me to a chair by one of the windows, fanning me as I chug the Evian, wishing I had a stick of gum and a redo of the last five minutes. I can't meet Drew Coyne with turmeric-flavored vomit breath.

And that's when I see him. *Lord,* of course, it is.

Drew Coyne walks past the window Harper and I are camped at. And even though I probably have puke on my face and smell like embodied stress, I fight the urge to stand and put my hand against the glass.

I've studied a million photos of Andrew Edward Coyne, and seen his movies more times than I can count, but seeing him in person is like seeing him for the first time all over again. All the things I thought I knew about him, *good God,* they're even better in person.

First, he's tall—even taller than I imagined. My dad is six feet and Drew is six-foot-four, but somehow those four inches seem more like feet. Second, his skin is darker than I pictured. Less tan more taupe. The combination with his ice-blue eyes is mesmerizing.

Next, his body. His. *Bodddddddyyyyy.* He's wearing a gray tank top and shorts that come about halfway down his thighs, and holy hell,

CHAPTER 7

his muscles are bulging. He could swallow me whole with his biceps alone. I severely miscalculated how many muscles he has. And how massive they are.

And then there's his face. *Sculpted by angels* might seem like an exaggeration, but it's not. Each feature – his nose, ears, smile, eyelashes, pupils, the ridges of his forehead, the dimples in his cheeks, the curve of his jaw, the fade on his hair, the arch of his brow – is textbook handsome. His face is so symmetrical, like that drawing Leonardo da Vinci did of the perfect man.

I stand up without realizing it, like I'm being caught up to meet Jesus.

"Holy shit, you're right, MB, there he is!" Harper squeals, grabbing my hand and tugging. "Come on."

The movement coincides with Drew's entrance into the lobby, and, as if being awoken from an exorcism, I wallop back into my chair.

"No." I shake my head, feeling the urge to run. I slide my clammy hand from hers. "No, I can't do this, Harp. This was a mistake."

"Yes, you can." Harper tries to take my hand again, but I grip the armrests of the chair with the strength of a million wildebeests. Harper hooks her arm through mine and pulls but loses her balance and nearly tumbles to the floor.

We repeat this fun little dance a few more times, exchanging varying forms of *no-I-can't-yes-you-can*, before our little squabble catches Drew's attention, and we both freeze. He only looks at us for less than a second, but I swear I see his eyes roll before he sighs loudly. Then he checks in at the front desk, orders a smoothie, takes a picture of it, tosses it into the trash without tasting it, and enters the locker room.

I've already blown it. Shit.

Harper crouches in front of my chair, bringing her face an inch from mine. "Mary-Beth, stop acting like a little pussy." She puts her hands on my shoulders and shakes, and I almost scream but cover my mouth at the last second. "You need to pull it together, or you're going to completely blow your one chance at meeting him."

I inhale a deep breath of her perfume and let it out slowly. Somehow, that's exactly what I need to hear.

"You're right." I roll my shoulders back and channel my inner Ariana. "Let's do this."

I stride up to the counter with my best sashay, throwing my hands down on the front desk with a whack.

"We'd like to open new memberships, please." I narrow my eyes and lift my chin. "And can you please make it quick?"

🐑 🐑 🐑

I am in the same room as Drew Coyne, and he has just removed his shirt to do the arm flexy machine, and I may never recover.

Abs.

That's the only way I can describe what I'm seeing right now.

"Okay." Harper pulls me to a weight bench, her eyes locked on mine. "Let's review what you're going to say."

"I'm going to ask him if he can help me rack the weights. And then when it's just him and me, I - I - I'll tell him I'm the author."

"And we are prepared for him to not believe you."

"We are prepared?" *I'm definitely not prepared.*

"And how will you prove it to him?"

I wipe my sweaty palms on my leggings and fumble to open my book sales page on my phone. "I'll show my Amazon KDP page. And then I'll ask him to speak in private."

I can barely say the word *private*. Speaking privately with Drew Coyne? What is this? Heaven? Hell? Both fit the description of today.

"Are you ladies using this?" a deep voice asks.

Like a lifeless, melting Jell-O mold on a hot day, I slide off the bench and into the arms belonging to the voice.

And just like that, my skin is touching Drew Coyne's skin. His hand is on my arm, and *oh, dear*, now another hand is on my waist. My forearm is touching his stomach. And it's sweaty, and now his *sweat* is on me. Liquid that was once inside his body is now on my skin. Would it be weird to lick my arm right now?

God, Mary-Beth, that's taking it too far.

"Shit, are you okay?" Drew asks, bending at the knee to support my weight.

I'm sick and well and hot and cold and awake and dreaming and not entirely sure if my body weighs a thousand pounds or is as light as a feather. I don't make any effort to come to my feet as I slink even further to the ground.

"Is your friend okay?" Drew unceremoniously drops me, but compared to the tiny drops of sweat still clinging to my arm, I barely feel it.

Dear Lord, from this angle, his thighs look like Mount Vesuvius.

"Yeah, she's fine." Harper crouches to coax me to my feet, pressing her cheek against mine. "Ariana Grande, remember? She'd never be lying on the *dirty-ass floor*," she hisses, hooking her elbow through mine and yanking so hard she practically dislocates my shoulder.

Somehow, I'm able to get my feet underneath me, and my legs remember how to bend and support weight. And now, I'm nose to bare chest with Drew Coyne. So close that I can smell how freaking amazing he smells. Like money and sex and wealth with just a hint of pine.

Or maybe it's Douglas fir.

I sniff again.

No, definitely pine.

Part of me wants to hug him, and part of me wants to run, and part of me wants to melt into the floor again. But instead, I do none of the above and just start giggling. Uncontrollable, explainable giggling.

"Yeah, she's fine." Harper speaks through nervous, gritted teeth.

Her rainbow hair reflecting off her red face only makes me laugh harder. "Aren't you Mary-Beth?"

Drew and Harper look at me expectantly, but I still can't control my irrational giggles. Drew's eyes go from concerned to pissed in an instant.

"Listen, I saw you two in the lobby. And if that has something to do with the Minnie Maple shit, I'm not fucking interested, okay? I've had enough girls like you trying to offer me *information.* So just save it."

And then, as if possessed by the spirits of all romance novelists before me, I somehow get up the courage and composure to whisper the words, "But I am Minnie Maple."

Chapter 8

Andrew Edward Coyne
Disappointed

I've had many effects on women over the years, but literal melting is a first.

The last five minutes have been like an NSYNC concert circa 2001. But fuck me, because Justin Timberlake never had to make any business deals with his teenage fans.

The girl looks up at me with saucer-like eyes, reminding me of a literal deer in headlights. A wobbly deer in headlights that hasn't learned how to walk. A wobbly deer in headlights that won't stop fucking giggling. This person, this *girl*—she can't be much older than eighteen—can't be Minnie Maple.

She can't.

She is short and scrawny with ribs that jut out more than her tits and elbows that are so bony they might impale someone. Her brown hair doesn't have any curves either and is pulled back into a ponytail so tight and straight, it almost makes her look bald. Her flushed face is covered with freckles, and her smile takes up the remaining facial real estate not already occupied by her giant brown eyes.

"Prove it." I narrow my eyes.

The ball in the girl's throat bobs as she swallows hard, her chest heaving frantically as she struggles to breathe. Okay, so maybe her boobs aren't *that* small, but smaller than what I'm used to.

The girl, Mary-Beth I guess is her name, finally blinks and takes a deep breath. She fumbles to take out her phone, her hands shaking so violently she drops it on the bouncy rubber flooring. I quickly swoop down and pick it up before she has a chance.

"All I need is the last four digits of your bank account," I say coolly, locking the phone and folding my arms. "Then I'll know you're the real Minnie Maple."

The girl's stare goes from the phone in my hand to my eyes in an instant, like a light switch being flipped. The pupils that were wide with shock before now contract.

"You know my bank account?" She struggles to free each word, like she's not only forgotten how to stand and breathe, but also speak.

For the first time since that TikTok video came out, my heart begins to race. This reaction is a first.

The friend with the rainbow hair and giant tits puts her arm around Mary-Beth. "Yeah, what the hell?"

"Only the last four digits," I say. "That's all my team could find when we were trying to locate the author. It's become the litmus test to filter the onslaught."

Mary-Beth chews on her bottom lip as she considers my request. I can't help it when my eyes flit to her mouth, her lips fuller than I first noticed—pink and plump, and an attractive shape, now that she's stopped squealing like a baby pig. I remember the scene from *Swallow Manor* where Ambrose and Susan first kiss, and I have a strange urge to grab Mary-Beth around the waist and do the same.

Just once. Just to see.

Ambrose skimmed his fingers across her full, rose-colored lips. Her cheeks flushed with desire, as he secured his grasp behind her neck, greedily pulling her mouth to his.

CHAPTER 8

My feet shuffle back a half-step.

"Three, four, four, two," she says softly, and I blink back to the present.

3442. *Holy shit.*

"Though she could have shown you without you hacking into her bank account," the friend says, tossing her ponytail over her shoulder. "That's a real douchebag thing to do. Is that even legal?"

Ignoring the friend completely, I turn my attention to Mary-Beth. Now I'm not staring at her lips or her chest or her elbows. Now I can't look away from her giant coffee-colored eyes, knowing all the brilliant and erotic thoughts that live behind them.

My heart pounds, pumping blood throughout my body. Some parts more than others.

I extend my hand, taking her dainty one in mine.

"It's nice to finally meet you, Miss Maple," I say with a wide smile I can no longer contain. Mary-Beth gives me a small smile in return, then snatches her hand from my grasp before I have a chance to shake. "My address is 23532 Wilshire Boulevard. Apartment 1602. I'll meet you there in two hours. I'll let security know to expect you."

I turn and leave the girls dazed in my wake. First, because I have to clean my filthy apartment, but mostly, because I don't want Mary-Beth to see the effect she has on me.

🐑🐑🐑

"You found her? No fucking way!" Will's voice echoes around the car as I drive home from the gym.

"Yessir!" I triumphantly pound the steering wheel. "I hope you've got the papers drawn up."

"I cleared everything with legal last week. How did it happen? She just walked up to you and said, 'I'm the author'?"

One eyebrow flits up as I remember catching Mary-Beth's tiny body as she slid to the ground. "Something like that." I laugh. "She kind of fell into my lap. Literally."

"That's the Drew Coyne way, I guess." Will chuckles. "And you're sure it's her? Did you ask her about the bank account?"

"Oh, it's her, all right. Although, she wasn't happy about your hacking."

At least, the friend wasn't.

"Understandable. That was borderline unethical," Will admits. Then, his voice lightens. "So, where's she from? What's she like?"

"I don't know anything about her, except that she's, like, four-foot-ten, weighs fifty pounds, looks like she's barely legal, can't contain her faculties, has a slight southern accent, and a best friend with rainbow hair."

"At least she's a *she*."

"I guess."

"You're disappointed she's not the sex goddess you were imagining." Will states it as fact.

Hearing the words out loud, I realize he's right. Mary-Beth isn't what I was expecting, and that is disappointing. But I can't seem to describe what I *was* expecting. And I'm not exactly sure why she isn't it.

I had women approach me that, on paper, fit the bill both physically and sexually of what I usually like. But I would have been disappointed with them too. I guess I wanted Minnie Maple to be someone…more. More *what*, I'm not sure. Not that I know Mary-Beth isn't. Like I told Will, I don't know anything about her. But I can't help feeling like there's a disconnect between Minnie Maple and Mary-Beth. Whoever she is.

"You got me," I admit, rubbing the back of my neck as I let out a long sigh. "Either way, she'll be at my house in two hours, so you need to get your ass over here. The housekeeping lady can't come today, and I need you to help me clean."

CHAPTER 8

"I just dropped Chloe off at Julia's mom's. I'm on my way."

Chapter 9

Mary-Beth Caroline Abernathy
Disappointed

"I can't do this, Harp." I'm lying on the bed at the hotel, my head propped up on the mountain of pillows; a pillow under my knees, and a pillow covering my face. I keep talking into the soft bamboo cotton, though I'm not sure if Harper can hear me or is even listening at all. "Can you book us a flight home?"

"Hell no!" Harper snatches the pillow from my face and wallops me with it. "We came to meet Drew Coyne and sell the rights to *Swallow Manor*, and that's exactly what we're going to do!"

"But, like, I can't go to his *house*." I sit up, causing my pillow mountain to come crashing down. I take Harper's hands in mine, pleading. "His house, Harper. You saw what happened at the gym. I'll never stand a chance inside his *house*."

"Drew Coyne is just like every other douchebag man on the planet, Mary-Beth," Harper says coldly. "Let's take him for all he's worth and then go explore Los Angeles for the rest of the week."

I drop Harper's hands, putting one of mine to my heart. "Drew Coyne is not a douchebag," I say defensively. "Yes, our first meeting didn't exactly go according to plan, but we ambushed him. Honestly, I don't know what we were expecting."

CHAPTER 9

"He hacked into your bank account, MB." Harper's glare could kill a small rodent.

"He was doing everything he could to find Minnie Maple."

"He dropped you on the dirty gym floor."

"He probably thought I had a rare, highly-infectious disease."

"He stared at my chest our entire conversation."

"To be fair, you have amazing boobs."

"And yours."

"Less explainable."

"Face it." Harper pushes a stray piece of rainbow hair out of her face and softens her eyes. "He's not as great as we thought he was. But that's okay. We can still make the deal."

"But he is." I roll off the bed and stand, emboldened by years of loyalty to Drew. "I'll prove it to you." I tug Harper over to the bags of new clothes we bought yesterday. "Help me get ready."

"Well, shit. If I knew it was that easy to get you to do what I want, I would have insulted a lot of other things. I hate your POS Kia and your shitty apartment too."

"Nothing rivals my devotion to Dream Coyne, Harp."

I remove a pair of jeans and a T-shirt from one of the Neiman Marcus bags, taking them to the bathroom to change.

"Not so fast." Harper grabs my hand and reels me in. She takes out a dress from the bottom of another bag and gives it a shake. A dress that cost two months of my teaching salary, and is so low cut, I'd never be caught dead in it back home. Once again, Harper worked her rebellious friend magic and convinced me to buy it anyway. "If nothing else, Drew Coyne is a horndog. And we need to use that to your advantage."

A cold sweat breaks out on my neck. "I can't wear that."

"Ariana Grande, remember?" Harper rips the tags off. "You need to use all the tools in your arsenal."

"But – but—"

Harper waves off my excuses and makes a beeline for the minibar. She looks back at me, kneeling in front of the tiny refrigerator. "Want a drink? Because I can already tell I'm going to need a few."

🐫🐫🐫

Ninety minutes, two miniature bottles of tequila, and a Snickers bar later, even I have to admit, I'm giving Ariana vibes.

The floor-length dress fits me like a glove and is the perfect shade of green to bring out the emerald specks in my eyes. My five-hundred-dollar four-inch stilettos sort of give me a butt and will help bridge the fifteen-inch gap between Drew and me. Harper did my makeup and styled my hair so instead of being plastered to my head like a helmet, it's now falling in soft waves down my back. I certainly don't look like I'm going to a business meeting; I look like I'm going to the VMAs.

As you'd expect Ariana Grande to be.

In the Uber, I cross and uncross my legs, slapping my shoe against the bottom of my foot.

"Relax, MB." Harper places a supportive hand over top my twitching, sweaty ones. "You got this. You look amazing."

I move a curl behind my shoulder and turn to her. "I look ridiculous," I correct. "And besides, looks are only, like, five percent of this battle, Harp. Ninety-five percent is not throwing up."

"Trust me, Mary-Beth. It's gonna be more than you think with this guy."

"You're wrong about him."

"This is it," the Uber driver announces, putting the car in park outside a swanky apartment building surrounded by a gate and a forest of giant palm trees. My insides feel like my organs are playing a game of musical chairs. I think the odds are more like ninety-nine to one percent in favor of puking.

I take in a long slow breath and let it out even slower. Placing my feet securely on the floor, I pop my knuckles like I'm preparing for

CHAPTER 9

battle. A battle against myself—composure versus collapse.

"You can do this," Harper repeats. She opens the door and takes my hand, squeezing it tightly. "I'll be right there with you the entire time."

The security guard leads us up to Drew's apartment, and before I've even finished knocking, Drew flings open the door. For a moment, we just stare at each other, him running his eyes up and down my body several times, like he doesn't remember what I look like at all, and me, well...trying not to fall over.

Drew looks even more glorious than I remember from two hours ago, but I'm getting used to being in his presence. Enough that I can stare at him and not faint or melt or vomit or giggle. However, if I felt self-conscious before, now I feel like a circus side show. Drew is dressed for a business meeting in black slacks and a sky-blue button-up shirt, and as previously stated, I look like I'm ready to accept the award for music video of the year.

"Uh, yeah, come in," Drew finally says, moving to the side and shaking his head like he just saw the Ghost of Christmas Future. Dressed in a prom dress.

Harper pushes me inside, and I take a few hesitant steps past the door frame, my heels making uncomfortably loud clicks against the smooth hardwood floors.

Much like Drew Coyne the person, his apartment is not what I expected. Of course, I've seen glimpses online—meals prepared in his beautiful state-of-the-art kitchen, and selfies in his bright, modern bathroom. But now that I'm actually here, something is missing.

"Where's Maggie?" I ask, realizing what it is.

"Oh, Maggie's not mine." Drew brushes off the question like he's done it a million times. "I'm actually allergic to dogs. Maggie is my best friend's dog."

"But online..."

"Yeah, my sister, Darcy, she's my social media manager, and she thinks it's good for my image to have a rescue dog." Drew shrugs. "So, I said, fuck it. I can take some Claritin and hang out with Will's dog a couple times a month to please a few thousand followers."

Harper catches my eye, her eyebrows darting up in an *I told you so*. Swallowing hard, I do my best to ignore the growing sour feeling inside my stomach, more determined than ever to prove Drew is not like he seems. I shake my head, walking a few steps in front of her as Drew leads us further into the apartment.

So, he's not a dog lover. And Darcy is probably the person who tweeted Harper and the rest of the Drew Coyne faithful. No biggie. I'm sure most celebrities do stuff like that.

The further we travel into Drew's apartment, the more impressive it becomes. The space is huge and open with an entire back wall of windows that overlook Los Angeles, filling the room with light and a stunning view. It's decorated with high-end, impersonal touches. A photo of a boat on the wall. A gray pot on the end table. A fake plant in the corner. Not much different than the décor at the hotel.

On the surface, it appears clean, but looking closer, I see a stack of dishes in the sink, a heap of dirty laundry peeking out from the bedroom, and a trash can filled with beer bottles and Amazon boxes. This certainly doesn't seem like the house of someone who puts their grocery cart away. Or recycles.

We reach the space dedicated to the living room, and a different man stands from the leather couch by the wall of windows, extending his hand as he walks toward me. "You must be Mary-Beth." He takes my hand in his and shakes enthusiastically. His hands are warm and soft, which matches his demeanor. "I'm Will, Drew's manager."

"It's nice to meet you."

Will has kind eyes set behind thick glasses. He's handsome, but in a cute, geeky-best-friend sort of way. In a tells-Dad-jokes sort of way.

CHAPTER 9

In a probably-still-builds-Lego-sets sort of way.

In an anxiety-reducing way.

"So you're the one who tried to hack into my best friend's bank account?" Harper takes a menacing step in Will's direction. She puffs out her chest and glares with a glare only Harper is capable of. I guess he had a different effect on her.

"And you must be the best friend with the rainbow hair." Will laughs. He extends his hand to Harper, and she hesitantly takes it. "Will Reed."

"Harper Watkins."

"I assure you, all of Mary-Beth's financial information is secure. We were only trying to facilitate this meeting."

"It better be. Because—"

"Which brings me to the first item of business," Will says. Harper clenches and unclenches her fists but surprises me by not charging like a rhino. He hands both Drew and me a thick stack of papers filled with legal mumbo-jumbo. "NDAs."

Like I've been thwacked over the head with a Moonman trophy, I suddenly realize how stupid I am.

I'm about to sign away the single most important possession I own. The thing I've spent the past five years perfecting. The thing that could ensure a ridiculous amount of wealth—the kind that lasts for generations. The thing that if anyone ever knew was mine, would ruin me.

My biggest accomplishment. My biggest secret.

And I didn't even have the slightest inkling to at least *consult* an attorney? Instead, I brought Harper, who is more equipped to castrate Will than translate his legalese.

I clear my throat, realizing I've missed the last thirty seconds of Will's explanation.

"I'm sorry." I lean against the kitchen island, staring at Will through glassy eyes. "Could you, um, explain that again? What's an NDA?"

"A non-disclosure agreement. It's a contract by which one or more parties agree not to disclose confidential information that they have shared with each other as a necessary part of doing business together."

"Will's basically a lawyer," Drew says. "Smartest son of a bitch I know."

"Well, I *almost* graduated from law school." There's a heaviness in Will's voice before he lightens it and continues. "But I assure you, we had our attorneys draft all the paperwork, and it's ironclad. We thought it might make you feel more comfortable, knowing your identity would remain a secret. If Drew tells anyone you're Minnie Maple, you can sue him for all he's worth."

"Which is a lot." Drew gives me a look that radiates superiority. "I invest in Bitcoin, in case you didn't know."

My gaze slips over to him again, the unpleasant feeling growing each time he speaks. He's making it harder and harder to find excuses for him. I try to meet his eyes, but he keeps looking away, pretending to act indifferent toward me.

"I know," is all I say. I read online that Drew invested in Bitcoin early on, so he's worth way more than a normal Hallmark actor would be. I purse my lips and turn my attention back to Will. "I feel silly that we didn't bring an attorney. Would you mind explaining this more in depth?"

"Of course," he says, guiding me to the expensive-looking table. The four of us sink into gray, velvet chairs.

Half an hour later, Drew and I have both signed away our rights—or at least, our right to tell anyone about our arrangement or any personal information. It should make me feel better, knowing my identity is secure, but the feeling gnawing inside me is approaching intolerable levels.

Drew is just so, so...not like I thought he would be. He's arrogant and crass and disingenuous. He's not a dog-lover or a grocery-cart-

CHAPTER 9

putter-awayer, or a recycler. And he's definitely not someone who cares enough to tweet his fans or protest that his female costars get equal pay. Instead, he's cold and self-absorbed and aloof. I guess I was expecting...more.

I grimace at my signature, scribbled on the dotted line, thinking Harper might be right about Drew after all.

Before the ink on the NDA has dried, there's a knock at the door. Drew ignores it, cursing quietly under his breath, until it finally stops. But then, it picks up again, this time with shouting.

"Drew, open up. It's Britta!" a voice calls from the other side of the door. "I know you're in there. I saw your car in the parking garage. I just want to get my earrings. I need them for an audition today."

"Britta?" Drew asks Will, looking very confused as to why a woman named Britta would be pounding on his door asking for earrings.

Come on, man. Even I can put two and two together on this one.

"Britta. You know, from last week? And twice the week before? Aspiring actress, blond hair, long legs." Will looks at Harper and me and lowers his voice. "Fake..." His voice trails off, hoping the boob motions he's making will convey his point.

"Oh, yeah, Britta," Drew says, like he's just remembering the name of a movie he saw last week and only sort of liked. "She knows my car?"

"Apparently."

"Can you help her? Her earrings are probably in my room. Whenever I find one, I put it in a bowl on the bookshelf."

Will excuses himself and goes to the door. I scooch out of view, not wanting the woman to see me. Drew slides in next to me until our arms are touching, hiding from his flavor of the week like a vegan in a meat market. His skin sizzles against mine, but it's nothing compared to the unsettled feeling in my belly.

"So...I guess Will is in charge of crowd control," I mutter under my breath.

"Not always. But this girl has stage-four clinger written all over her."

My tongue goes so far into my mouth, I can probably lick my brain. So, I guess we're talking now. "And you think that's okay? To not talk to her yourself?"

"Eh. That's why I have Will."

"And *Will's* okay with that?"

"There are worse things Hollywood agents do. At least I've never asked him to bury a body." Drew laughs, leaning further out of view. He's practically in my lap now. An hour ago, I would have keeled over and gone to heaven at the thought. But the more I'm around him, the easier it is to ignore his Da Vinci good looks.

"Worse than keeping inventory of your hookups' names and running the earring lost-and-found?" I slap my hand across my mouth, shocked I let such an only-meant-for-Mary-Beth-Caroline-Abernathy-and-no-one-else thought escape.

Drew turns and looks at me—really looks at me. The first time he's done so since he first opened the door. Under his scrutiny, my respiratory system ceases production. My heart almost collapses in cardiac arrest.

"What's with the dress?" He nods at my outfit.

"What?"

Drew's eyes are squarely on my chest as he asks again, "What's with the dress?"

"I don't know what you mean."

He drags his eyes across my collarbone and up my neck until they finally rest on mine, narrowing with condescension. "I want to know why you wore that *fucking* dress to our meeting today."

I drift back an inch. "I, uh, well." I swallow, wishing I had gone with the jeans. Or the vomit-splattered leggings from the gym. "I guess I

CHAPTER 9

wanted to look nice."

Drew pauses, like he's choosing his next words very carefully. "I have to believe you know a thing or two about casual sex, Mary-Beth. Perhaps you're even an expert." Drew lowers his voice to a sexy purr and cocks one eyebrow. "Why do you act so offended about my *earring collection* when you wrote *Swallow Manor*, and you wore *that*"—eyes on boobs—"dress?" His eyes return to my face, and he gives me a crooked smile.

Oh, dear Lord baby Jesus and the angels in heaven, is Drew Coyne *hitting on me?*

I sit up a little straighter and study him. He has that look in his eye, that *wanna get outta here?* look as he unabashedly undresses me with his eyes. Yes, he's definitely giving casual-sex-with-Mary-Beth-Abernathy vibes.

Excuse me? *Okay, Ariana. I see you.*

"I, um, I mean... I actually... Uh." I look around the swanky apartment for Harper, hoping she'll be able to give me some guidance for *Dream Coyne hitting on me*, but I don't see her anywhere.

"I'll be right there with you the entire time."

Ugh. One cute nerdy friend to banter with, and she's gone. Typical.

"Honestly, when a woman wears something like *that* to my house, there's really only one thing that happens next."

I clutch the fabric of my dress and offer up a silent prayer that when I open my mouth, I'll know what to say. Because heaven knows, I'm at a loss. Mostly, I'm disgusted. Offended. *Revolted*. But a teeny tiny little, microscopic baby part of me is intrigued.

Flattered.

Curious.

"Well, actually..." I wipe my sweaty palms, probably ruining the dress's expensive fabric. "There's, um, not any, uh, casual sex in *Swallow Manor*. Susan and Ambrose fall in love and –"

"But to write something like that, you've obviously—"

"And so um, and that's, um, because, I, uh, I don't believe in having casual sex. Because, you see, I um, I've never—"

"No fucking way." Drew bursts into laughter. "You're a *virgin*?"

Something about the way he's cussing or the way he's cackling or the dirty dishes in the sink or the lack of dog fur in the air is the final straw. The nail in the coffin. The coup de grace.

The unmistakable bursting of my Drew Coyne bubble.

I lurch in his direction, nearly tipping over my velvet chair. "I never said that," I hiss. "Because, actually, I do know a thing or two about sex. Enough to know that there's nothing casual about it. Or at least there shouldn't be. It should be about love. About connection. Virgin or not, I know how intimacy is *supposed* to work."

Drew looks a little taken aback but recovers quickly. "Maybe it's like that where you come from. But here in the real world, this is normal."

"So Hollywood is the real world?" It's impossible to keep the sarcasm from my voice.

"Hollywood isn't the kiddie table. It's where the adults sit."

"Well, maybe Hollywood is wrong." I stick up my chin. "Maybe *you're* wrong."

"Wrong about what?"

"Just, like, everything. How you are."

Drew laughs. "Oh, yeah? How am I?"

"You're just...different than you pretend to be. In your movies. Online."

"Is this because I don't have a dog? Shit, Mary-Beth, who cares?"

"This isn't about the dog."

"Okay, then what?" Drew's eyes coalesce on mine, and I suck in a breath. "How am I different?"

"You don't recycle." My eyes dart to the trash.

"Oh, *God*." Drew rubs his fingers across his short hair. "And guess what, I don't actually use those piece-of-shit hammocks either. Or the hiking boots."

"And you don't think that's wrong?"

Drew throws his arms up in defeat. "Okay, you got me. I should recycle. I usually do, but today, I was rushing."

"And what about promoting products you don't use? Smoothies and hammocks and hiking boots? Don't you think that's dishonest? Deceitful? Delusive? Deceptiv—"

"Smoothies?" He raises his eyebrows.

"You posted about a kiwi-blueberry turmeric pumpkin seed smoothie, and I tried it, and it made me puke. There's no way anyone could actually enjoy that. Today, you threw it away without taking one sip."

Drew brings his face just inches from mine. I instinctively hold my breath.

"Shit, woman. Are you stalking me?"

I try to hide my embarrassment, but there's obviously no point in denying it now.

"Just online." I crinkle my nose. "Though I'm regretting that now."

"Well, here's something you won't find online. I've been a slave to the Hallmark brand for six goddamn years. They expect me to be a certain way and portray a certain image. I don't have the luxury of doing what I want."

Drew's honesty takes me by surprise, and I turn away and take a few deep breaths. But like a vacuum, I'm sucked back into his cold, blue gaze.

"Well, neither do I."

"Okay, so then you should understand. I'll ask you again: what's so wrong about the way that I am?"

"You're wrong for sleeping with so many women that you can't remember their names and have a collection of their missing earrings.

You're wrong for not caring. I didn't think you were like that."

Anger flashes across Drew's face, and I realize something I said hurt his feelings. He narrows his eyes, inspecting me like I'm nothing more than a gnat that keeps buzzing in his ear. "How old are you, Mary-Beth? Eighteen? Nineteen, maybe?"

"I'm twenty-three." I put a hand to my heart to keep it from jumping out of my rib cage. "And I'll have you know, the last time I went out, I didn't even get carded."

"Is that because the stable hands were running security that night?"

I feel my nostrils flare. "What are you trying to say?"

"I'm trying to say you're a naïve hillbilly from a Podunk little town in"—Drew snatches the NDA off the table, studying it for a moment—"fucking Indiana, who knows nothing about me or how this business works. So please, if you could stop making assumptions, that would be great."

I let out a loud snort, clutching the edge of the table with white knuckles. "Oh, I'm the one making assumptions, am I? You don't know a thing about me. Do you even know my last name?"

"My guess would be *Virgin*." He draws out the two syllables to sound more like ten. "Mary-Beth Virgin. Want to talk about being different than expected? Fuck! How did you even write this book in the first place? You must watch a shit load of porn, because clearly you've never had sex with anyone."

"Well, joke's on you, because I never watch porn. Just your terrible Hallmark movies." I suck in a breath, preparing to go for the jugular. "That's right. When I was writing my books, I was thinking about my favorite celebrity. The one with a good heart and a dog named Maggie. I wrote them about *you*."

"I agree, the movies are shit." Drew chooses not to acknowledge the part about the books, but his reaction is clearly written on his face—somewhere between revolted and stupefied. "That's why I'm

CHAPTER 9

talking to your ass in the first place. Because I. Want. Out. I guarantee I would never speak to you in the real fucking world otherwise."

"Please stop cussing!" I push away from the table, nearly toppling over in the process.

Drew stands and takes a lap around the room before coming chest-to-chest with me. We are fuming at each other when I notice Will and Harper, matching shocked expression on their white faces.

"So, maybe it's time to talk about the rights to *Swallow Manor*," Will says calmly, reaching out his hand like he's trying not to scare a skittish animal.

I look up at Drew, towering over me despite my high-heeled shoes. I stick my chin up and meet his eyes. "You"—I poke his chest with my index finger—"will *never* have the rights to *Swallow Manor*. I would give them to a bum on the street before *you*."

"Oh, you'll be *swallowing*, all right. Just you wait."

"I think that comment was meant for Britta. If you can even remember who that is." I make a sound that is a mixture of throat and nasal and march over to Harper, hooking her elbow with mine.

"Oh, Britta's definitely a swallower. You should have seen her, taking every last drop." Drew's eyes are feral. "But you've got *spitter* written all over you."

"You're pathetic."

"You're a self-righteous bitch."

"You're a conceited tool."

"Ouch, *tool*—you really got me with that one!"

"I'm leaving."

"Adios, Virgin Mary."

"It's Abernathy!" I scream and all but yank Harper out the door.

Chapter 10

Andrew Edward Coyne
Conceited Tool

"What the hell happened, man?"

What the hell happened? What the *hell* happened? Virgin Mary-Beth Abernathy happened. Riding in on her high horse, she shows up looking like she's going to the fucking Oscars in a dress that made me notice the green in her eyes and the curves of her body that had seemed nonexistent before. Self-righteous, judgy, arrogant. *Beautiful.* Then, she proceeded to ruin my life in all the ways a life can be ruined.

How she ever wrote a book like *Swallow Manor*, I'll never know. And *God*, she wrote it about *me*.

"I'm not sure how that *she-devil* wrote that book," I say. "But we've got to pivot. I can't work with her."

"I'm afraid that's not an option at this point." Will won't meet my eyes. "We put all our eggs into the *Swallow Manor* basket, remember."

"Shit." I down the rest of my drink—the third since Mary-Beth left. I rub my chin. "Well, at least we know who she is now. We'll threaten to blackmail if she doesn't sign the rights."

"That's a no-can-do." Will points to the stacks of paper still on my dining room table. "The NDA, remember?"

CHAPTER 10

I slam my empty glass down, quickly pouring another. "I wonder if all my fans are this crazy." I wave my drink in the air, almost spilling the whiskey. "Or did we just find the one who's absolutely psychotic?"

"She did write at least five books about you," Will points out. "That is some next-level stalker shit. Maybe we should have seen this coming."

"I saw something coming..." I laugh. "But it certainly wasn't this."

"So, we either..." Will ignores my vulgar comment and pours himself a drink. "Completely abandon the *Swallow Manor* project, let down all your fans, and officially say goodbye to your acting career, or you have to figure out a way to work with Mary-Beth."

"God, why are both options so terrible?"

"Maybe you should apologize."

"*Apologize*?" I swallow and slam my empty glass down again. "For what?"

"For being so rude. You barely know the girl, and you called her a bitch."

"She was acting bitchy." My hands fall to my sides, not wanting to admit he's probably right. "What was I supposed to do?"

"Control yourself until she signed the book rights?" Will offers, like the answer is obvious.

"But she's so..." I finish the sentence with a sound somewhere between a grunt and growl. There is no word in the English language for how *grrr* she is.

"Well, she's clearly a fan of Hallmark Drew. Why not pretend to be him for a few days so we can get this deal done?"

"How so?"

"Enchant her with your wit and good looks. Butter her up. Be nice and down to earth until she signs away the rights."

"Mary-Beth is one hundred percent a tight-ass virgin who would rather shove a poison ivy-covered stick up there before sleeping with me." I shake my head and pour myself another shot. "Or work with me. She'd made that abundantly clear while she was here."

"I never said anything about fucking her." Will shrugs, the corner of his lips pulling up. "I mean, maybe romance her a little bit."

"Romance? What the hell man? You know I don't do romance."

"You may not do it in real life, but you're an expert in romance on screen. And if you want the rights to *Swallow Manor*, I think you're going to have to turn on the charm."

🐑🐑🐑

I've faced some challenging times in my career, but this has to be rock bottom.

Later that night, I'm lying in my bed, six drinks in, but wide awake. Every time I close my eyes, I see her—Mary-Beth in that *dress.* The dress that gave her just enough cleavage to pique my interest and bring out the green circling her huge brown eyes. How the heels she wore made me notice what a cute ass she has and put her at just the right height to fit perfectly in my arms.

But then, she opens her mouth, and the fantasy is gone.

She's a virgin. And a virgin for a reason. Virgins come with baggage. Virgins want commitment. Virgins are looking for *the one*.

I've stayed away from that type for a reason. A virgin would ask for too much, and I could never give it to her.

But you read what she wrote. Virgin or not, she's got a dirty mind.

And...now I'm hard.

So, yeah, I'll admit...I want to fuck her. But there are a lot of women in that category. What I don't want to do is *romance* her. I'd just as well stick my dick into a cactus as try and butter up Miss Indiana Chastity Junior Princess. I know I overreacted, but *that* seems impossible.

But my career is depending on this. It's depending on getting those movie rights. BookTok grows more and more hostile every day, eager for me to find Cinderella, put a glass slipper on that bitch, and declare

CHAPTER 10

Swallow Manor the movie is coming to a theater near you.

What comes after hostile? I'm too afraid to admit it's probably irrelevance. And irrelevance is the step right before, "I'm sorry, Drew, but the only thing I could get you an audition for this month is that foot fungus commercial."

The step before the end of my career. And my career isn't just about me. It's about Darcy and Will and Chloe too.

I guess I could say I wasn't able to find her. She's too elusive, too anonymous. Too not-giving-a-shit about making money or being famous or ruining my life. Then I could go back to making Hallmark movies until I die. I'm sure if we beg, Will could still get me slated for the lighthouse movie. But honestly, that sounds like a fate worse than Mary-Beth Abernathy.

No, I must strike now. While the iron is hot. While people still care. While viral videos and momentum are on my side. This is a turning point. Not just professionally, but personally. I'm not happy; I haven't been for a long time. And I can't help but feel like making this deal with Mary-Beth is the key to changing that.

This whole ordeal is just a lot more work than I anticipated. I figured once I found Minnie Maple, we'd sign the paperwork, I'd give her the night of her life, and I'd never see her again. Forging a relationship, even a fake one, seems...daunting.

I haven't had much of a relationship outside of Will, Chloe, and Darcy for some time. Sure, I have "friends" in the industry—costars and directors and whatnot. But we all have an understanding that we're trying to further the other's career and nothing more. And let's not even start on a *romantic* relationship. My parents' fucked-up relationship guarantees I'll never have that. I'll fucking die alone before I turn into my dad.

Yes, I'm a man, and I have needs, but I'm lucky enough that I can have those fulfilled without all the extra shit women sometimes need.

Women like Mary-Beth.

I roll over and put my pillow over my head, trying again for sleep. I've never been one to back down from a challenge, and I don't intend to start now. Even when the challenge acts like a child, writes like a porn star, thinks like a nun, and has the curves of a woman.

She's like a big walking contradiction. Actually, a small one. I'm pretty sure Mary-Beth is barely five feet tall.

Charm, Will said. Charm her.

I'll show her how goddamn *charming* I can be.

Chapter 11

Mary-Beth Caroline Abernathy
Self-Righteous Bitch

They say to never meet your heroes, right? That must include celebrity crushes too.

I'm awoken by strong perfume the next morning.

"MB, you have to get out of bed today." Harper flicks on the lights and pulls the drapes.

I hiss at her and slink under the covers like a vampire afraid of turning to dust.

"It's been almost twenty-four hours." Harper looks way too awake as she places a cup of coffee on my bedside table. "Drew, no matter how gorgeous he might be, isn't worth all this."

"He called me a self-righteous bitch." I look at Harper through my squinty eyes, swollen from crying all night, and take a precautionary sip of her caffeinated offering. "Drew Coyne thinks I'm a self-righteous bitch."

"I hate to tell you this, but you kind of acted like one."

"But he was just so...so..." I can't seem to find the word describing just how *grrr* he was.

"I tried to warn you. Your expectations were way too high. You put him on a pedestal."

"He put himself there. He dons this persona like he's genuine and cares and is a good person." My squeaky voice crashes, lowering at least two octaves. "But he's not. He's terrible. He isn't like his movies or his Instagram at all."

"To be fair to him, when we met in person, I could tell that from the jump. Clearly, anyone who knows him in real life knows his movies and Instagram aren't the real him."

"So you're on his side now?"

"MB, I'm your best friend. I'm *always* on your side." Harper gingerly sits on the edge of the bed. "But I tried to tell you he's not the saint you made him out to be. Yeah, so he sleeps around. I'm sure every man in L.A. does. Hell, if given the chance, so would I." Harper laughs, tossing her hair over her shoulder. "It doesn't make him a bad person."

"It wasn't that he's sleeping with so many women. It was that..." My lips purse into a line. "That he didn't know their names. That he had a bowl full of rando lost earrings. That he slept with that Britta chick last week and tried to avoid her like the plague yesterday. It's one thing to sleep with a lot of women. It's another to not care about them. Like, at all."

"Mary-Beth, I know you have a sensitive heart. And you're saving yourself for the One." Harper tries to keep the cynicism out of her voice and fails. "And when you do eventually have sex, it will mean a lot to you. But Drew is kind of right. To the rest of us, it's just...not that big a deal."

I pause, imagining a world where a man sticking his penis inside your body with one of the known potential consequences being a new human person in the world was not a big deal.

I've been taught my whole life sex is not only a big deal, but the biggest deal. And that after said deal is done, you're never the same again, which is why you wait to do the deed until you're sure you're making the right deal.

CHAPTER 11

That sounds like some sort of demented nursery rhyme.

But the truth is, I'm not waiting for the one, per se. I'm just waiting until I find someone worth having sex with. Someone who is sure about me. Who I'm sure about. Someone who won't treat me like just another earring. The longer I wait, the more I doubt that person exists. Especially after meeting Drew.

I'm probably destined to die a spinster virgin. Just like Lady Harriet Yvonne Barrington in *Swallow Manor: Book Four.*

"So you think I was too hard on him?" I cautiously look up at Harper through my eyelashes.

"I just think it's silly to miss out on selling the book rights and making"— Harper picks up the paperwork Will shoved at us on our way out the door. Her eyes grow wide at all the zeros— "a shit ton of money just because Drew Coyne didn't live up to your impossibly high standards." Harper flips her rainbow tresses over her shoulder. "So, he isn't what you expected. Fine. Don't let that influence a lucrative business deal with the man."

I almost completely forgot that's why we were at Drew's apartment in the first place. The book somehow seems secondary to the disappointment of Drew being worse than advertised. And not just worse. The *worst.*

"I can't give *Swallow Manor* to someone like that, Harp." I square my shoulders. "It's my baby. I want it to go to a good person. Someone who understands the book and will do it the justice it deserves. The person we met yesterday isn't it."

"Maybe if we gave him another shot? Everyone knows reformed rakes make the best husbands, right?" Harper laughs.

"Harp, Drew Coyne is past the point of reform. Clearly, he'll be a rake forever."

"No redemption? That doesn't sound like a preacher's daughter."

I give Harper my most menacing glare, and she rolls her eyes.

"Fine. At least let him explain? We know where he lives, and I've got all his info right here on the NDA."

I shiver, thinking about being in the same room as Drew again. Our first two rendezvouses hadn't exactly gone according to plan. First, I'd melted. Second, I'd imploded. I hate to imagine what could happen during visit number three. I'm not the type to castrate someone, but part of me thinks I'd be doing the entire female population a favor.

I shake my head. "Honestly, I never want to see Drew Coyne ever again. And if that means I never sell the book rights, I'm okay with that."

Chapter 12

Mary-Beth Caroline Abernathy
Unavailable:
Currently burning $500 shoes

After meeting Drew, Los Angeles also lost its luster. Harper and I stumbled through a half-hearted week of sightseeing, and now I'm grateful to be back in my hometown, at my mama's house, enjoying Easter dinner. Being here after the whole Drew Coyne fiasco feels like the big warm hug I needed. Around the table are people of a higher caliber. My parents, Nana, my Aunt Felicity, Uncle John, and three younger cousins: Reese (fifteen), Walker (ten), and Joey (six).

"The services were delightful today, Clark," Nana says, gumming a few bites of cheesy potatoes and swallowing hard. Aunt Felicity and Uncle John nod in agreement.

"Yes, Easter Sunday is always my favorite, honey," Mama chimes in. "It was beautiful."

"Well, that was all the Lord. It's His special day, after all." My dad looks around the table, taking a moment to grin at each of us, before settling his eyes back on his plate. I'm grateful he doesn't study me for too long. While I may have put Drew Coyne in his place for being a hypocrite, let's not forget that I'm one as well.

After the huge Drew TikTok surge, sales have slowed a bit. And by a bit, I mean a few hundred a week. I'm still very much riding the wave of self-publishing fortune, and still very much not knowing what to do about it.

"Great dinner, Aunt Lily." Reese excuses herself from the table, taking her plate to the sink and securing her AirPods underneath her sheet of long golden hair. Her younger brothers quickly follow suit, each ditching the grownups and pulling out a Nintendo Switch.

I relax into my chair and take a big bite of ham. My mother cooks the perfect ham, and it tastes like heaven. There's something about a cinnamon-orange glaze on a pig's butt that just squeals *home*. Yes, this is what I needed. A reminder of what's really important. Good food and good company, Jesus and family and—

"Mary-Beth!" Joey hollers from the entryway. "There's some dude here looking for you! He says he's your *boyfriend*?"

"Boyfriend?" I gag on the ham, coughing until a piece of it goes flying onto my mother's lace tablecloth.

"No way, is that Drew Coyne? What's he doing *here*?" Reese whispers. She turns to me, her eyes wide. "Mary-Beth, are you dating Drew Coyne? How could you not tell me you're dating *Drew Coyne*?"

I take a small sip of my water, striving with all my might to gain some composure. I should have known it wouldn't be this easy to get rid of Drew. He does have all of BookTok on a witch hunt for me.

"I'm not," I grind out, clutching the tablecloth so hard, my utensils begin to shift.

My mother's eyes dart to mine, a hint of panic swirling inside her golden-brown irises. "Mary-Beth, you didn't tell me you were expecting a visitor." I can practically see the wheels turning in her head. Everything from *Do we have the extra china?* to *Did I make enough ham?* to *Why is my daughter keeping so many secrets from me?*

I don't respond as I push away from the table, the napkin in my lap

CHAPTER 12

falling to the floor in crumpled abandonment.

"There she is!" Drew's entire face lights up when he sees me. "Hi, Mary!"

"Oh my gosh, he calls you Mary?" Reese squeals as I pass her on the way to the door. I clench my teeth into what I'm hoping is a passable smile. "No one calls you Mary."

Drew stands in the doorway, wearing a sweater that belongs on a chess champion and a smile that belongs on a clown. He's holding a bouquet of tulips in one arm and waving the other at me, like he's ready to pull me into a hug. Staying three feet away, I squeeze his hand as hard as I possibly can and give it an aggressive shake.

"What are you doing here?" I hiss between gritted teeth.

"Just here to meet the fam," he says, his perma-smile never flinching. They must literally teach you lying through your teeth in acting school.

"Well, Mary-Beth, aren't you going to invite your guest in?" My dad instantly appears behind me. He rests a hand on my shoulder and offers Drew the other. "I'm Clark Abernathy, Mary-Beth's dad. Please, come in."

"Drew. Thanks." Drew gives my dad's hand an enthusiastic jiggle before stepping into my parents' house. *My parents' house.* The house where I lost my baby teeth and started my period and got stuck crawling out the window on prom night looking like cotton candy.

The house I was sitting in when I first saw Drew Coyne on TV. Where I wrote the first draft of *Swallow Manor*, under the covers of my bed, strictly between the hours of midnight and 4 a.m., fantasizing about *Drew Coyne*.

The me from two weeks ago would be dead. Literally deceased. The me from today wishes someone were dead...but it isn't me.

"Lily Abernathy." Mama juts her hand straight past me and practically into Drew's abdomen. He offers her a dazzling smile when they shake.

"Drew." He hands her the tulips. "You have a lovely home, Mrs. Abernathy."

My mother blushes and smiles at Drew, then gives me a stern look that seems to say, "Why didn't you tell me your new hot boyfriend was coming over for Easter dinner?"

I feel like I'm on a love boat setting sail that I can't jump from. Everyone in the house crowds around us, introducing themselves, asking why I didn't tell them about our unexpected guest, and a million other things I wish they wouldn't be doing.

"Drew." I meet his eyes through the crowd. "I have to talk to you." I clear my throat and lower my voice. "Alone."

Reese raises her eyebrows and gives me a coy smile. I try not to throw up in my mouth.

"I, uh, wanted to give you that, uh, scarf I knitted for you. You know Southern California...still cold in April." I shake my head and grab Drew's arm, yanking him down the hall. "It's in my room."

I slink against the back of the door when Drew and I are alone.

"You didn't tell me you knit, though I have to say, it fits with the whole Virgin Mary bit."

"I don't *knit*," I seethe. "I *pretend* to knit so my family will leave me alone about my extra influx of cash."

"You can make that much money knitting?" For a moment, Drew actually looks like he's trying to compute how that's possible.

"Of course not, you idiot." I fight the urge to stomp on his foot with my high-heeled shoes. The same ones I was wearing the last time I saw him. Maybe I should burn them. You know what, five hundred dollars or not, I *will* burn them. "What are you doing here?"

"I'm here to apologize."

I stick my chin up. "Apology not accepted. Now, leave."

"I'm also here to convince you to change your mind about *Swallow*

CHAPTER 12

Manor."

"I already told you you're the last person on earth I'd trust with *Swallow Manor*. How is showing up at my family's house on Easter pretending to be my boyfriend going to change that?"

Drew's eyebrows dart up. "Shit, it's Easter?"

"Shhh," I chide self-consciously. "You can't cuss in my *parents' house*! How do you not know it's Easter?"

"Not really a religious guy." Drew shrugs. "I honestly didn't even think about it."

"Why else would my entire family be here? My aunt and uncle live an hour away."

"I have to admit, I wasn't planning on meeting your whole family. But I was just looking for you at your apartment and your neighbor across the hall said this is where you'd be. Right here on *Maple* Avenue."

I quickly move my hair in front of my shoulders to try to hide my blush. Glancing in the mirror above my dresser, I'm not surprised it didn't work. "Well, you found me. Congrats. And guess what? You're still not getting the rights to *Swallow Manor*. Now please leave."

Drew begins to stride around my small room, still filled with knickknacks from when I was a child. He picks up a stuffed cat from my bed and tosses it to me. I don't generate even an ounce of effort to catch it. It hits me on the shoulder and falls to the ground.

"That's a, uh, no can do, Virgin Mary. Because you've got a house full of people out there who want to know why Drew Coyne of all people is in their home. And dating their daughter."

"Boyfriend?" I run my fingers down my face. "Really?"

"Foolproof way to make sure you'd let me inside."

"Isn't this a violation of the NDA?" I rasp, grasping at straws.

"As long as I don't reveal that you're Minnie Maple, no."

"So, you *did* plan this."

"Not exactly..." Drew's lips curl into a nauseating smile. "I made it up on the way over here. But it's working out pretty well, actually."

"Mary-Beth! We're just about to cut the cake! Carrot cake, your favorite." My mother's voice peals down the hall, distant, but somehow right on top of us. I shudder and send Drew a scathing look across the sea of porcelain dolls on the bench between us. My family never eats dessert this soon after dinner, which means this must be a ploy to get me and my new mysterious boyfriend out of the forbidden territory of my unchaperoned bedroom.

I press my hands to my temples, trying to figure out a way out of this. Drew, while an idiot, is right. The only other explanation for him being here, outside of securing my book rights, is that we met in Los Angeles, and are now—*cue the dramatic music*—together. And now I either have to come clean about the real reason Drew is here or lie about dating the most awful person I've ever met.

What has my world become that I'm somehow fake dating *Drew Coyne*, and I'm not ecstatic about it? Probably the same reason I made twenty-five thousand dollars (actually forty thousand!) in one day and wanted to crawl in a hole and hide for the next ten years.

Life is weird.

"You better not embarrass me in front of my family." I grab Drew's hand and jerk him toward the door. "And I want to talk to Will about his crappy NDA. I feel like this should be against the rules."

Carrot cake is indeed my favorite, although I have a feeling it won't be, not after today. I push the cream cheese frosting around my plate, not taking a single bite. Instead, I'm fantasizing about stabbing Drew with my corn-shaped corn-on-the-cob holder under the table.

"So, Drew," my dad says between bites of his cake. "What do you do?"

"He's an actor!" Reese to my left blurts out.

Like the sun coming over the horizon to start the day, realization

CHAPTER 12

dawns on my mother's face. "I thought you looked familiar! Mary-Beth has always been a huge fan of your work."

Drew turns to me and smiles. No one else would be able to notice how fake it is, but he's given me enough fake smiles that I'm becoming somewhat of an expert. "Well, the feeling is definitely mutual."

Actor is right. And today's role is doting, respectful, down-to-earth boyfriend. Everything he isn't in real life.

"How could you not tell us you'd met Drew Coyne, honey?" My mother looks flabbergasted that I could leave such a life-altering event out of my Los Angeles vacation recap.

"Yes, how did the two of you meet?" my dad asks.

"Um, well, I.... He, uh..."

"She literally fell into my lap," Drew says with a sparkly laugh, and I slump into my chair. Around the table, everyone looks utterly captivated by him. Everyone but me. "She and Harper decided to hit up the gym while they were in L.A., and I was lucky enough that she picked mine. We were, um" — Drew smiles like he's reliving a happy memory. *Damn, he's good* — "both going for the same weight machine, and she truly did just fall into my arms."

My mother gives me a perplexing look. "You and Harper went to the *gym*?"

My butt cheeks clench. If I'd have known Drew was going to go with the actual story of how we met, I would have interrupted him. No one in my family is going to believe that Harper and I willingly went to the gym. Although naturally thin, I'm more likely to eat an entire pizza by myself than participate in organized exercise.

"We just thought it might be fun." I laugh nervously. "You know, sweat where the celebrities sweat."

Sweat.

I can't believe I wanted to lick Drew's *sweat*. Granted, the abs it came from were the closest thing to heaven I'd seen at the time, but still.

My mom and aunt trade a look, as if they're not buying my story, but don't really care.

"And then, you just, what? Exchanged numbers? Do people in Los Angeles do that?" Aunt Felicity asks, her eyes wide with curiosity.

Drew turns and gives me a genuine smile. "Yeah, uh"—he laughs a little, and my traitorous heart skips a beat—"Mary-Beth definitely made an impression. I knew I had to see her again."

I want to melt against my seat. I want to let my insides turn to mush. I want to believe this fairy tale.

But then I remember that everything is fake. Everything.

"Darling," my mother says. "Why didn't you tell us?"

I open my mouth to resume making inhumanly sounds and/or damning confessions, when Drew interrupts.

"I'm in the middle of promoting my latest movie, and the network doesn't like for me to be seeing anyone during the press tour. It can take away from ratings and all that. So I asked Mary to keep it quiet." Drew looks at me and winks. "For now."

I realize my mouth is still hanging open and shut it with a snap.

"Well, you won't have a problem with the press here, will you, Bethie?" My dad has a huge grin, like nothing could delight him more than seeing his daughter on the arm of America's sweetheart. *If only he knew.* "How long are you in town, Drew?"

"As long as Mary will have me." Drew laughs and the entire table, save me, joins in. "But in all seriousness, I don't have to be back in L.A. until the tenth. I've got all week to convince Mary to keep me around."

My dad laughs again, craning his head back. Laughing like I'd be a buffoon to say no to Drew Coyne. "That shouldn't be a problem!"

🐥🐥🐥

Two hours later, if I thought I hated Drew before, I really, *really* hate him now. Two hours ago, I had the intention of hating him privately, quietly stewing about his awfulness in the alcoves of my mind for the

CHAPTER 12

rest of my days. Now, I have to spend the rest of my week pretending to *like* him.

What's worse, the rest of my family won't have to pretend.

"Don't forget to call me with that tee-time!" Uncle John shakes Drew's hand, patting him on the back enthusiastically.

"I wouldn't dream of it, John!"

"Do you think you could get me a signed autograph from Heather Locklear? I just really love her," Aunt Felicity asks.

"I'll text Heather tonight. Shouldn't be a problem."

"Bethie, we're so happy for you." Daddy pulls Drew and me into a hug sandwich—Drew's cheek pressed against my Dad's left pectoral and mine against his right.

"Hey." Reese pulls Drew and I off to the side, her voice hushed as she looks back in paranoia. "Have you found Minnie Maple yet?"

I can feel the blood draining from my face, ounce by ounce until I'm convinced there must be a huge puddle of it by my feet. Drew must see it too, because he quickly reaches his arm under mine to help keep me upright. Against my will, my heart kangaroos back to life, pumping blood to the skin touching his.

"Yeah, uh, not yet," he whispers, his eyes darting to mine.

"Mama says *Swallow Manor* is a dirty book, but my friend, Margo, let me borrow it." Reese's eyes dance between Drew and me. "I hope you find her. I'd definitely risk getting grounded to watch that movie. The book's so good, right?"

I lean more heavily against Drew's arm. Good Lord, my innocent fifteen-year-old niece has read *Swallow Manor*? When will the madness end?

Amusement toys with Drew's lips, but he's not quite smiling. His eyes burn with intensity as they lock with mine. "I hope I find her too."

Chapter 13

Andrew Edward Coyne
The Worst Person Mary-Beth Caroline Abernathy Has Ever Met

"Are you talking about that dirty book again?" the aunt asks her daughter.

Mary-Beth jumps, then starts slipping from my grasp, even more limp than before if that's possible. I quickly hoist her up, resting her against my hip. If they keep talking about the damn book, I'm going to need puppet strings to keep her upright.

"It's not a dirty book. It's *mature literature*." The girl squares her shoulders with her mother and gives her a fiery look. I instantly like her more. "Not that I would know, of course. But Drew's been trying to find the author. He wants to make it into a movie."

I take back the liking part.

Seven pairs of eyes coalesce on me, waiting for an explanation.

Fuck. My. Life.

"You're going to make *Swallow Manor* into a movie, Drew?" Mary-Beth's mother asks.

Next to me, Mary-Beth springs to life, suddenly able to stand on her own. She turns to her mother, looking more surprised that she's heard of her book than if she'd sprouted a second head and it started rapping Eminem songs in operatic vibrato.

CHAPTER 13

"You know about that book, Mama?" Her voice is small, but clear.

Ballsy, Virgin Mary.

"Oh, some of the ladies at Bunco were talking about it. They say it's full of"— Lily Abernathy's voice drops a decibel or two as she raises a hand to shield her mouth from the children— "sexually explicit descriptions."

I swear an audible gasp goes around the room, and I have to bite the inside of my cheek from bursting into laughter. I'm beginning to see why Mary-Beth is trying so hard to keep Minnie Maple a secret.

Mary-Beth's pastor father turns to me, his blue eyes shining with betrayal. "Drew, is this true?"

Shit.

Why I thought this wouldn't get brought up today, I'll never know. I guess I didn't think they had TikTok this far out in the Indiana boondocks. Hell, it took Mary-Beth over a week to see my offer, and I have a feeling if Harper hadn't sent it to her, she still wouldn't know.

I dig my fingernails into my palm and try to think of an explanation. I'm almost regretting the whole boyfriend ploy, except Mary-Beth already seems resigned to the fact that she has to keep me around for at least a little while. Hopefully long enough to change her mind and convince her to sign away the rights. But if her family believes I'm the same douchebag Mary-Beth already thinks I am, I'll have no reason to stay here long enough to finish dessert.

I run my hand across my neck, then look down at Mary-Beth. Her eyes are dilated, and her chest is heaving. I snake my arm around her and shake her shoulders playfully.

"Well, it's, uh, something that my manager, Will, suggested to boost my career. He's always thinking of something, God bless him." I chuckle a little. "But I'm not sure if it's the right move. As I'm sure you know, I like to take on more wholesome roles. I don't like to compromise my values, so it's definitely something I'm reconsidering."

The group takes a collective breath as Mary-Beth's dad claps me on the shoulder. "You're a good man, Drew Coyne." He puts his arms around Mary-Beth and me, escorting us to the front door. "Easter is all about second chances. I'm sure you'll make the right choice."

"Well, I think Drew needs to be going." Mary-Beth nearly vomits the words out, seizing my arm and yanking. She sure does like to do that. "I'll walk you to your car."

A chorus of goodbyes erupt, and I'm pulled into several hugs on our way out. The grandma even kisses me on the cheek.

"Thank you so much for coming, Drew," the mom says. "You're welcome back anytime."

"This was lovely, Mrs. Abernathy. Thank you for having me."

I smile as I walk outside.

Even though charming Mary-Beth is damn near impossible, her family was cake.

By my rental car, Mary-Beth is throwing scalpels with her eyes. For such an innocent little thing, she sure is feisty when provoked.

"Go back to L.A. I'm not giving you my book."

I raise my eyebrows at my new fake girlfriend. "You've said as much. But I can't go back yet. I have a tee-time with Uncle John and his buddies from the office at the end of the week."

Metaphoric steam begins seeping out of Mary-Beth's ears. "You can't fool my family forever."

My lips pull up in a half-smile. "And you think you can?"

The ball in Mary-Beth's throat bounces as she swallows hard. Then she sets her jaw, meeting my eyes. "I swear, you will never have the rights to my book. Whatever game you think you're playing, I assure you, you won't win."

"I only need to fool your family for just long enough." I rub my jaw,

CHAPTER 13

looking up at the quickly darkening sky. "Then, when I'm gone making my dirty movie out in L.A., you'll have the perfect excuse to break up with me. I'll be the miscreant they feared all along. No parents would want someone like that for their little princess."

"It's true. No one would want someone like you."

"I can assure you many women do."

"Well...I can assure you not this woman. In any capacity."

"Oh, Mary." I lower my voice and take a small step into the no-man's land between us. "I think we'll see about that."

Mary-Beth's eyes are wide, but she doesn't retreat. I loom over her, at least a foot taller than she is, even in the heels. The same heels from before. The cute ass heels. And while her pink dress definitely isn't the green dress from before, it fits her well. With just enough makeup, long curled hair, giant brown eyes rimmed green, and pink full lips, she looks nice.

Plain. Ordinary. Innocent.

But nice.

For not the first time tonight, I have the baffling desire to grab her around the waist and pull her to my chest. To run my hands across her petite body and cover her mouth with mine. I begin bending down, narrowing in.

Mary-Beth licks her lips, and her eyes dart to the house behind us. Then she leans forward, as if she's going to accept my invitation. I lick my own lips and place my hand on her tiny waist in preparation, ready to release some of this pent-up sexual tension. But at the last minute, she reaches up and slaps me.

"You're the worst person I've ever met." She pushes away so quickly she almost trips on a crack in the driveway.

My hand flies to my cheek, and I flop back against the car in a fit of laughter.

"So I guess I'll see you tomorrow, then, babe." I reach for the car door, turning to give Mary-Beth one last agitating smile. She looks like she's about to spit on me, which only makes my smile wider.

There's something about annoying her that is strangely satisfying. After all the annoying she's done to me, it's nice to even the score.

Chapter 14

Mary-Beth Caroline Abernathy
~~Good~~ Different

"Mary-Beth, did you just kiss Drew Coyne?" Reese pulls me aside before the rest of the family can pick over my dead carcass.

My face instantly feels hot. "Well, um..."

No, I hadn't kissed Drew Coyne. But the fact that I had wanted to made me guilty enough.

He had just been standing *so close*. Close enough that I felt what every woman he's ever been with felt. The actresses from his movies and the earring ladies of the night. I was in *that* club. The club of women seduced by Drew Coyne.

I'd experienced the mesmerizing effect of his ice-blue eyes. The heat pulsing from his body onto mine. The spark of desire when his fingertips met my waist.

Drew Coyne was right there. And he was trying to kiss me. Part of me even thinks he wanted to. It happened so fast, in my parent's driveway, with my entire family watching behind the lace curtains in the living room.

So...I slapped him instead.

Because I know it's just an act. It isn't real. He doesn't really want me. He doesn't really want anybody. He wants to get off, and he wants the movie rights to *Swallow Manor*. Neither of which he'll be getting from me.

"Oh my gosh!" Reese squeals, taking my blush as admission. "What's it like dating a celebrity?"

I swallow, trying to collect my thoughts. In the space of one Easter afternoon, my entire world has changed. I will no longer be able to ride the wave of anonymity for the rest of my life. In Daisy Bluff, this news was going to travel fast. Like, faster than ice-cream-melting-on-the-Fourth-of-July fast. Fast like you can't even eat it and it drips down the cone and makes your hands all sticky fast.

And unfortunately, if Drew is going to be here, and I am going to keep my secret, I've got no choice but to play along until he gets frustrated and leaves.

This is a battle of wills, and I am going to win.

"He's so great, right?" I bat my eyelashes. "It's like a dream come true."

Reese swoons, catching herself on the wall before she falls to the floor. She puts one hand to her heart and fans herself with the other. "Mary-Beth, you're, like, the luckiest girl in the world."

"I really am."

"Darling, I want to talk to you." My mother's stern voice snaps me out of my Oscar-worthy performance. Reese's eyes widen in fear, and she gulps dramatically.

"Yeah, um, sure, Mama." I take a deep breath and give Reese a reassuring smile.

Mama leads me down the hall to the kitchen where my Aunt Felicity is already up to her elbows in suds and Nana sits in the corner having another slice of cake.

"Out, Reese!" My aunt's eyes dart to the shadows of the hallway, and my cousin slinks back from the kitchen at her mother's reprimand.

CHAPTER 14

"Aunt Lily and I need to talk to Mary-Beth alone."

I grab my untouched dessert plate from earlier and head for the trash, scraping the uneaten cake into the bin.

"Easter dinner was so great, Mama," I say, hoping to steer the conversation into safe waters.

My mother slams a stack of dishes down and turns to me, apron on, hand on hip.

So much for that. I hope they don't notice as my hands begin to shake.

"Tell us what's going on. How did you really meet Drew?"

I blow a stray piece of hair out of my eyes and cautiously set my plate in Aunt Felicity's soapy water. Since Drew decided to go with a version of the truth, I'll try and salvage as much of it as I can.

"At the gym." Three sets of eyes narrow on me with a *yeah, right.* "Really! We looked on Instagram to see if we could find where Drew worked out, thinking that might be the easiest place to run into him." My eyes turn pleading. If I can't convince them of this, they'll never buy the rest. This part is the only truthful part after all. "You know how obsessed with Drew Coyne I am. We went, and he was there, and I really did run right into him."

Aunt Felicity and Mama trade a look and then burst into laughter. I'm so relieved, I join in.

"I *knew* you didn't go there to actually exercise," my aunt says, plunging her hands deeper into the dish water.

"Of course not!" I flip my hair over my shoulder. "You guys know I don't exercise."

"But does Drew know that?"

"He does now." I grab a couple more dirty dishes from the table. "It was pretty obvious when I ended up on the gym floor."

My mother and aunt trade another look, but this time it's more serious. They have that sisterly bond, having an entire conversation with just a glance. It makes my blood run cold.

Mama already knows about *Swallow Manor.* And now they know Drew is looking for the author. And that we are somehow magically together. Can she see the truth just by looking at me? Do I have S for *smut* pinned to my dress, as red as Hester Prynne's A?

Anxiety works its way through my body and pools in my chest. Drop by drop until I can hardly breathe.

"We just don't want you to change who you are for a boy," my aunt finally says.

I open my mouth to speak, but Mama cuts me off. "Boys like Drew might have certain"—she puts leftovers in the fridge—"expectations. And we just don't want you to get hurt. He seems like a very nice young man. But I'm sure you know…"

I let out another long, relieved sigh, the drain pulled on the anxiety bathtub in my chest. Harper was right. Even when all the evidence points to me being Minnie Maple, people would never jump to that conclusion.

"Trust me, Mama. That won't be a problem. He knows"—I smirk down at the dirty plate I'm holding—"not to expect anything."

"But men like Drew might get bored—" my aunt cuts in, then stops herself, placing a wet, soapy hand over her mouth.

Get bored that I won't sleep with him? Get bored that I won't give him what he wants? Get bored and leave?

I'm counting on it.

I bite the inside of my cheek to hide my smile and instead wrinkle my forehead, pretending like I'm hanging on my aunt's every word.

My mother steps in to gracefully finish her sister's thought. "We just don't want you getting hurt, darling. Drew is obviously different than any other boy you've dated. And I'm sure you're caught up in the fairy tale of it all, but we just want you to be careful. Don't lower your standards." Her eyes narrow, and a shiver scampers down my back.

CHAPTER 14

"You *haven't* lowered your standards, have you?"

"Of course not!" I grab a rag and start wiping off the now empty table. "And I won't. Drew is just here for the week. He surprised me because he knows it's spring break. But I'm not naïve. I doubt it will last the week."

At least I hope it won't.

"Now don't sell yourself short, darling," my mother is quick to say in her cheerleader-mom type way. "You just keep being you and see where it goes. Drew seems absolutely lovely and very smitten. You're just the kind of girl he needs."

"You're beautiful and smart and pure." My aunt softens her eyes. "He's lucky to find a girl like you. I'm sure he doesn't meet girls like you very often."

"I'm sure that's what attracted him to you in the first place. Because you're different—good different!"

I slam the dishwasher shut to hide my snicker. Drew definitely thinks I'm different. But not in a good way.

"I think he's hot!" Nana's raspy voice startles me from the corner. My mom, aunt, and I all burst into giggles. "So good for you, Bethie!"

Chapter 15

Andrew Edward Coyne
Mirage

Virgin Mary: What hotel are you staying at?
   Drew: Why? Wanna finish what we started earlier?
   Virgin Mary: Gross, no. We need to set some ground rules
Drew: For?
Virgin Mary: For our fake relationship
Drew: Awww, babe
Virgin Mary: I hate you with the fire of a thousand suns
Drew: That metaphor's a little cliché for a bestselling romance author, don't you think?

The three little dots appear then disappear and then reappear several times, before they disappear altogether. I stare at the phone, finding myself hoping they'll return. There are only two hotels in this poky town so Mary-Beth could find me pretty easily, but I decide to save her the trouble.

Drew: Comfort Inn Suites Room 412

Less than three minutes later, there's a knock at the door.

"Holy shit, woman. Is this town really that small?"

Mary-Beth barges past, letting herself into the crappy room they call a suite. "There are only two hotels in Daisy Bluff, and I knew you

CHAPTER 15

wouldn't be caught dead staying at the Days Inn on State Street. All I needed was your room number."

"I'm glad you're here, Mary. It's good to see you." I wave at the small hotel room. "Come, sit down."

Mary-Beth stops and turns to face me, squaring her tiny shoulders with mine. "Do you have to talk like that?"

"Like what?"

"Like you're sweet and charming. We both know you're not. And when we're alone, you can save the act, okay? Just give me Drew from the first day, please."

"I thought you hated Drew from the first day."

"I do. But at least that's the real you. This"— she waves her hand in front of my face— "is a mirage I'd rather not deal with."

"Why?" I take a step closer and lower my voice to nothing more than a purr. "Is it working?"

Mary-Beth rolls her eyes and shoves me away. But I don't miss her blush, starting at her collarbone and traveling to her cheeks. I've never met a woman who blushes with her whole body before. I don't hate it.

"You know"—I lick my lips—"if you got to know the real me, you might be surprised you like me. Maybe even better than the Hallmark version."

I swallow and look away. I don't normally want women to get to know me. In fact, I try my damndest for the opposite. But something about being around Mary-Beth is like playing a game. The fuck-all-your-assumptions game. And I want to win.

Mary-Beth lets out a snort, then covers her mouth with her hand, like even *she* wasn't expecting to make that noise. "Believe me, there's no man on earth I could like more than Hallmark Drew Coyne. Part of the reason I hate *you* so much."

I laugh that comment off and follow Mary-Beth into the living room. She takes a seat on the couch while I claim the chair next to her. Mary-

Beth has traded her dress and heels from earlier and is now wearing sweatpants with a hole in the thigh and a hoodie, her long hair pulled into a messy bun and her makeup washed off. It's a far cry from our last secret meeting. I have a feeling the real Mary-Beth is somewhere between this and prom.

"I see you've dressed up for me, babe. What happened to the green dress?"

"Burned it. Shoes and all."

I crook up an amused eyebrow. "That's really too bad."

Mary-Beth carefully sets her hands in her lap and looks up at me with an emotionless face, like an attorney about to read their client's last will and testament. "If you're going to be in my hometown, we need to establish rules. This is my actual life you're screwing with now, and I refuse to let you ruin it."

"And you don't think you've fucked up my life enough?" I pat my chest and lean toward her. "*My* actual life?"

"This whole mess was your doing, not mine, and we both know it."

"Give me the book rights, and I'm gone. You'll never fucking see me again."

"And that...is a great segue into rule number one." Mary-Beth straightens her spine. "No cussing."

"Holy shit, Mary." I rub the back of my neck. "What is this, elementary school?"

"I don't like it when people cuss around me, and a man who I'm actually dating would be considerate enough to respect that."

"And why don't you like cussing?"

"Because I find it"— she looks away, like she doesn't really know why but is hoping she'll discover the reason on the other side of the room "—off-putting. Much like your personality."

"Fine." I wave my hand defeatedly. "It will be like living in one of my movies. I was trying to get away from Hallmark and now I'm living

CHAPTER 15

it. Fantastic."

Mary-Beth gives me a smug look. "Okay, second. I think there should be an end date. Like by Friday. You gotta go."

"I'll leave when I get the book rights I came here for."

"Which I've already told you you're not getting," Mary-Beth grates out. "I know you can't stay here forever. There's got to be someone in L.A. who would miss you."

"All right." I rest my elbows on my knees and my jaw on my palm. I carefully rub my chin, massaging the stubble that's already grown since this morning. "I'll give you two weeks. Two weeks to convince you I'm the right person to adapt *Swallow Manor*. One week here, and another in Los Angeles—"

In the middle of my sentence, Mary-Beth's phone buzzes and she pulls it out, typing distractedly. She doesn't even seem to notice I've stopped talking. I watch her, tapping my foot impatiently.

"Is that okay with you, Virgin Mary?" I ask, knowing she's not listening to me.

"Yeah, sure." Her eyes don't lift from the screen.

"Okay, then, time for one of my rules." I snatch Mary-Beth's phone from her hand and slam it on the coffee table between us. "When we're together, no phone."

"Hey!" Mary-Beth makes a grab for her phone, but I tuck it behind my back.

"Any woman actually dating *me* would be way more into me than whatever was on her phone. For this to be believable"— *and for me to convince you to give me your damn book*— "you can't be distracted when we're together. I want you focused on me."

"Ego much?"

I shrug. "It's just how it is being with me. You can ask around."

"Do you have a Los Angeles phone book? I'll start with A and work my way down to Z, though it might take me six months."

Despite trying to insult me, Mary-Beth's eyes keep darting to the phone hidden behind my back.

"What could possibly be more important than this conversation?"

She groans and slumps into the couch. "I was texting Harper. Apparently, ninety-five percent of the town already knows you're here and thinks we're dating. The story has morphed from us meeting at a gym to us meeting at an indoor trampoline park. The latest version is I got trapped in a game of dodgeball with a pack of rabid third-graders and you saved my life."

I let out a loud snicker. "So that's what it's like living in a small town, huh?"

"Ugh. The smallest."

"I think getting rid of your phone will be just as good for you as it is me. You can thank me later."

"You don't like social media? You post so much stuff."

"*Darcy* posts so much stuff," I correct. "And I allow it to help my career, but I think you've already figured out I don't give a sh—" I stop myself, rolling my eyes. "I don't really care about any of it."

"That's not really fair to your fans."

"You're not most fans, Mary-Beth."

She tilts her head slightly, as if to concede my point.

"So when you give up and leave—"

"*If* I leave –"

"*Once* you leave," she sneers, "that's it. No more contacting me. No more TikToks. You leave me alone. I'm only letting you stay now to quench the Minnie Maple rumors."

"I doubt us being together is going to quench any rumors, but sure." I snicker. "If after two weeks, you still refuse to sign over the rights, I won't ask again. But when you realize I'm not a terrible person—"

"*If* I realize –"

"*Once* you realize I'm not a terrible person going to ruin your beloved book forever, I get the rights. If I survive your small-town gambit, and you can still stomach me in two weeks, you sign, no questions asked."

"I can't stomach you now."

"Two weeks. If I can't convince you in two weeks, I'm gone. Just promise you'll give me an honest chance. Remember, I'm going to pay you. This is beneficial for both of us."

"Fine, if you promise to be the real you. No Hallmark Drew."

I dip my chin slightly. "Done."

"Okay, so to recap." Mary-Beth sits up in her seat again, counting her fingers as she reviews our new rules. "No cussing. No phones. Two weeks." I raise my eyebrows. "Two *genuine* weeks," she amends with a huff. "And...I have one last rule I'd like to propose." Mary-Beth shifts her weight like the couch is suddenly very uncomfortable.

I gesture for her to go ahead, and she lets out a puff of air, quickly sucking it back in again and holding. Finally, she lets out the last rule in a rush: "Nothing physical. No kissing. No hugging. No hand-holding. No groping. And, um...no sex."

"*Groping*, really?"

"I know about your earring collection!"

"I'm not a sexual predator, for Christ's sake!" I push out of the chair and begin stomping around the room. "Every earring was consensual, I assure you. With a condom and an Uber in the morning. You don't want me to touch you, I won't lay a fucking finger on you."

Mary-Beth stays completely still, except for one peaked eyebrow.

"A finger, sorry. Damn it, is this how it's going to be? The language police? Really?"

"We've had that rule for, like, two minutes." She puts her hands out in an invitation. "If you'd like to give up now and go home, you're more than welcome."

It only takes three long strides to reach Mary-Beth on the couch. Sitting down, I still tower over her, watching her suck in and pant out tiny breaths of air. Her mouth is open. Her pupils huge. Her cheeks red.

"Can't you just pretend I'm a little kid or something?" Her words are barely a whisper.

"You're not a kid, Mary."

And I realize at that moment, she's definitely not. Not even close. She's not a kid—chubby-cheeked and innocent like Chloe. She's a warm, sultry woman. A woman whose heart is beating so quickly I can see her blood travel. A woman with a dirty mind and a tight ass.

A woman I suddenly want more than anyone in the world.

I stand and take a step back, putting some much-needed space between us. She literally just told me not to touch her. I can't break another one of her stupid rules already.

Not yet.

"No more cussing. I'll try."

My words seem to startle Mary-Beth, and she shakes her head like she's coming out of a trance. "Two weeks, then."

Chapter 16

Mary-Beth Caroline Abernathy
Language Police

I need to get out of this hotel room before I do something I really regret.

Like kill Drew Coyne.

Or kiss him.

Both options seem equally likely right now.

I'm not sure which one I would regret more, but I have a sneaking suspicion if I kissed him, I wouldn't be able to stop. However, stabbing him repeatedly with a dull kitchen utensil would also be delightful.

I'm turning the doorknob when Drew says something that makes me stop.

"You know no one is going to believe we're actually a couple if we never touch, right?"

I take a step back into the small room and almost trip over the luggage rack. Taking a deep breath, I feel the blood rush to my face. Again. "Anyone who knows me would believe it."

I once "dated" Dominic Hostler for a month two years ago, and we barely even spoke on the phone. Granted, Dominic Hostler came out as gay six months later, but still.

"Well..." Drew moves the luggage rack with his foot and leans against the door frame. The tiny hallway by the door is suffocating. "Anyone who knows *me* wouldn't believe it. And any woman I'm seen with, especially in Los Angeles, is automatically going to be assumed to be Minnie Maple. Unless…" Drew leaves the sentence dangling there for me to fill in the blanks.

"I didn't agree to Los Angeles!" I take a few steps back into the room, leaving Drew to guard the door.

"Sure did." He smiles. "When you were texting with Harper."

"But I can't!" I begin pacing, running my hands down my cheeks. "I have to work next week."

"You have a job?"

"Of course, I have a job."

"I thought you were an author. And uh, what else?" Drew looks up at the ceiling. "A knitter?"

I freeze and glare at him. "Lord, really?"

"Whatever it is, I'm sure you can get out of it."

"It's not that easy." I rub my hand along my neck, thinking of how much work finding a sub and writing lesson plans for them would be. There's a reason I never take time off; it's easier to just go than not. I also have parent teacher conferences this week. And Harper's birthday the next. Not to mention the deadline with my editor.

"So…" Drew takes a step toward me. "What is it that you do?"

"You finally thought to ask?"

"Wait, don't tell me, don't tell me." He rubs his hands together. "I want to guess."

I put my hand on my hip and glare at him, already knowing he's going to guess correctly on the first try.

Drew massages his chin thoughtfully, mumbling under his breath. "Daughter of a preacher. Southern virgin with a dirty little secret. Barely taller than a small child. Uptight control freak with an undercurrent of Christmas cheer. Two weeks off in the middle of April for

CHAPTER 16

no reason..."

"For Easter," I correct.

Drew snaps his fingers and points at me. "Kindergarten teacher!"

I fight the urge to launch myself at him and claw his eyes out.

"I hate to tell you this, Mary, but you're a little on the predictable side."

"Good-looking man with no other talent beside pretending to be something that he's not. Ego the size of a small planet. Apartment decorated like an overrated four-star hotel." I raise my eyebrows. "Same to you."

"Again, I think you should get to know me better." Drew's hands fall to his sides. "I'm far more than a pretty face."

"And I'm far more than a southern virgin with a dirty secret."

"Clearly."

"Clearly."

We are silent for just a few seconds as we stop to reassess all the assumptions we've placed on each other. And ourselves. When Drew speaks again, his voice is noticeably more amiable.

"Come to California, Mary-Beth," he says, like he's asking a friend to come visit, instead of trying to coerce an enemy into surrendering. "It's only fair. Home court advantage and all that. You get to pick what we do here, and then it's my turn in L.A."

"Strip clubs and brothels, I'm sure."

"Only the finest brothels for you, babe."

I stand on my tiptoes and poke Drew in the chest with my index finger. "Fine. I'll find a sub. But I'm expecting you to compensate me. I don't get PTO."

"I think I can handle the sixty bucks. That should cover a teacher's salary in this godforsaken town for a week."

I sneer, trying to hide the fact that he's not really wrong about that. I'm gripping the doorknob when I turn back one last time. "And you can..."

I pause, considering what amount of physical contact is too dangerous.

Any. *None*.

"You can hold my hand. And hug me goodbye. While in public. Other than that, you can stay the"—*fuck*—"away."

Drew's eyes light with amusement. "Mary-Beth, did you almost cuss? Breaking your own rules already? I'm gonna have to report you to the language police."

"What can I say? No one infuriates me like you do."

"The feeling is mutual."

Back in my car, where I can breathe and think and type, I finally text Harper back.

Mary-Beth: This is a seriously bad idea

Harper: You're alive! I thought he'd eaten you or something

Mary-Beth: Or something

Harper: Holy shit, did something happen? Have you been deflowered?

Mary-Beth: No! Are you kidding me?

Mary-Beth: He's the worst. The absolute worst.

Mary-Beth: I hate him so much.

Mary-Beth: You should have seen him Harp. So conceited. So arrogant.

Mary-Beth: I'm surprised he doesn't tip over with how big his head is

Harper: You want him, don't you?

Mary-Beth: Ugh. So bad. Is it that obvious?

Harper: MB there's a fine line between love and hate. Especially with someone who looks like Drew Coyne.

Harper: And you've been obsessed with him for years. That doesn't just go away.

CHAPTER 16

Mary-Beth: I don't think I can do this
Harper: Then give him the book rights.
Mary-Beth: I can't do that!
Harper: Because...
Mary-Beth: Because then he wins

I shake my head and try again.

Mary-Beth: And he's still an awful person who doesn't deserve Swallow Manor

Harper: I just got a text from Kinsley Reader asking if Drew performed CPR on you after you got knocked unconscious during a dodgeball tournament in Las Vegas.

I slam my forehead against the steering wheel repeatedly before driving home. When I arrive, I rewrite four different sex scenes in four different books, before finally collapsing onto my bed in an aroused, fevered haze.

But before drifting off to sleep, I make one more rule for myself: no more being alone with Drew in dark bedrooms.

Neither I nor my book would survive many more nights like tonight.

Chapter 17

Andrew Edward Coyne
Human Pinball Machine

A loud knock startles me out of a restless sleep the next morning.

"Drew, open up. It's Mary-Beth."

I glance at the clock. 5:21. Fuck that woman.

"Why?" The word comes out more groan than English. I roll over and put a pillow over my head.

"Just want to spend every second with you, babe," she says in a sugary voice. "I've got big plans for your first day here."

I stumble from my bed to the front door, not bothering to put on pants or a shirt. I greet Mary-Beth in nothing more than my underwear.

"Hi. Oh, uh, what? Why? Uh, hi." Her wide eyes dart from my face to my arms to my chest to my navel to my package to my feet and back again, like she's playing a game of pinball with my body.

I open the door wider and gesture for her to come inside. "Hey, babe. Care to join me?"

Mary-Beth closes her eyes and thrusts a cup of coffee into my chest so forcefully some of the hot brown liquid spills onto my feet. I yelp and jump back.

CHAPTER 17

"Fuck! I mean, shit! I mean..." I finish my sentence with a growl. I should have never agreed to the no-cussing rule.

"Sorry!" Mary-Beth puts a hand to her head and takes a step back. I can see the blush starting to work its way up her chest and to her cheeks, even in the dark. "I wasn't expecting you to, uh, to be, um –" She opens her eyes, looking at me like I've personally offended her by not being dressed. "Dear Lord, don't you own pajamas?"

I bring my hands to my side as if to say, *These are my pajamas.* Mary-Beth's face goes from red to burgundy.

"Well, I, uh, I'll just, um, wait for you out here, then. I just, um, wanted to give you this." She hands me the coffee, this time more gently. "And tell you I've got something planned for today. If you could come out here. Um, soon. Ish. Soonish. When you're ready. I'll be waiting. Not for you. I mean, yes, for you, but yeah. Anyway, I'm here. For the love of God, get dressed!"

Mary-Beth turns on her heel and marches down the hall. I can't be sure, but I think I hear her mutter "shit" under her breath a few times. I take a half-step into the hallway, propping the door open with my leg.

"Sure you don't want to come in, babe?"

"Quite sure!" she calls from the elevator at the end of the hall. "I'll wait for you in the lobby. Wear a coat. And a hoodie. And probably a hat. It's cold out there. Maybe a parka, too. If you have one."

The elevator dings, and Mary-Beth all but jumps into it like she's trying to avoid an explosion in an action movie.

I smile and take a sip of the coffee. Americano with a splash of cream. She knows my Starbucks order. Of course she does.

Stalker.

🐑🐑🐑

It's not cold outside. Not even close.

By the time I've reached the lobby, I've taken off my coat. And by the time I've reached my rental car, I've taken off my hoodie and hat. When we get inside, I turn on the air conditioning.

"So, why the early wake-up call, babe? That eager to spend the day with me?"

Mary-Beth wriggles around in her seat, trying to squirm out of her jacket. Underneath, she's wearing a lavender tank top the same shade as her leggings and the swoosh on her Air Force Ones. A smile traces along my lips. The outfit looks good on her. The spandex hugs her cute little ass and perky tits perfectly. It's the middle of trying too hard and not trying at all.

"I have a deadline for my next book." She sighs. "And I'm completely stuck on my plot. I need some inspiration."

"Well...I'm your guy." I wink, but Mary-Beth isn't looking at me, her eyes firmly glued on the dark passing scenery.

What's going on in that twisted mind of yours, Virgin Mary?

We ride the rest of the thirty-minute drive in mostly silence, apart from Mary-Beth offering "turn here" or "veer left" with the occasional "slow down" or "you're gonna get a freaking ticket" thrown in. Each time she says something about my driving, I go a little bit faster.

We stop at the base of a small mountain, and she springs from the car like a jack-in-the-box.

"I should have guessed you'd be a terrible driver," she says, dusting off her pristine pants.

"Efficient," I correct. "I'm efficient."

"Want me to take your picture?" Mary-Beth's eyes are focused on the activity of choice behind me. "Darcy can use it for your Instagram. And for once, a mountain you've actually climbed. Not deceitful or crooked at all."

"Really, Virgin Mary? You want to stage a picture for my social media page I've told you I don't give a shit about?"

"I'm just trying to help you out. Although that might count as aiding

CHAPTER 17

and abetting when you inevitably get arrested for fraud."

I roll my eyes. Visibly.

"No phones." I snatch hers and toss it onto the passenger seat of my rental car. "You know the rules."

"Wow, somebody has their panties in a twist."

"No one twists my panties quite like you do, Virgin Mary."

"Well, untwist them, because it's almost sunrise."

Mary-Beth starts walking up the small trail on the opposite side of the parking lot, her little legs working overtime to stay ahead of me. Her ass jiggles, and I hang back for a good five minutes admiring. Finally, I put my hands in my pockets and catch up after only three strides. The side-eye she gives me almost makes it worth it.

"So where are we exactly?" I ask.

"Paxton Plateau." Her tiny little lungs already sound out of breath.

"And..."

"And it has the best views around. Believe me, if I'm going to get sweaty and gross, it will be worth it. You'll see."

"You don't get sweaty and gross for nothing," I tease and Mary-Beth blushes again. I dig my hands further into my pockets and try to divert my mind from all the filthy things I want to do with Mary-Beth's ass. "Noted."

We trudge along the empty path in silence, our feet crunching on gravel, the scenery around us lightening with the impending sunrise, the smell of a dewy spring morning hanging in the air.

The sun is close to blossoming over the horizon, and it casts a golden, almost magical, haze on everything around us. The side of the mountain is dotted with flowers and small thickets of trees. The breeze blows the tall grass lazily around us. Birds chirp. Butterflies float. The heavens fucking sing. Unexpected contentment lodges itself in my chest.

"So, what's wrong with your plot?" I finally ask.

"Not yet." Mary-Beth continues trudging upward like a sergeant marching troops into battle.

"Why the rush?" I notice a squirrel jumping from branch to branch. It seems wrong to not want to savor this view.

"Because today is going to be a nice day, and therefore, people will be here soon. And I would love not to run into half the town up here with you. I need some space. To think."

"Then why not come alone?"

"Because the last thing I need is for you to wander around town without me. Who knows who you'll run into." Mary-Beth physically shudders. "While you're here, I want to know where you are at all times. I want you with me."

I want you with me too, Virgin Mary. But I don't think we mean that in the same way.

"I must say, you make a delightful fake girlfriend. Not controlling or manipulative at all."

"Best you've ever had."

The higher we climb, the more my contentment grows. The town in the distance seems even smaller from up here—just a few dots for houses and snakes of gray for streets. A handful of lights glitter from the city center, but everything else is still and dark. I take a cleansing breath. The clean, warm air makes everything seem easier. It feels like I left my problems down there. From up here, they seem inconsequential.

It's been forever since I've been outside just to be outside. Mary-Beth is right—Darcy stages a lot of nature photos for my ad campaigns, but that makes the outdoors feel like just another photo shoot.

Like work.

Stare off into the distance, Drew.

Put your foot on that boulder, Drew.

Make sure we can see the hiking boot, Drew.

CHAPTER 17

Take a bite of that nasty-ass granola bar, Drew.

Can you stop making that face, Drew?

Change into this jacket, Drew. Now take it off. Actually, no, put it back on. Actually, sling it over your shoulder and take off your pants.

This is nothing like that. This is as comfortable as being alone without having to be lonely.

Maybe Mary-Beth is right about promoting products I don't actually use or even like. Products I actually *dislike*. Lord knows I don't actually want to swing around in one of those flimsy hammocks and undoubtedly fall on my ass. Or drink one of those God-awful smoothies I can't even bear to sniff. Or wear those hiking boots I know give people blisters.

To end my partnerships, I'd be sacrificing the ad campaigns and their royalties, but it would clear up more time to do things I want to do. And after seeing a view like this...that might be more important.

I make a mental note to call Darcy and schedule a meeting with my brand partners. When I get home, I'm going to reevaluate. I want more time for this. For quiet. And fresh air. For peace.

My eyes flit over to Mary-Beth, panting to stay a half-step ahead of me, ass still jiggling.

For producing *Swallow Manor*.

Just then, a huge sunbeam escapes from the horizon, shining directly on us. Mary-Beth stops and turns to me, her breathing heavy.

"See?" She smiles, seeming satisfied with the view.

We've reached the summit just in time. The sunrise is brilliant, the sky painted orange and purple and yellow and framed by wispy cotton candy clouds. It's beautiful. And somehow familiar, like I've been here before, though I'm sure that's impossible.

Next to me, Mary-Beth's tense body seems to slacken just a smidge. I feel my body doing the same.

"Worth getting sweaty and gross?"

She takes a long deep breath, putting her hands behind her head, her elbows flaring. "It usually is."

Chapter 18

Mary-Beth Caroline Abernathy
Sweaty
Gross

No matter how long I look into the blinding sunrise, my plot still sucks. Maybe I need to wait until it's at its peak and stare for long enough that I go blind. I've heard losing one of your senses can sharpen the others. That must count toward plot hole repairs, too, right?

"This is a scene from book three."

Drew startles me out of my masochistic thoughts. He has a smug look on his face, which instantly makes me frown.

He turns, studying the small purple and yellow flowers blossoming at his feet. "When Susan takes Ambrose to the meadow, and they bang in the flowers. I knew it looked familiar."

The heat rises from my toes to my chest to my head. I can even feel the tips of my ears turning red.

"Is not." I sound like a toddler sticking her tongue out. I wish I could snatch the words from the air and gobble them up.

Lord...as if Drew doesn't already think I'm immature.

His eyes turn humorous, but he doesn't laugh or even smile. He points to a gap in the flowers a few feet from where we're standing.

"So you're telling me that's not the 'small clearing among the lilac and saffron-colored wildflowers, just big enough for our bodies to fit as one'?"

Hearing Drew quote my book is a special kind of torture. One I simultaneously wish would end but also never stop.

I open my mouth, not quite sure which reaction will escape: indignation or begging for more. Drew's lips hint at a smile as he takes a half-step toward me. He's so close now, our chests almost touch. I bite down, afraid butterflies will swarm out.

Drew leans just a tad bit closer, his voice nearing a whisper. "The one 'in the mountains by my home, majestic yet gentle, with trees that caress the shaded cliffs and rocks shaped like hearts—as if Cupid himself consummated this place for lovemaking."

His eyes break from mine, darting to the rock by our feet. The heart-shaped rock.

Aw, hell.

"Fine. You caught me." I take a half-step back and cross my arms. "But I wasn't sure you'd even read past book one."

"Oh, I studied them, Mary-Beth. I read them over and over again. I *memorized* them."

The sixteen words (yes, I counted) seem innocent enough, but they hit my body like the spiciest smut I've ever read or written. Forget about breathing, now I'm just trying not to tackle him and do some lovemaking of my own.

A soft breeze rushes in between us, and a piece of my hair breaks free. Drew carefully reaches up and tucks it behind my ear, his fingers soft against the tender skin of my cheek.

Sirens erupt in my mind—*abort abort abort!* I should pounce back, point at Drew's dreamy cornflower eyes, and yell, "Stop! Liar!" I shouldn't let him touch me like this, not for even a second. But my body literally won't retreat. In fact, I find myself inching onto my tiptoes without meaning to.

"I know every single filthy thought that lives in your mind, Mary. I can't wait to bring them all to life." Drew's lips are a breath from mine when he turns and pretends to study the plateau, trying to hide a self-satisfied smirk.

Insert comment about hating Drew Coyne more than I thought I could. More than humanly possible. More than all the lava in all the volcanoes in the world. Than all the fish in the sea and stars in the sky and sand on the beach and words in my books. More than...*grrr*. More than ever.

He's playing with me just because he can. Like a cat that doesn't even plan on eating the mouse.

Drew walks around for a few minutes until he makes his way back to me. "We could film here, ya know. If that's what you want."

I put my hands on my hips. "*We* are not going to be filming anything anywhere."

"I promise to consult you as much as you want. About the movie. I will make sure we bring your vision to life."

"Again, I don't know why you keep using the word *we*."

"But there's already a *we*, right, babe?" Drew bumps me with his shoulder, and I growl and start walking away.

Drew catches up to me before I've even made it halfway to the *small clearing among the lilac and saffron-colored wildflowers.*

"So...what's your plot problem?" he asks for the second time.

"I don't want your help." I stick my chin up indignantly and turn like I'm going to walk away again. We both know I'm not. "I only brought you here to babysit you."

"Aww, come on, Virgin Mary. Try me." There's a laugh in Drew's voice that is equal parts sexy and enraging. "I am your muse, after all."

"Regrettably." I kick at the grass by my feet. My mouth is parched from the hike, my insides are in pretzels from Drew's touch, and my brain is scrambled from reworking my plot a million times. I've never had the luxury of brainstorming with someone, and it feels weird to let someone into this part of my creative process. Into this part of my life. Especially someone arrogant and hypercritical like Drew.

Especially after what just happened.

Or didn't happen.

But... I'm legitimately stuck—writers' block in the extreme. Even more blocked than when my cousin, Joey, got constipated over Christmas vacation last year and didn't poop during their entire visit.

I've never written on a deadline before, and it is much more difficult than allowing my creativity to spill onto the page whenever it damn well pleases. As much as it hurts my pride to admit, I can use all the help I can get.

"My main character and her love interest have nothing to do," I finally spit out.

"Nothing to do," Drew repeats slowly, cocking his head to the side.

"Yeah, I mean, like the story is mostly done. I know how they fall in love. I've already written the times they sleep together. And at the end, together they overcome the big obstacle and have their happily ever after. But in the middle, they're kind of stuck together in this old house with nothing to do. And it's"—I *hate* admitting this out loud—"painfully boring."

Drew rubs his jawline thoughtfully, as if he's really thinking about my problem. "How did they end up in the old house together?"

I take a deep breath and launch into my elevator pitch. "In a nutshell, Gabriel is hired to help Christine clean out her deceased husband's estate before she's shipped off to marry her older troll of a brother-in-law. Of course, Christine and Gabriel fall in love, and he saves her from the awful future of being married to an abusive spouse. But it's getting from the beginning to the end that's got me stuck."

"So...they do have *something* to do," Drew says carefully. "They're cleaning out the dead husband's stuff, right?"

"Yeah, but he was a boring dude. Just stuff from his wealthy family that's been collecting dust for a few hundred years. Their marriage was not a love match; it was for the money and propriety. The dead husband didn't treat her poorly, but he was kind of a wet blanket. Dull."

"Why not make him more exciting?" Drew asks. "Why not make him more flawed?"

"Because he needs to be boring to be a contrast to Gabriel. To help Christine see everything she's been missing."

"Maybe he doesn't need to be boring. Maybe he just needs to be different."

I pause, trying not to be too precious about the characters I've so carefully crafted. "But he just...he needs to be." I shake my head and open and close my hands. I don't like having to defend myself. Especially not to Drew. "I can't really explain it, but how I've written him, he needs to be boring."

"How about this?" Drew's eyes light up a little. "Back when I was taking acting classes, we used to play this improv game Yes, And. It's basically you take the given information, accept it, and add to it. Let's play that game with your plot and see where it leads us. We can take turns."

"Okay..."

"Just trust me."

"But I don't trust you."

Drew's jaw flexes. "Just trust me for the next five minutes so we can fix your damn plot?"

"Fine," I seethe.

"All right." Drew nods haughtily. "So the facts we are accepting are: Christine and Gabriel are stuck in this house. Her husband is dead.

They are going through his things."

"And the dead husband is boring," I add defensively.

"Christine *perceives* that the husband is boring," Drew amends. His eyes are downright twinkling now.

Despite my best efforts to control my fluttering heart, a tiny smile pulls on the side of my lips. "But he's not actually boring?"

"No, he's not. Because while Christine and Gabriel are cleaning out the house..." Drew pauses for dramatic effect. "They find something."

"He has a secret?"

"A big secret."

"That he's been hiding for years." My eyes grow wide.

"Something he's kept from everyone"—Drew smiles—"even Christine."

"Which is why he seemed so boring to her! He's been keeping her at a distance to protect his secret." I look at Drew desperately. "But wait, what did they find?"

"A book?" Drew suggests.

"A letter!" I'm so excited I almost trip over the heart-shaped rock. "A trunk full of letters. And gifts."

"From an old lover."

"Ooh, what about a current lover? He's a cheater." My forehead wrinkles. "But wait, a lot of men were cheaters back then. And if Christine doesn't love him, then why would she care?"

"What about if he has a lover who is a—"

"Man!" we both say in unison.

I smile.

Drew smiles.

And between us, a microscopic shift occurs.

"He's gay!" I say, relieved. "Yes, that explains why Christine would find him terribly dull. Because he can't let her in. And there definitely wouldn't be any chemistry. And Gabriel and Christine could find lots of little clues before the big reveal! That gives them plenty to do."

"Does that fix your problem?"

"Almost..." I pause, chewing on a fingernail and looking down the mountain at my little town. My very Pharisaic little town. "How would Christine react?"

"My guess is"— Drew beams down at me "—you'll find out a lot about her when you answer that question."

I nod, the words already starting to amass inside me, begging to spill. "Thanks, Drew. This was actually very helpful."

The words come out like we're friends or at least friendly. It feels a little wrong. But also a little right. I scratch my arm and take a half-step back.

"I could do the same thing for *Swallow Manor*, you know. I've got a lot of great ideas."

"I don't want to change anything about *Swallow Manor*."

"I never said I would change it. Just get it ready for the big screen." Drew's eyes change from amiable to piggish in an instant. "Ready to sign it over?"

"God, no!" I snicker and push his shoulder. "Did you really have to go and ruin the moment? We were actually getting along!"

Drew only shrugs. "I am the type."

Chapter 19

Mary-Beth Caroline Abernathy
Butter

Drew and I swing by my house to grab my laptop, pick up sandwiches from my favorite deli and snacks from the gas station, then head straight to the library. I'm hoping for privacy, but not *too* much privacy.

On his sandwich, Drew ordered every type of meat they offer, cucumbers, sprouts, and Sriracha mayo on Dutch Crunch bread, and then asked the employee to crumble up a bag of potato chips and an oatmeal raisin cookie on top.

I'm not saying you can tell a lot by a person's sandwich order, but I knew I couldn't trust Drew Coyne. In fact, I'm slightly concerned I've been associating with a serial killer.

When we reach the library, I head straight to the table in the back corner, tucked away behind a stronghold of bookshelves. Luckily, it's a warm, sunny day, and no one else is here.

"It's okay to eat in here?" Drew looks around our small, deserted sanctuary.

I nod. "The only library in the county."

"If you say so."

I carefully unwrap my turkey and cheese, with mustard, light mayo,

CHAPTER 19

and lettuce on wheat. Drew doesn't waste any time devouring a huge bite of his Frankenwich—cucumbers and bacon and chip crumbs oozing everywhere.

"Don't knock it till you try it," he says through his chewing. "It's the perfect salty-sweet combo."

Maybe it's from years of listening to Drew's recommendations, or maybe it's from his loud chomping, but suddenly, I'm dying for a bite. I open my computer and pretend to type, but all I can think about is what cookies taste like mixed with seven different types of meat.

"Fine." I snap my laptop closed and reach for the sandwich. "Give me that."

I stifle a moan when the ingredients hit my mouth. Drew's sandwich is so good, it's practically orgasmic. Not that I would know what that feels or tastes like. But I can't imagine it being better than this.

"So?" The smug look on Drew's face says he already knows my answer.

I force my features into disinterest. "It's all right." I say, fighting the urge to stuff the rest of the sandwich into my mouth. I reluctantly hand it back to him, my fingers clinging to the bread for just a split-second too long for my lie to be convincing. "Maybe you should endorse that sandwich instead of those smoothies."

Drew's left eyebrow flits up as a smile sneaks across his lips. "Maybe I should."

🐑🐑🐑

The words pour out of me at an exhilarating rate. I've been on a roll before, but right now, I'm butter. Hot and smooth and melting.

What I thought would take weeks or even longer now seems possible by the end of the week or sooner. Having Drew here helps, though I'd never admit it.

For example, I spent a half hour rewriting the big sex scene to include the details of Drew's hands. How they move, confident and graceful, rotating on the axis of his wrists, fingers long and nimble. The veins and the tendons and the tiny nearly invisible hairs clinging to the back. The wrinkles of his knuckles (fifteen) and the length of his fingernails (short). And Dear Lord Almighty, the size (*enormous*). I can't help but wonder if the correlation people always talk about between a man's hands and other body parts is true.

Without a doubt, it's the best chapter I've ever written. I have to get up and take a lap around the library to cool off when I'm done.

I was hoping when we reached the eighth hour, Drew would get bored and beg to go back to the excitement of Hollywood, but he seems to be enjoying himself as much as I am. He's aggregated a large pile of books and can't stop smiling as he guzzles through them.

I've always thought a person's book preferences tell a lot about a person, but I can glean about as much from Drew's book choices as his sandwich order.

Eclectic is putting it mildly. From fae smut to Machiavellian heroes to classics to biographies.

He started with *The Old Man and the Sea* by Hemmingway, tearing through it in just under two hours and quickly moved on to *Beach Read* by Emily Henry, finishing that one an hour ago. Without blinking, he picked up *Debt of Honor* (Jack Ryan book *seven*?) and is already at least one hundred pages in. He looks delighted to be holed up in a library reading, like Matilda just escaped from the Trunchbull.

I know it seems illogical considering the way Drew and I met, but I didn't peg him for a reader. The way he's ferociously turning the pages right now tells me I was very wrong.

Oh, I studied them, Mary-Beth. I read them over and over again. I memorized them. Drew's words from earlier echo in the tiny alcove of the library I've cornered us in. I'm instantly hot.

I slam my laptop closed with a loud *thunk*. Drew's eyes don't flinch from the page.

CHAPTER 19

"The library closes in five minutes," I whisper-hiss. "We need to go."

Drew's eyes jump from his book to my face to all four corners of the library, like he's forgotten where he is. "No shit?" He shakes his head, blinking. "I mean...really?"

I raise my eyebrows and nod at the darkened window.

"Wow, sorry." Drew rubs his eyes. "Were you waiting for me?"

"No, I've been writing."

"So you got your plot figured out, then?"

"I think so."

"Good."

"Good."

I stand, and Drew does the same. I tuck my laptop under my arm and rock back on my heels, trying not to stare at the book in his giant hands.

"End of day one," I say, mostly because I can't think of anything else. "You're still here."

"If you thought eight hours in a library was going to get me to leave, you're severely mistaken."

"How about twelve?" I stick out my hip and lean on the table. "We can try that tomorrow."

Drew only smiles. "I'm wearing you down," he says.

"If by *wearing me down* you mean I no longer feel physically ill in your presence, I guess."

"I helped you with your plot."

"I would have figured it out."

"I introduced you to your new favorite sandwich." Drew raises his eyebrows. "Or do you still want to pretend the moans coming from the back of your throat were because you didn't like it?"

The combination of Drew saying the word *moan* and mentioning the sandwich makes my mouth water. I swallow and jut my chin out. "I said it was all right. And it was."

Drew's eyes meet mine with heart-stopping blueness, and the corners of his lips pull up. "Was it *consummated for lovemaking?*"

🐥🐥🐥

Drew and I run through the Chick-Fil-A drive-thru on the way back to his hotel. His fast-food order has less serial-killer vibes, which disappoints me. A crispy chicken cobb salad with two packets of zesty buffalo sauce and one packet of garden herb ranch dressing is hardly a takeout hack. Neither of us eats until after we've said our goodbyes for the evening.

"Goodnight, Virgin Mary."

I pause, trying to find an insult just as cutting. I go with, "Goodnight, man who probably has fake testicles dangling underneath his car."

Drew's face lights up with the new banter. I try to keep my face neutral, but my smile dismembers my pride with teethy glory.

"Woman who probably has a fluffy cat named Duchess," Drew retorts.

"Man who doesn't hold the elevator for the person running across the lobby."

"Woman who says *if you know, you know*, when she doesn't really know."

"Man who doesn't do any of the work for the group project."

"Woman who pretends to laugh at dirty jokes she doesn't understand."

"Man who wears sunglasses at night...*inside.*"

"Woman who gets excited to stay in and do a puzzle."

Out of comebacks, I secure my computer and Chick-Fil-A bag. "You say that like it's an insult, but a puzzle alone actually sounds delightful after being stuck with you all day."

"Quitting so soon?" Drew asks, looking up at the dark sky. "I could go at least twenty more rounds."

CHAPTER 19

"I've got a whole week," I say, tromping to my car. "Gotta save some good insults for later."

"*Two* weeks!" Drew hollers.

"Yeah, yeah. Two weeks."

Chapter 20

Andrew Edward Coyne
Slytherin

I'm shocked, but grateful this crappy-ass motel has a minibar. I take out a small bottle of wine and don't even bother with the glass.

I need a celebratory drink. Because whether Mary-Beth admits it or not, her book is practically mine. Today couldn't have gone better. I text Will to tell him the good news.

Drew: Start chilling the champagne. The book is as good as mine.
Will: So soon?
Drew: $100 says I'll have it by the end of the week.
Will: You're on

It's been a long time since I spent this much time with a woman I wasn't working with, trying to fuck, or actually fucking. Or a combination of the three. But surprisingly, it hadn't been as appalling as I'd expected.

The hike had been nice.

The conversation stimulating.

The food good.

The library sublime.

The company tolerable.

CHAPTER 20

Actually, not just tolerable. Practically enjoyable.

Mary-Beth Abernathy. Virgin Mary. Minnie Maple. The pocket-sized hardass. The judgmental shrew. The woman intent on ruining my life.

She's actually not that bad.

When I touched her face and quoted the lines from her book, I wanted to kiss her. When her eyes went wide and her body went taut, I wanted to grab her tiny waist and dig my fingers into her ass and cover her mouth with mine. To unlock all those carnal thoughts she keeps locked away and show her it's okay to let them out. I know she wants me, no matter how many times she says she doesn't. Her body doesn't lie. She wants me just as bad as I fucking want her.

But I held back. When I kiss Mary-Beth, there better either be a bed or an audience.

🐑🐑🐑

The next day, Mary-Beth and I are back in the corner of the library with coffee, sandwiches, and enough junk food to feed an army of middle schoolers.

It's nice to spend time in a library again. I haven't been to a library since I was twelve. In a way, it feels like coming home. Peaceful. Quiet. Easy.

Well, easy except for the company.

Mary-Beth types insatiably from the opposite side of the table, pausing only to shovel in more peanut butter M&Ms. I look up from *The Goblet of Fire* to study her.

Today she's wearing jeans, yesterday's Nikes, and a plain gray hoodie. Her hair is in two long braids and more than once I've fantasized fucking her from behind, my fingers wrapped up and tugging gently.

Whenever Mary-Beth gets really into whatever she's writing, she bites on her bottom lip and her cheeks flush. It's impossible for me not to stare, wondering what dirty thing she's typing. Part of me even hopes it's about me. Okay...all of me does.

Mary-Beth's eyes dart up from the screen, meeting mine before I have a chance to look away. She nods at the book in my hands. "Why that book today?"

I carefully mark my place.

"Just in a *Harry Potter* mood, I guess." I swallow the emotion in my throat before it can find its way to my eyes. "It hits every once in a while."

There's something in Mary-Beth's eyes that tells me she can relate. I'd be shocked if she wasn't a fellow Potterhead, honestly.

"But why that one?" she presses.

I shrug, fanning the pages casually with my thumb. "Because I've read all of them several times. And this one is my favorite."

"The fourth?" Mary-Beth twists an empty M&M wrapper in her lap. "Really?"

"The Triwizard Tournament? Dragons? The sexy French witch? The return of Voldemort?" I list the reasons, counting them on my fingers. "Hell yes. It's easily the best *Harry Potter*."

"*The Goblet of Fire*?" She looks at her computer in disgust. "Ugh, you would be the type."

"To what? Prefer the obvious best book in the series? Of course."

"To like the book where bad prevails, and the hot guy dies in the end. You're so predictable, Drew."

"And which *Harry Potter* do you like best, Virgin Mary? No wait—don't tell me." I sit up and lock my gaze on hers. "Seven. You seem like the type who loves four hundred pages of camping."

Mary-Beth's eyes practically glow with chagrin, but her voice comes out phlegmatic. "The best Harry Potter book is number three: *The Prisoner of Azkaban*. Everyone with half a brain agrees."

My heart simultaneously skips a beat and twists painfully. On the outside, I roll my eyes.

"It's all in the characters." Mary-Beth folds her hands in her lap. "Remus Lupin. Sirius Black. And that surprise with Pettigrew at the end? Come on."

"Don't lie." I'm finding it impossible not to smile. I haven't talked to anyone about *Harry Potter* since... I was twelve. "That's your favorite because the smartass saves the day at the end."

"Hermione saved the day in every book."

"God, you're such a Hufflepuff."

"Hermione was in Gryffindor, in case you've forgotten."

"Pretty sure all kindergarten teachers are from Hufflepuff."

"And I'm pretty sure all actors are from Slytherin."

With that, Mary-Beth resumes typing, although I'd bet a small fortune she's just jamming random buttons.

"You know what the problem is with you, Drew?" Her eyes pounce up from the screen a few seconds later, and she closes the computer altogether.

"I'm sure you're eager to tell me."

"You never look at the big picture. You just see what's right in front of you, like a dog chasing after a squirrel. You're like 'Ooh, dragon!' Or 'Ooh, hot witch!' or 'Ooh, popular book I should torture a poor woman about until she signs over the movie rights!' Do you ever stop and think about the long term? Stuff like character development? Or people's feelings?"

"You certainly read a lot into a person's *Harry Potter* of choice."

"Tell me I'm wrong."

"You're not." I shrug. "My therapist tells me all the time."

"You see a therapist?"

"For the past ten years."

"And your therapist thinks I'm right?"

"I never said *my therapist thinks Mary-Beth is right*." I roll my eyes and take a shaky breath. "But...she's always telling me I compartmentalize too much. I think that's kind of the same thing."

"Compartmentalize?"

"Keep all the different parts of my life separated. Try not to mix it up too much." *That seems easier said than done these days.* "It keeps things...uncomplicated."

"What parts of your life?"

"My past, mostly. And work and my personal life. I've put in a long of hours trying to reconcile it all."

"What happened in the past?"

I shake my head. No fucking way I'm expounding on that one. "Let's talk about your book, Mary," I say instead.

She grips her computer like a feral animal defending the carcass it just killed. "I told you I figured it out."

"Not the new one. *Swallow Manor.*"

"No," she says automatically, though her fingers loosen just a smidge. "I haven't changed my mind."

"You said I never think about the future. But I've thought a lot about how I would adapt your book. Can I at least describe it to you?"

Mary-Beth's eyes narrow suspiciously.

"Come on. If you're actually considering signing it over, which *you said you would...*" I harden my voice and my eyes. I swear Mary-Beth twitches. "Don't you at least want to know my plan?"

She huffs and nods just slightly. I think anymore acknowledgment might have killed her.

"The reason people like *Swallow Manor* so much is because they've never read a story like it. And I think the movie should feel the same way..."

I spend the next twenty minutes describing my vision for *Swallow Manor*. From the soft lighting to the interesting cinematography to the modern music adaptations. How I want to film in Wiltshire in the summer (or Daisy Bluff in the spring) and which costume designer and intimacy coordinator I want to hire.

"I love how Susan takes control of her destiny in book two. But I think we could bring that out a little bit more in the first movie." I lick my lips and sit up in my chair. "She's stubborn and strong from the beginning. We could bring that scene in with the priest from book two to highlight that."

Mary-Beth doesn't say a word. Just nods.

"And with Ambrose...he's loyal to a fault. You know that scene from book four where he fights that one dude?"

"Lord Brighton?"

"Yes! That scene shows that he's loyal, but also vulnerable. I think if we brought that into an earlier movie, it could really bring that out of him. And then by the end of the series, we could show how he's really opened up to the viewer. How he's changed. Everyone who has read *Swallow Manor* is a little bit different afterwards. I promise we can do the same with the movie."

Mary-Beth's lips part, but instead of speaking, she looks down, blinking away tears.

I fight the urge to take her hand, and instead fold mine in my lap as I get lost in her brownish-green stare. "Come on, Mary. I know you can see it. What's your biggest fear about this? What's holding you back?"

She takes a long time before answering, studying her hands as they strum along the top of her computer. Finally, her eyes thoughtfully meet mine, her lips pulling up at the ends slightly. "My biggest fear is that the actor who plays Ambrose turns out to be a total douchebag."

I laugh. I can't help it. "Well, I'm afraid that might be unavoidable."

Chapter 21

Mary-Beth Caroline Abernathy
Hufflepuff

Shake Shack is tonight's drive-thru of choice, but we barely speak on the way back to the hotel. I slurp on my shake anxiously, unable to think of anything but Drew's question from earlier.

What's your biggest fear about this, Mary?

The answer I'd given him had been honest. But it hadn't been everything.

I'm scared to admit the entire answer. Even to myself.

My biggest fear is letting Drew in, falling for him, and then realizing he was just playing me to get my book. It's falling into the trap of believing this fantasy, this Drew Coyne's girlfriend fantasy, is real. It's getting used and getting my heart broken. He'd be a douchebag, and I'd be a fool.

I feel like I'm already at least halfway there.

We pull into the parking lot, lit by a single streetlight. My shake is gone, and I swallow down my anxiety instead. I arm myself with a heavy dose of cynicism as Drew and I both exit the car.

"Adios, man who eats the last slice of pizza."

"Woman who ate the other nine."

CHAPTER 21

"Man who spoils movies and gives no warning."

"Woman who wants movies to be spoiled."

"Man who probably has a hidden tribal tattoo."

Drew looks taken aback but then smiles. "Actually, I don't have any tattoos."

I subconsciously rub the inside of my wrist. "Really?"

"Afraid of needles." Drew shrugs. "And could never think of anything I wanted."

I roll my eyes and shift my weight to my hip. "You are the type."

"Am I?"

"To not want anything that lasts?" Even I have to admit my insult lacks its usual sting. "Yes."

"I like to think of it as not messing with perfection."

I snort and take a step toward my car. "Lord, of course."

"Do *you* have any tattoos?" The way he says it, I know he's assuming the answer is no.

Grinning triumphantly, I flip my wrist over, revealing my tiny black tattoo—half-covered by my watch.

Drew gingerly takes my hand in his, bringing it to his face to inspect. Electricity shoots up my arm.

"*Penicillin allergy?*" Drew practically cackles.

I nod my head so forcibly, I almost get whiplash. "When I was a baby, I had an infection and nearly died from an allergic reaction to penicillin. I used to have to wear a bracelet when I was younger, but it was always falling off or getting lost or giving me a rash. I don't really like to wear jewelry because I have sensitive skin. Anyway, when I was eighteen, I went and made it permanent."

"Good God, Mary-Beth." Drew's smile stretches wide across his face. It makes his sapphire eyes dance. "Leave it to you for the one rebellious thing about you to also have a medical purpose."

After my hamburger and fries, I'm tucked into my bed with a half-gallon of ice cream by 9:30. I'm alternating between staring at the puzzles I dragged out of the closet yesterday, texting Harper, and rubbing my tattoo.

Harper: Leave it to you to be pretending to date the hottest guy in the world and spend two days hiding in the library.

Mary-Beth: Drew Coyne's fake girlfriend or not, I have a deadline

Mary-Beth: Plus, he enjoyed it. He likes books

Harper: Maybe he is Dream Coyne after all. If reformed rakes make the best husbands, what do BOOKISH reformed rakes make?

Mary-Beth: I guarantee earrings > books. Hard pass.

Harper: Are you coming to the Persimmon Festival? You know it starts tonight.

"Ugh," I say out loud, not really meaning to.

I've been going to the Persimmon Festival since before I could walk, and I've never missed a year. I was even crowned Little Miss Persimmon Queen when I was eight and Junior Persimmon Queen when I was thirteen.

But going to the Persimmon Festival would mean bringing Drew out in public, and having him meet no less than ninety-two percent of the town (aka ninety-one-point-nine percent of people I know). As much as I hate breaking tradition, that sounds worse.

Mary-Beth: I think I'm gonna skip this year. Extenuating circumstances

Harper: Come on! You get to have Drew Coyne for the week. DREW COYNNNNNEEEEE. At least come show him off.

I groan into my pillow.

Mary-Beth: The next two weeks...

Harper: Wait...what? Two weeks?

Mary-Beth: I may have agreed to go to L.A. next week

Harper: Shit, MB. You'll never survive. Might as well sign away the book rights and your virginity right now.

Harper: Also... does this mean I get to have my birthday party in L.A. this year? You'll let me tag along, right?

Mary-Beth: Of course! You better come. You got me into this mess in the first place.

Mary-Beth: And believe me, I'm not going willingly. It's part of our fake dating agreement

Harper: Ooooooh, fake dating agreement. Pray tell

Mary-Beth: He stays here for a week. I go there for a week. If I don't sign over the book rights by the end, we never speak again

Harper: And what about the sex?

Mary-Beth: Harper Elizabeth! Do you not know me at all?

Harper: What? Every good fake dating contract has a no-sex rule the couple is bound to break. It's in the rom-com handbook.

Mary-Beth: We may or may not have a no-sex rule. But we certainly won't be breaking it

Harper: Right...

I take a break to stare at a cat puzzle that looks particularly enticing. *Do you think her name is Duchess?*

Harper: There's not that many people here. Come onnnnnnn

Mary-Beth: And by not that many, you mean everyone

Harper: Just Charlotte and Josie. But they're already drunk

I growl and shove my phone under the blankets, fully intending to keep it buried until morning. The absolute *last* people I want to see are Charlotte and Josie.

But then...

An idea crawls into the back of my mind—like an evil goblin constructed from the puzzle pieces hiding in the corner. It's a bad idea. It's playing dirty. *Filthy.* It's definitely breaking our fake-dating rules. But based on how this week is turning out, and how I can already feel my resolve slipping, I think it might be my last chance.

I get out of bed, unbraid and curl my hair, wash my face, put on makeup and actual pants.

And a bra.

A sports bra.

Actually, a push-up bra.

Chapter 22

Andrew Edward Coyne
Beyoncé

How had I never noticed? I can't believe I never noticed.

Black ink on soft skin. On *sensitive* skin.

Even if it is the most Mary-Beth tattoo in the world, it's still doing things to me. Maybe because it is so... *Mary-Beth.*

After I finish my dinner, I take off my shirt and jeans, slip into basketball shorts, then march over to the mini bar. Tonight, I skip the wine and go straight for the whiskey.

It's not that I shouldn't continue the celebration. The book is so close, I can practically taste it. I might even be home sooner than expected.

It's that...part of me doesn't want to go.

I shake my head and down the tiny bottle in one swallow.

No. *No.*

If the past three days have told me anything, it's that I need to go. The sooner the better. I don't do heart-to-heart conversations or corner of library dates. I don't do banter or inside jokes or hikes in the mountains.

I don't do relationships or commitments or romance.

And I definitely don't do women like Mary-Beth Abernathy.

I need to stick to my original game plan.

Convince Mary-Beth, sign the paperwork, and never see her again. That's the only way my life will ever go back to some semblance of normal.

I'm just about to open a second bottle of Jack Daniels when there's a knock at the door.

"Drew, it's me. Please tell me you're dressed."

I chuckle and swing open the door. Cue the second game of human pinball.

"I told you to get dressed!" Mary-Beth shrieks and closes her eyes.

Since she can't see me, I take the opportunity to stare at her chest, which looks larger than it did earlier today. Her tits are pushed up and showing a hint of cleavage at the V of her tight black shirt. She's wearing tighter jeans and the same cute ass heels as before. I smile. So, she didn't burn them.

Damn.

Mary-Beth opens her eyes and gives me an annoyed look. I lean against the door frame, my smile growing wider each time her eyes flit below my neck.

"You said"—I lift my voice to my best falsetto—"'Please tell me you're dressed.'" I bring my hands to my sides. "And I am, mostly."

"Well... get all the way dressed." Mary-Beth sighs like she's about to deliver bad news. "We have to go out."

"Out?"

"It's the Persimmon Festival this week. And people will be suspicious if I don't go. I always go. And since you're my boyfriend now, that means you have to go, too."

"Persimmons? Like the fruit?"

"Yes, our town grows them. It's like...our thing, I guess. Anyway, there's a parade and a carnival and a pageant and all kinds of recipe contests. You'd be amazed how many things you can do with a

CHAPTER 22

persimmon."

How many things can I do with a Mary-Beth?

"But yeah, tonight is opening night." Mary-Beth runs her hands through her hair, loosening the spiral curls. "There's probably a local band playing and a street fair with a bunch of fried food and MLMs trying to sell you stuff."

"What's the weather like?"

My question seems to catch Mary-Beth off guard. "Warm," she answers. Her eyebrows pull together suspiciously. "I'm not gonna bring a jacket."

"But jeans? Should I wear jeans?"

"Yeah, I guess."

"Got it." I drop my basketball shorts, and Mary-Beth physically pounces away from me, her eyes glued on my tight boxer briefs, bulging a little from staring at her boobs.

"Shit, Drew!" She covers her mouth, which seems to be smiling against her will, and takes another step back. Her back is almost touching the opposite wall of the hallway. "You can't just do that!"

"Oh, sorry, Virgin Mary, I thought you said to get dressed." I cough to hide my wicked cackle. "Also, who do I talk to about a language infraction?"

🐑🐑🐑

Downtown-Middle-of-Fucking-Nowhere, USA.

Growing up in Los Angeles, I've never really been to a place like this. Sure, I've been on plenty of movie sets made to look like this, with narrow roads and cozy storefronts, but really being here feels different.

A tall, brown-skinned celebrity from Hollywood in a sea of white country bumpkins. I stick out like a sore thumb. People don't even pretend to not stare.

In Los Angeles, I'm used to getting recognized, but nobody makes that big a deal about it. I'm famous, but I'm not A-list. Here, I might as well be Beyoncé. Only half a block in, I've signed autographs and taken selfies with Mary-Beth's old cheerleading coach, her postman, and the nurse who administered her last flu vaccine. Just to name a few.

The two main roads in town are closed, with vendor booths twenty deep in each direction selling everything from leggings to Tupperware. In the center, a band raised on a small stage plays covers of classic rock and country songs. Right now, they're playing a mediocre version of Lynyrd Skynyrd's "Sweet Home Alabama." Of course, they are.

There are lights strung overhead and a slight breeze in the air. Dads carry small children with stars in their eyes on their backs and packs of unruly preteens dart through the crowd. There's something about the whole family-friendly scene that makes my stomach corkscrew and emotion lodge in the back of my throat.

When we reach the town's local brewery tent, Mary-Beth nearly dives in line. "Lord, I need a drink."

"Mary-Beth!" a high-pitched voice screeches to my left, and I swear Mary-Beth visibly flinches. I have a feeling that voice is part of the reason she needs a drink so badly. "I thought I saw you!"

She draws in a long breath and turns to the voice, plastering on the fakest smile I've ever seen. "Charlotte! Josie!" She pulls the girls into a hug that involves a lot of jumping.

Mary-Beth's "friends" are different than any other people I've met here. While not unattractive, they look sort of like the Walmart version of the girls I normally hook up with in L.A. "Don't look too close" type of girls. "Go get tested for STDs the next day" type of girls. "Fake boobs in pink pleather" type of girls.

The blond one looks like she's had a bad nose job and the other one's left boob is noticeably bigger than the right. They are each holding a 7-Eleven big gulp cup, and I smell the alcohol inside from here.

CHAPTER 22

Mary-Beth, standing in the middle, couldn't look more out of place. Or more beautiful.

"So the rumors are true! I thought Kinsley was shitting me. Mary-Beth is dating the guy from all those Hallmark movies. Wow. I, like, never ever would have thought you could, like, do it." The girl with dark hair sticks out her fake lopsided tits and offers me her hand. "Hi, I'm Mary-Beth's friend, Charlotte."

"Josie," the shorter blond one with the bad nose adds. When she sticks her hand out, her cheap, dangly earrings almost get caught in her friend's black rat's nest hair.

Earrings.

Earrrrrringsss.

Well played, Virgin Mary. Well played.

I step back and take Mary-Beth's hand instead. I press her knuckles to my lips, then wrap her arm around my waist as I casually sling my other arm around her shoulder.

Mary-Beth fights the gesture at first, stiff in my arms until she finally succumbs with a *harrumph* I feel more than hear. Melting into my side, she fits perfectly into the space between my feet and my shoulder, like her body was made to be next to mine. And damn—I'm more and more convinced that's true.

I smugly plant a kiss on her hair just because I can, daring her to bring up her stupid rules. When she doesn't, I bend down and laugh in her ear. "Nice try, Virgin Mary."

Now to get the bitchy friends she thought I would flirt with on my side too.

"Hi." I slap on my best Hallmark Drew smile and wave. "It's so nice to meet you. I'm Mary-Beth's boyfriend, Drew."

"Hi," they say in unison, their eyes bulging almost as much as their nipples.

Mary-Beth's fingernails are practically drawing blood through my

T-shirt. But what I'm sure she doesn't realize is...it's turning me on. I've been wanting Mary-Beth to claw her nails into me for weeks. I pull her so close I can feel her heartbeat, and she mutters, "I hate you" through the clenched teeth of her fake-ass smile.

"It's so nice to meet more of Mary-Beth's friends. I've been keeping her all to myself for way too long." I shake her shoulders, and she twists in a weak attempt to escape. I loosen my grip to allow her to leave, but she doesn't. *That's what I thought.* "And God, what a beautiful night. Persimmons, am I right?"

The girls trade confused looks, before agreeing about the fruit and/or festival and/or weather.

"So how long have you two known each other?" Lopsided Boobs asks.

"A few weeks," Mary-Beth says at the same time I say, "A few months."

"Feels like months," I quickly correct.

"Sure does," Mary-Beth says under her breath.

"In a good way," I add.

"Yep," Mary-Beth agrees sarcastically.

"You guys are so cute. Aren't they so cute? Like in an opposites-attract sort of way," Bad Nose Job says to her friend, swaying a little. "How did you guys meet? Was it really dodgeball, because that is, like, so fucking romantic."

"In Los Angeles," Mary-Beth says when I say, "At the gym."

"At a gym in Los Angeles," we say together.

"Oh my God, Mary-Beth, do you, like, work out now?" one of the girls asks, though I'm not sure which one. "You're, like, so different than in high school. You always skipped the gym during cheerleading."

"Um, I guess? But anyway, we didn't meet at a dodgeball tournament in Las Vegas," Mary-Beth clarifies, rolling her eyes. "Not sure where that one came from."

CHAPTER 22

And then, I just can't help myself. "Probably because we love to visit Las Vegas. Don't we, babe?"

"We do?" Oh, Mary-Beth—if looks could kill.

"Yeah, silly!" I fight the urge to ruffle her hair. "We have another trip planned for Las Vegas next week."

"We do?"

"She's so cute, isn't she?" I say, and the girls openly gape at me.

Mary-Beth gapes a little less openly, but only slightly.

I beam down at her with my most adoring smile. "We love to travel together, don't we, Mary? But this is my first time here. Babe, you have such a great hometown. I can't wait for that thing we have planned later this week. What was that again?"

Mary-Beth practically hisses at me. God, she's so easy to mess with. Not only can she not keep her cool; she reacts with her entire body.

Her *entire* body.

Even though she's an uptight virgin, I bet she'd be amazing in bed. A filthy mind with skin and muscles that reflect emotion. Fuck...

"We were, uh –" Mary-Beth clears her throat. "Just gonna go to the libra—"

"Oh my God, I love the library!" Bad Nose Job cuts in. "We have the best library in the county. Did you know you can eat in it? I mean, it's cool to visit even if you don't like books. But Mary-Beth, you still like books, right?"

Oh, this is just too easy. I give my favorite fake girlfriend's shoulders a squeeze. "Mary-Beth loves books. Absolutely *loves* books. Don't you, babe?"

Right now, Mary-Beth looks like she loves books. Books on decapitation. Or castration.

"Speaking of books. Drew, have you found Minnie Maple yet?" Lopsided Boobs asks, her voice hushed. "Those books are so hot, right?"

"So hot," the other girl agrees.

"I haven't found her. Not yet." I look down at Mary-Beth, who has a green tinge to her skin. I hold her tighter to my hip. "But I'm gonna keep looking. Hopefully soon."

When the girls finally leave, I press my lips to Mary-Beth's ear, my breath hot against her skin. "I'm a lot of things"— my voice is dark and menacing— "but I'll *never* be a cheater. Not even on you."

Chapter 23

Mary-Beth Caroline Abernathy
Property of Andrew Edward Coyne

I'd severely underestimated Drew Coyne.

Because not only am I so mad I can barely see, but my knees are also wobbly, my heart is fluttering, and the skin behind my ear may never stop tingling.

And apparently, I'm going to Las Vegas next week. I can only hope it's better than L.A.

Worst of all, I'm stuck to Drew's hip while he shakes hands and kisses babies with everyone I know like the politician he played in *A Candidate from the Heart.* Is there a contest for how many townsfolk you can win over in less than twenty minutes? If so, give Drew the trophy.

"So, who were Tweedledee and Tweedledum?" Drew asks after he buys us each a beer and we make our way from the loud music of the stage. His arm is still slung across my shoulders, and dear God, the weight of it feels unnaturally good, despite wishing I could rip it off and catapult it to the next state. "Other than girls you planted to try and seduce me. It's gonna take a lot more than the town Playboy Bunnies to get rid of me, Virgin Mary."

"I didn't plant them," I clarify carefully. "They just...*happened* to be here." I leave out the part that I *knew* they were here, and I ran into them on purpose despite abhorring them to no end.

"They don't seem like people you would be friends with."

"Another one of your assumptions?"

"Sure. But it was pretty obvious there's history there."

I quickly take a swig of my beer, hoping Drew doesn't catch the pain of an old wound being ripped open.

"So, I'm guessing that's a yes."

I swallow, keeping my eyes trained on the fried Oreo stand behind him. I try to steady my voice when I finally speak. "If you call telling the whole high school my boyfriend, Sutton Heard, dumped me because I wouldn't sleep with him, then having a threesome with him the next weekend at Chozen Halstead's house party, and ruining my high school social life forever a history, then I guess, yeah. We have a history."

"Wow, that's pretty shitty," Drew says, leading us past a local photographer's booth.

I don't bother correcting his language.

"And you said I'm the worst person you've ever met." Drew chuckles, but his voice still somehow sounds serious. "At least I didn't fuck your boyfriend."

I wince at the f-word, but again, don't say anything. "Charlotte, Josie, and I were on the cheerleading squad together, but I knew deep down that I shouldn't trust them. And Sutton had a reputation, but I thought things would be different with me. So..." I let out a heavy sigh and take another drink. "I was just as much to blame. I knew I shouldn't do it, but I did anyway."

"Just because you expected it doesn't make it any less awful."

"I guess when you're not expecting it, it just hurts more."

Drew stops walking and looks down at me, that sentence heavy between us. "You're the type," he finally says.

"Lord, what type am I now? The type to have more plants than

CHAPTER 23

friends? Or to have *Cooking for One* sitting on my counter?" *Both true, I'm afraid.* "The type—"

"The type to forgive girls like that," Drew interjects. My breath catches in my chest as my eyes dart up to meet his. The lights of the street fair reflecting in them flicker.

"Who said I forgave them?"

"Forgave them to the point you use them to try and get rid of me."

A hint of a smile plays at the corner of my lips. "You have no idea how badly I want you to pack up and go home."

"You have no idea how badly I want the rights to *Swallow Manor*." A sincere smile breaks free on Drew's lips, and I cough and look away, trying to hide my own.

"MB!" Harper comes barreling through the crowd like a bull in a china shop. "You came!"

With her rainbow hair and billowing low-cut red dress, Harper is like a bright, bouncing beacon of relief. I slither out from Drew's arm and run to meet her. When we embrace, she pets my hair lovingly.

"All the pieces still there?" Harper looks me over with excessive concern. The stench she's giving off could disinfect a wound. Luckily, when Harper gets *drunk* drunk, she turns into a lovely Mother Goose type of friend.

"I'm fine, Harp. Still intact. Mostly."

"You!" Harper's eyes slide to Drew, and she takes a menacing step in his direction. He puts his hands up in surrender, and I almost feel sorry for him. "Come here."

Harper pulls Drew into a drunken hug, pressing her boobs into his stomach. He shoots me a surprised look and tentatively pats her on the back.

"While I do absolutely detest you and your *friend*," Harper spits out the word *friend* with unusual disdain, and I'm not really sure why. "Tonight is the fucking Persimmon—" Harper stops and crinkles her big blue eyes at me. "Sorry, Mary-Beth."

She turns back to Drew, shoving her pointer finger into his chest, her words slurring. "The Persimmon Festival. And we are gonna celebrate that magnificent nasty-ass orange fruit no one else gives a shit about tonight. And when you celebrate a forgotten fruit together, you become family." Harper turns back to me and smiles, her eyes turning to little slits. "So let's let bygones be bygones and go dance!"

Harper seizes our hands and tugs us toward the stage, like an executioner dragging her next victims to the gallows.

"Livin' on a Prayer" by Bon Jovi, or some semblance of it, blares from the band. Harper screams, "I love this song!" and rushes forward, leaving Drew and I standing on the outskirts of the crowd.

Drew tries to take my hand, but I snatch it away instinctively. I only sort of regret it.

"People are looking," he says.

"They're not."

"Why don't you want to dance with me?" Drew gives me a wicked look, raising his eyebrows. "Scared?"

I don't favor him with a response, just a huff and a scowl.

"Or is it that you can't dance?" He starts fiddling with one of the belt loops on my jeans.

I cross my arms, trying to muffle my earsplitting heartbeat and attempt to make my voice sound indifferent. "It's not that I don't like to dance. Or that I'm not good at it. I love to dance, and actually took dance lessons until I was thirteen when I started cheerleading. I'm a freaking amazing dancer." I jut my chin up stubbornly. "I just don't want to dance with *you*."

Truthfully, I'm absolutely petrified of dancing with Drew. My body is slowly betraying me; it's Russian Roulette when it will finally snap.

Drew drops his hand from my jeans and leans closer. "Might like it if you try it."

CHAPTER 23

"American Girl" by Tom Petty is playing now.

Harper is a blur of flailing limbs and rainbow hair by the stage. She grabs an equally drunk girl, and they start grinding on a pair of men at least double our age. I begin to wonder if my attendance tonight has lasted long enough.

But then, across the crowd, I see *him*. Blond hair, a lopsided smile, a Coors Lite, and a flannel shirt I'm pretty sure he's had since high school. I would recognize it anywhere.

Sutton Heard looks like he joined Harper, Charlotte, and Josie at the pre-game. His cheeks are flushed, his hair is greasy, and his eyes are hazed. Staring right at me, he looks like he's toying with the idea of approaching.

Heck to the no.

"Fine." I grab Drew's hand, yanking him toward the stage. "I'll dance with you."

Drew's chuckles chase me into the heart of the crowd. The song changes to "Piano Man," and his hands find my waist. Looking over my shoulder, I place mine clumsily on his shoulders. Sutton is still watching as we begin swaying to the music.

"Who's the farmer?"

"Sutton Heard."

Drew nods like he's just received a top-secret assignment. "Roger that."

He draws my body to his, inch by erotic inch, until our chests touch. He takes my hands and snakes them up to his neck, then digs his hands into my lower back, applying pressure until my leg is in between his. His hips move across mine, hard in all the places I'm soft. Our eyes lock, and all I see is Drew's eyes, a strange voraciousness clouding them, like a storm moving on a sunny day. A tightness comes over me, settling in my lower belly.

"This is against the rules." I cough and look away, trying to dispel the temperature rising between us. "This is cheating."

"Is it cheating?" Drew pulls me closer. Dear Lord, I don't fight it. I don't even try. "Or improvising?"

My mouth is as dry as a withered persimmon. My legs are as shaky as a withered persimmon branch.

"That guy—" Drew nods to Sutton, standing right where we left him—"is a total ass. I can tell."

"Takes one to know one?" The heat between my thighs won't let me deliver the insult with any amount of fervor.

"Any guy who would leave you for those girls"—Drew's forehead wrinkles—"can't be trusted. Show him what he's missing, Mary-Beth. You look hot tonight. Your ass looks incredible in those jeans."

To prove his point, Drew gives my butt a squeeze, his eyes daring me to stop him.

"Let's show you off," he says, the squeeze turning into more of a knead. My entire butt cheek fits into the palm of his hand, which both terrifies and excites me. I've never really registered our size difference before now. Drew could manhandle me if he wanted to. Eat me alive.

My entire body is overtaken by desire. With just one touch, Drew is stirring up all the feelings I try to keep hidden. The feelings I tell myself I don't have. The feelings I'd *never* act on.

"He can't hear you," I rasp. "But thank you."

"I didn't think he could."

The song continues, Drew holding me against his body possessively, his hands inside the back pockets of my jeans, his hot breath on my hair. His erection –his *erection!*– near my hip bone. Me, trying not to lose my shit. I'm quite certain I've never been this turned on in my life. Drew is an ocean consuming me, and I want to freaking drown.

About halfway through the song, Drew starts singing along, his voice low like subdued thunder. My fingers bore into his shoulder muscles, gripping him with the little self-control I have left.

CHAPTER 23

I force myself to pull away, but only enough to see his face. To see if I can tell what he's thinking. Is this a game to him? Or is he wanting to do this just to...*do* it? His eyes burn into mine, their blue irises dark with something unholy. In all the lighting and poses and situations I've seen Drew in over the years, he has *never* looked like this.

What on God's green earth could it mean?

I find myself playing with the hair at the back of Drew's neck, and he starts playing with the hem of my T-shirt. It's hard to concentrate on much more than that.

"You're a Billy Joel fan?" I ask, forcing myself to think of something other than how horny I am.

"My dad was."

"Oh." I wait for him to expound. He doesn't. "Billy Joel is cool, I guess."

"He's not."

"Okay."

"Just one of the many, many shitty things about him."

"Billy Joel? That he's not cool?"

"My dad. That he liked Billy Joel."

"Oh."

"So what, um, other crappy things does he like?" I laugh a little, only because it feels necessary.

Drew doesn't answer, just shakes his head with a conversation-ending grunt.

Don't ask about Drew's dad. Noted.

Toward the end of the song, I glance around for Sutton. I don't see him anywhere. I smile to myself. Revenge is sweet, even when it's fake.

Out of nowhere, a woman bumps into Drew and me. His hands wrap all the way around my waist when he pulls me against his side.

"Oh my God, Drew Coyne!" the woman, clearly drunk, says. Then she turns to me. "Is this her?"

"Yes," I sigh. *How many times must I answer this tonight?* "This is my boyfrie—"

"Minnie Maple?" She keeps talking as if I didn't speak, tangling me into a sweaty, unwieldy hug. "I'm such a big fan of your books. I've read all of them. I can't wait for the movie."

"I, uh…" I struggle for words, anxiety clenching my lungs with unforgiving forceps. I've lived this moment over and over in my nightmares, but reality is even more lurid. My life flashes before my eyes, all ending here at the intersection of Main Street and Station Road with Billy Joel playing in the background.

"This is actually my girlfriend, Mary-Beth," Drew says coolly, taking my hand in his. "I haven't found the author of *Swallow Manor* yet."

"Girlfriend?" The woman is looking at me like it can't be true.

I panic, needing to prove to her and everyone else that might be listening or watching or even in the vicinity that she's wrong. That I am not Minnie Maple; I am Andrew Edward Coyne's freaking girlfriend.

"Yes, girlfriend," I grind out.

Without thinking, I thrust onto my tiptoes, throw my hands around Drew's neck, and press my lips to his.

It takes about two seconds before I realize what I've just done. That my mouth is pressed to Drew Coyne's mouth. That our bodies are connected from our lips to our thighs. That one of his hands is grabbing my butt and the other is tangled in my hair. That Drew is biting my bottom lip and his tongue is sliding into my mouth.

This. Is. Happening.

I'm kissing Drew Coyne. Sweet Jesus, *I'm kissing Drew Coyne.* And he's kissing me back. And he's pulling me closer. And going deeper. And I'm feeling things. Amazing, horrifying, new, exciting, immoral things.

And now, his tongue is definitely inside my mouth, tasting, exploring. It's been a while since anyone's tongue was in my mouth, and I can't say I've ever really enjoyed it. But that was because no one has ever kissed me like Drew is kissing me right now.

Drew Coyne's tongue. In my mouth.

It tastes like whiskey and need.

Holy shit.

"God, Mary-Beth, you're a good kisser." Drew practically breathes the words into my mouth. "Do it again."

I do. I don't even think twice.

Or once.

Kissing Drew feels more like a conquest than kissing. Like Drew is trying to find all the hidden parts of me and claim them as his own. My butt—Drew's. My hair—Drew's. My clothes—Drew's now. My bottom lip, the corner of my mouth, the tiny little ridges on my tongue, all property of Drew Coyne.

The back of my neck as he pulls my face back to his—Drew's. The skin at the edge of my breast as he runs his fingers down the side of my body—his. The breathlessness of my lungs and the heat on my skin and the frenzied desire at the apex of my thighs. My nipples as they perk and my lips as they swell and my mind as it spins and my toes as they curl.

They're all Drew Coyne's.

Chapter 24

Andrew Edward Coyne
Mistake

I should have opted for the bed over the audience. Because damn, I want Mary-Beth right now.

Kissing is not enough. Clothes are too much. I want to devour her. Consume her. I want to bend her over and brand her mine. Take ownership of her. Fuck Sutton whatever-the-hell-his-name-is. And fuck that lady who thinks Mary-Beth is Minnie Maple. Tonight, she's only one thing.

Mine.

The tiny moans coming from Mary-Beth's throat are what make me finally pull away. She doesn't have a freaking clue how sexy she is and what noises like that can do to a man. Her eyes are huge and rich chocolate brown, and her lips are pink and swollen. Her skin is flushed from her cheeks all the way down to the cleavage disappearing beneath her shirt.

What other parts of Mary-Beth are red?

The woman who accosted Mary-Beth is long gone, but that doesn't mean no one is looking. On the contrary, we've amassed quite the audience. Harper, front and center, looks like she's about to start slow-clapping. Mary-Beth gives her a small hug, then grabs my hand

CHAPTER 24

and pulls, shielding her face with her other hand.

"Let's go."

Fuck yes.

In the car, before Mary-Beth has even closed the door, I lean across the console to kiss her. I'm eager to pick up where we left off, especially with more privacy, but Mary-Beth pushes me away.

"Thank you for helping me tonight." Her voice sounds unsure.

"Helping you?" I grip the handle of my seat to feign control.

"With Charlotte and Josie. And with Sutton. And with that woman." Her eyes fall, and she shakes her head. "I'm sorry, you didn't need to do that."

She's *apologizing*? I don't know whether to be pissed or offended. Or something else.

"You're my girlfriend."

The crease in Mary-Beth's forehead deepens. "*Fake* girlfriend."

"Still. Did you really think I was going to fucking cheat on you?" I growl, the passion from before fueling my anger. "That I wouldn't kiss you back when you kissed me?"

"Language, Drew." Mary-Beth's voice is a shiv.

"So we're back to that?"

"You're a super great actor." Mary-Beth keeps her eyes on her squirming hands. "You're even better than I thought you were. You've won the whole town over. Congratulations."

"You think that's what I was doing? Acting?"

"Of course. It's what you do." Her words are staccato ice cubes. "You act."

"Mary-Beth, when are you going to give up the damn fantasy? Yeah, so I'm not a Hallmark boyfriend in real life. And I don't have a dog, and I don't *always* recycle and no, I'm not a virgin. Far from it. I'm sorry who I am is not who you were expecting. But maybe if you gave the real me a chance, you might be surprised how much you like it."

There I go again. Demanding Mary-Beth get to know me. Why do I want her to *know me*? No one knows me.

Probably because I want to know her so fucking badly.

"Doubtful."

The word lances me. My voice drops to a snarl.

"Then there's always the 'sign the book rights' option." My fingers grip the steering wheel, wishing I could rip the leather to shreds. "That's the fastest way to get rid of me. It's not parading me around to everyone you know. Because I can guarantee I'm going to win that fight every time. I've made a living acting like the perfect guy. I know *exactly* how to do it."

"And *that* is the problem." Mary-Beth's eyes finally leave her hands, jumping over the seat to meet mine for just a split second. It's not long enough to figure out what the hell she's thinking.

"Shit, Mary-Beth." I slam the steering wheel. "Just because I'm an actor doesn't mean I'm always acting. For the postman and your bitchy friends, yes. But when it was just me and you..."

"Drew, don't. There was a crowd watching. I'm not stupid."

"Mary-Beth, I talked about my dad. I never—" I stop myself before I say too much. I narrow my eyes and start again. "I don't do that. And when we kissed—"

"The kiss was a mistake," Mary-Beth cuts in. Her words are like ice water. "I, I broke our rules." Her hands are shaking now, along with her voice. "And I'm sorry. It won't happen again."

"A mistake," I repeat.

Mary-Beth nods. I wish she would fucking look at me.

"Why was it a mistake?"

"Because it was fake. And, and I shouldn't have put you in that position, where you felt like you had to pretend."

"It was real, Mary-Beth. I did it because I wanted to. And don't lie to yourself, so did you. Shit, how could you think *that* was fake?"

CHAPTER 24

My voice sounds like I'm begging. I swallow hard. I don't beg.

Mary-Beth finally turns to me, her brown eyes on the verge of tears. I look away, not wanting to watch them spill. "Please, just don't, okay? It's not gonna help you get the book rights, I promise. This is my fault. I messed up, and I won't do it again."

And with that, I slide the car into drive, my hands clenching the steering wheel so tightly they turn bone-white. "Okay, Mary. If that's what you want."

If Mary-Beth doesn't believe that kiss was real, there's no fucking way I'll be able to convince her of anything else.

Chapter 25

Mary-Beth Caroline Abernathy
Hypercritical
Smartass
Black Heart
Closed Mind

The next two days are some of the most awkward of my life. Drew and I fall into somewhat of an offbeat rhythm. We meet in the hotel parking lot, me with Starbucks cups and a bag of junk food from the gas station, him with a scowl and books to return to the library. We climb into his Mercedes rental. We pick up sandwiches from the deli, both ordering the Frankenwich. I've perfected saying, "I'll have what he's having," and ignoring the worker's annoyed side-eye. We spend the next twelve hours in our bookshelf fortress. We hit a drive-thru before he takes me back to my car.

We don't talk. We don't touch. We don't even look at each other. I write. He reads. Rinse. Repeat.

Yesterday, Drew added *Jurassic Park* by Michael Crichton and *It* by Stephen King to his book tower.

This morning, he added *Scythe* and *Dry* by Neal Shusterman.

I'm pretty sure he's researching different ways to off me. Everything

CHAPTER 25

from feeding me to a dinosaur or a cannibalistic clown, to beheading me with a sickle or depriving me of water till I die of thirst. The book he's reading now, *14 Ways to Die* by Vincent Ralph, is a bit too obvious if you ask me.

What he doesn't know is I've already contemplated doing the job myself. I'm pretty sure death is preferable to spending another anxiety-laced moment with Drew Coyne, my thoughts teetering between the memory of his lips seared against mine and the black in his eyes when I told him it was a mistake.

That I wouldn't kiss you back when you kissed me?

I'm sure in the history of humanity, no woman has analyzed ten words more than me and that sentence.

I hate myself because I caused this. I gave into the fantasy and pretended this was real with it clearly isn't. We both agreed this was *fake*; it's about the book. I hate myself for forgetting about the damn book altogether.

But I think I hate myself most of all for admitting it was a mistake. For breaking the fragile friendship Drew and I somehow formed. We hated each other before, but this feels different. This feels more like disdain.

Why couldn't I just keep playing along? Let Drew kiss me until I was dizzy and breathless and falling off an abyss I'd never climb out of. Keep parading around town on his arm, holding his hand so tightly no one would ever question our relationship status again, even though they'd all be wrong. Let him squeeze my butt and bite my lip and lie about wanting to. Let myself be Drew's, even for just a week, even just for pretend.

Oh right, something about my pride and my heart and my virginity and my book.

But one question remains—

And that's the question I'm asking myself when Drew and I enter

Chipotle.

There's a long line, which we join.

I turn to him, gulping a breath I'll surely need. "Why are you still here?"

Drew's eyes slide to me, so narrow I can't even see the blue. "You know why."

"But if we're not going to speak to each other..."

"All I have to do is survive two weeks." His voice is clinical, like I have an ear infection and he's telling me about the medicine I need to take for the next two weeks to clear it up. "You obviously want me to leave you alone, and that's what I'm doing."

"But aren't you supposed to be, like," — I laugh nervously— "proving to me you're a good person or something?"

Drew takes a step forward, placing his hands in his pockets. "And what exactly makes someone a good person?"

I open my mouth to try to answer that, but Drew keeps talking. He keeps his voice quiet and his face neutral, aware of the people around us. No one would suspect, except me. I'm the only one who can see the murder in his eyes.

"Because I could sit here and tell you I treat my employees fairly. Will and Darcy and my therapist and my personal trainer get all federal holidays off. And they're very well-compensated. That I never take anything from hotel rooms. Not even a hand towel or the remote-control batteries. That I never steal my neighbor's Wi-Fi or a distant relative's Netflix password."

Drew's words are pouring out like a dam sprung a leak. Why did I have to go and pull the plug?

"That I recycle ninety percent of the time and donate ten percent of my income to charitable causes. That I never cheat on my taxes, and I'm a very generous tipper. That I've never touched a woman who wasn't begging me to. Never a woman who wasn't one hundred percent single. That I've *never* done it in anger. That I *do* hold the elevator. And I *do* save the last slice of pizza. And I *would* rather stay in and do a puzzle or read a book. That whether you believe me or not, I do actually give a shit about the planet and my job and people's feelings and—"

"Okay, I get it." The air inside the restaurant is stifling—hotboxed by Drew's subdued anger. I want to run outside. "I don't want a laundry list of things you think make you a good person." The sentence comes out sounding like a plea for silence.

"You're right. You don't. Because you've already made up your mind about me. You're not even trying to get to know the real me. When you look at me, all you see is a fuckboy and nothing else."

"That's not true!" I nearly shout, and the woman in front of us looks over her shoulder. I grab Drew's hand to make sure she doesn't suspect. He lets me hold it, though it feels like a dead fish in mine.

"I assumed the best about you, Drew," I whisper. "I tried to give you the benefit of the doubt. I even defended when Harper called you a douchebag."

"So, what changed?"

"I saw who you really are. That everything I thought I knew was a lie. I saw that you're just a big hypocrite."

"And *you're* not a hypocrite?" Drew laughs. "You think you're exactly who you pretend to be? What's worse, Mary-Beth? A hypocrite who wishes they could be authentic like me? Or a hypocrite who wants to keep their secret life a secret forever like you?"

"At least I'm a hypocrite who is a good person hiding one bad thing about herself. You're a bad person pretending to be good."

I've struck a chord. I see it in the way his eyebrows lift, just a smidge.

"And who says *you're* a good person?"

I put my hand on my heart, prepared to recite my list of "good person achievements" even though I literally just told Drew not to do that. It doesn't matter, though, because he cuts me off again, his whisper one of a fire-breathing dragon.

"Because I think you're judgmental. And controlling. And you use your upbringing and your purity as a weapon. A way to look down on people with different values. You're afraid to let people know the real you. And you know why? It's not because of your books. Your books bring people joy. Help people. They aren't bad. They're one of the best things about you.

"No, it's because the *real* you is a hypercritical smartass with a black heart and a closed mind who thinks she's better than everyone else. Who shames everyone you deem less than. Anyone who isn't exactly like you."

"Wow, tell me how you really feel." The words fall flat and don't even begin to cover the hurt in my voice. "I suppose now you're going to tell me why you're not an egotistical pig-headed womanizer?"

"Is there anything in this world I could tell you to convince you otherwise?" When I don't answer, Drew's voice gets even quieter. "I'm never going to be the man you imagined, Mary-Beth. That isn't me. It's not who I am."

Drew licks his lips and starts leaning toward me, something unnamed in his eyes. My mouth goes completely dry.

"Will you ever change your mind about me, Mary-Beth? Because if not, you're right. I should leave."

Drew steps up to the counter. It's our turn. His order is boring: a chicken burrito. I'm glad I can't see my reflection in the shiny tinfoil. I'm hoping he'll at least add chips or extra guac. He doesn't.

He pays for our food but doesn't wait for me before he begins marching to the car. After a few gulps of air, I cautiously follow—like a lost kitten, not knowing what else to do.

We ride back to the hotel in dead silence—his hands in a vice grip around the steering wheel, mine shaking violently in my lap. It's a

CHAPTER 25

struggle not to cry before I reach the sanctuary of my car. When I do, it feels impossible to stop.

Chapter 26

Andrew Edward Coyne
Egotistical
Pig-headed
Womanizer

Like I've done the past three mornings, the next day, I go to the sorry excuse for a gym in the hotel basement and grab an apple from the continental breakfast in the lobby.

I go back to my room, shower, and start reading a book while I wait to hear from Mary-Beth. I finish *Shoe Dog* and raid the minibar's peanuts and whiskey around lunch time. I start on *Jurassic Park* around two o'clock. Four chapters in, I finish the whiskey. After the T-rex eats the park's publicist, I realize Mary-Beth isn't going to call.

I realize I've royally fucked up.

Not that she didn't deserve to hear what I had to say, because she did. And not that I didn't mean every word of it, because I did. And not that it wasn't one hundred percent true, because it was.

I tell myself it's because I probably just lost the last shreds of hope I had for securing *Swallow Manor,* but I know that's not true.

It's because I hurt Mary-Beth's feelings.

For some reason, I *hate* that I hurt her feelings. It's just like she said: I'm an egotistical pig-headed womanizer. And although I've been that

CHAPTER 26

for years, I'm not sure I want to be anymore.

I grab my phone and pull up the conversation labeled **Virgin Mary**.

I scroll back through our conversation from the past few days.

Virgin Mary: Hey man who goes to the car wash every Sunday and blares bad rap music no one wants to hear...

Virgin Mary: Hey man who needs to get his mysterious mole checked by a doctor...

Virgin Mary: Hey man who won't stop talking about his fantasy football win from three years ago....

She'd been trying to get to know me. And trying to give me a chance. I accused her of not trying, but here it is. Proof that she was.

I'm such an ass.

I type out: **Hey woman who has multiple Instagram accounts so she can like the same thing more than once.**

But quickly delete it. Too on the nose.

Hey woman who gets excited when people cancel their dinner plans with her.

I delete that too. *You're trying to make dinner plans, dipshit, not cancel them.*

Hey woman who asks for a new mop for Christmas.

I reread it three times, nod, and am about to hit send when I get a phone call from Will.

"What's up, man?" I say.

"Do I need to put out a casting call for *Swallow Manor* yet?" I can hear the smile in Will's voice, which instantly makes me frown. "I read online that actress from the Netflix movie we watched a couple weeks ago is hoping to play Susan. She seems like a fun time."

"Yeah, I guess."

"Jesus Christ, what's wrong with you? I'd ask if someone shot your puppy, but Chloe is having a tea party on Maggie's back right now."

"Mary-Beth," I grind out, hoping that explains things.

"What happened? On Monday you said things were going so well, you thought you'd be home by the end of the week. I've been stockpiling champagne."

"That was before we kissed."

"Well, shit." Will's voice is not surprised. "I figured it was only a matter of time."

"And then she said it was a mistake."

"I know that's a major blow to your ego, but it probably was from her perspective. She's not exactly the type to—"

"And then I called her a hypercritical smartass with a black heart and a closed mind."

"Nice. I'm sure she loved that. Probably even more than the kiss."

"She deserved it."

"Why? Because she's already regretting you?"

"No." I dig my fingernails into the flesh of my palm. "Because it's true."

"And you care because…"

"Because she can't get over our first impression. She can't reconcile the person in her mind and the real me. She's convinced I'm the worst person in the world and every word out of my mouth is a lie."

"Has it been?"

"Surprisingly, no. Before the kiss, we were getting along. And I was actually being myself. And it was nice to be myself for a change. I was enjoying it. I was enjoying…her."

"And the book rights…"

"Yeah." I pause. The book rights. *Why don't I care about the damn book rights?* "That too. That was happening too."

"Well, shit." Now Will's voice couldn't sound *more* surprised. "I can't believe it."

"Believe what?"

"You have feelings for her. You *actually* have feelings for her. Also, you owe me a hundred bucks."

"What? No." I harden my voice and try again. "*No.*"

"Is this because she won't sleep with you? Because she's holding you hostage with her body? Is this some twisted version of Stockholm Syndrome? Because I never thought I'd see the day."

"I don't know what you're talking about. I just told you she's a smartass with a black heart and closed mind. Which is exactly what she is."

"I'm shocked this charm hasn't worked."

"She told me to be myself. It's not my fault she hates everything about me."

"Just be honest. Speak from the heart, man."

"Fuck off."

Will laughs for too long, then thankfully changes the subject. "Anyway, I hear we're taking a trip to Las Vegas next week."

"How did you hear that?"

"Should I book the Chateau Nightclub for the fourteenth?"

"What the hell, man?"

I get a notification I have a new text message. My heart feels like a jackhammer against my ribs.

Virgin Mary: Hey man who drops his weights on the ground so people will know how heavy they are.

I tip the glass previously holding my whiskey but find it empty. I quickly rewrite my text draft from earlier, a smile threatening.

Drew: Hey woman I'm surprised knows that's a bad thing.

Virgin Mary: I googled

Drew: Googled what?

Virgin Mary: Things douchebag guys do.

Virgin Mary: You hungry?

Drew: I've been living off Jack Daniels and peanuts from the minibar

Virgin Mary: That was number 12 on the douchebag list

Virgin Mary: You could have gotten something to eat, ya know

Drew: Girlfriend says I can't leave this hotel room without her. Something about wanting to know where I am at all times

Virgin Mary: She sounds like a real bitch

I smile for real.

Drew: Best I've ever had.

Virgin Mary: Dinner in 20?

Drew: Parking lot?

Virgin Mary: My house

My blood pulses. Hard and heading south.

Drew: Chick-Fil-A delivers?

Virgin Mary: I'm cooking.

Drew: Doubling something in *Cooking for One*?

Virgin Mary: Something like that.

Now, I have a full-on grin. And a boner.

"Drew? Still there?"

I fumble to bring the phone to my ear. I'd completely forgotten about Will. I'd completely forgotten about everyone.

"Shit. Sorry, man."

"So, Las Vegas..."

"Yeah, sure. Book the Chateau. I gotta go."

"Just tell her how you fe—"

Click.

Chapter 27

Andrew Edward Coyne
Ass
(Again)

I hear "Brass Monkey" by the Beastie Boys before I even turn the corner to Mary-Beth's apartment. Through the slits in the blinds, I see her dancing around her microscopic kitchen as she chops something. She's singing every word, which, to a song like "Brass Monkey," isn't an easy thing to do.

I watch for a good two minutes, staring at her ass as it wiggles to the beat. She's wearing a green dress. Not *the* green dress, but still. I know what Mary-Beth in green does to me.

Just when I think I've figured her out...*this*.

I carefully knock, almost wishing I didn't have to. Almost.

Mary-Beth licks something off her finger, and I can't control my own tongue when it licks my lips. She rushes to the door, and I jump back, trying to pretend I haven't been spying on her through the blinds like a creep.

She flings the door open, and her heart-shaped face, long shiny hair, and big brown eyes greet me. This dress has a lighter hue and higher neckline, but it does the same thing to her eyes. They're electric. A pink polka dot apron hugs her hips and says, "Will Cook for Shoes."

And she's got the cute ass heels on again. Tonight, in the green, they make her ass look fucking adorable.

My lungs deflate. My muscles twitch. My mouth salivates.

The song changes to "No Sleep Till Brooklyn."

"Beastie Boys, huh?" I laugh.

Mary-Beth's blush is immediate. From her collarbone to her forehead. "Yeah, um. I like eighties and nineties hip hop. The Beastie Boys are my favorite." She tucks a curl behind her ear.

"I'm more of a Tribe Called Quest guy myself." I lean on the door frame.

Mary-Beth's eyes light up and my heart sputters. "'Check the Vibe' is one of my favorite songs."

I cock my head to the side. "'Can I Kick It?' is better."

Mary-Beth's eyebrows converge. "Maybe the *instrumental*," she concedes reluctantly. "But the lyrics on 'Check the Vibe' are infinitely better."

"Quote one line, and I'll consider changing my mind."

She licks her lips, a smile threatening. "*Now here's a funky introduction of how nice I am. Tell your mother, tell your father, send a telegram. I'm like an energizer 'cause you see, I last long. My crew is never ever wack because we stand strong.*"

Well...*damn*. Now Virgin Mary is a rapper?

I think Mary-Beth likes playing the fuck-all-your-assumptions game too. And she just scored a point.

"You're not the hip-hop type, Mary." I bite my cheek to keep from smiling.

She shrugs. "I know good music when I hear it. And I heard it when I was thirteen and never got over it."

I lean closer as I finally take a step inside. "I still think 'Can I Kick It?' is better."

"Lord, of course you do." She shakes her head and turns toward the

CHAPTER 27

kitchen.

Mary-Beth's apartment is shitty. And tiny. And cluttered. She has too much shit for such a small space. But it's so perfectly her. You could have shown me pictures of fifty different apartments, and I would have known this one was hers instantly.

The shelf beneath the big window has peeling paint and seven plants in bright pots, each at varying stages of health. There's a basket filled with green and blue yarn and a half-completed creation next to the small, obviously secondhand couch. On it, there are at least four blankets and ten pillows. One has a dog wearing glasses and another says, "Kindness is my superpower."

Two different depictions of Jesus, four Scripture quotes, and innumerable snapshots hug the walls. I study a photo of the Wildcat cheerleading squad from six years ago, recognizing Mary-Beth and her bony elbows instantly. Today's version looks practically geriatric. But her smile, taking up her whole face, and her eyes, bright and brown, are the same. A photo of Mary-Beth as a toddler, wearing nothing but pink rain boots, a diaper, and a scowl makes me smile.

Secretly, she's always been a stubborn smartass.

There are so many crayon drawings stuck to the fridge, I can barely see it. Each one says something in the neighborhood of, "i LUv ms AvRnFy." A letter board on the counter next to two more dying plants reads, "Today is a good day to have a good day!"

The tiny Ikea table is set for two with chair cushions that are mustard yellow and plates featuring barn animals. There's a basket of crescent rolls and a bottle of wine at the center.

Mary-Beth pulls a casserole from the oven, and I half expect her to kiss my cheek, light my cigarette, and ask me how work was.

"What's all this?" I motion to the table.

Mary-Beth sets the casserole (lasagna) on a coaster next to the wine (Merlot). She braids her hands together and rests them in front of her like a woman trying to avoid a nervous breakdown. "A ceasefire."

"A what?"

"A ceasefire. A redo?" She raises her eyebrows like she's talking to one of her kindergartners. "A second chance at a first impression? Whatever you want to call it. I want to start over."

My eyes narrow. This must be some sort of trick. At any moment, new women in pleather will jump out of the closet. Mary-Beth will run outside shrieking into a bullhorn I've slept with them.

She sighs, like what she's about to say will be painful. "Drew, you were right. I haven't been fair to you. And I apologize." Her mouth pinches at the sides. "Truce?"

"Truce," I say immediately. I don't even consider saying anything else.

She gifts me a tiny smile and rushes into the kitchen, grabbing a salad bowl and parmesan. She tinkers with each object on the table, arranging it until she seems satisfied. Then she offers me her hand.

"Hi, my name is Mary-Beth Abernathy. I'm a virgin and a kindergarten teacher who dabbles in erotic literature. I suck at knitting." She glances at the table. "But I'm an okay chef. I hope."

The smile I've managed to suppress escapes. "Hi, Mary-Beth." I don't let go of her hand, running my thumb across her knuckles. "My name is Drew Coyne. I'm an actor who specializes in subpar made-for-TV movies, so I'm attempting to break into production. I endorse too many products that are complete shit. I also suck at knitting, but I'm definitely not a virgin."

I let go of her hand and instantly miss its warmth. We both sit.

Mary-Beth cuts the lasagna, and I serve the salad. I grab a roll. She grabs two. I pour the Merlot. She fetches ice water and four different salad dressings from the fridge. We both choose ranch. With the exception of the Beastie Boys' greatest hits playing in the background, we prepare our plates in silence.

CHAPTER 27

The song switches to "Sabotage." Fitting for the past few days.

Mary-Beth takes a huge bite. She stifles moans as she chews, licking sauce from her lips and squirming in satisfaction against her seat. My mouth hangs open, unable to do anything else but stare.

"Where does it all go?" I mutter to myself. Mostly to keep the drool from dribbling down my chin. And the blood from rushing between my legs.

Mary-Beth's eyes lift from her plate. Her eyebrows lift in "*huh?*"

Realizing she heard me, I clear my throat and try again. "The food?" *What a batshit crazy thing to ask.* "Where does it all go?"

I've literally never seen a woman eat as much as Mary-Beth. From the fast-food to the sandwiches to the snacks to this. I'm used to aspiring actresses and models who live off celery and pre-workout, starving themselves to have a body half as good as Mary-Beth's. They'd never dream of M&Ms and lasagna.

The joy she gets from eating. The glow of her healthy body. The perfect curve of her waist. And holy hell, *her ass*. I didn't know it was possible. And *God*, it's sexy.

"I have a high metabolism." Mary-Beth rips off a piece of roll and runs it through the pasta sauce on her plate. She shrugs and pops it in her mouth. "It's genetic."

I ogle her for an obscene amount of time without blinking. I could watch her eat for hours. Days, maybe. She has absolutely no clue what she does to me. None.

"And what about your culinary preferences?" Mary-Beth asks, and my gaze is pried from her mouth to her eyes. I finally take a bite of lasagna. It's fucking delicious. "Like that sandwich. Are you an aspiring sandwich artist or something?"

I shovel in two more bites and swallow without really chewing. "When I was younger, there were times I was on my own a lot. So...I used to put everything I could find on bread and eat it." I load up my roll with a wide, cheese-covered noodle and take a big bite.

"Do you do that with pizza, too? You seem like the fruit-on-pizza type."

"I'm an everything-on-pizza type. If you haven't noticed, I'll eat anything," I say. Mary-Beth glances from her empty plate to the lasagna like she's contemplating taking more. "I think we might have that in common."

"But pineapple, really?" Mary-Beth makes a sour face as she reaches for the spatula, scooping a second helping.

I shrug and hold up my plate, too. "I learned really quickly not to be picky."

Mary-Beth's mouth twitches like she wants to ask another question. I fill the silence before she can.

"So, what did you do all day without me?" I ask. Mary-Beth serves me another square of lasagna. "Go buy a new lamp? Or a plant? Deep clean your microwave? Finish a knitting project?"

"No..." Mary-Beth sits up straighter, smoothing the napkin in her lap. "Actually, I finished my book."

"Well, look at you, Miss Maple." A weird sense of pride swells inside me, knowing in a small way, I helped. It's followed by a twinge of sadness realizing I wasn't there when she typed *THE END*. I slap on a smile to hide both emotions. "So...what did you end up learning about Christine? Homophobic asshole or ahead-of-her-time gay rights advocate?"

Mary-Beth takes a bite of her salad, chewing thoughtfully. The crease in her forehead deepens. "Neither. She was hurt and confused at first, of course. But then"— Mary-Beth's smiles to herself—"she comes to peace with it."

"Peace? Yeah?"

"Ultimately, she understood why her husband had to hide his true self. She felt sorry he had to live his life that way. She vowed to live more authentically in his honor. It gave her the courage to run away with Gabriel. She realized everyone should be able to do what they want, regardless of..." Mary-Beth finishes her sentence with a shrug.

"And is that why you texted me? Because you're sorry I have to live this way?"

She laughs at my shitty attempt at humor, but her revelations still dangle between us. It's obvious they mean more than either of us cares to admit.

"Something like that," she concedes. "It *would* be terrible to be you."

I glance around the small apartment. "That seems strange coming from a woman with ten throw pillows and nine dying houseplants."

Mary-Beth raises her glass and tips it in my direction. "I am the type."

I lift my glass too, and we drink and set down our wine without blinking, like a weird version of the staring game.

"And you're the type to..." Mary-Beth pauses, no doubt mentally reviewing the Google douchebag list.

I fill in the blank: "To be a total ass?"

Mary-Beth's surprised eyes pounce up to mine. "Well, yes," she says. Then her eyes fall. "But...I'm pretty sure I deserved it."

"I didn't say you didn't. But I was still an ass. And I hurt your feelings. Even with the kiss..." I eagerly watch Mary-Beth's blush travel across her skin. "I shouldn't have gotten so butt-hurt about it. And I'm sorry."

"I take it you're not used to girls telling you you're a mistake?"

"You were the first."

"Do you just, like,"—Mary-Beth picks up her wineglass, giggling nervously before taking a small sip— "assume every woman you meet wants to sleep with you?"

My eyes meet hers over our wine. "Yes," I answer honestly. "I can't remember a time when a woman wanted anything else."

"You've never had someone just want to get to know you?"

"Not really, no."

If I didn't know any better, I'd say Mary-Beth was personally offended by that statement. Her eyes wrinkle at the corners with something that looks like anger. "They just, like, want one thing?"

I nod. "In my experience, yes."

Mary-Beth huffs, blowing a piece of hair from her eyes. I get the feeling she's doing it to hide the emotion on her face. To hide how much she cares. It surprises me.

The dry emotion in the back of my own throat surprises me too. I'm used to being wanted for my body and nothing else. And I've always fucking loved that. It's convenient when that's the only thing you want too.

I'm six-pack abs. I'm biceps and blue eyes and a million-dollar smile. I'm big dick energy. I'm the one-night stand you brag to your friends about. I'm used to sex without strings attached, and women who want that too. It's the only thing I know. The thing I tell myself I want. I *know* it's the only thing I can have.

It's never bothered me before.

I grab my water, gulping hard.

Why is it bothering me now?

Chapter 28

Andrew Edward Coyne
Unsure

Dinner and the wine are both long gone, yet Mary-Beth and I are still glued to the table. In the last three hours, I've learned more about her than any woman I've met in the last ten years, easily. Maybe ever.

And to my surprise, I'm having so much fucking fun.

Loving 80s and 90s hip-hop might be where our similarities stop.

She sees numbers in color. For me, it's letters.

She's never done drugs. It's been a few years, but I have. Lots of them.

Her go-to drink is a bay breeze. Mine is whiskey.

Her favorite animal is a dog. Mine, obviously, is not.

When making a peanut butter and jelly sandwich, she spreads the peanut butter first, and then puts the butter knife straight into the jelly. I do the jelly first and put the knife straight into the peanut butter.

We argued about that for, like, ten minutes. I'm still convinced I'm right. What psychopath wants peanut butter in their jelly?

Around midnight, we finally move to the couch. Mary-Beth pulls the blinds and throws all the pillows on the floor so she can sit as far away as possible. The dog with the glasses smiles up at me as if to say,

"*If you get naked, can I watch?*"

Mary-Beth kicks it across the room.

We start by arguing about In and Out Burger vs. Shake Shack for fifteen minutes...

"God, Mary-Beth, you've got to go back and order it animal style. With fries well done, salt on the side. When we go to California, I'll help you."

"What good is a restaurant when half their menu items are part of a secret society?"

Until finally, I sling my arm on the back of the couch and muster the courage to ask the question I'm really wondering.

"Mary, why did you decide to write *Swallow Manor*?"

She blinks a few times, her long eyelashes fluttering against her freckled-covered cheeks. "I don't know if it was ever a decision or if it just kind of happened," she finally says. "I've read romance novels for years. When I had the idea for the plot, I started writing and just...never stopped, I guess."

"You knew you could do it better than anyone else?"

"Ha. I wish."

"It's true."

"Thank you."

"I'm glad you finally published it." I smile. *How different would my life be now if she hadn't?* "What made you pull the trigger?"

"It was the right time, I guess."

"What made it the right time?"

"Harper." Mary-Beth laughs. "And more alcohol than any one-hundred-pound woman should ever consume."

"I call bullshit." I sit up a little straighter, creeping my hand across the back of the couch until it's nearly touching Mary-Beth's shoulder. "It has to be more than that."

She toes the yarn at her feet, taking several deep breaths before answering. "Yeah, I guess there was a part of me that wanted to see. See if it was really as good as I hoped it was."

"It is." My voice doesn't leave any room for disagreement. "And now that you know that, why not just own it? Do you really think your books are that bad?"

"I don't think they're bad." I can tell by the way she says it, slow and careful, that it's the first time she's ever admitted that to anyone, even herself. "But I know I *should*. That I am expected to. And I feel guilty about that. That, in a way, I'm letting people down. Betraying a part of myself."

She licks her lips. I stare.

"That probably sounds dumb to you."

"No," I say earnestly. "It sounds incredibly brave, actually."

Mary-Beth's mouth turns up at the corners. Only slightly.

"Why should you think your books are bad?" I press.

"Because they talk about *relationships* in a way I've always been taught was…wrong."

I quickly read between the lines. The shame in her eyes fucking kills me.

"You were taught sex is bad." It's not a question.

Mary-Beth stares at the ground for so long, I'm not sure she's going to respond. Finally, her gaze thoughtfully meets mine. "The only sex ed I ever had was 'Don't do it.' Period. I think they meant don't have sex before marriage, but I internalized 'don't do it at all.' I was taught, especially by my mother, if I did have sex, I would be forever ruined. A licked cupcake. A chewed piece of gum. That no matter what I did, I would be damaged goods. Sexuality of any kind was shameful. A part of yourself to hide."

I think about our kiss. If you look up the word *sexuality* in the dictionary, you'd find a picture of us at the corner of Main Street and Station Road three nights ago. Is this part of the reason she thought it was a mistake?

"And do you believe that?"

Mary-Beth shrugs. "It was never explained that sex *could* be good. But inside I sort of thought, intuitively, it was. I think that's what I'm still figuring out."

I stay silent, hoping she takes that as a sign to keep talking. Finally, she does.

"I think that has been part of writing these books for me. Exploring the part of me that's always wondered *why*?" Her voice catches on *why*, her eyes growing wide. "Why is it so forbidden? Why is it so wrong? And is there ever a situation when it could be *right*?"

I think of Mary-Beth and me together. That would be forbidden and wrong. But in all the right ways. I shift my weight so I'm sitting a little closer.

"And what have you decided?" I rasp. Clearing my throat, I try again. "What is the right way?"

Mary-Beth's eyes harden. "Not earring sex, if that's what you're wondering."

"You've made that abundantly clear."

"At least not for me," she amends, smoothing down her skirt. "I'm trying to have less of a black heart and a closed mind regarding other people's sexual inclinations."

"Fair enough." I chuckle. "If Christine has taught us anything, it's that."

Mary-Beth smiles. So big it makes her eyes sparkle.

"So...you're waiting, then? For marriage or whatever?" I recline a little, trying to hide how interested I am in the answer to that very loaded question. "Do you think that's the right choice for you?"

"I don't know..." She chews on the inside of her cheek as she picks at her fingernails. I hold my breath for what seems like forever. "All I know is I definitely want it to be with someone who is sure about me.

CHAPTER 28

Someone I won't regret. That probably means marriage, but maybe not."

I nod. Slowly. Processing.

Someone sure.

Probably marriage.

But...

Maybe not.

Mary-Beth laughs and shakes out her shoulders. "Lord, how'd we get on this subject? How about, what's your favorite color?"

My eyes capture Mary-Beth's, searching for the green flecks inside them.

"Green." My entire life before last week, it's been red. But now, green.

"Blue," she whispers.

We stare at each other in smoldering silence before Mary-Beth finally speaks again.

"Can I ask you a question, Drew?"

"Anything."

"Why did you pick *Swallow Manor*? Of all the books you've read—and now I know that's a lot—why do you want mine so badly?"

Before I can even think of a less revealing answer, the truth scampers out: "Because I was dying to meet the author."

Mary-Beth's eyes dilate, brown quickly inking to black. "And when you met the author?"

"She wasn't what I was expecting."

"And you were disappointed." Her gaze falls to her twitching hands.

"I was." I slide closer. "But I was wrong."

God, *so wrong*. I could have never dreamed up Mary-Beth, and that's a fucking fantastic thing.

"How much does it hurt your giant ego to admit that?"

"So much."

The ball in her throat bobs as she swallows. I lean even further forward without making the choice. I'm so close now, our shoulders touch. When she looks at me, it feels like lightning.

I take a strand of Mary-Beth's hair, rubbing it between my fingers. Then my hand goes to the back of her neck, my thumb under her chin. I apply the smallest bit of pressure as I tilt her jaw up.

"Mary, what are you waiting for?" The words escape before I can stop them.

"What do you mean?"

"You know what I mean."

She doesn't. How could she? *I* don't even know.

"I guess, I'm waiting for the right person," she whispers. The words practically float into my mouth.

"Why can't that be me?"

Mary-Beth's lips part, but instead of speaking, she leans closer.

The small movement feels like an invitation. And holy hell, how I want to accept. I want to explore every inch of Mary-Beth until I'm a certifiable expert. I want to feel her. Inside, outside. Up, down. Around. I want to make her mine to the point no one ever questions that fact again. My mind goes to when Susan and Ambrose first sleep together.

His hands were unsure until my skirts fell to the floor, and I found myself unabashedly nude. Then, he knew exactly what to do—like a flip switched between mind and body. Skin to skin, he was no longer hesitant. He was powerful. He was sure. He took me in his arms, his thumb grazing my sensitive bare nipple, and kissed me for the first time, knowing he didn't have to stop.

Fuck, yes. That. I'm dying to do *that*.

I run my thumb across Mary-Beth's lips. Plump, pink, open. I want to kiss her. God, I want way more than that.

Yesterday, I would have. I would have done anything she'd let me do.

CHAPTER 28

But as I look down at Mary-Beth, giving herself to me—eyes blinking closed, hand gripping the couch, green fabric at her collarbone shifting—I realize... I want her, but I'm not sure about her.

And that absolutely terrifies me.

Chapter 29

Mary-Beth Caroline Abernathy
Woman Who has had an Orgasm

My lips are millimeters from touching Drew's when he pulls away. Slightly, but it's enough.

"Sorry." He looks down, rubbing the back of his neck. "The, uh, the rules."

"Yeah." I blink, silently cursing myself from five days ago. "The rules."

Drew stands. "Well, I know you're not the type to have a guy spend the night." I try to decipher if he's sad or happy about that. Nothing. "Even on a couch made for one with a dog pillow and four rainbow blankets. So, I should probably go. It's late."

Drew's right—I'm not the type, and everyone knows it. The entire town would be talking if he stayed the night, even if nothing happened. I'd probably wake up to FORNICATOR spray-painted across my door in the morning.

Still...

The thought of watching Drew leave tonight feels worse.

After our Chipotle fight, I spent the next twenty-four hours teetering between self-loathing and self-reflection. And I came to the conclusion...Drew was right about me.

CHAPTER 29

But yesterday, when I was drowning in tears and peanut butter M&Ms and finishing my book, I realized I don't want to be like that anymore.

Especially about Drew.

I wanted to start over. I wanted to give him another chance. I wanted to get to know Drew Coyne the person instead of Drew Coyne the actor. I wanted to stop hating him so much.

Now, I'm afraid I might have the opposite problem.

All these years, I thought Drew and I were the same—recyclers who love a good Hallmark movie and snuggling with a puppy—but he's actually my antithesis in every way. From our values and the way we were raised –*obviously*– to the things we like, to the way we make a PB&J—peanut butter first is better, and I will die on that hill.

But somehow, along the way...differences became a good thing. A great thing.

I don't know if I've ever enjoyed talking to someone as much as Drew. He brings out something in me no one else has: my voice. I'm used to nodding and doing what I'm told. But it's not like that with him. He challenges me. Makes me take a stand. Makes me want to prove him wrong. About me. About him. About everything.

Every conversation is a contest. A contest I have to win.

Forget those women who don't want to know him. He's clever and insightful and freakishly honest when he wants to be. I hate that I fell into the category of women who didn't see the real him before. Before I looked past the exterior. The façade.

He was right—now that I have, I might like him even more than Hallmark Drew.

Hallmark Drew is the man of my adolescent dreams. Real Drew is the man of today's.

I know this means I should sign over *Swallow Manor*, but much like letting him walk out the door right now, that seems like an impossible task.

I want more. Way more.

And I find myself hoping Drew does too.

"Well, I mean, I guess you could stay." I sweep my hand toward the couch. "As long as you sleep on the couch."

Drew's eyes narrow with a flash of blue. "Is this some sort of trick?"

I smooth out my dress, then open my hands at my sides innocently. "No trick. Promise."

"This feels like breaking the rules. Like cheating."

"Cheating? Or improvising?" I laugh. It's high-pitched and shaky.

"Oh yeah, Virgin Mary?" Drew laughs too. It's low and sexy.

"Maybe we need new rules."

"And what do you suggest?"

"I just want one rule." I swallow and meet his eyes. "Don't do anything unless it's genuine. Unless you mean it."

Drew's jaw flexes. My stomach flips like a gymnast lives inside.

What did I just do?

He licks his lips, studying me from my high heels up to my eyes and back down. "I meant it before. All of it. I told you that."

Did I say gymnast? I meant circus, complete with acrobats, elephants, lion-tamers, and dancing poodles.

I take a few steps toward Drew until we are chest-to-chest. When I stand on my tiptoes, our lips nearly touch. He keeps his hands strictly at his sides, even as I place mine on his chest. The muscles underneath my fingertips tense. I stop breathing.

I take his hand and guide it to my waist, nudging his nose with mine.

"Why don't you want me now?" The words escape from somewhere deep inside before I can stop them.

There's a pause. A long one.

And then something shatters inside him.

The hand at my waist contracts as he pulls me against his hips. He

CHAPTER 29

reaches under the layers of my dress and grabs an entire handful of my ass, lifting my leg up to wrap around his. A gasp escapes from my mouth and into his when he kisses me.

Our kiss from three days ago was tame compared to this. That kiss was controlled. This kiss is hungry.

Drew's tongue slips inside me, and his teeth claim my bottom lip. Moving hard and intentional against me, he makes the roof of my mouth tingle. The hand on my butt forces my hips to grind with his, his erection hard and huge on my hip bone. I'm swallowed by desire, unafraid of drowning.

When Drew pulls away, he runs his fingertips over my left nipple through my dress. Like there's an invisible string from my breast to between my legs, a jolt of desire pierces me.

Drew looks down at me, something primal in his dilated, icy eyes. "You have no idea what I fucking want, Mary. None."

I know I've lost all control when I say, "Show me."

Drew jerks me back to his body, and I jump, wrapping my legs around his waist. My dress comes up in the back, and he squeezes my butt with both hands. His arousal is squarely between my legs now—hot and hard and terrifying and amazing. He holds me solidly against his hips as his fingers begin to fiddle with my satin underwear.

He kisses me again, his mouth crashing into my mine so hard, our teeth scrape. He pins me against the wall between the kitchen and living room, and the picture of me wearing my pink rain boots falls to the ground. It doesn't make us stop, though. If anything, we accelerate. I clench my legs around him, and he kisses my neck, his body turning into a rock against me.

"What have you done before?" he asks breathlessly between kisses. "I know you're a virgin, but what else have you done? Oral?" His eyes meet mine hopefully.

I try not to look away as I shake my head. "No one has ever touched me like this, Drew. But…Sutton did try. He, well, he…"

Drew shushes me and nods, as if that information gives him some sort of green light. "Fuck that guy," he growls. "Mary, you're perfect the way you are. You don't need to change a thing. Okay?"

I nod, though I don't know what I'm agreeing to, exactly.

"But fuck if I'm going to let that asshole be the last person who touches you."

The circus inside me turns full-on pandemonium. Before I can stop myself, I'm nodding again.

"You'll tell me if you don't like it? If you're uncomfortable?" Drew's forehead ruffles.

"I promise."

He slowly sets me down and plunges his hands into my hair. He kisses me again, this time with more control. It's gentler, sweeter. Like he's savoring me, tasting every drop. There's more breathing. More swaying. More pressing against each other. His tongue slips inside and out. His hands run down the side of my breasts with careful fingers.

Each time he tries something new, he pulls back, waiting for me to tell him to stop. His control only makes my need grow. Something is tightening inside me, parts of me coming to life I didn't even know were there.

I get turned on when I write. Imagining things I secretly want for myself but know I could never have. Envisioning what it would be like to have a man desire me. Pleasure me. Trying to paint a picture in my mind of what it might be like. Someday.

But the feeling has never been like this. That was tingles and flutters. It disappeared after a nap or a walk around the block. This desire is tight and heavy and urgent. It feels like there's only one release, and the need to have it has taken over.

"Touch me, Drew." The words don't sound like mine, but they are.

CHAPTER 29

I see the curse word flash in Drew's eyes, although he doesn't say it aloud. Like I've just given him permission he doesn't know he can contain. I bite my lip, and he swallows and nods.

With the sexiest control imaginable, Drew runs both hands along the front of me, his thumbs brushing past my perky nipples. The invisible string pulses, drawing tighter. I moan and lean closer.

"Do you like that, Mary?" He seems encouraged by my response. I nearly buck in his arms when he does it again, harder. Then again, catching me in between his fingers and pinching gently. "Do you like it when I touch you there?"

Words fail me, but I manage to nod. Drew's hands go to the back of my dress, slowly pulling down the zipper.

"I don't want you to regret this in the morning," he says, kissing my naked shoulder. "I promise, I won't do anything you don't want me to do. If you don't like this—"

I shake my head, not wanting to imagine a world in which he stops. "I like it."

"I'm not going to fuck you tonight, Mary. So don't be scared," Drew says as my dress falls to my ankles. His eyes travel across me greedily. "I'm just going to touch you. A body like yours deserves to be touched."

"But what about y—"

"Don't worry about me," he interrupts with finality. He takes my hand and kisses the back of it as I step out of my dress. "Tonight is about you."

And just like that, Drew Coyne is staring at me in my underwear and five-hundred-dollar heels.

Holy shit.

"Do you always wear lingerie?" Drew's eyes snag on my matching pink satin and lace underwear.

I look down at myself, feeling self-conscious. Drew has been with actresses and models. Probably foreign royalty and mythical goddesses too. I'm sure my boobs are the piddliest he's touched in years. Ever?

But then my eyes dart between Drew's legs. His erection is so swollen, I'm amazed his pants are containing it. I must be doing something right to elicit that kind of reaction. The need between my own legs grows more severe, if that's even possible at this point.

I giggle a little to hide my embarrassment and nod. "I like pretty underwear. I can splurge on it, and no one will know."

Drew smiles, and it's a wicked one. "Your secret is safe with me." He places a hand on my waist and pulls me in. "And only me."

His hand reaches from the dimples in my back all the way up to my bra clasp. The size difference between us is staggering. If we did want to have sex, I'm not even sure it would be physically possible.

Drew fiddles with the hem of my panties, and I reach my hand up under his shirt, spreading my fingers across his abs. I can feel goosebumps forming under my fingertips when his muscles contract. Rock hard, like the rest of him.

He helps me guide his shirt over his shoulders, until he's standing before me in all his muscley glory. I run my hands along the peaks and valleys of his wide chest and down his arms, until I'm tracing the muscles disappearing below his waist.

"I love it when you touch me, Mary. I can't even begin to tell you how much I love it." Drew repositions us so he's standing behind me. When his chest comes flush with my back, I gasp. Skin to freaking skin. "Do we need a safe word? I promise I'll stop if you want me to."

"How about *Azkaban*?" I suggest, one eyebrow darting up.

"Like *Prisoner of Azkaban*?" He laughs and bites my earlobe. His fingers flare out around my belly button, his index fingers sliding under the hem of my panties. His fingertips apply pressure against my skin, and my hips begin to move with his. "Not a fucking chance."

"Fine," I concede. "*Goblet*. But only because I don't want you to

CHAPTER 29

stop."

"Good choice, Mary." Drew's hand stays at the edge of my panties, and another creeps up my rib cage, to the edge of my bra.

"Tell me where to touch you," he whispers against my neck. "I won't move my hands until you move them."

I suck in a breath and hold it. When I exhale, the rest of my will melts away.

I slowly braid my fingers with Drew's—our left hands just below my breast, our right hands just below my navel. My heart is pounding, and my vision is blurred. But somehow, this feels right. It feels good.

Lord, who am I kidding? It feels freaking incredible.

For a few moments, I leave his hands where he placed them, moving them in slow circles across my skin. I writhe in his arms as Drew kisses my neck and shoulders, his mouth leaving trails of fire in its wake. His erection is hard against my backside, throbbing through his jeans.

When I just can't take it anymore, I slowly move one hand under my bra and another down my panties.

When Sutton Heard tried to do this six years ago in the backseat of his car on a deserted backroad, for a moment, I wanted him to. Wanted to be cool. Wanted him to like me. Wanted to give it a try. But when his rough fingers found my most sensitive parts, it hadn't felt good. He wasn't gentle, and he wasn't slow, and I wasn't ready.

This experience could not be more different. Drew isn't rushing or assuming or pressuring me. He's letting me take control. Making sure I know what I want. Making sure my mind and body are in agreement.

Before, I felt scared. Now, I feel safe.

"Have you ever touched yourself, Mary?"

I shake my head sheepishly. "I've thought about it, but never actually done it."

Oh, I've thought about it, all right. Late at night when I've just finished writing a sex scene and my body gets that tingly feeling. When

I'm lying in bed fantasizing about what I just choreographed. Wishing I could do it with Drew. When I think of him and me together, I've wanted to more times than I can count.

Drew nuzzles my hair with his neck and kisses my collarbone. "That's okay. If you want, we can do it together."

"Yes. Please."

I take my nipple in his hands, rolling it slowly between his fingers. When he touches me like this, it makes the invisible string feel like it's about to break. And holy hell, how I want it to.

I take his other hand and guide it down, until his fingers sink into the wet folds of my arousal.

"You shave?" He traces his fingers along my smooth skin.

"Laser hair removal, actually." I laugh. "Another one of my secrets."

"Shit, Mary, I want to know all your secrets." His hands dip lower, moving across my slit slowly. "You're wet. So wet. Fuc—" The curse word trails off in a whoosh of breath.

I giggle. "I thought that was pretty obvious."

"You have no idea, Mary. No freaking idea what you do to me." His fingers part me as he continues to explore. "Tell me what to do next."

Slowly, I move his hand to the part of my vagina that feels like it's ten times bigger than the rest and is throbbing for release. My clit, I assume. I glide our fingers around and over top, doing the same with my nipples.

"Do you like that?" I hear the smile in Drew's voice. I can't deal with words right now, so I only moan, moving his fingers faster. Tension builds. Heat rises. I writhe in his arms, staring at our interlocked fingers as they pleasure me. "Because I love it. I fucking love how you feel."

"Drew..." My voice sounds like it's falling off a cliff.

"Do you trust me, Mary?" Drew asks, sensing I'm close.

"Yes," I moan, arching my back against him, dropping my arms to grab the fabric at his thighs. "Please, do it."

And with that, Drew slips one finger inside me, just an inch, then two. In and out, pumping slowly, gently, then faster and faster while still managing to stimulate my clit. The fingers at my nipples move to the same rhythm, urging my body to do something it's only dreamed of.

"Drew, oh my God!" I scream, then go tense in his arms. "Oh my..."

All at once, the invisible string snaps, and a flood of pleasure rushes over me. Starting at the apex of my thighs and bursting to all the other secret parts of my body. Drew keeps stroking, cradling me in his arms when I collapse, letting the blissful waves keep coming and coming.

And coming.

Holy shit. Is this what I've been missing all these years?

When my body finally stops shaking, Drew turns me in his arms and brings his forehead to mine, his hands clutching my ass.

"Was that an..." My words trail off, too embarrassed to finish that sentence.

"An orgasm. Yes." Drew's voice is controlled, but a smile pulls at his lips. "Did you enjoy it?"

Orgasm. I'm a woman who has had an *orgasm*.

I don't answer, instead looking down bewildered at my naked flesh. It feels foreign, like it isn't even mine anymore. "I didn't know my body could do that."

"You have no idea"—Drew kisses me roughly—"what your body is capable of."

He kisses me again, softly, his hands combing out the tangles in my hair.

Then, he pulls away and puts on his shirt. He hands me my dress.

We dress in silence, then Drew takes a few steps toward the door.

"You're leaving?"

"I can't stay." Drew motions to the impressive tent still pitched in his jeans. "It would be a bad idea."

"I'm sorry." I shift my weight from one leg to the other.

It only takes Drew two strides to reach me from the door. He takes my chin between his fingers, forcing me to look at him.

"I'm not." He kisses my cheek with rough lips, his blue eyes boring into me. "Don't you for one second think I didn't want this or didn't enjoy it. Because it was fucking everything."

Drew stalks back to the door and opens it.

"I'll see you tomorrow, Virgin Mary."

Chapter 30

Andrew Edward Coyne
Hot for Teacher

The next morning, I get a text.

Virgin Mary: Hey man who has ruined all other men for me. I'm in the parking lot.

A smile unfolds across my face, as much as I wish it wouldn't.

Virgin Mary-Beth Abernathy. *Fuck*, I'm in trouble.

I've never had a night like last night. Of course, there was dinner and our conversation, which was a first all on its own. But what came next—God, it was torture. And ecstasy. A combination I'm realizing might fucking ruin me.

We'd barely done anything. But somehow, it felt like everything.

I've never had to control myself like I did last night; I've never had a reason to. Definitely never wanted to. But holding Mary-Beth in my arms and touching her, simply for the pleasure of touching her, of giving *her* pleasure, had been transcendental.

I'm good in bed. I've been told more times than I can count. And I absolutely know how to pleasure a woman. But I've never done it like that. With care and control. Without concern for myself at all.

It was wild. And it was hot. And I fucking loved it.

Thankfully, I'd made it back to the hotel in time to take care of myself.

Part of me thought I might have to do it in the car. Her ass rubbing against me had almost made me come all on its own.

Mary-Beth might kill me. But I'd die a freaking happy man.

Drew: I need to take a cold shower. A very cold shower. I'll be down in 10

In the parking lot, Naughty by Nature is blaring from Mary-Beth's POS Kia. She waves a coffee cup out the driver's side window.

"Get in," she says. "Today, I'm driving."

If I thought Mary-Beth's apartment was shitty, it's because I've never seen her car. It rattles just idling and the breaks squeak without moving. Inside, the fabric on the ceiling droops, the seats are stained, and I'm pretty sure nothing on the dash works. I cautiously get in, sliding the seat all the way back.

"Virgin Mary, you need a new car." I take a small sip of coffee.

"Good morning to you too." Mary muscles the car into drive and clutches the steering wheel hand over hand to make it turn.

"Please tell me we're heading to the dealership. Nobody in the twenty-first century should drive without power steering."

Mary-Beth smiles and shakes her head. "It works most of the time, but sometimes it just gets stuck." Whatever was stuck seems to unstick, and the car jolts forward. Mary-Beth exhales and puts her blinker on, careening the opposite way of the library. "Today, I have to work."

"It's Saturday. Isn't that one of the only perks of being a teacher? Weekends off?"

"I have to work two weekends a year. Parent-teacher conferences. And lucky for you, that's today."

"I'm honored to tag along."

"Well, I am your controlling fake girlfriend, after all."

Silence settles over us as we both nurse our coffees. Over my cup, I peer at Mary-Beth, searching for any signs of remorse. Any sign that

CHAPTER 30

she thought last night was a mistake. I hate to admit how much it would gut me if she did. But...she's as chipper and stubborn-looking as ever, mumbling the lyrics to "Hip Hop Hooray" under her breath between sips. I hide my smile as I wipe my sweaty palms on my jeans.

"Drew..." Mary-Beth finally says. Once the silence between us is gone, I realize how awkward it had been. "About last night..."

And here it is...the thing I was fearing. She's regretting it. Regretting me. Again. She's going to retreat into her shell. Put her walls back up.

Why am I so fucking afraid of that? I'm the king of walls up.

I force my expression to be neutral and turn to look at her. She's wearing black slacks and a purple shirt. Besides green, purple is my favorite color on her. It makes her hair and skin glow. I stare at her, wondering what fun surprise is hiding underneath. She always wears lingerie? Every day? Even now? If I'd known that a week ago, she sure as hell wouldn't be Virgin Mary anymore.

"Last night..." I prod.

"It was..." Mary-Beth stops at a red light and looks at me. I swallow, physically preparing myself for the blow. "It was really fun. I'm glad you came over."

My eyes dart across the middle console to hers. "Yeah?"

Mary-Beth smiles, and my whole world comes undone. "Yeah. Turns out you're not the worst person in the world after all."

I take Mary-Beth's hand in mine, kissing her knuckles gently. "Jury's still out on you, Virgin Mary."

🐥🐥🐥

I sit outside her classroom during Mary-Beth's conferences. The hallways are wallpapered with art projects—cotton ball sheep and Fruit Loop rainbows and construction paper ladybugs. Her door is decorated with a big flowerpot that reads, "Ms. Abernathy's Garden" with flowers sprouting from the top with each child's name and picture in the center.

I watch as parent after parent hugs Mary-Beth, thanking her for loving and teaching their child. The kids that tag along run down the hall and jump into her arms. She beams as she leads them into her classroom, chattering on about how smart and kind and wonderful they are.

A few kids stay in the hallway while their parents speak with Mary-Beth. I probably shouldn't, but I ask about their hot teacher anyway.

"So, do you like Ms. Abernathy? Is she a good teacher?" I ask a little girl about the same age as Chloe, with the same chubby cheeks and mischievous eyes.

"Ms. Abernathy is the best teacher in the whole world," she coos. "I love her."

"What do you love about her?"

"She is so nice." She bats her eyelashes. "The other kindergarten teacher, Mrs. Highwater, yells. But Ms. Abernathy never yells. She says it's because we are all angels. But that's not true, because Colin isn't."

I laugh, impressed by this precocious little girl. "Which ladybug is yours?"

Looking positively giddy, she points to a picture on the wall labeled *Emilia*. "And this is my rainbow," she says. "And this is my bunny."

"Wow! That is a very fluffy bunny. I love it."

"Are you Ms. Abernathy's boyfriend?"

I'm taken aback by the girl's candor. But then I remember when Chloe called me an ass, and the picture of Mary-Beth in the pink rain boots. I chuckle to myself. All these badass little girls. They will change the world one day.

"Yes." My forehead wrinkles. "Is that okay with you?"

Emilia narrows her eyes, pointing at me sternly. "As long as you're nice. Ms. Abernathy can't have a mean boyfriend."

I raise my right hand like I'm about to pledge some sort of oath. "I

CHAPTER 30

promise to be nice to Ms. Abernathy."

"Is that right?" Mary-Beth asks, her hip leaning against the door frame, her toe tapping.

Without really meaning to, I imagine Mary-Beth swatting her hand with a ruler, wearing her pink bra and panties and the cute ass heels from last night. With glasses. And thigh highs.

I have a new kink.

"Thanks for everything, Ms. Abernathy," Emilia's parents say, following her out. "Come on, Emilia."

Emilia runs over and gives Mary-Beth a huge hug. A small grunt escapes from her when the little girl's arms constrict.

"I love you," the little girl says into Mary-Beth's side.

She pats her head lovingly. "I love you too, sweet girl." She pries the little girl off her, turning to her parents and shaking both their hands. "Thanks for coming in today, Mark and Jeanene. I really appreciate it."

"We appreciate you so much, Mary-Beth. You're the best." Jeanene's eyes flit to me, and she smiles but doesn't say anything. "We'll see you Monday."

"Actually, I'm out all next week." Mary-Beth looks over at me and smiles. I lick my lips and smile back. *Yes, she is.* "But I'll be back the week after."

As Emilia and her parents turn to leave, the little girl puts two fingers to her eyes and then points them at me. I nod gravely, understanding her warning. I burst into laughter when she rounds the corner.

"I think Emilia is going to hunt me down when we break up."

Shit. As soon as the words leave my mouth, I know I shouldn't have said them.

Mary-Beth shakes her head, like she's trying to make them go away. "Yeah, she's a spitfire." She steps away awkwardly. "She was, um, my last conference, so I'll pack up and we can go."

Her classroom is even more magical than the hallway—filled to the brim with bright colors and fun books and glittering art projects. The bulletin board in the corner says, "Amazing Things Happen Here," and the sign above her desk proclaims, "Ms. Abernathy Loves You."

"I wish I had a teacher like you." I spin around slowly. "The kids love you."

"You didn't love your kindergarten teacher?" Mary-Beth gives me a surprised smile.

"I think she was more like Mrs. Highwater."

Mary-Beth chuckles. "Deborah is great. She's just a little more...old school."

"Then I guess all my teachers were old school. Like...medieval."

"You didn't like school?" She says it like it shouldn't even be a possibility.

"I *hated* school."

"Makes sense, because I loved it." She shrugs. "Why did you hate school?"

"Probably because I went to so damn many. I never had a chance to get settled."

"Why did you—"

"High school was a little better, but only because I found drama club."

Mary-Beth's eyebrows rise. "Drama club, huh?"

"You sound surprised. I *am* an actor."

"I guess you strike me as more of a high school sports kind of guy. You're six-foot-four."

I tut. "Making so many assumptions, Mary-Beth." I shake my head. "Christine would not approve."

Mary-Beth rolls her eyes and opens her mouth to say something. I interrupt before she can.

"I played sports when I was really young. But I always liked to read

CHAPTER 30

more. And my dad really liked sports, so not playing was kind of a fuck-you—" I pause to choose my words more carefully. It's a little too easy to open up to Mary-Beth which both terrifies and comforts me. "Anyway, when I got to high school, drama club became my escape."

Mary-Beth chews on the inside of her cheek like she's choosing her next question carefully. I change the subject before she can ask it.

"Cheerleader who used to make fun of the drama geeks behind their backs." I point at her. "The kind of popular girl who was nice to everyone to their face but wouldn't be caught dead with them at a party outside of school."

Her eyes flicker. "Wow, speaking of assumptions..."

"I'm making a very liberal amount, yes."

"You're about half right," she admits, shifting her weight from one foot to the other. She points at herself. "Cheerleader who everyone knew didn't smoke, drink, cuss, or have sex so she never got invited to any parties, drama geek-attended or otherwise. Oh, unless you count using me as the DD."

"A noble title."

Mary-Beth shrugs and looks up at the ceiling. "I did that for the first half of my senior year. Drove and tagged along. That's when I started dating Sutton. But then...yeah. Everything happened with Josie and Charlotte, and I stopped getting invited. And if I did, I didn't want to go."

"I think you're cooler than you want people to know. Beastie Boys and Air Force Ones and erotic romance novels? That's pretty badass, Mary."

I can tell Mary-Beth is trying to hide a smile. And a blush.

"Well...I think you're more intelligent than you want people to know," she retorts, bringing her hair in front of her shoulders. "I've literally never seen anyone read more than you do. I call BS on hating school."

"I said I hated school, not learning. School was a prison. Learning is an escape." I take a step toward Mary-Beth and grab her by one of her belt loops, reeling her in. She protests at first, but eventually gives. I place my hands on the small of her back, applying just enough pressure so her hips are flush with mine. "Seriously though, if I would have had a teacher like you, I think I could have loved it too."

"I'm nothing special." Mary-Beth shrugs and brings her hands to rest on my shoulders. We start to sway. "I just really love the kids."

"I never had a teacher who gave two shits about me. Pretty sure more than half were racist assholes. Seriously, Mary-Beth, in some of the neighborhoods I've lived in, you could make a real difference."

I look away, knowing I've finally said too much.

"Why so many neighborhoods?" Mary-Beth's tone is gentle but prodding.

An alarm on my phone chimes. I'm grateful for an organic way to flee the conversation.

"Shit." I let my hand fall. "I forgot I made a tee-time with your uncle this afternoon."

Mary-Beth's eyebrows rise. "You actually followed through with that?"

"Yes, *I followed through with that.* When I make a plan, I'm a follow-through kind of guy." My fingers inch under the fabric of Mary-Beth's shirt just an inch. "Is that okay?"

"Yeah, that actually works out. Today is my day to visit Nana in the nursing home."

"I liked Nana," I say, remembering the old lady from dinner. "She seemed spunky."

"Yeah, she's the best. I usually stay pretty late when I go." Mary-Beth sounds like her mind is far away. She takes a step back, out of my arms. "And then I've got church in the morning. I'll need to head straight to the airport afterwards. Wanna just meet me there?"

CHAPTER 30

"At the airport?"

"Sure."

The disappointment weighing down my chest surprises me. It's just one day. Why does it feel like more? "Yeah, Mary. Sounds good."

Chapter 31

Mary-Beth Caroline Abernathy
Rethinking Everything

"Knock, knock." I step into the sun-drenched bedroom. "Hey, Nana, it's me."

"Oh, Bethie." My grandmother's eyes light up from her chair by the window. She sets her book down and waves me inside. "Come in, sweetheart."

I bend down and kiss her forehead, setting a bouquet of flowers on her bedside table.

"I wasn't sure you were coming today." Nana laughs. "I thought your hot new boyfriend was still in town."

My cheeks instantly warm.

"Ah, so he *is* still around." Her eyes twinkle with mischief, pointing at the chair next to her. I sit obediently. "Why didn't you bring him?"

"He's, um..." I chuckle. "He's actually golfing with Uncle John and his work friends this afternoon."

"He's a good boy, Bethie. I liked him."

My eyes fall to my hands, and I begin picking at my fingernails. "Yeah, he liked you too, Nana."

"Well, of course." Nana places her weathered hands over mine and smiles warmly. "Everyone likes the Abernathies."

CHAPTER 31

My lips pucker. "So, what's new around here?" I look around the room for something other than Drew to talk about.

The lunch tray is still on the table by the door. Of course, she didn't touch her vegetables. She never does. Her photos are displayed proudly next to her bed—one from my mom and dad's wedding, my senior portrait, a snapshot of the four of us from my college graduation, and my grandfather's army portrait before he left for Vietnam. Her keepsakes line the shelves on the far wall: a silver tea pot, a marble chess set, a painting she got in Venice on her honeymoon. An entire life boiled down to a few shelves in a small room.

My eyes settle on the bookshelf next to her chair, filled with stacks of romance novels.

Nana's love of reading romance novels inspired mine. I used to sneak books off her shelf when I was a teenager, becoming addicted to their stolen glances and heaving bosoms. Nana has also been a huge part of my justifying *Swallow Manor*. Of course, she has no idea I'm the author, but I'm hoping one day I'll come here and see them on her bookshelf. Mine are significantly spicier than her usual bodice-rippers, but I truly think she'd enjoy them. She's a sucker for love interests like Ambrose.

Above the bookshelf, a flier about a seniors aerobics class—a class she undoubtedly will not be attending—is tacked onto her bulletin board. An invitation for a dance next week dangles next to it.

"So"—I shake my shoulders a little—"is Ben Graham still trying to ask you out? You gonna go to the dance with him?"

Nana rolls her eyes. "Oh, Ben. Yes, of course, he's already asked. But now there's Tim and Gerald, too. I'm a hot commodity around here, you know."

It's true that Nana is stunning. As a youth, she had fire-engine red hair, but now it's a pretty shade of gray, still long and shiny. Her eyes are a beautiful dark blue and sparkle just like my dad's. I was gifted my mom's boring brown, and I've always been jealous of the Abernathy blue. Her features are delicate, her eyelashes long, her cheeks rosy. I've been told I get my uncanny blushing ability from her.

Along with a love of bodice-rippers, junk food, and not exercising.

"Grandpa was a lucky guy, that's for sure."

Nana's eyes go distant as a small smile plays at the corner of her lips. "I was the lucky one."

My dad's dad died when I was a little girl—almost twenty years ago—from a brain aneurysm. Nana has had multiple suitors since then but has never treated their attention as anything other than a minor annoyance. It's her lot in life as a beautiful widow—to have men she's not interested in fawning over her.

I lean closer, breathing deeply of Nana's rose perfume. "How did you know Grandpa was the one?"

Nana gives me a toothy grin.

"I guess it was when I got pregnant," she says matter-of-factly.

Lord, did I hear that right?

She laughs. "What, is that not what you were expecting?"

"Uh..."

"Your dad was born seven months after we got married, Bethie," she croons, her blue eyes shining. "I thought you knew that."

"No, I, uh. No." I shake my head. Words. Sentences. I should say sentences right now. "But, like, you, um..."

"Your grandpa was all wrong for me, Bethie." Nana giggles. "I was a lady of good southern breeding, you know. And he was from the other side of town, rough around the edges, to put it nicely." She smiles roguishly. "But he had dark hair and piercing green eyes. And we couldn't seem to keep our hands off each other."

"I just...I thought—"

"Thought people didn't do that back then?" Nana fills in the blanks I can't seem to stop leaving open. She waves her hand like she's throwing away the words. "Oh, everyone did at least a little fooling

CHAPTER 31

around. Most went all the way but wouldn't admit it. And...a few were forced to admit it, like us." She laughs, seeming amused by my reaction.

Everyone?

Certainly not everyone.

"When you find the right person, you can't really help yourself, right?"

Her words swirl around me, like leaves carried on a brisk wind, almost knocking me over.

"But I guess to answer your question, I knew he was the one because your grandfather always made me laugh. He had a quick wit and sharp tongue. And he was playful and fun. Always ready for an adventure. More than anyone else, I just loved being around him. I liked who I became." Nana's eyes soften. "And he was very spiritual even if he wasn't necessarily religious. And always kind and gentle. A wonderful father to your sweet daddy."

My dad always talks about how much his dad influenced his decision to go into ministry. Nana, of course, had raised him in the church, taken him to Sunday School every week, and made sure he was baptized. But it was his dad's stoic, quiet support for his wife and her beliefs that really solidified things for him. "A man of faith, even if he didn't know it," my dad always described him. "He was the most Christlike man I've ever known."

"You *can* have it all, Bethie." Nana's eyes twinkle. "If it's the right person, it's okay to let yourself fall."

Lord, I'm begging to ask her what she means by that. But I feel like prodding for more information would be way too telling.

"Where is your mind, Miss Mary-Beth?" Nana places a gentle hand on my cheek.

"I just never knew." I lean into her touch like a little child. "I had no idea."

When Nana's mouth folds into a line and she nods, I realize my grandmother knows what I really mean.

I'm rethinking everything.

🐑🐑🐑

It's weird to spend a morning without Drew. It's only been a week, but I've gotten used to having him around. I packed my bags and dressed for church alone, the two actions conflicting. Like church and Drew Coyne don't mix. Lord, how I wish what Nana said was right.

Unfortunately, there's one thing Nana doesn't know... Drew Coyne doesn't do relationships. He doesn't commit. He does one-night stands—repeat booty calls at best. There's no way he would ever want to settle down with anyone. Least of all...*me*.

He's already talking about when we "break up." When I sign over the book rights and this thing we've been doing, whatever it is, inevitably ends. That's the end of our story, already written and published, no matter how much I'm wishing I could suggest edits.

After Friday night, I'm terrified to admit how much I want to do with him. How fast I'm falling. Maybe this is why I told myself he was awful, and the whole thing was fake. Because letting myself believe it's real, letting myself know the *real* Drew, letting him know the real *me*... I already know he's going to break my heart.

The wooden pews feel harder than usual. I cram into my seat, the one in the second row with the best view of the pulpit, right between Mama and Nana. It's the same spot I've sat in since I was a little girl when my feet didn't even reach the floor. Today, my toes tap anxiously under my light blue dress.

"Darling, glad you made it." Mama's voice is colder than usual, practically Antarctic. I smile at her and try with all my might not to squirm. "I wasn't sure you'd make time for us today."

"My flight doesn't leave until this afternoon. I'd never miss church."

"That's our Bethie," Nana says, patting my knee.

CHAPTER 31

"I see that Drew didn't make it," Mama bites off.

"He's not religious." No sense in making excuses for him at this point.

Mama doesn't say anything, but her mouth pinches in disapproval. I pretend not to see.

The prelude music is coming to an end when prickles travel from my neck down my spine and into my belly. I hear the snickers next, little whispers that crescendo into full-on chatter. I chew on my bottom lip to try and hide my grin as I turn in my seat, already knowing what I'm going to find.

Drew is walking down the aisle, looking unfairly hot in a dark gray suit and a shirt the exact shade of his eyes, the top two buttons undone. I stare at the patch of brown skin between his chin (freshly shaven) and his exposed clavicle (protruding) remembering how soft his skin at been. How it had felt pressing against my shoulder blades as his hands stroked me to climax. How he had commanded my body, enveloping—

"Darling, you need to slide down." Mama's voice snaps me from my reverie like a bucket of ice water. "Looks like Drew decided to come after all."

The shuffle to get him into our pew is ridiculously cumbersome and takes longer than Moses getting the Israelites to the Promised Land. First, Mama scootches down, then me. Then Nana, even though she didn't need to. Drew starts climbing over the three other people in our row (Tim, Gerald, and Ben from the nursing home, each wearing a fedora and holding a cane) while they awkwardly try to stand and sit at the same time. Then Drew realizes he won't fit overtop them and tries to crawl back. He gets stuck. He stands. Backs up. They stand, shuffling into the aisle like a barbershop trio about to perform. Then Nana, painfully slow in her slide along the never-ending bench, also stands.

Now, Drew is stuck behind the four geriatrics in the aisle, his butt in the face of the young mother and her baby in the row across from us. The baby is screaming, but the mom looks like she just saw the resurrected Lord and might start speaking in tongues at any moment. Her husband looks pissed.

To make room for Drew to slide around, Nana and her suitors are forced to march up to the stand, where my dad is now waiting for the spectacle to conclude before starting his sermon. The organ has stopped. Except for the soundtrack of grunts, groans, baby cries, and whispered "excuse me," the room is painfully silent.

Finally, *finally,* Drew toboggans across the vast, empty pew, until his shoulder collides with mine. He slings his arm around me like he didn't just cause the church's biggest spectacle in twenty years.

"Hey, Mary."

I have to surgically remove my hands from my eyes to look at him. "What are you doing here?"

Drew smiles and leans closer. "Turns out this is the only thing to do on a Sunday morning in this town."

"But you're not religious." I say it as much to myself as I do to him—a reminder to my racing heart.

"Yeah"—he shrugs and squeezes my shoulder—"but you are."

And with that, everyone is back in their respective seats, and the service begins.

And once again, I'm rethinking *everything.*

Chapter 32

Andrew Edward Coyne
Somewhere in the Middle

I don't know how I ended up here. Wedged into the middle of a church pew between Mary-Beth and her grandma, who smells like old books and rose water, listening to her dad pulpit-pound about some dude named Nehemiah, with her mom eyeing me every five seconds across her daughter's lap.

But I do know I shouldn't be.

I should have asked Mary-Beth about the book by now. At this point, it's unspoken, but we both know it's mine. I should be declaring victory on TikTok and searching for a screenwriter. I should be back in Los Angeles banging that Netflix actress and sweet-talking her into taking the role of Susan. I should be securing my next round of social media endorsements and shamelessly cashing the checks. Life should be getting back to normal.

I shouldn't be in church fantasizing about what Mary-Beth is wearing underneath her blue dress or what she packed for our week in California. Or wondering what she's thinking or how her piece of shit car made it the two-minute drive from her apartment to here. Worrying if it will make it to the airport. Trying to figure out a way to justify buying her a new one. I shouldn't have changed my outfit three times before finally Googling, *What do men wear to church?*

I shouldn't feel like a piece of me is missing when Mary-Beth isn't around. I shouldn't be dreading a week from now, hoping normal will never come.

"I'm so glad you came to the service," Mrs. Abernathy croons across Mary-Beth's lap, and I realize church is over. Chatter and organ music erupt around us. "It was nice to see you again."

I nod graciously. "You as well, Mrs. Abernat—"

Mary-Beth stands and yanks me up by the collar of my suit jacket.

"We have to go if we're going to make it to the airport in time." Mary-Beth turns away from her mom and not-so-gently shoves my chest, trying to shuffle me out of the tiny pew.

Her mom doesn't take the hint. "I hope you've enjoyed your time here in Daisy Bluff." Mrs. Abernathy smooths a lock of askew hair.

"It's been great, thank you."

"John said you guys had fun yesterday."

"Oh, yes." I laugh a little. "They were a fun group."

Read: a tipsy group of middle-aged white guys who suck at golf and love to talk about barbecuing, their lawn, and the weather. I'm sure each owns at least one pair of white New Balance shoes.

"Well..." Mary-Beth re-inserts herself into the conversation, turning to her mom and giving her a hug that feels more like a muzzle. "We really should go. We don't want to miss our flight."

Mary-Beth basically steamrolls me, Nana, and the three grandpas until we manage to escape into the aisle. But her mother catches her before she can run away.

"Beth, wait." Mrs. Abernathy's voice is ice-cold.

I place my hand on the small of Mary-Beth's back to try and be reassuring. "I'll wait for you outside."

"I'll walk you out, Drew," Nana says, taking my hand and yanking. Now I know where her granddaughter gets it from.

CHAPTER 32

Outside, the parishioners gather on the grass in front of the church.

"I needed to get away from them." Nana motions to the men gathered on the other side of the lawn. They grin at her, and she gives them a slight finger wave, speaking through a scowling grin. "They're insufferable. The lot of them."

I chuckle a little. I knew I liked Nana. "You're in high demand."

"Yes, well, it's my cross to bear." She flips her hair. "You know, everyone says Mary-Beth takes after me."

I smile at Nana, noticing the unmistakable likeness. Similar bone structure and facial features. Freckles and rosy cheeks and a petite figure. Same long, shiny hair. And Nana's eyes, although a startling blue compared to Mary-Beth's umber, have the same drowning effect.

"I see it."

"You better be careful with our girl," Nana warns, but then she smiles at me warmly. "But I suspect you will."

I look away. It's harder to lie to Nana than most people. Especially myself. I'm pretty damn good at lying to myself. "I'll certainly do my best."

"I'll tell you the same thing I told Mary-Beth last night. When it's the right person, it's okay to let yourself fall."

"What?"

"Don't act stupid, Drew." I have a feeling if she was carrying a cane, she would whack me with it. "You know what I mean."

"Um, sorry. I don't."

"Well, then, I guess you two have some thinking to do." Nana blows a stray hair out of her eyes with an annoyed huff.

Just then, Mary-Beth comes rushing toward me from a side door, tears streaming down her face. She offers Nana a hasty goodbye, then links her arm with mine and pulls.

Shit.

"Mary, is everything okay?" I try to take her hand, but she's two steps ahead of me now. I race to catch up. "What happened?"

She sniffles but doesn't answer, marching toward her car and not looking back. She unlocks the trunk and hefts her suitcases out. I quickly take them from her.

"Can we ride together?" Her brown eyes shine up at me, somehow even more striking through her tears. "In your car?"

"Yeah, of course."

Mary-Beth composes herself as we pull onto the freeway.

"What happened?" I ask again when she seems calm.

"My mother," is all she says, like that should somehow explain things. She sinks into her seat.

"She was nice to me," I try.

"Well, she's not quite as good an actor as you are, but she's close."

"So..."

"She was asking about sleeping arrangements and where I'd be staying and what we'd be doing and telling me not to go. Accusing me of things that haven't happened and..." Mary-Beth's eyes pinch with fresh tears. "I'm twenty-three years old, for Christ's sake. I'm not a freaking child."

My heart falls to the floor, and I place my hand on Mary-Beth's knee, rubbing gently. I stay silent, waiting for her to be ready to talk again. It takes her a few minutes.

"She told me to 'remember who I am,' and that she 'didn't raise me to be like this,' but I don't even know what that means anymore." Mary-Beth shakes her head, her eyes clouded with confusion and hurt. Something hollow in my chest aches.

"We don't have to go to Los Angeles, Mary."

"Yes, we do. I *have* to go. I don't care what she thinks. I need to do this for me."

We sit in silence. I wait until it turns from tense to comfortable before speaking.

CHAPTER 32

"Does it bother you that I'm not religious, Mary?"

"No," she answers. She looks at me and doesn't blink.

I raise my eyebrows, hoping she'll elaborate.

"Really, no." She smooths her hair and looks away. "Obviously, religion is a big part of my life, and always will be. But really the only thing I care about is that people respect that."

"I'm sorry if you felt that I didn't."

"You never *not* respected my religion..." Her voice trails off with a small laugh. I raise my eyebrows again. "I mean, the sex thing is separate," she clarifies. "At least I'm trying to keep it separate."

"How so?"

"Like, can I still be a religious person and also be a sexual person?" Her face flushes at the intimate question. My blood is pumping just as quickly.

"I think so." I swallow hard, choosing my words carefully. "Because you're already both of those things, Mary-Beth. Obviously, you're religious. But Mary, you've always been a sexual person, too. Your books"—*and every fucking time we're together*—"prove that. Just because you've never had sex doesn't mean you're not sexual. You are. You've always been. And that's not a bad thing. It's a natural part of who you are."

Mary-Beth's mouth puckers as she considers my words. Finally, she gifts me a small smile. "I guess," is all she says.

"You have it all, Mary. Everything anyone could ever want." I try to keep the jealousy out of my voice.

"I guess if having an overprotective mother is everything."

Emotion hits the back of my throat. I'd give anything to have an overprotective mother again. I swallow and change the subject.

"I mean, having your books and also having something to believe in." Such a small portion of the things Mary-Beth has that she has no fucking idea how lucky she is to have. "I think that would be really nice."

"What do you believe in?"

I sigh. "I believe in 'who the hell knows?'" I finally say. "I've never really been taught to believe in anything. So... I don't, really. That's why I said it would be nice."

"And sometimes I think it would be nice to start with a blank slate like that. To be able to figure it out for myself."

"You know, Mary." I take her hand and kiss the back of it, then rest it on my leg. She doesn't move it, even when I lift my hand to flick on the blinker. "I think you and I are not as different as you think we are."

Her eyes narrow. Her hand contracts. "How so?"

"I think we've fallen into the exact same trap. The trap of being who people expect us to be."

"And how exactly do people expect you to be? Because as you'll recall...you were nothing like I expected."

"That's fair." I laugh and switch lanes. "I guess, people who know me in real life expect an arrogant, rich fuckboy."

Mary-Beth nods. "That tracks."

"And in my professional life, in the public eye, people expect America's sweetheart."

"I certainly fell for that one." Mary-Beth chews on her bottom lip. Her fingers resting on my leg twitch. "But I think the real you is somewhere in the middle."

"I don't think even *I* know who the real me is, honestly." I shrug. It's the first time I've admitted that. Out loud, and to myself. "I think I'm still trying to find him. I think making that TikTok to find *you* was the first step."

Mary-Beth's gaze locks with mine, and I can't tear my eyes away. The car veers, making the rumble tracks screech before I can right it.

"Well...if anyone has fallen into that trap, it's me." Mary-Beth sighs defeatedly, running a hand through her hair. "I've been expected to be a certain way my entire life, and I've been exactly that. Except, well...the obvious."

"*Swallow Manor.*"

"Right."

"Well, for what it's worth, I think the woman who pushed 'publish' is the real you." I squeeze her hand, braiding my fingers with hers.

"What?" Her eyebrows rise. "The erotica author? Really?"

"No. The twenty-three-year-old woman who does whatever the hell she wants. Who is brave and smart and gets everything she deserves."

Chapter 33

Mary-Beth Caroline Abernathy
Twenty-Three-Year-Old Woman Who Does Whatever the Hell She Wants

"I saw his car there, Beth. I know about what happens in apartments with men like Drew Coyne late at night. I know you think I'm stupid, but—"

"No, Mama. I don't. Please, it's not what you think."

"Charity saw you at the Persimmon Festival with him. The words she used to describe it were 'borderline X-rated.' I'm disappointed in you."

"Seriously, Mama. Nothing happened. We just kissed, nothing else—"

"If it hasn't happened already, it will happen if you go. If you stay at his house. Sleep in his bed. Remember who you are, Beth. I didn't raise you to be a whore. You need to end things before it's too late."

"Mary, the plane is gonna land soon. I have to talk to you about something."

Drew shakes my shoulder, and I jolt awake, wiping a puddle of drool from my chin. My eyes blink against the stark airplane lighting. My skin prickles with the dream of my mother.

She thinks I'm a slut.

One can only say, "Nothing happened, Mama," so many times before realizing she is going to see what she is going to see. And she sees a

CHAPTER 33

slut. I'm a twenty-three-year-old virgin, for crying out loud, yet my own mother thinks I'm a slut. All because I'm planning to stay at my pretend boyfriend's house for a week, undoubtedly sleep on his couch, sign away my book rights, and return home a virgin.

A heartbroken virgin for sure, but still a virgin.

Since Friday night, I've been waiting for the regret to come. To feel guilty that I'd gone that far, done that much. Let Drew touch me like that. *Had an orgasm.* That not only had it happened, but I'd enjoyed it. Liked it. Loved it. Went freaking wild for it, honestly.

But the guilt never came.

Especially after my conversation with Nana. Especially looking deep into my seemingly perfect mother's eyes, the same brown as mine, and wondering. Wondering what secrets she's hiding.

Besides, if she's going to judge me and treat me like a whore when I've done nothing, why not do it all?

Unfortunately, I've already told Drew I want commitment before I have sex with anyone, *even Drew Coyne*, and his face had said enough. Hell would freeze first.

So heartbroken virgin I shall remain.

"I just got a text from Will." Drew's voice has an unusual tightness to it.

I sit up in my chair. "Is everything okay?"

"The paparazzi knows we're coming. They know I've been staying with you for a week. And..." Drew takes a deep breath and lets it out in one big puff. "There are rumors you're Minnie Maple."

It feels like my heart lurches into my nostrils. Mama is already convinced I'm sleeping with Drew. She will probably disown me if we add *romance author* on top of that.

"What do we do?"

"Well, there are also rumors you're my new girlfriend." Drew puts his arm around my shoulders and pulls me to his chest. He kisses the top of my head when I melt into his side. "We're gonna show them which rumor to believe."

I nod into his chest, trying to keep fresh tears from spilling.

"Don't worry, Virgin Mary." His voice is a rumble in my hair. He rests his chin on my head and squeezes my shoulders. "Remember, boyfriend Drew is my specialty."

The words feel like Drew just ripped my heart out of my chest and threw it out the airplane window.

The charade continues.

🐦🐦🐦

"Here, put these on." Drew hands me a pair of oversized sunglasses, putting on his own.

"Didn't I say you were the type to wear sunglasses inside?" Neither of us laughs at my joke.

He grips my hand tightly and leads me through the airport. So far, people are staring and whispering, but no pictures or finger-pointing. No public flogging or tomato-throwing. So far.

"Follow my lead." Drew bends down and kisses my cheek before making a sharp left toward the baggage claim escalator.

Halfway down, a wall of blinding flashes accosts us. The lights make me temporarily blind, and my feet trip when the stairs disappear from underneath me. My fingers dig into Drew's forearms as I try to stand. If he wasn't hugging my shoulders to his chest, I would have been sucked inside the escalator like a meat grinder.

"No matter what they say, don't talk to them," Drew whispers, tugging me around the large cluster of photographers. He puts up a giant hand to block my face from the intense lights and tries to shield my body with his.

The shutters sound like a firing squad, and the flashes are like fire pokers, but their words are the worst.

"Mary-Beth, is it true you wrote *Swallow Manor*?"

CHAPTER 33

"Mary-Beth, is it true Drew inspired *Swallow Manor*?"

"Drew, is it true you're moving to Indiana?"

"Minnie Maple, what can you tell us about the new movie?"

"Drew, when can we expect *Swallow Manor* the movie?"

"Mary-Beth, what is it like dating the star of your new movie?"

I'm pretty sure this is what hell is like.

We finally find a bit of refuge near the baggage carousel by the wall. Drew turns me in his arms and brings his forehead to mine.

"Showtime." He looks down from behind his sunglasses and smiles. Then he kisses me.

It's a very short, sweet kiss, with no tongue and no rubbing, but it brings me right back to my apartment. Back to the unfulfilled need. Drew pulls away first and carefully guides my head to his chest. He wraps his big, strong arms around me, and rests his chin on top of my head. I hug him back, breathing in his pine-tree-scent.

If hell is an airport infested with paparazzi, heaven must be a forest of pine trees.

I hide in Drew's chest, pretending they aren't taking photographs of us. Pretending my mom and the rest of the world won't see them.

Pretending this means as much to Drew as it does to me.

🐑🐑🐑

After finally outrunning the paparazzi and stopping for life-changing food truck tacos in a sketchy neighborhood, I follow Drew into his dark apartment. Still holding our suitcases, he marches past the kitchen and living room and straight into his bedroom. I stop at the threshold, only getting a glimpse of the giant bed inside.

"What are you doing?"

Drew drops the suitcases with a *thump*. He loosens his tie and takes off his suit coat, throwing it on the bed. "Mary-Beth, you look like hell. You need sleep."

"Sleep?"

"Yeah, you know, it's a thing people do when they're tired?"

Of all the things I thought might happen at Drew's apartment, I'd never considered sleep. Wild all-night parties. Yes. Fighting so much we accidentally kill each other. Obviously. At least one night of mind-bending sex so amazing I can't see or walk straight ever again. Duh. But sleep? Did women ever *sleep* when they stayed the night at Drew Coyne's house? I guess it makes sense I would be the first.

You are the type, Virgin Mary, to come to my house and want to sleep.

"What? Did you think I was going to hold you hostage?" Drew's laughter lightens his voice. "Force you to stay up watching porn? Drink ten beers and not recycle them? Go to a strip club and force you to strip?"

"I guess I just didn't think I would, um"—I blink several times—"sleep."

Drew shakes his head, but he's still laughing. "Jesus, Mary-Beth. One of these days you're going to realize I'm just a normal person. Sleep and all."

He methodically takes off his shoes. One and then another. Then he unbuttons the rest of the buttons of his shirt, letting the light blue fabric fall open, revealing his perfectly defined, miracle-inducing, close-to-heaven torso. I go so long without blinking, my eyes water.

"I can take the couch," I quickly say.

Drew shakes his head. "Not a chance in hell, Mary."

Without another word, he shuts the door. Him inside, me out.

I slump against the wall and take out my phone, something I haven't done in what feels like ages. After texting my parents I arrived safely and praying I don't get a response, my thumb hovers over the Google app. I've never googled myself. Never done anything worthy of a google. But after today, I have a feeling something would pop up if I dared.

I start with Mary. Suggestive text fills in the blanks with Mary J.

CHAPTER 33

Blige, Mary Poppins, and Mary Magdalene respectively. I laugh. *What would that dinner party be like?*

When I add the letter B after Mary, I get Mary Blake, food blogger, Mary Bell, child serial killer, and Mary Boquitas, singer. I'm glad I'm still less famous than that trio.

I hold my breath and reach for E when Drew opens the door. He's changed into sweats and a T-shirt that look like they were tailored to fit his body, smelling like laundry detergent and a sexy lumberjack. I lean on one side of the door frame, and he leans on the other.

"So, is it always like that for you?" I fumble to put my phone away. "Getting accosted at the airport?"

Drew laughs, shaking his head. "God, no. I'm not as famous as you think I am. I get recognized pretty often, and I sign quite a few autographs, but the paps usually leave me alone. It's really picked up since, uh, the Minnie Maple stuff."

"And you've been loving it?" I assume. "Being instantly more famous?"

"Hell no. I absolutely hate it." The knuckles gripping the door frame grow white.

"Then why'd you become an actor? Don't all actors want to be famous?"

"No," Drew says with finality, and I drift back an inch. "Most actors I know hate the fame aspect of acting. We just want to be left the fu—" Drew pauses, then starts again. "To be left alone. But we aren't allowed to say that because then it sounds like we are complaining about being celebrities and having successful careers.

"But I couldn't care less about the fame. Or even acting, honestly. I became an actor because I liked pretending to be something I'm not. And I like to read and can memorize things easily. Acting comes easily to me, but it's not my passion."

"You don't care about acting?" My eyes go wide. "But isn't that what this whole thing is about? You wanted something new for your acting career?"

"I wanted something new." Drew rubs the back of his neck. "But I'm realizing that might not be acting. Acting has always been just an escape. And I'm not sure I need an escape anymore."

"An escape from what?"

"From my shitty life."

"Oh."

I get a ping on my watch telling me I have a new text message. Thank God, it's not my mother.

"It's Harper." I'm grateful for a change in subject. I sense Drew is dangerously close to shutting down.

Harper: I know I was supposed to get into town tomorrow morning, but it's gonna be tomorrow night instead. But don't worry, I've got a place to stay and a ride all worked out. You just have fun with Dream Coyne, yeah? Wanna meet for dinner?

"When does she get into town?" Drew asks.

"Tomorrow?" I shake my head, not convinced this plan will stick. This is the fourth time her itinerary has changed.

"Do we need to pick her up from the airport?"

"No. She said she had it all figured out. She even has a place to stay."

"I guess that settles it," Drew says.

"I guess it does."

Without meaning to, I yawn.

Drew cocks his head toward the bedroom. "I assure you there will be no unsolicited advances."

"I am perfectly capable of thwarting any and all advances."

"Is that so?" A wicked smile dances across Drew's face as he takes my hand and leads me into his bedroom. *His bedroom.* "Let's test that theory."

Inside the room, the walls are high and white except for a patch of

CHAPTER 33

exposed brick by the large window opposite the bed. The back wall is completely covered by a large floor-to-ceiling bookshelf with books of all shapes, sizes, colors, and genres shoved into every nook and cranny. I spot the *Swallow Manor* series immediately, front and center, on the floor next to the bookshelf. I turn away, not wanting to invite that elephant into the room.

The bedside tables are empty except for two expensive-looking bronze lamps and two glasses of water Drew must have filled earlier. Above the bed, several black and white photographs in simple frames hug the wall. A whale's tail fluke. A boat. Half of an old woman's face. A dog.

I turn back to Drew, standing closer to me than I expected. He's been watching me. "A dog, really?" I laugh.

Drew smirks. "Darcy helped me decorate."

"Clearly."

The side of Drew's mouth pinches into a devious half-smile. "You're a smartass, you know that?" he says, almost like it's a term of endearment.

I'm thinking of some semblance of comeback when Drew picks me up and tosses me on the king-sized bed. My shoes go flying, and the crisp white comforter puffs around me like a cloud. Before I even have a chance to register *I'm lying in Drew Coyne's bed,* he climbs on top of me.

His body is long and heavy and startlingly form-fitting against mine. Practically Legos. My chest pushes against his, and his leg fits perfectly between mine. Even our eyes seem to connect—his light blue gaze capturing me and not letting go. His heaviness compared with the softness of the bed rips the breath from my lungs. Drew kisses my neck, and his hands find their way to my waist. He tickles my ribs, and I squirm underneath him.

"A *ticklish* little smartass?" His eyes light up. "How did I not know?"

I find his hands and hold them. "I'm not ticklish. I'm trying to escape," I lie. I'm neither *not* ticklish nor trying to escape.

"Bullshit."

Drew runs his hands down the side of my body, wiggling his fingers across my skin, jabbing between my ribs, kissing my neck, eager to solicit a reaction. I try my best to hold still, demanding that my body stop betraying me. I bite the inside of my cheek to keep from squealing.

His hands move across the top of my thighs, tickling me through the fabric of my dress. When he reaches my knees, his hands stop, and he explodes in laughter.

"Pantyhose, Virgin Mary?" He buries his head into the crook of my neck, laughing into my hair. "Really?"

"What?" I whack him on the shoulder. "It was a little chilly this morning, and it's always cold in the church."

"God, you are the type."

I sit up on my elbows and glare at him, waiting for the insult, but it doesn't come. Instead, he creeps to the end of the bed until he's kneeling beside it—his head hovering just above my belly button. His hands return to my legs, slowly moving upward until they crawl under my dress and find the waistband of my tights. I gasp when his fingertips touch the skin at my hips, inching under the elastic.

"The type to want to put as much clothing between us as possible." Drew slides the fabric over my hips, his fingers digging into the sensitive skin of my butt.

Arousal hits me like a physical blow to the chest. His touch feels like hot coals as he painstakingly guides the flesh-colored nylon down my thighs, then my knees, and my calves, before tugging them off my feet and throwing them across the room. They land scarily close to *Swallow Manor*.

Lord, give me strength.

I'm so shocked, I don't know whether to panic or celebrate, so I do

CHAPTER 33

nothing, laying absurdly still. The only body part that even shifts is my nipples peaking.

Drew kisses the inside of my left thigh, just above my knee, below the hem of my dress, and then stands and walks over to my suitcase.

I'm a puddle melting into the white linen on Drew's bed. The left side of my body feels like it's just been electrocuted, leaving a new invisible string behind. One from his kiss to the throbbing between my legs. My heart races, remembering exactly how it feels when the string snaps.

Drew lays my suitcase on its back and carefully unzips.

"Shit, Mary-Beth," he says when he flings it open. "What are you trying to do, kill me?" He carefully takes a black lace thong in one hand and the matching bralette in the other.

I can't help but giggle. "I've actually already worn that this week. Three days ago. You had no idea."

Drew growls and throws the lingerie back in my luggage. He rummages until he finds something else.

The sweatpants with the hole in them –*why did I pack those?* – and a T-shirt. Pajamas.

Sleep, remember, Mary-Beth?

"Sit up," Drew directs, and I obey, coming to my knees. He sits on the edge of the bed and helps guide my dress over my shoulders, until, once again, I'm in my underwear with Drew. He throws my dress aside and grabs my pajamas. His eyes running up and down my skin burns almost as much as his touch.

"Goddamn, Mary-Beth." His hands are gripping my sweatpants so tightly, he looks like he might rip them to shreds. "Lay down."

I again obey without questioning what exactly I'm agreeing to. His jaw flexes.

Drew pulls the sweatpants over my feet, and up my calves, then reaches both hands to my butt and squeezes hard, forcing my hips upward before he guides the pants to rest at my waist. His breath is hot on my skin, and his fingers are rough and barely controlled, like he's fighting the fabric to make it move.

I didn't know putting clothes *on* could illicit this reaction, yet here I am, hornier than ever. It's unfair what he does to me. If he made a move, I'm starting to believe I wouldn't stop him.

Drew pulls me up and grabs my T-shirt. The backs of his hands skim my breasts as he slides it down my belly. I arch my back and close my eyes, feeling the familiar zing of the string tightening. Drew pushes me back to bed, and I gasp. But then, something else tightens around me.

"Are you *tucking me in*?" I slump against the pillow as Drew pulls a blanket over me, jamming it under my legs and back.

"You won't find a finer turn-down service in all of Los Angeles." Drew kisses my forehead and tucks the blanket under my feet and at my shoulders, pinning my arms to my sides.

"Lord, sometimes I really hate you."

When I'm sufficiently burrito-fied, and Drew is standing in the open door, I sit up again, reaching under my shirt. His hand hovers above the light switch as he freezes, staring at me.

"What are you doing?"

I unsnap my bra and thread it through the neck hole of my T-shirt. I throw it on the ground, squirming around in the tourniquet he made for me.

"I don't sleep in my bra."

His eyes bore into me like I've just done something...unholy. "Sometimes I really hate you too, Virgin Mary."

Chapter 34

Mary-Beth Caroline Abernathy
Psycho Jealous Pretend Girlfriend

I'm seriously considering pleasuring myself. Drew left me in such an aroused haze, I'm unable to get comfortable, unable to silence my racing thoughts. I drift in and out of sleep for hours, the unsatisfied pulse between my legs playing drill sergeant. Knowing Drew is in the next room doesn't help either. How dare he touch me like that and then leave, daring me to *sleep*.

My body screams for release. My mind is going berserk. But I'll be damned if I'm going to be in Drew freaking Coyne's bed and give *myself* an orgasm.

My feet hit the cold hardwood floor with a tiny squeak. Not knowing where I'm going and barely able to see with only moonlight to guide me, I inch toward the door, creaking it open and slipping into the hallway in silence. I cling to the wall as I make my way toward the kitchen, but nearly topple over when I realize Drew isn't alone.

"On second thought," Drew says. I hear ice tinkling inside a glass. "I don't know if having Chloe here tomorrow is a good idea."

Chloe? Who the hell is *Chloe*? Jealousy conks me over the head like a falling coconut. I hold my breath and tiptoe another step closer.

"You think Mary-Beth would have a problem with it?" another male voice asks. Will, I think.

Hell yes, Mary-Beth would have a problem with it. A big problem. What happened to *Drew Coyne is not a cheater*? Not even on his psycho jealous pretend girlfriend?

"No, I don't think so." It sounds like Drew is setting his drink down and pouring another. "I just don't want Chloe getting hurt, ya know?"

Oh, Chloe is gonna get hurt all right. That's for damn sure.

"She'll be fine," Will says. "I mean, if Mary-Beth is going to be here, she's gonna have to get used to having Chloe around. And vice versa."

Holy shit. I know Drew said he was going to take me to a brothel, but is he actually running one? A harem, perhaps? A polygamist colony? The Playboy mansion?

"Yeah, you're right. And Mary-Beth's a kindergarten teacher. She'll know exactly how to handle it."

A Playboy mansion full of kindergarten teachers? What twisted fantasy have I found myself in?

"So..." Will pauses, and I hear him swallow. "Mary-Beth is going to be around, then?"

More ice tinkling. More glass slamming. Then the distinct sound of Drew's mouth puckering and sighing. "You were right, Will. What you said before."

What did he say before? Lord Almighty, *what did he say before?*

"I think I should get a recording of you saying that," Will teases.

"Seriously, though. And I'm fucking terrified, if I'm being honest. This has never happened. I've never felt—" A swallow and then the sound of glass meeting mahogany. "I'm just afraid of fucking losing her, man. I don't know how to do this. You know this isn't me."

Losing me? Or losing Chloe?

"You say that like it's a bad thing. Maybe it's not."

"Maybe not bad..." Drew's voice drifts off. I lean a smidge further to make sure I don't miss anything. "But impetuous."

CHAPTER 34

"This wasn't the plan," Will clarifies.

"Fuck no! You know this wasn't the plan. This is never my plan."

"So what are you going to do about it? Honestly, this could actually be a really good thing for you."

"I have no fucking clue. I'm freaking out. She's going to be here all week. Who knows how screwed I'll be by Saturday."

How is me being here until Saturday going to screw him? If tonight is any indication, it's certainly not screwing in the literal sense. *He tucked me into bed, for crying out loud.*

"Start with tomorrow," Will says. "Take it one day at a time."

"With Chloe." I hear the dread in Drew's voice.

"With Chloe." And the delight in Will's. *Jackass.* "See how that goes. Maybe it'll be complete shit."

"Mary-Beth and Chloe together is not going to be complete shit. But it will make things a million times worse."

"A million times worse because..."

"She's in my bed right now, Will. Sleeping. Without a bra on. Fucking sleeping. And she'll be there tomorrow. And the next day. And the day after that. But you know how she is. How I am. I'm going to fuck everything up. Someone will get hurt. How is this not a problem?"

"Does this have something to do with the book?"

"Fuck the book." My legs nearly buckle, and I lean against the wall for support. "You know what I mean."

After a long break in conversation, Drew speaks again.

"Is this how it was with Julia? When you first got together? Like this...all the time?"

"Well, shit." Will laughs, but it doesn't sound like it's because he thinks Drew said something funny. "This really is a problem, isn't it?"

"Why do you say that?"

"Because I know you wouldn't bring up Julia if it weren't."

Drew and Will grow quiet. After a few minutes, footsteps threaten, and I slink back to Drew's room, mostly because I don't know what else to do. I rip at the bedding, clawing my way into the butter-soft sheets. The blanket he tucked around me falls to the floor with my bra and my pantyhose and my books. I curl into the fetal position, turning my back to the other side of the bed.

Tears spill down my cheeks and into my mussed hair. I don't bother wiping them away.

I've completely misread this situation. And my heart might never recover.

Eventually, sleep finds me, and morning comes, despite my prayers that it won't. I don't know how I'm going to face Drew today. And not just him, but Drew and *Chloe*, whoever the hell that is. Fake girlfriend is a hard enough role to play. I won't be able to handle fake mistress.

Drew isn't in bed when my eyes finally split, feeling like sand was ground into them during the night. But...the sheets on his side of the bed are out of place, so I know he eventually did come to bed and sleep next to me.

I slept next to Drew Coyne last night. My seventeen-year-old self would be screaming. I punch the pillow instead.

The smell of bacon and something burning levitates through the air, and I fling my legs over the side of the bed. Better get this over with. But first, my bra. I'm never finding myself braless or shirtless or pantsless or dressless or without any and all of my clothing securely on around Drew again. I even put on socks.

I make my way from the bedroom to the kitchen with fists clenched. But when I round the corner, there's a little girl sitting at the counter.

"Aw, you're awake." Drew greets me with a huge smile as he flips a pancake in the air.

It lands on the floor, and the little girl covers her mouth and giggles.

CHAPTER 34

I take two more steps into the room.

"Mary-Beth, this is Will's daughter, Chloe." He gestures between the girl and me. "Chloe, this is Miss Mary-Beth."

Chloe.

Dear Lord, have mercy. *Will's daughter, Chloe.*

I scurry into the room and take Chloe's tiny little hand in mine, squatting so we're closer to eye level. "Hi Chloe, I'm Miss Mary-Beth. It's so nice to meet you."

"Hi, Miss Mary-Beth."

Chloe looks to be about the same age as my kindergartners, maybe a year younger. She has adorable chubby cheeks, big brown eyes, and chestnut ringlets. She's missing two of her bottom teeth.

"Are you Uncle Drew's girlfriend?" she asks with wide, curious eyes. Count on a five-year-old to get straight to the point.

I look at Drew, unsure how to answer.

"Mary-Beth is Uncle Drew's very good friend. And the rest is"—Drew blinks a few times—"complicated." He walks around the kitchen island and hands me a plate of bacon, eggs, and mutilated pancakes. He kisses me on the forehead. Against my better judgment, I let him.

"I can't lie to Chloe," he whispers. "But she can't keep a secret for shit, so I wouldn't say too much if I were you."

I nod, already knowing this about most five-year-olds.

"Daddy said don't freak out if you kiss Miss Mary-Beth," Chloe says nonchalantly in a little raspy voice, taking a bite of her breakfast. "But I won't. I've seen lots of people kiss. Grandma and Grandpa even kiss sometimes. So you guys can kiss if you want."

I take the seat next to her and grab a fork. "Say, Chloe. Are you in school yet?"

"I go to preschool three days a week," Chloe declares proudly, shoveling in another bite of a weird-shaped pancake.

"What's your teacher's name?"

"Miss Jennifer."

"Is she so nice?"

"She's the best!"

"And are you going to go to kindergarten next year?"

"Yes!"

"Are you excited?"

"Excited…" Chloe's little mouth turns down at the sides. "…and a little nervous."

"Did you know I'm a kindergarten teacher?"

Chloe's eyes light up like *I'm* the celebrity. "Really?"

"Yep. I know everything there is to know about kindergarten. Would you like to ask me a question?"

"Will Marcus be in my class?" Chloe makes a salty face.

"Is that punk still giving you trouble?" Drew positively glowers from behind the griddle. He's wearing a gray T-shirt and a blue apron that brings out the fire in his eyes. I swallow nervously. Protective Uncle Drew is a hot look for him. Dangerously hot. "Do your dad and I need to go talk to Marcus and his mom again?"

Chloe shakes her head and looks up at me through her thick, long eyelashes. "Marcus put glue in my hair once," she explains. "Daddy had to cut it."

"Oh, Chloe. That's terrible. I'm so sorry that happened to you."

"Will he be in my class?" she asks again, a tremor in her little voice.

"Yeah, will he?" Drew adds, though he knows I have no freaking clue. The most recent batch of pancakes look like they're starting to burn.

"Well, I don't know about that." I take her little hand in mine. "But I can tell you there's definitely no hair gluing in kindergarten. I've been a teacher for two years, and that hasn't happened. Not even once."

"Miss Mary-Beth, will you be *my* kindergarten teacher?"

CHAPTER 34

I shake my head. "No. But...there's a rule that all kindergarten teachers have to be super-duper nice. They don't let mean people be kindergarten teachers."

"Only the nicest," Drew adds. I can't tell if he's complimenting or mocking me.

Chloe's face relaxes, and she takes three more bites of pancake. When her plate is empty, she looks up at Drew. "Can you make me a ballerina unicorn next?"

"Of course. We're gonna turn these unicorns into anything you want. Anything but green monsters, darlin'."

My insides go numb. My ovaries practically fall out of my body. *Darlin'.*

Drew waves the spatula at me. "Sorry, you, uh, got the mess-ups of roller-skating unicorn and ice cream cone unicorn."

"It took a few tries to get it right," Chloe explains.

I look down at the disfigured pancakes and smile over at the little girl.

"You're right, Chloe. These definitely look more like *alien unicorns*." I say the last two words in a spooky-robot voice, and she squeals in laughter. Drew smirks and throws the latest burnt pancakes into the trash, scraping the griddle clean with the back of his spatula.

"All right, all right, enough out of you two." Drew's voice booms as he prepares to pour the batter, brandishing the bowl in the air. "This time, I'm gonna get it on the first try!"

Chloe tugs on my shirt and brings her hand to my ear. "He won't," she whispers. We burst into giggles.

After breakfast, I take a shower and get ready while Drew and Chloe watch cartoons on the couch, her little head tucked securely under his arm.

File this morning next to *sleep* in the "things I did not think would be happening this week" folder.

File this view next to *everything in the past week* in the "things that are making me fall in love with Drew Coyne" folder.

When I emerge from his bedroom in cutoff jeans and a hoodie, Drew and Chloe are standing by the door, wearing matching conspiring smirks.

"Uncle Drew says we're going to the finest brothel in all of Los Angeles," Chloe announces. She's added a unicorn-shaped purse and pink sparkly shoes to her already rainbow-heavy outfit. The way she says *brothel* sounds more like the *Brussels* in *Brussels sprouts*.

I hold in a snort. "Is that so, Miss Chloe?"

"Yep!"

Chloe leads Drew and me out of the apartment, marching assertively in front of us.

"You are the type," I whisper, low enough that she can't hear.

"The type to be a kickass uncle?" Drew smirks. "Yeah, I am."

"The type to bring a child to a Brussels."

We both laugh.

Drew slings his arm around my waist casually, tickling my ribs. I wriggle and try to escape, but he holds me tightly to his hip. "I love that you're ticklish. I'm going to exploit that."

"You wouldn't be you if you didn't."

Chloe is extra squirmy when we pull on I-5 South.

"Have you been to this brothel before, Chloe?" I ask. What a strange sentence to say to a five-year-old.

Chloe nods enthusiastically. "Yes, but Uncle Drew says we have to keep it a secret."

The *brothel* is over an hour away with traffic. For the first fifteen minutes, Drew and I are mostly quiet in the front seat, holding hands and listening to Chloe prattle on about Maggie the dog and Marcus the bully and the new stuffed animal she got yesterday named Nelly the Narwhal.

CHAPTER 34

"Daddy had to buy her for me because he didn't know narwhals were a real animal, and we made a bet. But come on, it's the unicorn of the sea!"

I laugh and look over at Drew. "Will didn't know narwhals are real?"

His eyebrows rise, and he glances at Chloe in the rearview. "Uncle Drew is smarter than Daddy, isn't he?"

Her face scrunches, and she holds up her index finger and thumb in a pinch. "Only sometimes."

Five minutes later, the girl is dead asleep.

"Will had to drop her off really early this morning." Drew's lips turn down. "I thought she might crash."

"She's adorable."

You guys are adorable.

Drew stares at Chloe in the mirror with a look that makes my heart feel like it's falling off a cliff. "Yeah, Chloe's the best."

"What happened to her mom?"

His eyes constrict into slits. "How did you know something happened to her mom?"

"Because if her mom was around, there's no way Will would be the one cutting glue out of her hair."

Drew concedes with a small shrug. "Julia died in a car accident when Chloe was two months old."

I gasp and bring my hand to my mouth. "Oh my gosh, that's terrible."

Drew nods. "Yeah, it was."

"Poor Will. How did he handle it? Did you know him back then?"

His hands constrict around the steering wheel. "Will and I have been best friends since high school. He was the one who knew what he wanted for his life—the white picket fence and the minivan full of kids. He fell in love with the cheerleader he sat next to in Geometry when we were sixteen and married her when we were twenty. He graduated college by twenty-two and headed back east to become an attorney. Julia and Will had Chloe when he was in his last year of law school. Everything was going according to plan. Until...it wasn't. The universe can be pretty fucked up sometimes."

I look back at the sleeping girl in the backseat. I can't help but agree. That does seem incredibly unfair.

"Meanwhile, I'd left community college after several failed semesters and decided to pursue acting. Will dropped out of school and moved back home to live with his parents and to be close to Julia's family. I hired him to be my agent, and the rest is history. He helped me capitalize on my freakishly good memorization skills, and I helped him pay off his student loans and funeral expenses."

Drew exits the freeway, making a swift left turn at the end of the on-ramp. "Will is like my brother, the closest thing I have to family." His eyes soften as Chloe stirs. "So...for the past five years, Chloe's been part mine too. Will's mom and Julia's mom take turns watching her when Will is busy. But I'm not a bad pinch hitter."

"You're a wonderful hitter." I place my hand on his thigh, and he clutches my hand. "I've never seen anyone make unicorn caricature pancakes like you do."

"Roller-skating unicorn was a challenge. But I'm somewhat of an expert."

Chloe pops up from the backseat.

"We're here!" she screeches, holding her hands up. "The finest Brussels in Los Angeles."

Chapter 35

Uncle Andrew Edward Coyne

"Disneyland?" Mary-Beth bursts into giggles. "This is the finest brothel in all of Los Angeles?"

"Well... I guess this is technically Anaheim." I squeeze her hand. "But it's kind of mine and Chloe's spot. Isn't that right, darlin'?"

Chloe nods. "Are you surprised, Miss Mary-Beth? Uncle Drew really, *really* wanted to surprise you. I think he has a crush on you."

I give Chloe a *what the hell?* look in the rearview. She puts her hands over her mouth and giggles. I guess I did warn Mary-Beth she couldn't keep a secret.

Mary-Beth turns to smile at the little girl. "I don't think I would have been more surprised if we had blasted off to the moon."

That makes Chloe beam with pride.

Mary-Beth's eyebrows rise in a you're *so-not-the-Disneyland-type* look, and I can't keep myself from smiling. I love surprising her. Not with Disneyland or unicorn-shaped pancakes, but by revealing more of myself. Scoring points in the fuck-all-your-assumptions game.

There was something about seeing Mary-Beth in my bed last night. First, in her underwear, obviously. Shit, she gets more tantalizing by the second, I swear. If she hadn't been wearing those goddamn pantyhose, who knows what I would have done to her.

But there was something else, too. Something about seeing her in her pajamas, asleep in my bed with her freckles and scrunched nose and fluttering eyelashes. It made me realize…I wanted her there. Not because I wanted to fuck her – which, duh – but because I simply just wanted her with me. Asleep. Next to me. The promise that she would be there in the morning. That she wasn't going to disappear from my life.

I've never been so fucking scared.

It's why, at one in the morning, I'd called Will and begged him to come over.

"I can't come over, man. What about Chloe?"

"Bring Chloe. She can sleep on the couch."

"But I need to take her to my mom's in the morning. I'd hit traffic if I had to come all the way from your place."

"I'll watch her tomorrow. Please, I need to have a drink and talk to someone. I'm losing my fucking mind, man."

Will sighed. Twenty minutes later he was here. Thirty minutes, two Gogurts, and three *Bluey* episodes after that, Chloe was asleep.

And then I'd told him everything. Around 3 a.m., I finally got up the courage to ask what I've been wondering all along.

"How did you know you loved Julia? That she was the one?"

"Because she made me so damn happy." Will's smile was heartbreaking. "Made me the best version of myself. And because the thought of losing her felt like the worst fucking thing in the world." His voice chokes. "And when it happened, it was."

"Shit, man. I'm sorry for bringing it up."

"It's okay. Honestly, I would go through it all again to have the seven years I had with her. Fuck—to have just one day with her. It was all worth it. And of course, that's how we got Chloe. But, Drew, when you love someone, time is the most valuable thing in the world.

I'm telling you right now, if you care about Mary-Beth, don't fucking waste it."

And so, as I'd lain next to Mary-Beth last night, studying her fucking gorgeous face and watching her sleep, that's what I'd decided to do. If we're only getting another week together, or even just a day, I was going to make every moment count.

Five minutes into watching her with Chloe, with the pancakes and Mary-Beth's sleepy smile and how she knew exactly what to say about that punkass-kid who's been plaguing Chloe for months, I already knew I was fucked. More than before. More than ever.

And as I buy them matching Minnie Mouse ears and the three of us matching T-shirts from the shop at the entrance of the park, I feel the ultimate shift. My chest tightens. My gut throbs. My heart inverts. A realization my life will never go back to the way it was settles deep inside me.

Uncharted territory is putting it mildly. This is a part of the map that previously had a giant red *stay the fuck away* written all over it.

I want a future with Mary-Beth. I've never even considered a future with anyone, but I *want* one with her. And now I'm scared shitless that if I open up to her completely about my past and who I really am, she'll run for the fucking hills.

"Chloe, I've never been to Disneyland before. Will you show me where to go?" Mary-Beth asks, taking the small girl's hand.

"Oh, yes." Chloe positively beams up at her. "Me and Uncle Drew come all the time. I know exactly where to go."

Chloe tugs Mary-Beth past the Mickey Mouse-shaped-flowers toward Main Street. I adjust my backward Mickey Mouse hat, staring at Mary-Beth's ass in her cutoff jeans as she saunters away with the little girl I love more than anything in the world.

I hurry to catch up.

We round the corner, and the castle materializes. Chloe raises her hand to present the view.

"This" –Chloe pauses for dramatic effect– "is Sleeping Beauty's Castle."

Mary-Beth puts her hands on her cheeks and makes her eyes wide. "Wow, this is magical! It's so big!"

My cock twitches. I could listen to Mary-Beth saying *it's so big* on a loop for hours.

Pleased with her guiding skills so far, Chloe skips off in a rainbow blur.

Mary-Beth presses her lips to my ear, and my skin turns hot. "Honestly, I thought it would be bigger."

And...there goes that fantasy.

I roll my eyes and sling my arm across her shoulders as we chase after Chloe. "Lord, you are the type."

"To never be satisfied?" she guesses.

"No, smartass." I tickle her side, and she blushes and bucks in my arms. I get hard again. "To seductively whisper the one thing no guy ever wants to hear."

Mary-Beth laughs so abruptly, she practically snorts.

"Also, you just lied to a child," I tisk. "Not very kindergarten-teacher of you, Ms. Abernathy."

"What? It *is* magical. Just a little...small."

"I thought you would love Disneyland. You're totally the Disney type."

"And you're the type to worry I'm not enjoying something that I'm thoroughly enjoying." She raises her eyebrows, and my mind instantly goes to the night in her apartment. Now I have a full-scale hard on. I adjust, shifting my weight from one leg to the other.

"Seriously, Drew, this is really great. Best brothel ever." Mary-Beth laughs. The blood rushes from my groin to my heart. "Thank you."

The rest of the day passes, for lack of a better analogy, like a Hallmark

CHAPTER 35

movie montage. A blur of churros and rides and stolen kisses and sarcastic conversation. Cotton candy and balloons and princesses and seductive glances.

Chloe is too short for the best rides, so we hit all the standard kiddie favorites. Mary-Beth gets spit on by an animatronic elephant on Jungle Cruise. She and Chloe kick my ass on the Buzz Lightyear ride. Chloe names her horse Mary-Beth on the carousel. Mary-Beth names hers Chloe. I happily name mine Third Wheel.

On It's a Small World, I convince Chloe to ride in the front row alone so she could "have the best view." But nothing could beat my view while I made out with Mary-Beth in the back. I hum the song and keep my hand in the back pocket of her shorts the rest of the afternoon.

On the scarier rides, Mary-Beth offers to let Chloe hold her hand. "And you can put your head in my lap and close your eyes if you get scared."

"Can *I* put my head in your lap if I get scared?" I mumble under my breath. I didn't really mean for Mary-Beth to hear me, and even though she doesn't say anything, I know she does when her blush spreads past her collarbone.

For the first time, Chloe doesn't cry on Alice in Wonderland when the Queen of Hearts pops out, or on Pirates of the Caribbean after the first drop, or when we go into the whale's mouth on the Storybook boats. For the first time ever, I convince her to ride the Haunted Mansion. Eventually, she even opens her eyes and lets the circulation return to Mary-Beth's hand.

We ride Dumbo just after sunset. Mary-Beth's blowing hair and rosy cheeks in the evening Disneyland lights is goddamn magical. Chloe and Mary-Beth's laughter ringing through the air makes my eyes water. I'm not sure why it makes me emotional—actually, yes, I do.

Maybe I don't need to be afraid of commitments and relationships and attachment. Maybe not if it's with Mary-Beth.

After Dumbo is the teacups. Chloe finishes her third cotton candy of the day in line. She picks the pink cup with hearts as our chariot.

The ride starts out all right. The annoying teapot song plays above us, drifting in between the strings of lights.

"Uncle Drew likes to spin fast!" Chloe says, grabbing the frisbee-shaped spinner in the center. "Mary-Beth, help us!"

Together, the three of us spin the teacup. Slow at first, but accelerating. Still, Chloe is not appeased.

"Come on! I could fall asleep on this ride." The little girl pretends to sleep, her shoulders jerking back and forth violently. Mary-Beth and I spin the center wheel faster.

"This is the slowest you've ever done it, Uncle Drew. Faster, faster!" Chloe's little hands work double time trying to turn the wheel.

Mary-Beth and I oblige as best we can. The teacup catapults past spinning and practically corkscrews right off the ride floor. Mary-Beth and I let go of the wheel and trade concerned looks.

All at once, Chloe's little face turns from pink to white to gray. Even her lips lose color. And then she slumps back in her seat and goes limp.

Chapter 36

Mary-Beth Caroline Abernathy
In Love
(I think?)

I realize what's going to happen about thirty seconds before it does. Poor little Chloe's face drains of color, and her body looks like a wet sock in the dryer. She barely has time to turn her head before she vomits. Chunky and pink and smelling like cotton candy and rancid pancakes. All over my legs.

"Oh shit!" Drew grinds the teacup to as much of a halt as possible, though we're still spinning a little. Unfortunately for us, the change from whirling to swaying makes Chloe throw up again. I slide across the bench to her side, holding her hair and rubbing her back. Drew's shoes are the next victims.

"Oh, sweetie. You poor thing. It's okay." I reach into my purse for a napkin, dabbing it on Chloe's chin. "The ride's almost over. I'm so sorry."

The girl lets out a retch of a scream and finally begins to cry.

"I don't like spinning anymore," she says between sobs.

"Me neither," Drew and I say in unison.

Finally, the ride comes to a stop. I take Chloe in my arms and carry her to the nearest bench, where she throws up again.

Drew looks at me in a panic, appearing slightly gray himself. "What do we do?"

"Poor thing just has motion sickness. The two churros and three cotton candies probably didn't help. She'll be okay in a few minutes."

"I just wanna go home," Chloe cries, and Drew winces. Every tear she sheds seems like daggers to his heart. Lord, seeing him wounded over a sick little girl might be his sexiest look yet.

He swallows, giving his puke-covered feet a once over. "Should I carry her to the car?"

"Why don't you go rent a stroller, and we can wheel her out of here. If you try to carry her, it might just aggravate the motion sickness."

That happened to Mrs. Highwater last year. When the kid inevitably puked all over her, she accidentally dropped him on top of another kid. Who then began puking.

"Stroller, got it." Drew looks relieved to have a job that involves getting the heck away from us.

After he's gone, an empathetic cast member comes by with paper towels, a clean T-shirt, hand sanitizer, and two bottles of water. Together, we're able to get the poor little thing cleaned up, and by the time Drew returns, Chloe is dead asleep on the bench, her head in my lap.

"Oh, thank God." He collapses next to me. "I'm glad she's resting."

We transfer Chloe to the stroller, and I help him get cleaned up. Five minutes later, we're strolling toward the castle like nothing happened.

"So, I take it you've dealt with puking kids before? You seemed to know exactly what to do." Drew pushes the stroller with one hand and takes mine in the other. His warmth travels through my fingertips, up my arm, and straight into my chest. It's a feeling that hasn't gotten old all day.

"Comes with being a teacher." I shrug. "Kids are notoriously disgusting."

Drew shudders like he's already reliving the teacups episode. "You've been yacked on before?"

"Just like...a couple times." I giggle and look down at Chloe, dead asleep.

Something about my laughter seems to reset Drew. He laughs too. "God, Mary-Beth you are the type."

"The vomit-inducing type?"

"The type to know you're going to get thrown up on and still want to do it."

"I just love kids. I couldn't see myself doing anything else."

"So..." Drew's eyebrows raise. "I take it you want your own kids, then? Probably a whole basketball team. Or a breakdancing crew?"

I can't tell if Drew is saying it like that because he doesn't want kids or does.

My eyes fall. "I would love to have kids of my own. But I don't know if I ever will."

"Why not?"

"It was really hard for my mom to get pregnant. Even harder for her to keep the baby. She had something like ten miscarriages. She has endometriosis, and so do I. So I don't know if I'll be able to have kids or not."

Drew squeezes my hand. "Shit, Mary. That really sucks. I'm so sorry."

I quirk up a shoulder and offer him a tiny smile. "It's all right. I've known for a long time I might not have kids. If it happens someday, I'd be so happy. But if not, I'm at peace with it."

"Your students are so damn lucky to have you."

"What about you, Drew?" I glance at him through my eyelashes. "Do you want kids?" I push. Hopefully not too hard.

Drew's jaw tightens. "I think I'm more of the fun-uncle type. I'm definitely not the dad type."

My bottom lip juts out, just a smidge. "I don't know..." Imagining all the what ifs I want with Drew turns my voice whimsy. "If today is any indication, I think you'd be amazing."

He smiles down at me, then Chloe. "I mean, I guess having a daughter wouldn't be the worst."

"It's having a girlfriend that's the worst," I tease. But also, kinda don't tease.

"Now you're seeing things my way." Drew slaps my butt, and I squeal and jump away.

He laughs, but then takes my hand and reels me back in. Putting his arm around me, he nuzzles his face into my hair. "Although, I'm starting to think that's not the worst either."

The space right below my chest aches. I've never wanted to be Drew's more. I want to be his so badly, it's painful.

Today will easily go down as one of the best days of my life. Disneyland with Drew Coyne and a super cute little five-year-old girl? I couldn't write a better day if I tried. And trust me, I've tried.

It's in the way he treated me—different than any other day. For the first time, he's treated me like his girlfriend. Not his pretend girlfriend. Not some rando lady he's trying to coerce into a business deal. Not even someone he wants to hook up with.

His girlfriend. With matching shirts and stolen kisses and Disney magic and vomit and all the other strings attached.

My heart aches with the memory of today even though it's not technically over yet. I know that I'll be looking back at today years from now. Remembering my one perfect day as Drew Coyne's.

"So...is this how you seduce all the ladies?" We meander toward a ride shaped like a snowy mountain, lit up in the night sky. "Bring them to Disneyland with Chloe?"

"I've never introduced anyone to Chloe." Something about his voice is both hard and soft at the same time. A bobsled rushes past where

CHAPTER 36

we are standing and the people inside scream. We turn toward the carousel.

"I mean, it makes sense that you would save the vomit for me." I bump my shoulder against Drew. "Just like the smoothie, right?"

I laugh. Drew does not.

"I've never brought anyone to Disneyland either."

"So I—"

Drew cuts me off again. "I haven't been on a date at all in, like, five years, Mary-Beth."

My face probably looks like someone just punched it. "But—"

"I've been with a lot of women, Mary-Beth. But as you know, I never get to know any of them. It's never been like this."

"So how do you meet them? If you don't date?" Sometimes I forget how completely different our two worlds are.

"Through work or work events, mostly." Drew shrugs and darts around a family with a bubble machine. "Sometimes online. If someone slides into my DMs or something like that. Or, occasionally, I go to a club with Will or people from work. Sometimes I meet people that way."

My mind goes back to when Drew told me women only want him for one thing. Anger erupts inside me and I swipe at the bubbles blowing toward me.

"Well, those women suck." My words are louder than I was expecting. "They're idiots for not getting to know you."

Drew's face lights up. He stops and turns so we're facing each other, then brings his hands to the pockets of my shorts and squeezes. My heart is pounding so hard, I can feel it behind my eyeballs.

"Is that so, Virgin Mary?"

"Yes," I say defensively. "Because you're...you're great."

Drew's eyebrows rise like he's waiting for me to add something. "What?"

"Just waiting for the caveat."

"What caveat?"

"The caveat as to why I'm not actually great. Or why you don't like me. Or how I'm some sort of *type*."

"No notes." I laugh and meet Drew's eyes. They twinkle with the overhead Disney lights. "I just...like you. I thought that was pretty obvious."

The side of his mouth twitches, like he's suppressing a smile.

"What now?"

"It just sounds nice. That's all. To hear that you like me. Not Hallmark Drew. Just me."

"Let me guess, you've got the book papers stuffed in your back pocket for just the occasion."

Drew's eyes harden. His voice drops at least an octave. "Me and you has nothing to do with the book. Not anymore."

Music and fireworks burst from the front of the park, and Chloe stirs but doesn't wake. We steer her away from the quickly building crowd, finding our own little sanctuary next to It's a Small World while we wait for the crowds to disperse.

The fireworks reflect in Drew's eyes as he grabs my belt loops and pulls my hips to his.

"I like you too," he says, bringing a hand to my jaw and tilting it upward. "Not Minnie Maple. Not Virgin Mary. Not Ms. Abernathy. Just...Mary-Beth. My Mary."

His mouth lowers to mine, and I swear my knees actually buckle, and my heart actually drops. I've written dozens of kissing scenes and read hundreds more, but there aren't words to describe this kiss. It's long and deep and leaves me with swollen lips, deflated lungs, and misty eyes.

The fireworks finally end, and I pull away, afraid that if he looks into my eyes, he'll know I'm a liar.

CHAPTER 36

Because I don't just like Drew. After today, I'm pretty sure I love him.

Chapter 37

Mary-Beth Caroline Abernathy
Flavor of the Week

I wake up around eleven the next morning. Drew is gone.

When we'd finally made it back from Disneyland and dropped Chloe off at Will's house, it was after two in the morning, and I was dead on my feet. Jet lagged, smelly, exhausted. Drew let me shower first, and I was asleep by the time he was finished.

There's a note on the pillow next to me. I get shivers at his intimate thoughtfulness.

MB-

I have a business meeting with Darcy this morning. I'll be home around five. Gonna write another book about me? If not, feel free to buy a new plant or lamp at your discretion. The photogs camped outside will love it.

And so will I.

-D

Five hours alone in Drew Coyne's apartment. I don't know whether to laugh or cry. Or run around naked. That's what I'm leaning toward.

I clutch the paper to my chest, then smell it like a creep.

In the night, Drew had held me. In my half-awake, half-asleep subconscious, I don't even think I realized it was happening at the time. It felt so natural, so right. But now that I'm awake and alone, I

CHAPTER 37

miss his warmth. His long body pressed behind mine. His heavy arm wrapped around me.

It's the first time I've ever slept in someone else's arms, and it was heavenly. It wasn't sexual by any stretch of the imagination, but I felt safe. And wanted in a deeper way. A so *not* Drew Coyne way.

I go to the kitchen to scrounge up something for breakfast. After the huge unicorn-themed feast yesterday, there isn't much left. I decide on a cup of coffee and a Kind Bar.

It feels weird to snoop around the apartment without Drew being here, but he knows I will. I figured he wouldn't leave me alone if he wasn't okay with it.

"I am the type," I say, raising my coffee in the air and taking a sip.

After digging through all the fancy gadgets in the drawers of Drew's kitchen, adding two bottles of his shampoo (Paul Mitchell Tea Tree Lavender Mint Moisturizing Shampoo) and body wash (Wild Pine Shower Gel by The Body Shop) to my Amazon cart, and staring out at the L.A. skyline for half an hour, I find myself strolling in front of his humongous bookshelf, running my fingers along the worn spines.

Drew must have a soft spot for the classics, because they constitute a large portion of his collection. *Wuthering Heights* and *The Sun Also Rises* and *The Great Gatsby*. *Animal Farm* and *The Adventures of Huckleberry Finn* and *Moby Dick*. *Brave New World* and *The Invisible Man* and *All the King's Men*.

I really think he was screwing with me back in Daisy Bluff. Chick lit? Really?

Most of the books seem well worn, like they've been read at least twice. Some have dog ears, - the humanity! – some have broken binding, and others have sticky tabs. Against my better judgment, I pick up book one of *Swallow Manor*.

Oh, I studied them, Mary-Beth. I read them over and over again. I memorized them.

Let's see about that.

The cover and the first three pages are curled at the bottom right corner. The long-haired fella and his lady that had the unfortunate fate of starring on the cover are cracked from wear, the paper underneath the matte-coating peeking through. The name, Minnie Maple, at the top is smeared and fading, like Drew ran his fingers across the letters dozens of times.

There are no dog ears or sticky notes, but the pages are far from crisp. Wrinkled and smooth around the edges. Drew wasn't gentle with my book. It looks more like he was hungry and tried to devour it. Then came back later for more.

Inside there are no notes in the margin or underlined passages, but I swear, at the end...there appear to be tear stains. At least I'm hoping that's what it is, and not...another bodily fluid.

More than anything, the book looks loved. And honestly, I couldn't ask for anything more.

I set it down, my own tears threatening. My reaction startles me, and I jolt up, bumping the bookshelf above me. Something spills from a shelf above my head, raining down on me like a twisted version of Flashdance, but instead of water, it's the evidence of my fake boyfriend's past escapades.

The earrings land in a pile by my feet, the metal bowl rolling toward the door.

I slump to my knees to gather them. I don't know if I was expecting more or hoping for less, but there are seventeen earrings total. A few are simple studs, but not many. Most are outrageously showy—long dangly glittering monstrosities that look terribly uncomfortable and terribly cheap. One is made of feathers. Two are made of wood. One pair are bejeweled flamingos with long crystal legs that would hang almost to my shoulders. There is no event I would ever be tempted to wear something like that to.

CHAPTER 37

As I drop them into the bowl one by one, I try to visualize the women they belong to. Gorgeous, tall, experienced, confident women with perfect six-pack abs and giant fake boobs. Women the complete opposite of me. Models. Influencers. Actresses. Sex goddesses. Probably at least one stripper. I'm sure I'd recognize at least one of their names—especially if Drew starred opposite them in one of his movies.

Drew.

Jealousy takes hold of my stomach and twists. I hate to imagine sharing him with someone, let alone seventeen different someones. At least. The real number is probably ten times that.

But am I really sharing him? These women have had all of him, and I've had none. I've been here two nights, and the first night he tucked me into bed and the second we washed cotton-candy-flavored vomit off our feet. If that doesn't scream "friend-zone," I don't know what does.

It's not fair to be jealous of something you'll never have.

Right on cue, there's a knock at the door.

I scramble to clean up the rest of my mess and go hide under the covers of Drew's bed.

"Drew, open up! It's Britta!"

Britta.

This is the worst kind of déjà vu.

"Drew, I can hear you. I know you're home. Open up."

I stay as still as I can, praying she'll go away.

Five minutes later...she's still knocking. Girlfriend is persistent.

"Drew, we need to talk. Open up."

Eventually, I just can't take the banging anymore. In all senses of the word.

The first thing I think when I swing open the door is Drew and Britta would make beautiful babies. She is the most striking woman I've ever seen in person. If an angel were also a stripper and also had RBF, her name would be Britta.

This is the kind of woman you'd picture Drew Coyne with. She has flamingo-earring energy.

Even though she's wearing flip flops, she towers over me—barefoot and still in my sweatpants. The ones with the hole. Her body is long and lean and looks *Sports-Illustrated-Swimsuit-Edition*-good in her shorts and tank top. Her extension-upgraded golden hair cascades perfectly over her shoulders, coalescing into the perfect curl resting in the cleavage of her perfectly sculpted boobs. Her eyes are a bright blue, almost too bright, like they're somehow enhanced. Her eyelashes are definitely fake but the expensive kind that look real.

Honestly, if I were to go for a woman, it would be Britta. Ten out of ten, no notes.

"So...you must be the flavor of the week." Britta's eyes rake up and down. "Not his usual choice, but—" She finishes her sentence with a flip of her hair and a scowl. "Where's Drew?"

"Out."

Britta shoves past me though I didn't invite her in, and my anxiety kicks into high gear. I trail behind her, not knowing what else to do.

"What do you want?" I cross my arms. "I can give him a message for you."

"Oh, honey, like you'll still be here when he gets back." Britta laughs, heading for the kitchen. "I'm sure he read you the riot act and told you to lock up on your way out."

"Actually—"

"Any idea where I could find a pen? I'm just gonna leave him a note." She rummages in a drawer, closes it, and opens another.

"I'll give him the message." I summon all the boldness I can rally. "I'm his girlfriend."

Britta stops mid-search and looks up. "Aw, girl. It's all right." Her eyes crinkle, and her lips pout. It makes her look like a fish. A sexy fish, but it makes me feel marginally better. "Drew's an amazing fuck, I know. I get it. But you don't need to pretend with me. I already know he doesn't do relationships. We all know."

"But—"

"Drew doesn't do relationships," Britta says again, more defensive. "And honestly, if he did"— she steps back, motioning to herself, then motioning to me— "I think his choice would be pretty obvious."

"I think you should leave."

"As soon as I leave him a note."

"No. Now."

"Watch it, bitch." She takes a menacing step in my direction. But then...she stops, her eyes narrowing. "You know...you look familiar."

I lean on the counter, trying to hide my shaking knees. I wish there was a way to hide the quiver in my voice too. "We've never met," I try. "I'm from out of town."

It's true. The day she was here, I'm positive she didn't see me. Drew made sure of that.

"Okay, but still..." She stares at me like she's dissecting a frog and trying to locate the different organs. I can pinpoint the exact moment she finds the heart. "Oh my God, you're the author!" She exhales, looking grateful to have an explanation as to why I would be here instead of her. "You're the author Drew's been looking for."

I get a full body chill, like someone just cut a hole into a frozen lake and dunked me under. Before I speak, I pull my shoulders back and lift my chin, calling upon my inner Ariana Grande. I've only got one shot to convince Britta, so I better make it count.

"God, why does everyone keep saying that?" I laugh and roll my eyes. "Like I would know the first thing about writing a book. Drew and I have been dating for weeks. We met while I was here on vacation. He spent the last week in my hometown, for Christ's sake."

Britta's eyes narrow, not seeming to buy my story for even a second. "Drew doesn't do relationships," she says for a third time. I can't tell if she's trying to convince me or herself. Probably both.

I shrug and force my voice to be casual. "I guess not with you."

Wrong. Answer.

"Bitch," Britta tightens her jaw into a menacing scowl. "I don't know who the fuck you think you are, but you sure as hell aren't Drew Coyne's girlfriend."

She ditches her quest for a pen and starts walking toward me. If this comes down to a physical fight, I stand zero percent chance of winning. She's got at least eight inches and thirty pounds on me. Not to mention her razor-sharp bright pink manicure.

I widen my stance and loosen my locked knees, preparing for the blow, but it's her perfume that hits me first. It's so strong, it seems to suck all the oxygen from the room, almost more effective than an actual punch. I take a half-step back, trying not to gag on the artificial vanilla stench. She's practically on top of me when she speaks again.

"You know that thing Drew does right before he's about to climax?" She laughs to herself, tossing a golden curl over her shoulder. "No, I guess you wouldn't, would you?" I swallow. It tastes like fake vanilla. "Because Drew Coyne doesn't fuck around with girls like you." She pats my shoulder. "Which means there's only one explanation. Don't worry, Minnie Maple. Your secret is safe with me."

And just like that...she's gone.

I crumble into the nearest chair, taking big gulps of air to reoxygenate my body. It takes a few minutes before my heart rate returns to normal and the blackness around my vision dissipates.

You know that thing Drew does right before he's about to climax? No, you wouldn't.

But she would. It's killing me that she knows something about Drew that I don't. Probably a lot of somethings. And I feel like if I don't find

CHAPTER 37

those things out soon, I might lose him forever.

I pull out my phone.

Mary-Beth: Are you in LA yet?

Harper: MB!! I was just about to text you. I'm here!

My body physically relaxes. Thank God.

Harper: Wanna grab a late lunch?

Mary-Beth: I'm at Drew's. Can we have lunch here?

Harper: Is everything okay?

Mary-Beth: I'm okay. Just a million things we need to talk about.

Harper: I'll be there are soon as I can. Any requests for lunch?

Mary-Beth: I've been told I need to try In-N-Out again. Something about animal style? How does that sound?

Harper: In-N-Out animal style. Sounds kinky.

Mary-Beth: I am rolling my eyes right now...

Harper: Alright, I'm on my way, but it might take a while. This traffic is the worst, right??

Mary-Beth: I don't think we're in Daisy Bluff anymore, Harp.

🌼🌼🌼

Kneeling on Drew's carpet and using his coffee table for a dining room, I finally tell Harper everything. From our fight at the Persimmon Festival to Drew's psycho book stacks at the library to the night at my apartment to church with my mom to the airport to Disneyland to Britta.

"Wow, what a bitch!" Harper says, stuffing in a handful of fries. Well done, salt on the side.

"The most beautiful, most terrifying bitch I've ever seen," I say.

"Don't worry, MB." Harper pats my hand sympathetically. "She's not gonna do anything to you. What could she do? Drew is obviously in love with you. She's got nothing."

"Ha!" I laugh so abruptly I start choking on my milkshake. *Still not as good as Shake Shack.* "Drew is not in love with me. When we're alone, he won't touch me with a ten-foot pole. You heard the part about how he *tucked me in*, right?"

"The man is probably scared shitless. You're a virgin who has made it very clear she is not interested in having casual sex, which I'm guessing is the only kind of sex Drew Coyne has ever had."

"But I've made it pretty obvious I would—"

Harper cuts me off by dropping her cheeseburger into her lap.

"Shit, you would?" Her mouth hangs open.

"I'm assuming that's what Drew is expecting. And I'm pretty sure I love the man, Harp. It seems like the next step."

"Hold up—so you're not waiting anymore?"

I flop back dramatically on Drew's carpet, and fries fly everywhere. "I don't know, Harp. I feel like everything I've ever been taught has been a lie or at least some sort of weird cover-up. Nana was pregnant when she got married. She said everyone fools around before they get married. And Mama is already convinced Drew and I are sleeping together. I feel like at this point...why the hell not?"

Also, if I don't, I might lose Drew to women like Britta forever.

"Ho-lee. Shit." Harper's eyes grow so wide, it looks like they might turn inside out and swallow her face whole.

"Not that it matters." I sigh and grab a french fry from my hair. "Pretty sure I'm in the friend zone. I'll just live out the Drew Coyne girlfriend fantasy a few more days, sign the book away, and be done with it. He can go back to banging girls like Britta and whoever they find to play Susan."

"And you're okay with that? With letting the first man you've ever loved, ever wanted to be with, just slip away?"

"Well, obviously my heart is gonna get broken."

"Then fucking fight for the man!" Harper pounds her fist on the coffee table, and her milkshake topples over. "I'm sorry for my language. But shit, Mary-Beth. Come on!"

"You already said I'm basically poison because I'm a virgin." I come onto my knees. "Drew seems less and less like he wants to be the one to do something about that."

"We could always find you a male prostitute."

The look I give Harper could melt steel.

"Or not," she mumbles, righting her milkshake.

"What about you?" I very much need to change the subject. "You've been very MIA lately. Who's the guy?"

Harper rolls her eyes like I just asked about the new foot fungus growing under her big toenail. "He's coming to my birthday party, so you'll see him there. But he's got...a lot of issues. He's a hard nut to crack."

I'm just about to pry for more details when Harper swerves the conversation back to me. It's like we're both gripping the wheel and trying to muscle the car in our direction.

"Speaking of hard nuts to crack, are you sure you're ready for this, MB? Do you think Drew will do it?"

"Harp, it's like"— I stuff in the rest of my fries. "It's like the closer we get, the more I want him. *Sexually*. But the more I want him like that, it's like the *less* he wants *me*."

"Again, I think he's just scared." Harper pats my hand. "But the man has eyes, MB. You just need to remind him what he's missing out on. Show him you're ready."

I swallow down a lump that's been building, along with the fries. "What do you mean?"

"I mean...let's go buy you some sexy-ass lingerie, get you all dolled up, and when he gets home, you can be draped all over his big-ass kitchen island looking fine as hell. We'll go all Ariana on his ass. Drew can only have so much willpower."

"You think so?"

"Hell yes! If this is really what you want, then let's do it." Harper pauses, her eyes shrinking to little slits. "This is what *you* want, right?"

Chapter 38

Andrew Edward Coyne
Free

It was torture untangling from Mary-Beth this morning, and I cursed myself from six days ago for setting up this meeting. Time is limited. I don't want to waste it. But at least I'm not coming home empty-handed. Or, actually, maybe I am.

I'd completely cut ties with every single one of my social media advertising partners. The hammocks, the granola bars, the smoothies, the skincare, the boots. All of it. In one fell swoop. Gone.

I thought signing away those dollar signs would give me some sort of remorse, but instead I feel a huge sense of relief. I won't miss the partnerships and their handcuffs at all.

I'm free.

"You do realize you're ending the one steady form of income you have, right?" Darcy had asked, looking very surprised and very skeptical when I'd given her the news. "Your followers have come to depend on your advice."

"Combined with the loss of your Hallmark movie roles, this is a very risky time to be doing this," Will chimed in. He'd liked the idea less than Darcy. "I know you're assuming the *Swallow Manor* rights will—"

I cut Will off before he can make this about Mary-Beth's book. It's not about the book. Nothing is anymore. "I'm done promoting products that are complete shit and that I don't use. In the future, I want to test products before agreeing to endorse them. I want stricter guidelines and more flexibility to end things. If people really do give a shit about what I promote"— I had a feeling that list began and ended with a five-foot smartass from southern Indiana— "then I should promote things I believe in. Things I believe will help people."

Will and Darcy traded a look.

"Does this have something to do with Mary-Beth?" Will asked.

"Of course it does." *Fuck, everything has to do with Mary-Beth these days.* "She helped me see how wrong endorsing products I hate is." I shrugged, like there was only one logical thing to do next. "So, I want out."

I can't wait to get back to my apartment and tell Mary-Beth the news. I want to score another point in the fuck-all-your-assumptions game. I even grab a bouquet of tulips to mark the occasion.

The sun is low in the sky when I open the door to my apartment, casting the kitchen and living room in a golden haze.

Actually, the golden is from the sunset, the haze is from something else.

The smoke detector starts beeping the second I'm inside.

"Aw, shit!" Mary-Beth's voice peels over a cacophony of banging pots and pans. "Shit, shit, shit! Damn it!"

"Mary..." I walk hesitantly toward the burning smell coming from the oven. "Is everything okay?"

Mary-Beth's head pops up from behind the island. She's holding something smoking in gloved hands...and isn't wearing much else. My mouth goes cotton-dry. I drop the flowers.

"Drew!" She jumps so high I'm surprised she doesn't drop whatever it is she's holding. I'm even more surprised it isn't burning her. *She's*

CHAPTER 38

basically naked. "When did you get home?"

"Like, thirty seconds ago?" I lick my lips and rush over to help her. "Someone has a dirty mouth when they're alone."

Her lips turn down in a full-out frown. "I wanted to have everything ready when you got home. I tried to cook dinner, but..." She shakes her head, finally dropping the smoking failure into the sink. "I couldn't figure out how to work anything in your fancy kitchen. What even is an induction stovetop or a convection oven anyway?"

Mary-Beth is wearing a light green bra so sheer, I can see her nipples through the fabric. Pink, round, hard, perfect. The exact size for my mouth. Her thong matches, showing me her entire ass. God, it's amazing. Smooth and round and bubbly. The exact size for my hands. Her body was made for me. This is indisputable proof.

Her hair is curled and hair-sprayed in place, and she's got more makeup on than I've ever seen her wear. Perfume. The heels. Green. She's like my own personalized cocktail, a mixture I can't refuse. Like a fucking tease in the best way.

I'm instantly hard. But I try to have some semblance of restraint. As in, I don't immediately bend her over the counter.

"What's all this?" I ask with a laugh.

She tugs off the oven mitts, letting them fall to the floor. She motions to the sink and bites her lower lip. The tiny flick of her mouth does away with my shitty attempt at self-control.

"I'm sorry—"

Mary-Beth barely gets the words out before I snatch her around the waist, grab her ass with both hands, and bring my mouth to hers. She moans and melts against me, winding her hands up to my neck. I plunge one hand into her hair, deepening the kiss.

I want to fuck her right here in the kitchen, with smoke in the air and sirens blaring.

I lift Mary-Beth onto the island, and she wraps her legs around me.

I run my fingers down the front of her, watching her nipples as they perk. Her eyes as they widen. Her mouth as she sucks in a breath. I kiss her collarbone, and her head falls back, giving me more access.

Every curse word I've ever spoken floods my mind.

"Of all the things I thought I'd come home to," I say between kisses. My lips can't seem to leave her skin. I want to worship it. Lick it for hours. Suck on every inch. Her neck. Between her breasts. Her shoulder. Her ribs. Other places she would probably object to. "I never thought I'd find this. Fantasized, yes. But—"

Mary-Beth cuts me off, pulling me in for another kiss. I laugh and grip her around the ribs. She pulls me closer, locking her ankles around my thighs. Our mouths part. We breathe. Her eyes look so green in this light, the brown is almost gone. Neon. Explosive. I nudge her lips with mine.

"I wanted to surprise you." Her gaze goes to the burned dinner in the sink. "I'm sorry about dinner."

I take her face and turn it to meet mine. Our eyes connect. The space below my chest twists.

"Forget dinner." I press my lips to hers again, slipping my tongue inside, sucking on her bottom lip. She answers, wrapping her arms around my waist and pulling me flush against her hips, deepening every connection.

As more control is lost, I reach down and squeeze her left breast harder than I ever have, kneading her with my palm. Her back arches. Her fingers dig into my shoulder.

"Do you like that?" I feel like I'm high.

"Yes." Mary-Beth looks at me with fuck-me eyes. I grab her other tit too, going under the fabric. Her nipples slide in between my fingers with pert perfection. In her hooded eyes, I see how much she's enjoying it. Probably almost as much as me.

But then, she pulls back, taking an unsteady breath. My hands drop.

CHAPTER 38

"I want you," Mary-Beth whispers. Her voice is shaking. "All of you, Drew."

I blink and take a step back, unsure if I heard her over the fire alarm. "What?"

Mary-Beth hops off the counter. She stands right in front of me, looking up with those electric eyes. Her knees are unsteady. She's barely breathing.

"I'm ready to go all the way."

The smoke detector finally goes quiet, bringing me back to reality. Something isn't right. This isn't the Mary-Beth I know. The Mary-Beth I care about. Mary-Beth doesn't strut around in see-through lingerie. She doesn't throw herself at anyone. Not even me.

What happened while I was gone?

"Is everything all right, Mary-Beth?"

The hurt in her eyes is immediate. I fucking hate it.

"Yes." Her mouth pinches, a telltale sign she's lying.

"Let's slow down a little." I hate the words, even as I'm saying them. Slowing down is the last fucking thing my body wants right now.

"Why?" She reaches up, placing a hand on my cheek. Emotion floods her eyes. "Don't you want me? Isn't this what *you* want?"

And there it is. She's doing this because she knows I want to. That hollow part of my chest sputters again.

I motion to the three-ring circus going on below my waist. "I think it's pretty freaking obvious I want you, Mary."

I pull her into a hug and kiss the top of her head. She feels limp in my arms.

"But this isn't you. And as much as I goddamn want to, I'm not going to take advantage of you like this. I care about you too much to do that to you."

"What do you mean, this isn't me?" Her eyes harden, and she puts her hands on her hips. "Maybe this is me now."

Smartass. Such a stubborn smartass.

I shake my head. "No. I know you well enough to know this isn't you. You don't get sweaty and gross for nothing, remember?"

"But I will. If this is what you want, I will..."

"Mary, maybe you think this is what I want, but really, I just want you." I carefully move a stray piece of hair from her eyes. "Virgin Mary-Beth Abernathy. Exactly as you are. The real you. The you that doesn't need to change a damn thing."

Her shoulders relax as she lets out a long, slow breath. I guide her head to rest against my chest, wrapping my arms around her waist.

"Who *is* the real me?" she asks, almost to herself.

And that's a question I just have to answer. I pull away and meet her eyes.

"Mary, the real you is a freaking pain. But that's what I like about you. Because you don't make anything easy. And the best things aren't. The real you bites on her bottom lip when she's really into what she's writing. The real you can eat more than a sumo wrestler. The real you has sweatpants with a hole in the thigh and a creepy dog pillow on her couch. The real you wears pantyhose to church and cutoffs to Disneyland, and your ass looks incredible in both. Mary, you're a damn good teacher and an amazing friend and a brilliant writer and a ticklish smartass. You're forgiving. And funny as hell, Mary. Sarcastic. Witty. You're a challenge. And I freaking love to be challenged."

Mary-Beth tilts her head up to mine and smiles. I kiss her softly.

"And what about when I *am* ready?" Her words are barely a whisper against my lips. "Will you be the one?"

My insides feel like they just fell five stories down, leaving my shell of a body up here. Two days ago, I told Will I was going to try and wait. Maybe forever.

"When you're ready." I grab Mary-Beth's face with both hands, forcing her to look at me. "Really ready. When it's what *you* really

CHAPTER 38

want." She blushes. I swallow. "I would kill the bastard if it wasn't me. When it's right, you better believe it's gonna be me. On every fucking wall and door and bed in the room."

I release Mary-Beth's face, and she looks away, like she's trying to catch her breath.

"So..." She looks down at her skin awkwardly. "What do we do now?"

"Right now"—I trace along Mary-Beth's rib cage with my fingertips—"I want to take my girlfriend to dinner."

"Don't you mean *pretend* girlfriend?"

I shake my head. "Not pretend. Not anymore."

"But you don't do relationships."

I look straight into Mary-Beth's emerald-rimmed eyes.

"I do when it's with you."

Chapter 39

Mary-Beth Caroline Abernathy
Andrew Edward Coyne's ~~Pretend~~ Girlfriend

The paparazzi are having a field day with us. They follow us from the parking garage of Drew's apartment to the front steps of the restaurant, and I can still see them out the window from our table.

Instead of hiding like I did at the airport, I look straight at them, holding my head high. I hope they take a million pictures of Drew and me together, and I hope Britta sees every single last one of them. I hope she sits on a bench with our faces plastered all over it. Or gets whacked in the head by a flying tabloid cover. Has to drive by a billboard of us on the way home from work every day. I hope she sees so much of us, she can't escape.

Because I *am* Drew's girlfriend. Not pretend girlfriend. Just... girlfriend.

I'm Drew Coyne's girlfriend.

Once again, my brilliant plan mostly backfired. I wanted to recreate our night in my apartment, plus lingerie, minus half the town knowing he was there. I hadn't counted on not being able to work a damn induction stovetop.

But at the end of the day...Drew was right —*as painful as that is to*

CHAPTER 39

admit. I'm not the type. And I'm not ready. At least not to go all the way. I wasn't trying to seduce him for the right reasons. When I'm having sex for the first time with the man I love, it shouldn't be because a tall hot blond woman beat me to it.

And...other than the glaringly obvious thing keeping us from doing the deed, there's something else, too. The thing keeping him from letting me in. The thing holding me back from trusting him completely.

"Drew, tell me about your family."

He sets down his wine, peering over the glass with slitted eyes. "What do you want to know?"

"Why don't you ever want to talk about them?"

"Because there's not much to say, honestly. Not anymore."

"What's your mom's name?"

"Shari."

"And your dad's?"

"Joe."

"Are they still together?"

Drew snorts and leans back in his chair. When he doesn't say anything, I try again. "How did they meet?"

Just then, breadsticks arrive, and the waiter asks for our orders. Beef risotto for him. Saffron shrimp gnocchi for me. Calamari and an antipasti platter to share.

"I love that you love to eat." Drew rips off a piece of breadstick and pops it into his mouth. "It's sexy, you know that?"

"Don't change the subject, Drew."

His eyes narrow. Now I can barely see the blue. "Why the third degree, Virgin Mary?"

"Because I like to know a little something about the people I'm dating. You know, besides fast-food restaurant of choice and favorite *Harry Potter* book."

"Honestly, those things are way more important to me than my family."

I sigh, realizing he's shutting down again. "Well...family is important to me." I raise my eyebrows and force my voice to be gentle. "Humor me?"

Drew takes a long pull of his drink, setting the glass down carefully. The look he gives me says, *You want to know about my family? Well, here you go.*

"My mom was the other woman," he finally says, shrugging. "Or maybe the other woman was the other woman. Hell if I know. When I was younger, I thought my parents were good together. To a kid, they seemed like they were. Yeah, we had problems. We moved around a lot. They fought about money and other stupid shit. But I guess they seemed happy, mostly. My dad was an electrician. My mom was a librarian. We had a pretty normal life. But when I was twelve, my parents were killed in a car accident. And that's when the shit hit the fan."

Drew looks away, the hurt in his eyes like shards of glass. "Turns out my dad had another family on the other side of town. My pale-ass blue-eyed dad had another Black wife. Two more brown-skinned, blue-eyed kids, just like me. He was a fucking liar. A cheater. And when he was gone, he took fucking everything from me. I had fucking no one, and his other shitty family refused to take me in. The other wife was the one on his life insurance policy, so their family was set. I guess having me around was just a reminder of the fuck-up that was my father."

My eyes water, and I look away, guilty to have pried. To force Drew to unearth such painful memories. My hands begin to shake, and I put them in my lap. Drew looks across the table, his ice-blue eyes drilling into me. He looks hauntingly beautiful.

"I'm sorry, Dre—" I start to apologize, but he cuts me off. Like matches and gasoline, now that he's talking, he can't seem to stop.

CHAPTER 39

"For three years I was in and out of a lot of shitty foster homes, a lot of shitty neighborhoods, a lot of shitty schools, until I was finally placed with Darcy's parents, George and Colette Covelle. He's a doctor, and she's a lawyer. If nothing else, they had a shit ton of money." Drew laughs, but it's a rough sound.

"Darcy's not your biological sister? I didn't realize..."

"Most people don't know, thank God. We look enough alike, I guess. She's Black, not mixed-race like I am, but...yeah."

He lets out a breath that sounds like a deflating balloon. "Anyway, that's how I ended up at the private school with Will. Looking back, the Covelles tried their best with me. They were actually fucking good parents and good people. But I was just"—Drew picks up his fork, grips it tightly, sets it back down, opening and closing his fists a few times—"really angry. I shut them out. I started shutting *everyone* out. That's when I got into acting. I craved the escape of being something I wasn't. It made it easier to forget."

His fingers nervously strum along the tablecloth as he shakes his head, then he looks up at me. "And this is why I didn't want to tell you, Mary. Why I don't tell anyone. Why I don't do relationships. I don't let anyone in. I've spent my entire adult life trying not to be my dad. If I don't have a relationship, I can't be a cheater. If I keep everyone away, I can't hurt them..."

Drew's mouth pinches and he clasps the tablecloth. "Mary, I see where you come from, and I see where I come from. And I'm *jealous*. I'm so freaking jealous of you, Mary-Beth. Since my parents died, I've wanted nothing more than to have my old life back. To have what you have. But, with help, I've learned to deal with that. To compartmentalize that part of life and move forward.

"But now, with you, I'm scared shitless. Because I want to be with you, Mary. I've never wanted anyone, but I fucking want you. Like I've never wanted anyone before. But you deserve the life you're used to. You deserve stability and love and a normal fucking person. And honestly, I don't know if I can give that to you. I want to. But I really don't know if I'm capable." Drew shakes his head and looks away. "It doesn't make sense that someone like you, with the perfect family and the perfect life and a healthy understanding of love and family could ever want to be with someone as fucked up as me, Mary. Someone who could never be the person you need me to be. Someone who is destined to fuck everything up."

Our appetizers arrive, but neither of us reaches for them. Instead, I take Drew's hand under the table. His eyes jump to mine, so breathtakingly blue and deep, I want to drown. We sit like that in silence for a few moments while I collect my thoughts.

"Drew, you don't have to be scared." I squeeze his hand, hoping he'll believe what I'm about to say. "I want to be with you because I like who you are. Not where you came from. Not your dad. You're nothing like that, Drew. *Nothing*. You never will be. No one has ever given me what you give me. For the first time, I feel accepted. Able to speak my mind. Be myself. I feel enough. As I am. Virgin. Uptight. Black heart. The whole thing. And I feel the same way about you. Just you, Drew. Not perfect Hallmark Drew. But the real you. The imperfect you. The you that doesn't have everything figured out.

"If you can overlook my super closed-minded family and my strict upbringing and values, and Daisy Bluff and all the crap that comes along with that, and see the real me, I can do the same for you. Where you come from. *Your* past."

"Who is the real me?" Drew runs his hand along the back of his neck. "I feel like I've been trying to answer that damn question since the day my parents died. Since I learned the truth about what I come from. I'm afraid that's my destiny too."

"The real you..." I pause, wanting to say the exact right thing. "Is passionate. And funny. And empathetic and accepting. You work hard for what you want. You're intelligent, but not in a pretentious way. You're a problem-solver. A dreamer. You keep your cards close to your chest. You don't let a lot of people in, but when you do, you're freaking loyal. And honest. You're someone the people you care about can trust.

"You're someone who steps in to help take care of his best friend's daughter when his world turns upside down. Someone who makes freaking unicorn pancakes. The real you takes care of people, Drew. Even when you're scared...you put on a brave face and do it anyway."

I've barely finished when he reaches for me across the table and urgently brings his mouth to mine.

"God, Mary-Beth." He strokes my cheeks gently. "You see me. No one has ever seen me like you see me."

"You control who you become, Drew. And I trust who you're becoming."

Drew kisses me, so deeply, so purely, my heart feels like it's floating above the table. I feel this kiss from the tips of my toes to the end of my hairs to the depth of my soul.

"Now I know why you like books so much," I say softly, braiding my fingers through his. "It's your mom."

Drew nods, and his eyes start to water.

"What was she like?"

"She definitely wouldn't let anyone eat in her library, that's for sure." Drew laughs, wiping away tears. "But she was amazing. She was everything to me. I think that's why I hate my dad so fucking much."

"Is it hard to remember your mom without remembering him?"

Drew nods again. "I've been trying for ten years, but it's hard to separate the anger."

"I'm sure."

"But yeah, she loved books. That's how I remember her, mostly.

When I'm lost in a story, it always reminds me of my mom." Drew looks at me, a smile hinting at the corner of his lips. "Her favorite *Harry Potter* was number three."

"She sounds like a smart lady."

"Yeah." Drew squeezes my hand. "She would have loved you, Mary-Beth."

🐥🐥🐥

The rest of dinner passes with lively debate. Arguments about who is better: LL Cool J or Run- D.M.C. Jordan Ones versus Jordan Fives. Which pasta shape tastes the best. The ideal temperature setting for a thermostat. The best show on Netflix. The acceptability of eating ice cream straight from the container or drinking milk from the carton. Sunrises or sunsets. We even revisit the peanut butter and jelly argument for, like, ten minutes.

Conversation with Drew is like an extreme sport. Like MMA fighting or paragliding. Filled with head-to-head combat and stomach-dropping adrenaline rushes. We disagree about every single thing we talk about. We order dessert and finish the bottle of wine and close down the restaurant, laughing all the way to the car, even when the paparazzi flashes blind us.

I've never had more fun.

I barely close the door to Drew's apartment before he pushes me against it and kisses me, tugging at my jacket until it slips from my shoulder. We bang around in the dark, kissing awkwardly while we kick off shoes and rip off layers of clothing. I'm sure we look like that scene in every rom com. You know the one.

Once all outerwear is removed, Drew takes my hands in his and holds them above my head, pinning them to the wall beside his bedroom door. Then he kisses me again. Harder. Less playful, more intentional. My mouth and my cheeks, then working his way down to my neck, my shoulder, my collarbone. Every kiss is kindling to build a bigger fire.

CHAPTER 39

"Mary, I've been thinking," he says between kisses. He pushes his hips against mine, and I gasp when I feel how hard he is.

I bite my bottom lip, staring into his eyes, lit with the city below. His pupils are so dilated, they are almost black.

"I want to hear you scream my name again. I've been dreaming about it for three nig—"

"God, yes." I bring Drew's hands to my chest, encouraging him to touch me. "I thought you'd never ask."

He kisses me again, hungrier, less restrained. His hands go straight under the fabric of my dress and my bra to my skin. I moan and arch as my nipples harden under his touch. Everything between my breasts and my knees tightens.

I tear Drew's shirt from his wide chest, and he unzips my dress, guiding it to my hips. I'm still wearing the see-through lingerie I bought with Harper earlier, and Drew's hungry eyes take me in. He mutters a string of curse words under his breath.

"You are so goddamn beautiful, do you know that?" He kisses me right above my bra, his chin tickling my nipple through the sheer fabric. Sensation zips through me, and suddenly, I want his mouth in a million more places.

Actually, not want. *Need.* I need it. I need it all over me.

Drew drops to his knees as he tears my dress past my hips, ripping the fabric. He grabs my butt with both hands and squeezes, crashing my stomach against his mouth. I lean against the wall for support as he explores my torso. Sucking, biting, licking. My need escalates to nearly intolerable heights.

"Tell me what you want, Mary-Beth," he hums against my ribs. He bites the fabric of my bra, tugging it down, almost exposing me completely. He lets it go with a snap, smiling up at me wickedly. "And tell me to stop if you're uncomfortable. Remember our safe word?"

"Azkaban?"

"Smartass."

Drew stands and scoops me up, carrying me over his shoulder. I kick and squeal, and he slaps my ass. All of it just makes me want him more. He stalks into his room and throws me onto the bed, which is still unmade. It's darker in here without the light from the big window. Drew flicks on the bedside lamp before joining me. I scooch up until I can rest against the pillows, and he leans on his elbow next to me, lazily running his fingers across my stomach.

"Tell me what to do to you, Mary. Tell me what's going to make you scream my name."

"Your mouth," I say before I even realize what it is I'm saying. "This time, I want you to use your mouth."

"You're sure?" He shifts his weight closer to me, and I'm able to see the enormity of his erection.

Holy shit.

While my body may not show it like his does, I'm just as turned on. The pounding between my legs is wet and demanding. Even more than before, knowing how amazing the release feels.

I nod. "Yes. I'm sure." I lean toward him, allowing him access to any and all parts of me.

He starts at my mouth, using his tongue to part my teeth, working his lips with mine in perfect rhythm. His fingers glide over my bra lightly, and my skin twitches with desire. I nip at him.

"Patience, Mary." He laughs.

Eventually, he moves his hands to my hair, tilting my head back. His lips trail across my neck to my collarbone to finally, the sensitive skin just above my breasts. With careful fingers, he curls the fabric back from my left breast, exposing it. I gasp when his breath hits my nipple. Instinctively, I move my hands to cover myself, but Drew stops me.

"Perfection," he says, bringing me into his mouth. Now, the string between my nipples and my legs feels more like a lightning bolt. A

CHAPTER 39

pulsing lightning bolt that is both on fire and also dripping wet. I bite the inside of my mouth to keep from screaming.

Drew teases me, nibbling, biting, licking, sucking. I writhe against his body, tangling myself in his sheets.

"Is this all right?" He stares up from between my breasts, and my breath catches in my throat.

"I might kill you if you stop," I rasp.

"Just wait."

Drew carefully reaches behind me, unhooking my bra and tossing it aside. He drags his large hands up my rib cage and my breasts bounce against his fingertips as he holds me with both hands. He kisses me a little while longer, taking time for both sides, before moving down. To my ribs. My belly button. My hip bones. Then he reaches underneath me, forcing my hips up. With gentle fingers, he slides my underwear off. And then, I'm completely naked.

Breathe, Mary-Beth. Just fucking breathe. This is Drew. You're safe.

Drew settles in between my legs, nudging me to open them wider with his head. I feel the stretch as they fall open, resting against the soft, white bedding. I suck in a nervous breath and hold it, grabbing the blanket with white knuckles. He places gentle hands on top of mine, untangling my fingers from the fabric.

"Relax, Mary," Drew whispers against my inner thigh. "I won't do anything you don't want me to do. I promise."

"I want your mouth inside me." The thick words come from a place deep within. From a chasm housing my most primal desires.

His blue eyes meet mine from between my legs, and he gives me a mischievous smile. "You are the type."

Drew kisses the inside of my thigh, then the other. Then, he runs his tongue along my wet slit.

I have to bite my knuckle not to scream. Drew notices and reaches up, pinning my arm to the bed.

"If you want to scream, Mary-Beth, you better fucking scream."

His breath is hot against my legs when he kisses me again.

"You taste so good." He slides his tongue up and down, around. Lapping. Swallowing. Like he really does like the way it tastes. "So fucking good."

The thing that is *fucking good* is this sensation. Like what he did with his hand, but better. Warm, wet, and soft, his lips and tongue and teeth knowing exactly what to do to make the feeling build. A bullseye exactly where it feels best.

"Oh my Lord. Please, Drew. Please don't stop."

With every flick of his tongue or graze of his teeth, I feel like I'm edging closer and closer to the side of a cliff. My hips grind against the rhythm of his mouth. My hands grip the sheets. I writhe and twist and buck, my body not knowing what to do with this sensory overload. I'm just about to come when Drew slips a hand underneath me, changing the angle so he has perfect access to my clit. Then, with the other hand, he reaches up to stimulate my nipples.

It only takes two or three strokes in that new position before I explode, screaming his name.

I grip his head, holding it between my legs as the pleasure washes over me, coming in waves. The feeling makes me thrash, then relax, then thrash again. When I just can't take it anymore, I push him away and collapse in euphoria.

Chapter 40

Andrew Edward Coyne
In Love
(I think?)

"I think I'm gonna be hoarse tomorrow." Mary-Beth laughs, her shoulders and tits shaking. I laugh too...*other* parts of me shaking.

"Just means I've done my job."

Now that her high has crashed, she seems self-conscious. She buries herself in my sheets.

"Not so fast." I place a gentle hand on her shoulder. "You'll ruin the view."

Mary-Beth blushes, and for once I get to watch it travel all the way down. From her temple to her belly button. *Holy shit, what a sight.*

I stare, and thank God, she lets me.

Perfect. I'm trying to think of another word to describe Mary-Beth, but *perfect* is literally the only thing that comes to mind.

Mary-Beth's tits are perfect. They are the perfect size and shape. Her nipples are the perfect color and diameter and perk in the absolute perfect way. The way they complement the rest of her body, the curve of her waist and her perfect ass, is perfect. The way she tastes. Perfect. The way she moves. Perfect. The way she screams my name when

I'm making her climax. Perfect. And shit, the way she's looking at me right now, flushed, content but shy, and biting her bottom lip self-consciously, it's perfect.

Mary-Beth, she's just...perfect.

Me, on the other hand... I'm a fucking mess.

I don't know if I've ever been this hard. This close without being inside someone. I stand, my body telling me I *have* to do something about that. And since fucking Mary-Beth against the wall isn't really an option right now, I need to get out of this room before my body takes over and I do it anyway.

"Where are you going?"

I turn to the side so she can see how much I'm bulging.

"I'll be right back, Mary." I kiss her on the forehead and walk toward the bathroom. "Don't you even think about getting dressed."

"Drew?" Mary-Beth sits up, her wide umber eyes looking up at me, her bottom lip jutting out. "Stay?"

I wasn't built to sustain this level of control. But God, seeing her naked in my bed, begging me not to go—I can't. Not yet. She needs to know just how perfect she is.

I take a slow, cautious step back to the bed, not trusting myself. Mary-Beth moves her hands across her stomach and to the edge of her tits. God, she has no clue what such a simple movement can do to a man.

When I reach the bed, I grab Mary-Beth by the waist and spin her until her ass rubs against my leg, her head fitting perfectly just under my chin. Slowly, I slide my hands over her shoulders, to her tits.

I don't pray. I never have. But I offer a silent one that I'll be able to stop when I need to. After she came, clutching my head to her stomach, it took every bit of control I had left not to drop my pants and take her right there. I'm walking a very tight rope. I care about Mary-Beth, but shit, it would be easy to slip. Too easy.

CHAPTER 40

Her nipples slide effortlessly between my fingers, hardening under my touch. I move slowly, exploring the texture, the weight, the feel, trying to memorize every detail. Her entire breast fits in my hand. I don't know how I could ever want more; it seems like such a waste.

I knew Mary-Beth's tits were real, of course, but I'd forgotten how fucking fantastic real tits feel. Firm and soft at the same time. The perfect amount of droop, of sway. Before I realize what I'm doing, I'm kneading her, taking all of her in my hands and squeezing, massaging, twisting, caressing. More than before. I'm not gentle or careful. I'm losing control already.

Mary-Beth moves her hips against me—grinding and arching, making me want her even more, if that's humanly possible at this point.

"You're perfect, Mary. You're so perfect for me. I've always thought so."

"Even when you hated me?"

I slide my hands down the front of her, letting her nipples pop between my fingers, until I reach the curve of her waist. I turn her in my arms so she's facing me.

"Especially then."

I place my hands on the dimples of her back and tug her toward me, watching with greedy eyes as her naked tits bump against my chest. Perfect fucking fit, as always.

I kiss her, long and slow, then pull away. "Do you taste yourself on my lips? Do you taste how delicious you are?"

Mary-Beth swallows and nods. She blushes again.

Then, I just can't help myself. I follow the blush, kissing her neck. And her collarbone. Then the top of her breast, the spot where it starts to curve. Then each nipple, taking it inside my mouth and sucking gently.

Then, when I can hardly stand the urgency between my legs, I take a step back.

"Mary, I need—"

"Let me."

I take another step, positive she has no idea what she just volunteered to do.

"Mary, you don't have to—"

Before I can say another word, I'm back at the bed, and Mary-Beth's fingers are unbuttoning my pants, unzipping the zipper, tugging at the waist.

"I want to, Drew." Her eyes are full of steely resolve. "Please. I can't stand the thought of you going into the other room to..." Her voice trails off, and she shakes her head. "When, if you stay here with me instead, I could do it. We could do it...together."

The thought of Mary-Beth touching me. Even just wanting to touch me.

Fuckkk...

"Are you sure?'

Mary-Beth sits up on her knees and nods. "Yes."

"All right."

I step out of my jeans, and my cock springs free, precariously held in place by my boxer briefs. Mary-Beth's eyes are a mixture of curiosity and fear.

"Still think this is a good idea? It won't hurt my feelings if you change your mind."

"Get that huge dick over here, Drew," she says roughly. "I want to see it."

My huge dick – her words – spasms. The rest of my restraint flies out the fucking window.

I drop my underwear with one swift motion, the entirety of my erection freed. Mary-Beth's eyes jump from my cock to my eyes.

"Holy *shit*, Drew."

"The reaction every man dreams of." I laugh and come to kneel next to her.

I'm naked in my bed with Mary-Beth. Nothing has ever felt more right.

"Can I?" She lifts her hand, then pulls it away.

"God, yes." I take her hand in mine and guide it to my shaft. I have to admit her tiny hand does make me look huge.

"Show me what to do," she says, gripping me. I grit my teeth so I don't come immediately. A woman's touch has never felt like this.

Slowly, I move her hand up and down with mine. From the base to the head, already starting to leak. As we stroke, she looks like she's taking mental notes. How hard to squeeze, how fast to go, what angle to hold her hand at. She bites her lip in concentration, her eyes studying me. Again, the simple movements almost do me in. I drop my hand, letting her take the lead.

"Am I doing it right?" she asks, looking up at me with wide eyes.

"Yes," I growl. She needs to stop talking. Her sexy questions are going to embarrass me with how quickly I come.

Instead, I grab her around the back of her neck and bring her lips to mine. Then, I slip my other hand between her legs and into her warm, wet pussy.

The hand on me falters, and she breaks our kiss.

"Drew," she gasps.

"Is this okay?" I slip two fingers inside her, moving in and out gently. She's tight. The tightest thing I've ever felt.

"More than okay." She grinds against my hand. "I love that you know exactly how to touch me."

Damn it. Again with the sexy words, Mary-Beth.

"Together." I help her readjust her grip on my cock. My fingers pulse inside her just a little faster.

She nods, and I go back to kissing her. Our tongues and hands work into a rhythm—sublime and slow at first, until everything becomes a frenzy of desire. I go deeper with my fingers, the deepest I've been inside her, and curl them just a little, trying to reach the perfect spot. In return, she grips me tighter, stroking my length with more intensity.

"Drew, I can't. I'm gonna—"

I feel her pussy tighten around my fingers just as I spill all over her hand. The liberation is sweet, heavenly, emotional even. I've never felt this connected to anyone. I hold Mary-Beth's body against mine, cradling her as I slip my hand away. When I'm sure she's finished, I grab my T-shirt from the floor and wipe Mary-Beth's hands, then we both topple onto the mattress.

"How do you keep doing that?" she says, rolling onto her side. "That time felt different than before. Which was different than the time before that. Like, how many ways can you make my body do that? How many hidden spots do I have inside me?"

"An infinite amount, Mary." I take her face in my hands and kiss her. "I promise I'm gonna find every last fucking one."

🌱🌱🌱

An hour later, I'm watching Mary-Beth sleep. Her mouth is slightly parted, her hair is spread across the pillow, her eyes are fluttering. She's exposed from the waist up, and I feel that word again—perfect.

But then another word enters, crashing into me with so much force, it knocks the wind out of me.

Love.

Love?

I think I love Mary-Beth.

I didn't even realize I was capable of loving a woman, honestly. I've been with so many of them, and only had lukewarm feelings at best. Lust, but never love. But that's how it is with Mary-Beth. She yanks my hand and throws me into the abyss headfirst. I've only known her for a few weeks. And yet...

CHAPTER 40

"I love you." I say the words out loud, testing them out to see how they feel.

Natural. New and foreign and scary as hell, yes. But easy too. Organic. Like of course, that's what I should be saying to her.

If it's the right person, it's okay to let yourself fall.

I smile, remembering Nana's words. If ever there was a right person for me, it would be freaking Mary-Beth Abernathy.

I weave one arm under Mary-Beth's shoulders, resting the other across her stomach, and she curls into me in that perfect-fit sort of way. I kiss her hair and stroke her skin gently, then say it again, just because I can. Because I want to.

"I love you, Mary-Beth."

Chapter 41

Mary-Beth Caroline Abernathy
Hoarse

I wake up first the next morning. Hoarse. Naked. In Drew Coyne's bed. With Drew Coyne. Also naked.
    Also hoarse?

Maybe.

What the hell?

Last night feels like a dream. So much so that I'm not entirely sure it actually happened. I got naked? Drew went down on me? I saw his penis? I made him come with my hand? I had *two* orgasms?

No. Way.

I lift the covers, peeking underneath.

Yep. Still there, still huge, even relaxed.

Last night wasn't some X-rated fever dream. It really happened. *Damn.* I'm going to have so much new material for my books.

Begrudgingly, I hop out of bed to use the bathroom. I study myself in the mirror, wondering if I should look or feel different. Wondering if I'll soon regret last night. Feel guilty? Dirty? Defiled?

I've never done any of this. Been naked. Had a man kiss me there. Held a man's dick in my hands. Made it explode like a volcano thousands of years in the making.

CHAPTER 41

I wash my face and brush my teeth.

Do you taste yourself on my lips? Do you taste how delicious you are?

Had Drew really said that to me? Had he really liked the way I tasted? I had oral sex. *Sex.*

I stare at myself in the mirror, waiting. Waiting to feel...like a licked piece of gum? Or maybe a partially digested cupcake?

But the longer I wait, the more I just see...me. The same old me. The same straight brown hair, messy from sleep and *everything else.* The same boring brown eyes, not a speck of green to be had in this drab bathroom lighting. The same bony shoulders and elbows. The same flat chest. The same freckles, the same ridiculous rosy cheeks. Same lips, same teeth. The same...everything.

Mary, you've always been a sexual being.

Is this who I've always been? Deep inside? Has this always been me?

The twenty-three-year-old woman who does whatever the hell she wants. Who is brave and smart and gets everything she deserves.

I smile. Looking in the mirror, that's who I see.

When I come back to bed, Drew is gone. I slip on new pajamas and head out to look for him.

I find him in the kitchen, shirtless and wearing black sweatpants, looking like the definition of a hot-ass man, making—oh, *hell no*—

Making a PB&J, jamming that butter knife, covered with jelly, straight into the peanut butter.

"Mary!" Drew's smile stretches all the way across his face, making his dimples pop. I scowl back at him. "Just in time. We didn't have much to eat, but I still wanted to make you breakfast."

He tries to hand me the sandwich, but I cross my arms.

"You're out of your mind if you think I'm going to eat that."

"Aw, come on." He waves the sandwich at me. "You're really going to reject my generous offering?"

"In case you've forgotten, I have lots of practice rejecting your generous offerings."

Drew drops the sandwich and pulls me into his arms. I pretend to fight, but can't help it when I melt against his naked torso. He kisses my hair and grabs my butt. My body betrays me, already turned on.

"What about if I offered to lay you on this table and give you an encore of last night?" he whispers. "To put my tongue between your thighs and taste you until your legs grip my ears and you scream my name. Could you say no to that?" His ice-blue eyes dare me to reject him, a smirk pulling at his lips.

Damn it, I'm undressed and gripping his kitchen table so quickly, you'd think I'd never said no to anything in my entire life. My willpower is a very pitiful force indeed.

Drew stands at the end of the table and carefully pries my legs apart so he can stand between them. As they stretch, I notice how sore I am. My inner thighs haven't had a workout like that...ever.

Drew moves a stray piece of hair from my eyes, kissing my cheek softly.

"You're so beautiful, Mary-Beth." He kisses me again, looking straight into my eyes. I wrap my legs around his waist, feeling his erection right on top of me. "This might be my favorite look of yours. Everything is real."

"I'm sure you're not used to *everything* being real," I tease. I clutch the back of his neck and lean back, looking down at myself. "I mean, these are probably a lot smaller than what you're used to."

"Quality over quantity, Mary," he says. I feel his cock pulse through his sweatpants, and a flash of hot desire spears me. "You have the most perfect tits I've ever laid eyes on."

As if to prove his point, he bends down and takes one nipple into his mouth, sucking and biting while he pinches the other, rolling it between his fingers. My internal string grows needy in a hurry, and I push away and shove his head between my legs.

CHAPTER 41

"You are not a very patient lover. Did you know that, Virgin Mary?" Drew laughs as he kneels in front of me.

"I'm sorry. I just want it." I scootch closer to the edge of the table, resting my legs on top of his shoulders.

"God, same," he says, before lifting my hips off the table and diving into me.

This time, Drew goes straight for my clit, teasing with his tongue. But then, oh Lord, then he slips his fingers inside me, pleasuring me from the inside out. I nearly come with the first stroke but manage to hold on a little longer.

"Touch yourself, Mary," Drew says from between my legs. He takes my hands and guides them to my breasts, then puts his hands back where they were and starts kissing me again.

Unsure at first, my hands stay still. But then, that insistent connection between my breasts and my vagina teases me, and I begin to rub my nipples. They harden against my fingertips, and my body reacts, fire erupting from his tongue all the way up. I look down at my body in wonder, amazed at all the things it's capable of. All the hidden nooks and crannies Drew is helping me explore. I writhe against his mouth, my body jerking against the table, feeling empowered.

Feeling sexy as hell, if I'm being honest.

Drew's blue eyes stare up from between my legs like he's high. I lean my head back, trying to give him a better view, and the hand underneath me grips tighter. His pace increases, less gentle, more insistent. Decadent. Greedy. And then, it's all too much. I climax gripping his head with my thighs and his kitchen table with my knuckles.

This orgasm might be the best one yet. It's inside from his hand. And outside from his mouth. It's shivers across my skin and vibrations inside me. When the pleasure finally subsides a little, Drew stands and draws me against his chest, kissing me wildly. I wrap my arms around his waist, feeling the huge bulge against my stimulated body.

If he tries, I won't say no.

Drew rips his pants from his waist, and his enormous dick is freed like a reckless animal.

"Mary, God, I want you." He takes himself in his hand and thrusts a couple times. His erection is so hot and hard, it even looks large in his giant hand. "I want to bend you over this goddamn table and make you mine. I want to fuck you right here, right now."

He thrusts again and again, and it's clear that he's not going to make good on those desires. He's just going to take care of it himself even though I'm sitting right here.

He's still scared. Unsure.

"Wait," I say softly, sliding off the table to stand next to him. I carefully pry his hand away from his cock, taking it securely in my own. It throbs and is wet. I can tell he's already close. "Let me try something."

I drop to my knees.

"Mary, you don't have to do th—"

The rest of Drew's sentence is swallowed up in a mixture of profanity and growling as I kiss his head. Obviously, I have no idea what I'm doing, but I'm guessing his reaction means I'm on the right track.

There's no way the entire length will fit in my mouth, but I am able to take the head and a few more inches, gagging as it slides to the back of my throat. I grasp the base and pull it out, then back in again, trying to mimic the motion I'd studied last night.

It doesn't take long. Just a few strokes in and out. And then Drew erupts in my mouth, pulling my hair and nearly toppling us both over.

"Fuck!" he roars when I pull away. I smile, loving that *I* do this to him.

I look up at him, wipe my mouth, and swallow. He helps me to my feet and holds me tightly against his chest, still covered in

CHAPTER 41

goosebumps.

"Holy shit, Mary-Beth. Where did you learn to do *that*? That was like...the best head of my life."

Chapter 42

Mary-Beth Caroline ~~Abernathy~~ Coyne

Today is Harper's birthday. And apparently, we're having her party in Las Vegas.

Which is why, one airplane ride, two all-you-can-eat buffets, one Cirque du Soleil show, five-hundred lost blackjack dollars, one grand suite at the Bellagio, two shots of whiskey, and two orgasms later, Drew and I are walking hand in hand to the Chateau Nightclub. It's a warm night, the desert breeze comfortable in only my black sparkly mini-dress and heels. While Harper and I were shopping for lingerie, I bought new ones, an inch taller than the others and patent leather black.

Drew pulls me against his hip and buries his face in my hair. "You look amazing, Mary-Beth. I love the new shoes."

He looks incredibly sexy tonight in a perfectly tailored black suit, white shirt, and pristine white Air Force Ones. I wrap my arm around his waist, and we fall into step, like we've catwalked the Strip a million times.

The air is buzzing, and the streets are crowded, although it's only a Wednesday and not quite midnight. Several people stop us, asking Drew for autographs and selfies, asking about the book and/or our relationship status. He's polite but frank each time.

CHAPTER 42

"This is my girlfriend, Mary-Beth." Drew never lets go of my hand. "And she'd really appreciate it if you'd stop asking about that fucking book."

Finally, we make it to the Paris Hotel. Outside, there is a neon balloon and a replica of the Arc de Triomphe, and then above us, of course, the Eiffel Tower.

"I've always wanted to go to Paris." I crane my neck back to take in as much of the spectacle as I can.

"I went a few years ago when I was filming—"

"*The French Flirt?*" I cut in, and Drew nods.

"Someday, I'll take you. You would love Paris, Mary."

"How do you know?"

"Because I hated it. Too damn hot. And the French are assholes." Drew laughs and kisses my hair, holding the door. "But I have a feeling I might like it if I went with you."

The ceiling inside the hotel is painted to look like clouds, and the Eiffel Tower's legs jut straight through the casino. Drew makes a sharp turn at the slot machines.

"The nightclub is at the base of the Eiffel Tower," Drew explains. "I've been here quite a few times for work events. I think there are better nightclubs in Las Vegas, but Will is particularly fond of this one for some reason. He got shitfaced drunk and hooked up with a bottle girl here once."

We're greeted by security at the top of a black marble staircase. They usher us to an elevator that takes us up the inside of the Eiffel Tower. When we exit, more security is waiting to take us to our VIP party area.

From up here, we can see the entire Strip, and the view is stunning. I've never been to Las Vegas, but somehow, it's exactly what I expected. Bright lights and gaudy hotels and music pouring into the streets. Slot machines and drinks and hordes of drunk partygoers.

The DJ sits atop a ten-foot-tall fireplace, and there's a giant screen behind him. It's still early, so the dance floor isn't crowded, with packs of cologne-heavy men and groups of girlfriends huddled around the edges that haven't found each other yet. I smile. There aren't nightclubs like this in Indiana, but I guess some things are universal.

Drew doesn't look at the Strip or the DJ once, just looks at me looking at it. "You like it?"

"I've never been anywhere like this."

He grabs me around the waist and kisses my cheek, holding me with gentle fingertips. The way he's looking down at me, I swear, makes my heart stop beating for a half-second. Drew opens his mouth to say something but is cut off by Harper barreling at us from across the room.

"Mary-Beth!" she screams, launching herself at me. I untangle from Drew just in time to catch her.

Harper looks like a fairy princess. Complete with a flowing white dress, taller-than-mine magenta stripper heels, sparkly silver makeup, and flowers in her braided rainbow hair.

"Happy birthday, Harp!" I crush myself against her, breathing in her familiar scent. Tonight, it's mixed with Black Cherry White Claw. "You look gorgeous!"

Harper shimmies, and her boobs bounce so much I'm afraid they might fly out of her dress and hit me in the face.

"I could say the same about you two!" She takes my hand and spins me around. "Hot damn, MB!" She turns to Drew. "Whatever you've been doing to her, keep doing it!"

"Oh, I fully intend to." Drew gives me an errant smile.

Harper's mouth falls open like she's about to ask for a play-by-play.

Before she can pry for details about my very tenderfooted sex life, Will joins us. He's wearing a navy suit, but he's already lost the jacket and rolled up his sleeves. His left arm is covered with tattoos I've never noticed, and he's holding two glasses of amber liquor.

CHAPTER 42

"Mary-Beth." He steps forward and gives me a warm hug with his forearm. "My daughter hasn't stopped talking about you."

"Oh, poor Chloe! How is she?"

"She was totally fine the next day. Was ready to go back and do it all again. Thanks again for taking care of her." Will hands Drew one of the drinks. "Can we talk?"

Drew kisses my cheek. "Be right back."

"I don't think I'll be able to top this next year!" I shout over the loud music once they're gone.

"Your twenty-third sucked in comparison. I'm sorry." Harper hooks my arm and pulls me in the direction of the bar. "You can count this one too if you want. I don't mind sharing."

"Feels like my birthday, honestly." I giggle. A legit schoolgirl playground giggle.

"So..." Harper leaves the word dangling as she orders us both Cosmopolitans.

"He asked me to be his girlfriend, Harp. His *actual* girlfriend." I try not to squeal the words. I fail.

I'm expecting Harper to be more surprised than she is. She's looking at me like this is old news.

"So...I take it Drew liked the lingerie?" she asks instead.

"He did." My giggling turns to chuckling with the words *Drew* and *lingerie*. Our drinks arriving saves me from having to say anything else.

"Mary-Beth..." Harper clinks her glass against mine, her eyebrows rising. "Is there something else you need to tell me? Has the cherry officially popped?"

"No..." I take a small sip and cock my head to the side. "But I did steal third."

Harper nods approvingly, but again looks unsurprised. "Nice. Was that orgasm as life-changing as the first?"

"Lord, yes."

"And are you still planning on rounding for home?"

I take another sip and shrug. Put that way, it doesn't sound like a big deal.

"I guess we'll see."

Harper smiles in her bad-influence-best-friend sort of way. "I'm expecting at least a text in the morning," is all she says.

"What about *your* new guy?" I try to remember if she ever told me his name. "Is he here yet? How is it I don't know anything about him? It's not Jake Ursley again, is it? Or someone else from the D&D club?"

Before Harper can answer, Drew and Will return. Drew sets his empty drink down and pulls me toward the dance floor without a word. I wave to Harper and gladly leave my half-finished Cosmo behind.

"Whenever he gets here, come find me!" I shout.

Harper doesn't answer but raises my glass and takes a sip.

The house music slows from rave to more bump and grind. Drew places his hands on my ass.

We fall into an easy rhythm. Twirl. Grab. Release. Tease. Drew is an awesome dancer and an even better dance partner.

He pulls me against his hips. Holds my hand. Plays with my hair. Touches my body. Sings along when he knows the words. Sings along when he doesn't. Kisses me. Kisses me again. We get into at least ten arguments about random, unimportant things. I don't know if we ever stop laughing. The hours pass in bliss.

Around three a.m., Will wheels out a giant pink cake for Harper, and we sing "Happy Birthday" with four hundred of our new best friends. Her new mystery man never showed, but she's been happily dancing with Will all night instead. I even spied them drunkenly making out an hour ago. They give each other a silly look over the sparkler candles before Harper blows. I'm glad she had a birthday kiss, even if it was with Drew's dorky best friend.

CHAPTER 42

After the birthday celebration, Drew and I choose a table overlooking the Bellagio fountains.

"I have a surprise for you." He hands me a much-needed bottle of water.

"You've changed your mind about *Harry Potter*?" I chuckle then take a sip.

"Smartass," Drew says, grinning. "Nope. Try again."

"Jordan Ones? Peanut butter and jelly? Run-D.M.C.? Shake Shack? Check the Vibe?"

"God, Mary-Beth. Must you?" Drew kisses me again, holding my face with both hands, stroking my cheeks. I take another sip. "I canceled all my social media partnerships. All of them. Will just confirmed they're done."

I choke on my water. Like, up my nose, down my throat, eyes watering, cough for thirty seconds *choke*.

When I finally start breathing again, I wipe my eyes and look over at Drew. "Really?"

"One can only be lectured about being a dishonest hypocrite for so long until they're forced to do something about it." He laughs and tilts his head in my direction.

"So you...you aren't going to do ad campaigns anymore?"

"I will eventually. But I'm going to choose things I actually care about. And for right now..." Drew reaches down and takes my hand. "There are other things I want to spend my time doing."

He stands and pulls me back to the dance floor. The music has really slowed now. To more of a prom-night sway. We spin around the club together, Drew lazily running his fingers up and down my back.

"I like dancing with you, Mary." Drew nudges my nose with his.

I feel mine crinkle. "I like dancing with you too."

"I don't normally like to dance." Drew spins me and pulls me back into his arms, this time even closer. "But with you, it's easy."

"You don't like to dance? You tried so hard to get me to dance with you at the Persimmon Festival."

"Well...someone kept talking about what a freaking amazing dancer they were. I was influenced."

"And?"

"Better than advertised."

"But you don't like to dance?"

Drew shrugs, then brings his hands to rest at the small of my back. "Always seemed unnecessary."

I fill in the blanks. "Man, you wouldn't even give the girls a dance before taking them home?" I joke, wrinkling my forehead. "Harsh."

"I've never danced with someone like you." Drew's fingertips apply the slightest bit of pressure, bringing my hips flush with his.

"Someone you mildly hate and know you won't get past third base with?"

Drew spins me again and then looks right into my eyes. So deep, so intense, like he can see into my soul.

"With someone I love."

We stop spinning. In fact, I'm pretty sure the world has stopped spinning.

"What did you say?" I whisper.

"I love you, Mary-Beth." Drew takes my hands in his. He's shaking. I start shaking too. "Damn it, I tried not to. And you didn't make it easy. Nothing with you comes easy. But yeah. As much as I hate you, I'm pretty sure I love you more.

"And to be honest, I'm freaking scared as hell, Mary. You can be so difficult. And we disagree about everything. And nothing about us makes sense. Not a damn thing. And I'm not sure how it's all going to work. And I'm pretty sure I'm doing everything wrong." His voice softens. He moves a piece of hair from my eyes. I blink, finding tears there. "But I want things with you, Mary. All the things. All the things

CHAPTER 42

I never thought I wanted or would ever have. I want them with you. Because I've never felt like this about anyone. Like I can't catch my breath when you're around. Like a part of me is missing when you're not. Like if I can't be with you, no one else will ever be enough. You've fucking ruined me, Mary."

"You've ruined me to—" The rest of what I wanted to say is swallowed up in Drew's kiss. I laugh against his lips, and he steadies my face with his hands.

"Say it, Mary," he whispers, stroking my cheek.

"I love you, Drew."

He smiles. "You are the type."

He kisses me again, breathing me in like air. Like he needs me just as much.

When we part, glitter is raining from the sky. It's in our hair. On our eyelashes. In my mouth.

Glitter. Everywhere.

I know that's not really true. It doesn't actually rain glitter, not even in Las Vegas. But somewhere, someone or something is dumping glitter on us. I look up and laugh, trying to catch the sparkles on my fingertips. The air feels like magic. Like enchantment.

And there's something about that glitter, that magic in the air, that destroys the last of my inhibitions.

"Drew, I'm ready." My voice is completely sure and steady. I press onto my tiptoes and wrap my arms around his neck. Our lips are just a breath apart when I say it again. "I'm ready. Tonight. I don't want to wait any longer to be with you."

"I don't want you to regret this, Mary." Drew kisses me again. He has glitter clinging to his collar. To the back of his hands. To his lips. "I'll wait, Mary. I'll wait as long as you want if it means I can be with you."

"I won't regret this, Drew. I promise." I swallow and press my body against his. "I love you. You're the one I've been waiting for."

"You're sure?"

I nod. "Are *you* sure?"

He stops. Looks at the glitter raining down. Swallows.

"Mary, I know you want a commitment. And I want to give it to you." Drew laughs and looks at the legs of the Eiffel Tower. "We're in Vegas. Fuck it! Let's get married!"

🐤🐤🐤

The next hour is a blur.

Searching.

"Where are Harper and Will?"

"Fuck if I know."

Giving up after ten minutes.

Googling.

Nevada marriage laws

"We need a marriage license."

"And a chapel."

Marriage licenses

Wedding chapels

"There's a twenty-four-hour one-stop shop fifteen minutes from here."

"This is absolutely insane."

"One hundred percent."

"Las Vegas weddings never last."

"Of course, they don't."

Percentage of Las Vegas weddings that fail

"Fourteen percent."

"That's actually lower than I thought."

"This is still a stupid idea."

"Of course."

"I'll call the Uber."

CHAPTER 42

"For the chapel?"

"Yeah."

"Wait. I've got a better idea."

24-hour pawn shops

"A pawn shop?"

Drew takes my hand and kisses the back. "I'm gonna buy you a ring, Mary. Probably a shitty one. But if we're gonna do this, you're gonna have a goddamn ring."

Twenty minutes later, we rush from the store hand in ringed hand. His is probably gold. Mine is definitely cubic zirconium.

"In the morning, I'll buy you something better," Drew says. "Whatever damn ring you want."

I feel my lips pull to the side. "*Any* ring?"

"Bankrupt me, Mary. I know you will."

Drew pulls me into another Uber and kisses me fiercely against the door, gripping my five-inch stiletto with one hand and my butt with the other. "Your finger will be green tomorrow. I hope it never washes off."

"God, Drew. I love you."

It feels so good to say that out loud.

"I love you too."

The Uber pulls onto Las Vegas Boulevard.

Drew pulls me against his chest. "Marry me, Mary-Beth Abernathy," he whispers, rubbing the ring on my left hand. I crush my lips to his, sure I've never wanted anything more in my whole life. "Annoy me for the rest of our lives."

"I am the type."

The next thing I know, I'm holding a bouquet of fake flowers and staring at Elvis and Drew down the aisle of the Las Vegas Little White Wedding Chapel.

Elvis starts singing "Fools Rush In."

Fitting.

I feel like it's pretty obvious, but I'll clarify in case anyone is unclear: I'm not the type to elope in Vegas.

I always imagined my wedding would be in the chapel in Daisy Bluff. My dad would walk me down the aisle, then stand in the front of the congregation to perform the ceremony. Mama would be crying in the front row. Nana would be grinning. I'd be wearing a white strapless A-line gown with a modest neckline, a long train, and a chiffon veil. I'd be clutching a bouquet of fresh tulips and Mama's handkerchief, the one she held on her wedding day. The one embroidered with her mom's initials and the blue heart.

It would be morning. Maybe midday. Light would pour through the stained-glass window above the organ. Harper would be my maid of honor and Reese my bridesmaid, both dressed in something pastel and flowy. The pews would be filled with half the town. Charlotte and Josie would be feeling envious. Sutton would be feeling foolish. I'd be feeling like a princess.

Tonight, my wedding night, I'm realizing, is nothing like that.

Instead of my dad, I have Elvis. Instead of Harper, a lady playing Wordle on her phone to keep from falling asleep. Instead of tulips, fake carnations. Instead of Daisy Bluff, Las Vegas. Instead of a long white gown, a short black party dress.

Lord, am I really getting married wearing *black*?

But there's one thing that's the same, both in my dreams and in reality: the groom. As wrong as this whole situation feels, Drew feels right. So right.

Since the moment I first saw him on my TV when I was a teenager, it's been Drew. Even when I hated him. Even when I was sure he was the worst person alive, it's always been him.

I hold my breath and take two cautious steps down the aisle. Step, together, step. Just like I practiced when I was a little girl.

CHAPTER 42

The aisle is short, and before I can even exhale, I've reached the altar.

Drew.

And Elvis.

I am so lightheaded, I feel like I might pass out.

Drew takes my hand, rubbing my knuckles gently. "You okay?" His eyes narrow.

I swallow. I think I nod.

"Thank you, thank you very much!" Elvis says.

"No!" I shout, the word escaping before I even make the choice to say it.

I look up at Drew as tears threaten. "I'm sorry. But I can't do this. Not like this." I gasp for air. "I love you. I love you so freaking much, Drew. And I want to marry you. But not here." I look at Elvis apologetically. "Not by Elvis."

Drew laughs, and it's such a relief, a tear slips down my cheek. He brushes it away.

"Thank God, Mary-Beth. I thought I was going to have to peel you off this nasty-ass carpet. Let's get out of here."

Chapter 43

Andrew Edward Coyne
Sure
So So So Damn Sure

The second we walk outside the chapel, the color returns to Mary-Beth's cheeks. Cars zoom past as they race down Las Vegas Boulevard, rustling her hair.

"Why didn't you say something sooner, Mary?" I tuck a wandering strand behind her ear. "I'm so sorry."

"I just, um...got swept up, I think. Because"—her big brown eyes jump to mine—"I do want to marry you, Drew. I've dreamed about marrying you for years. But I just..." She licks her lips. "I always wanted to get married in my daddy's church. I wanted him to do it. And as mad as I am at my mom right now, I want her there. And Harper. And..." She looks down at her dress. "And I can't get married wearing *black,* for God's sake."

I laugh and grab Mary-Beth around her waist, spinning her into my chest. "No. You can't. Not if it's not what you want." I kiss her. "But that doesn't mean I wouldn't have said yes."

"I would have said yes too. That's why I had to stop Elvis before he asked."

"We're fucking crazy, you know that?" I slide my hands down to

CHAPTER 43

her ass.

"We are. Certifiably." She runs a hand across her face.

"I don't give a damn, though." I lean down and kiss her. "I want to be crazy with you."

I hardly recognize myself. The words coming out of my mouth. The feeling in my chest. I'm pretty sure someone came and rewired my brain last night. Because I am not the elope type. The marriage type. Fuck, I'm not even the girlfriend type. But damn, I love this woman. And now, that's the only thing that seems to matter.

"Drew..." Mary-Beth slips her hand into mine. She's still wearing the ring I bought her at the pawn shop. "I meant what I said before. I'm ready. I really am."

That probably means marriage, but maybe not.

I was ready to marry Mary-Beth tonight. To show her I'm sure. But if that's not what she needs...

My heart begins to race. After all the buildup, the back and forth. The fighting and making up. From falling in hate to falling in love, is the moment really here?

All I know is I definitely want it to be with someone who is sure about me. Someone I won't regret.

I wasn't sure before. All the times I could have had her, when Mary-Beth wouldn't have stopped me, I was still unsure. But tonight, I'm sure. I'm so, so, *so* damn sure. After watching her walk down the aisle, I've never known what I want more.

"You won't regret this tomorrow?" I ask again. She's probably getting sick of hearing it.

Mary-Beth looks up at me and shakes her head. "I'm sure I won't."

I kiss her forehead, then lean mine against hers. "I'm sure too."

🐑🐑🐑

I've been picturing this moment in my mind since the day I read *Swallow Manor*. In those fantasies, I was aggressive. Rough. I fucking man-handled Minnie Maple. Twisted her into a pretzel. Pounded hard. In reality, I'm so ridiculously scared to hurt Mary-Beth, I can barely look at her. I hope I can maintain control for a little longer. Enough to go slow. Enough to be gentle.

When we step into the hotel room, I flick on the lamp, and Mary-Beth kicks off her shoes. Without the extra inches, she looks even tinier, more delicate.

The air in the room is suffocating. I shrug out of my jacket, then undo the rest of my buttons and take off my shirt, hoping that will help.

"So..." Mary-Beth waves her hands in front of her waist, swinging them nervously.

It takes two long strides to reach her. I place my hands on her shoulders, and she moves her hands to my chest.

"I love you, Mary-Beth," I say. " But the rules still stand. If you're uncomfortable, I will stop, no questions asked. I'm going to try and be as gentle as I can."

She nods. "I know you will."

I plunge my hands deep into her tangled hair, angling her mouth up to mine.

"I love you so goddamn much, Mary-Beth. I didn't know it was possible. To feel like this about someone."

Then I kiss her, so deeply, so purely, using my lips to show her how I feel. Her hands travel across my chest and down my stomach, before she wraps them around me.

"You know what this reminds me of?" I whisper, pulling down one strap of her dress, and then the other, kissing each shoulder.

She looks up. "What?"

"Ambrose and Susan's first time."

Mary-Beth blushes. Her flushed skin disappears underneath the black sparkles of her dress.

CHAPTER 43

"Is that how you pictured your first time?" I whisper against her skin.

Mary-Beth laughs. "I mean, that was before I met you. Before...a lot of things. But yeah. When I wrote it, that's how I imagined it, I guess."

"And who did you picture it with?" Now I'm just being greedy.

"Lord, you know it was you." She laughs, put-out.

"You have no idea how many times I've imagined it too. Pretty much every second of every day since I read your books. I've been wanting this."

"*Really*?"

"Jesus Christ, yes."

I carefully unzip the back of Mary-Beth's dress. It falls to the ground, revealing a black lace bra and thong. The one from the suitcase.

"God, I knew you were trying to kill me." I grab her around the waist, and she laughs. "Let's see what I can remember."

"I have high expectations. There will be a grade at the end."

My teacher fantasy from a few days ago returns. After tonight, when Mary-Beth is truly mine and I can have her anytime she'll let me, that roleplay is first on the list.

"All right." I lick my lips. "I seem to remember that Ambrose's hands were unsure until Susan was unabashedly nude. Is that correct?"

A smile plays at the corner of her mouth, and she nods. I run my hands along her collarbone, from the left to the right, sliding my fingers under the black fabric of her bra, and her breathing increases. I can't tell if it's because she's getting more turned on or more nervous. For me, it's both.

"So... I guess that's where we should start." I raise one eyebrow. "Don't you think?" I place one hand on the back of Mary-Beth's head and one at her waist, sliding down to her ass, as I lower my mouth to hers for one short kiss. My fingers do indeed shake as they fumble to unclasp her bra. When it falls to the floor and her naked tits rub against my chest, it feels heavenly. My dick is hard, but the urgency is tampered. I know there will be a release tonight. I can take my time. I *will* take my time. I'll savor her.

My fingers slide around the waist of her thong, running over her hip bones and across the curve of her ass. Finally, I slide the black lace over her thighs and down to the floor.

"Perfection," I say, stepping back to admire her. "There's no other word for you."

Mary-Beth is getting used to being naked in front of me, but she still blushes and goes to cover herself. I take her in my arms before she can, running my fingers over one of her nipples. It hardens under my touch.

"Is your nipple sensitive?" I ask, stroking her. "Just like you thought it would be?"

"So sensitive." She arches into my touch. Now I *know* she's turned on.

I touch her again, both of us watching as my hands slide over her naked body. I lean down and bring my lips a breath away from hers. "I think now I'm supposed to kiss you knowing I don't have to stop."

It's Mary-Beth who brings her lips to mine first, crashing into me. She wraps her arms around my neck and yanks me down to her.

I'm a fucking goner.

I pick her up and throw her on the bed, shedding the rest of my clothing. When I spring free and crawl over to her, her eyes grow wide.

"Do I look like you imagined I'd look, Mary-Beth? *Every bit the man you'd hoped?*"

"More, Drew," she says, scooting up toward the headboard. "Holy shit, more."

I try to remember exactly how she phrased it, because it was so goddamn sexy. "Am I *raw* and *carnal*? *Calling to the parts of your body you've saved just for me?*"

CHAPTER 43

"Lord, that's so corny." She laughs, shaking her head. "But that's exactly how I feel."

I position myself next to her, leaning down for a kiss. "I didn't realize I was saving parts of myself for you too, Mary. There are so many parts of me no one else has ever seen. Ever touched." The words are tumbling out before I can even really think them. Straight from my heart to Mary-Beth's skin, bypassing my brain completely. "You've saved yourself physically, Mary. But I saved my heart for you. No one has ever held it the way you do. I didn't realize all I needed was a smartass from southern Indiana."

I notice tears in Mary-Beth's eyes. My heart stops, and I retreat.

"Is everything okay?"

"It's just..." A tear falls down her cheek, and I wipe it away. "I thought you would be one way. And I thought that's what I wanted. But I'm so glad you're more."

I let out a sigh of relief and kiss her again, running my hands lightly across her perfect breasts. "Next, I think I'm supposed to *kiss the very heart of you. Your center of existence. The part of you screaming for bloody release.*"

"God, this is both torture and so damn hot." Mary-Beth's eyes are clouded with both emotions. "But yes, I definitely want that."

I place my hands on her shoulder blades, holding her up as I kiss her from her sternum to her ribs to her belly button, to her hip bones to the top of her pubic bone, raking my hands down to her ass just like she described in her book.

"I'm going to do a little rule-breaking, if that's all right with you," I say against her inner thigh, pushing it against the sheets to open to me. Mary-Beth arches her back and bites her lower lip. "Or should we call it *improvising*?" We both laugh. "But this isn't my first time pleasuring you. Fucking you with my hand. Or my mouth. I'm starting to know exactly what you like."

Mary-Beth nods, and I slide my hand to her warm, wet pussy. I glide my fingers inside, pumping in and out slowly, while my other hand creeps from her stomach up to her tits. I take one, twisting her nipple, then massage her with my whole hand.

"I can be a little rough, don't you think?" I stare at Mary-Beth as she begins to writhe against my hand. I pump harder, jerking my hand against her apex. "I think you like it like that. Don't you, my little smartass?"

I go deeper, and Mary-Beth bucks beneath my touch. I pound inside her, an appetizer of what is to come.

"You feel so good. So tight. So perfect in my control."

"Drew!" Mary-Beth screams. She's climaxing already. I feel the tightening around my fingers, wet and so fucking incredible, it's dizzying. When she relaxes, collapsing against the bed sheets, I keep my hand inside her and one hand on her chest, as I finally bring my mouth between her legs.

"I wasn't kidding when I said you taste amazing, Mary-Beth." I lick her from her entrance to her clit. "Damn."

My tongue laps Mary-Beth in time to the pulses of my hands, watching the show from between her legs. She bites her bottom lip, occasionally grasping whatever she can reach. The sheets. My shoulders. My ears. My head. The closer she gets to completion, the more her body writhes in pleasure, her hands moving across her rib cage as she twists against my mouth. I always knew she would be great in bed, but how could I have ever foreseen this?

Dancing with her tonight showed me she knows exactly how her body moves. What to do with it. That definitely translates into the bedroom. She's a fucking goddess.

A few more minutes and Mary-Beth comes again, digging her fingers into my deltoids and screaming my name. I hold her there, on the edge, for as long as she lets me. Finally, she pushes me away, panting as she

CHAPTER 43

sinks into the sheets.

"Yes." Her voice is slightly annoyed but content. "It was *ecstasy personified.* Like *I'd been taken to the brink of heaven and brought right back again.*"

"Your words." I laugh and kiss her hip bone. "Not mine."

My erection is at the point of no return now. And I know her body is ready for me. She's as wet and stretched as she's going to get.

"Mary, you've always been a sexual person," I remind her. "Before you've even had sex, this is who you are. And I'm so goddamn lucky to get to be the person to help you experience it. I won the fucking lottery."

I kiss her again, still staying to the side. Mary-Beth's hands travel down the front of me, until she's clutching my cock. I twitch when her eyes meet mine.

"Drew, I want it. I'm ready."

Chapter 44

Mary-Beth Caroline Abernathy
~~Virgin~~ Mary

Drew stands and turns off the lamp before he pulls the curtains open. The sunrise is just coming over the Las Vegas skyline, and it bathes the entire room in orange light.

"You did say you prefer sunrises, right?"

Before I can even get a snarky comment out, I hear the zipper of his suitcase and then foil ripping.

A condom.

Holy shit.

My heart begins to pound in time with the need between my legs like I'm one big metronome. My body is begging me for something deeper. Something only Drew can give me.

All my doubts and inhibitions are officially gone.

I'm about to make love to Drew Coyne.

"Mary-Beth, I want you to know I'm sure about you." Drew sits and smooths my hair away from my forehead. "You said you wanted to lose your virginity to someone who was sure. And as crazy as these past few weeks have been, they've made me sure. Sure you're the only person I want to be with. Ever."

Each time Drew tells me he loves me or wants to be with me, I have to fight a silly grin. In all my fantasies, in all my dreams and girlhood ideals, I've wanted Drew. But actually having him, the real him, is better. It's pure happiness. It's everything I never knew I always wanted.

I know that saying is very cliché for a romance author.

I don't care.

It's true.

"Drew, you're the only person I've ever imagined this happening with. I promise, I'm sure too."

He lays down, his weight shifting the mattress. This time, he positions himself on top of me. Taking my hands in his, he nudges my legs open with his leg and my inner thighs stretch to open to him. He rests most of his weight on his elbows next to my ears, but Lord, he's still heavy. All the strings inside my body go taut, buzzing with anticipation.

"I'm going to try and be gentle, Mary-Beth, but this might hurt."

I look down at his huge cock resting above my tiny body.

"You think?" I giggle. I can't help it.

"You can take it," Drew says, sliding his dick up and down my slit. It feels like a sparkler on the Fourth of July. Holy shit, it feels good. He kisses my neck as one hand finds its way to my breast. He massages me gently, more gently than before. "I'll go slow. Every inch of you was made for me, Mary-Beth. This won't be any different."

"I don't know, Drew. That's a lot of inches."

More nervous giggling.

"You know exactly what to say, don't you? My little smartass." Drew laughs as he nibbles at my ear. He continues to tease his cock against me, until finally, he freezes and locks his gaze on mine.

"You ready?" he whispers. His tip is hovering right over my entrance.

"Yes."

I try to relax, but I feel like it would be easier to transform into a different species at this point. How do you relax at a moment like this?

"Here." Drew takes my hand and positions it at the base of his cock. "Help me guide it in. We'll do it together."

Heart pounding in my ears, I roll my hips forward. He helps me get in the perfect spot, adjusting our bodies until I assure him I'm comfortable. Then, ever so gently, he pushes forward, his dick sliding from my hand to inside me. Just an inch, maybe two. My body expands in a whole new way to make room.

"How are you doing, Mary? Are you all right?" He adjusts again, pushing on my hip bones and shifting the majority of his weight onto his elbows.

"Good," I manage to say.

Drew moans and pushes a hint more. His heavy body rests on top of me, his chest rising and falling against mine. I run my hands up the side of his body until they find his biceps, holding on. Drew takes one of my hands and kisses the back of it, then holds it in his, pinning it against the mattress.

He eases forward a little bit more, then stops and readjusts again, pushing my legs a little wider with his hand. His eyes are still on mine as he sighs contentedly and smiles. So wide his dimples pop.

"I love you, Mary. You're everything."

Drew lowers his mouth to mine, kissing me as he continues down below. I find myself relaxing into his touch, when finally, I feel him go deeper, more inside me.

Officially virgin no more.

I jolt at the sensation. Not quite pain. More like a throb. A pinch.

"Are you all right?" Drew pulls away, concern in his eyes.

I stop to take inventory. "It's a strange feeling. Odd." I move around Drew, inside of me, testing it out. "But I'm okay."

"I'm gonna move now." Drew pulls out just a little and comes back in slowly. "Tell me to stop if it's hurting you."

"Not hurting. Just...different."

"Good." Drew kisses my nose as he moves again. He smiles down at me, his face glowing from the orange light. "You look so beautiful right now, Mary. God."

Each time he comes back inside me, he goes a little deeper. I know he's still not all the way in, and I'm not sure I can take the rest of him. My insides already feel stretched to capacity. But...I want to try. I want to be connected as much as we possibly can.

"Go deeper, Drew." I apply a little pressure to his back, forcing him to sink into me more. He moves again, in and out. Faster, but only just a little. Each time, getting closer and closer until... Finally, he bottoms out, settling himself fully inside me. I feel myself pull him in, and he moans.

I scream.

"Shit, Mary-Beth, are you okay?" Drew pulls out a little, but I grab his ass and bring him back.

"Drew, that spot. Holy shit, it feels good."

Drew thrusts again, a little more confident now. "That spot, Mary?" he asks, bottoming out again. I lift my hips to meet him. "Is that the fucking spot?"

"Yes, Drew. God. Yes. More."

"Your body was made for me, Mary. Just like I always knew." With his hand, he lifts my face to his. When our eyes meet, he flits his gaze down. "Look down." Drew moves inside me again. "Look how perfect we are together."

I do what he says, studying as I watch him move in and out of me. The thrill is indescribable.

Having my permission, Drew becomes a tad less gentle. He stares into my eyes as he thrusts again and again, each time hitting that magic spot that, as I said in my book, *I've saved my entire life for him.*

Our bodies jerk against each other, working into a rhythm, but our eyes never stray. I've never felt more connected to anyone. Ever. I'm positive I never will.

The more he thrusts, the more my body responds, the strings inside me coiling.

"Drew...what the—" I feel like my entire body is stretching and straining and bending to fit around him in a new way. The friction brings me to the edge, begging for release, pleading for it, demanding it, until finally, my whole world ruptures, shattering.

I moan as the pleasure washes over me from the inside out, filling me. It's a fire and an ocean and a warm cozy bed all at once. It's the feeling of being complete. Completely in love. Completely content. Completely connected. Completely me.

A split second later, Drew arches his back and sheaths himself so deep inside me, I'm not sure how I don't split in two. Then he growls and collapses on top of me.

My legs fall to the side as I slump against the mattress. Drew rises onto his elbows and kisses my eyes. My heart feels like he's holding it in his hands.

The room that, seconds ago was overfilling with passion, feels quiet. Peaceful. I let out a long, slow breath, and Drew lowers his mouth to mine, kissing me sweetly. Still inside me, I feel him pulse as he starts to relax.

"I love you, Mary." Drew rests his forehead against mine as he strokes my hair. "How are you feeling?"

I'm surprised when my eyes begin to water. I'm even more surprised when Drew's do too.

"I love you, too," I choke out, wrapping a hand around his neck. "That was perfect. Even better than the book."

Chapter 45

Andrew Edward Coyne
~~Actor~~ Producer

I've slept with countless women, but it's never been like this.
That was fucking.
  This is making love.
The two actions don't even belong in the same category.

Fucking is body only. Pleasure and lust. Taking, not giving.

Making love is all-consuming. Mind. Body. Heart. Soul. Connection and fulfillment. Giving and receiving.

It's so fucking cheesy, but honestly, tonight feels like the first time for me too.

Mary-Beth and I sleep a few hours until we're woken by the sun beating in through the window. She yawns and shifts in my arms, putting a hand to her eyes.

"I think everyone in Las Vegas can see us," she says groggily. She rolls onto her belly and puts a pillow over her head.

"Don't worry, we're too high up." I hop out of bed and yank the curtains closed.

When I return, Mary-Beth rolls onto her side, resting her head on her elbow and lifting her eyes to mine. Her little sleepy smile and her scrunched nose make the hollow part of my chest throb.

She's mine. Really mine. I still can't believe it.

"Drew, we need to talk about the book."

I take her free hand in mine, rubbing my fingers lazily across her tattoo.

"What book?" I tease.

Mary-Beth's eyes narrow. "Drew. Tomorrow will be two weeks. Obviously..." She sighs like what she's about to say is going to be painful. I don't even try to hide my smirk. "I'm going to sign over the rights to *Swallow Manor*. Let's just do it and get it over with."

She hops out of bed, rustling around in her suitcase. I watch her shadow, in awe of her. All of her. Her brilliant mind. Her sultry body. Her wit. Her sex appeal. Her sass. Everything. She returns to bed with paperwork and a pen.

"Roll over."

I obey, and she puts the papers on my back, pressing the pen against me to sign them.

"There," she huffs, setting the papers on the bedside table. "Done."

I kiss the inside of her wrist as she turns to me. "Told you I'd convince you."

She rolls her eyes and tosses a stray hair out of her face. "I sincerely hope that's not what all this was about."

"Much like Ambrose and Susan in book two..." I pull Mary-Beth closer, running my fingers across her naked back. "My initial intention became a trivial side effect of what I really desired."

"Lord, do you really have the entire series memorized?" She laughs, and her face falls into the space between my neck and my shoulder.

I lay back and guide her to rest on my chest. "I told you I did."

"Drew, as much as it pains me to say it, there's no one better to adapt my book than you." Mary-Beth's fingers dawdle across my chest. "I really mean that. You'll be the perfect Ambrose."

"About that..."

CHAPTER 45

She shifts her weight so she can look me in the eye. The crease in her forehead deepens. "About what?"

"I want to cast someone else to play Ambrose, Mary."

"What?" She shakes her head. "Why?"

"The more I think about it...the more I think I want to get out of acting. I'm ready for something else."

"But Drew, you're—"

I shrug, and Mary-Beth quits talking mid-sentence.

"Someone told me recently that I should start looking at the big picture, and I realized I don't want to do it anymore. I want to be behind the camera. To be honest, I'm freaking sick of the spotlight. I don't need to pretend to be something I'm not. Not anymore."

Mary-Beth blinks a few times before nodding. "If that's really what you want, then of course that's okay with me. After everything, that's a really brave choice."

"Well...you helped me make it. So, thank you."

She leans up and kisses me before resting her head back on my chest. "Someday, I hope I can be brave like that."

"What do you mean? You're like...one of the bravest people I know."

"I mean, going after what I really want. Like...out in the open."

"Publishing under your own name?"

Mary-Beth nods against my chest. "I think someday I'll be able to. Be okay with people judging me. To not hide anymore. I've imagined it a million times. It's going to feel so good. So liberating. Like, empowering, you know? I'm excited for that. One day."

I pause for a moment, considering Mary-Beth's words, my fingers trilling along her back.

Not taking the lighthouse script, making the TikTok, going to Daisy Bluff, ending my sponsorships, falling in love with Mary-Beth, and now leaving acting. Each choice feels like a step on the path to claiming who I want to be.

"I'm excited too." I pull Mary-Beth closer. "For the world to finally see how brilliant you are. If you give people a chance, it will be obvious."

She looks up at me and smiles. It's my final undoing.

"Now, if I remember correctly, I made you a promise about every door and wall and bed in the room."

Chapter 46

Mary-Beth Caroline Abernathy
Fool

At some point between the bed and the wall and the door...I finally fell asleep. I think my body finally reached its breaking point, and I just couldn't take any more pleasure. Also, I'd like to walk again in this lifetime.

I wake up to find a note on the pillow next to me.

MB-

Went out to scrounge up some food. There's a kickass sushi place on the other side of the Strip. You probably hate sushi (because I love it) but I'll be back with all the California rolls you can eat. And then you can tell me how much you hate them.

I love you. My smartass Virgin Mary. Can I still call you that?

-D

I smile and place the note on the bedside table. Next to it, my cell phone buzzes. I realize it's been buzzing. Even in my sleep, it was buzzing.

I have twenty-seven missed calls and double the texts. Mostly from Harper.

Anxiety chokes me, and I scroll through them, only pausing to read a few.

Harper: Shit has officially hit the fan.

Harper: What the hell is Drew thinking?

Harper: R u ok? Call me

My fingers are shaking as I dial her number, knowing I'm not going to like whatever she has to say.

"Mary-Beth. Thank God. Are you okay?"

"I think so..." I swallow a lump that's been building. "What's going on?"

"Holy shit. I've been trying to get a hold of you for hours. Have you not seen?"

"I've been asleep..." I don't know how long I've out. Or how long Drew's been gone. I glance at the clock. Nearly 8 p.m. My heart races. "For a while."

"Shit, MB. Shit. Shit. Shit. The news is out."

"What news?"

"The Minnie Maple news. Drew. He...he confirmed it."

Now my heart feels like someone just ripped it from my chest and chucked it through this thirty-six-story hotel window. My lungs feel like deflated punching bags.

I hang up the call without another word. My shaking fingers take me to Google.

I don't hesitate this time. I type **Mary-Beth Abernathy** without stopping once. I click *enter* without breathing.

Pages of articles and hundreds of pictures of me and Drew fill the screen. At the airport. At dinner. From last night. Each picture and headline makes my stomach turn more sour.

"She's Finally Been Found! Mary-Beth Abernathy Confirmed Bestselling Author of *Swallow Manor*"

"TikTok Sensation Mary-Beth Abernathy Has It All: A Bestselling Book Series AND the Movie's Star"

"*Swallow Manor* Author Mary-Beth Abernathy Confirmed Hours

CHAPTER 46

After Marriage to Hallmark Star Drew Coyne in Intimate Las Vegas Wedding"

I smack my forehead and run my fingers down my face, my eyes stopping to study the ring on my left hand. Like Drew predicted, it's already turning my finger green.

Funny how things can change overnight.

After scrolling through pages of articles, I finally get up the courage to click on one titled: "Drew Coyne Confirms *Swallow Manor's* Author Is Girlfriend, Mary-Beth Abernathy."

The article is short.

Swallow Manor fans, rejoice! After weeks of TikToks and false alarms, it seems Drew Coyne's search to find Minnie Maple has come to an end, and the movie is a go! Coyne's quest to find the bestselling Swallow Manor *author began when he made a TikTok asking for the anonymous writer to come forward, offering her the opportunity for his inchoate production company to buy the movie rights for an undisclosed amount of money.*

Two weeks ago, rumors flew when Drew was seen spending time with kindergarten teacher, Mary-Beth Abernathy. The two were photographed kissing at the airport and also at dinner, and a source confirmed that he had met her family when he spent a week in Mary-Beth's hometown of Daisy Bluff, Indiana. While repeatedly denying claims that Mary-Beth was the author in question, Drew finally confirmed the rumors Thursday afternoon.

"Mary-Beth is the author. It's obvious at this point. And I'm going to be the one to adapt Swallow Manor, *so I'll be making those decisions. Mary-Beth signed this morning."*

Drew failed to comment on his relationship status with Mary-Beth or their rumored Las Vegas nuptials.

My eyes pinch with tears as the boulder of betrayal crushes me.

There's a video attached to the article. I can barely see through my blurry eyes to click it.

Drew is standing somewhere along the Strip, holding what looks to be a takeout bag and scowling as he talks to someone off-camera. It seems like the video picks up mid-conversation.

"Mary-Beth's the author. It's obvious at this point." He practically spits out the words, his ice-blue eyes glaring to the right of the camera. The video seems to cut and paste here, picking up in the middle of his rant. "*I'm* going to be the one to adapt Swallow Manor, so *I'll* be making those decisions. Mary-Beth signed this morning."

I scream and throw my phone across the room. I curl up in a ball and pull the covers over my head. Then, the sobs come.

A douchebag and a fool. Just like I feared we'd be.

I'm not sure exactly how long I lay in bed crying. Could be minutes, could be hours. Eventually, I make my way to the bathroom. Everything from my lips to my nipples to my hips to my thighs is sore, and each step feels like emotional torture. More evidence of all Drew took from me. I dress and wash my face. Then I hear my phone buzzing again in the next room.

I miss the call but have a voicemail from work. I hold my breath as I listen.

"Hello, Mary-Beth, this is Charity Greene calling. As you know, here at Chapel Bluff Elementary, we hold our staff to the highest level of conduct and accountability. We want to set an example for our students and for our community of what strong Christian leadership looks like both here at school and also in our personal lives. With the disturbing information that has recently come to light about your personal life and hobbies, Mary-Beth, I'm sorry, but I have no choice but to suspend your employment until the board can meet and discuss further action. Effective immediately, your class will be taken over by a long-term sub. I'll reach back out about getting your room cleaned out and what you can expect going forward. Please, don't hesitate to call me if you have questions. God bless."

CHAPTER 46

I crumple to the floor, and the tears return tenfold.

My job. In all the worst-case scenarios I've imagined, I never thought I'd lose my job. My dignity, yes. My squeaky-clean reputation, duh. Even my family temporarily, maybe. But never my job. My body shakes as the shock settles.

My kids.

Who will make sure Colin doesn't use too much glue? Or that Henry makes it to the bathroom in time? Or reminds Ainsley the difference between B and D? Who will make sure Liam doesn't cry at parent drop-off? Or make sure Emilia gets tested for the gifted program? Who will teach them CVC words? Or sight words? Or how to count by tens? Or backward from a hundred?

Damn it, I love those kids. There's no one better to teach them than me. No one.

This isn't fair.

My phone buzzes again, and I jump, almost dropping it.

Drew: I'm sorry, Mary-Beth

Drew: It's not what you think

Drew: I'll be back soon, and I'll explain everything.

Drew: Please

There are twenty similar texts.

Panic seizes me. Followed shortly by blind rage.

Fuck Drew Coyne.

There's no way I'll be able to face him. He clearly knew what he was doing. The day after we sleep together and I sign the book rights, he tells a reporter I'm the author. There's no freaking way that's a coincidence.

He didn't care about the NDA or the money or even the book. He knew this would hurt me. Ruin my life. And he did it anyway.

New tears trickle down my cheeks.

Drew Coyne doesn't do love. He doesn't do relationships. He doesn't do women like me.

He does business deals and hookups. And he's used to getting what he wants. And I was the forbidden fruit, and now that I'm not...he knows the best way to get rid of me.

Brusquely wiping away the last of my tears, I rush around the room, stuffing what I can find into my suitcase. I rip off the piece-of-shit ring Drew gave me last night, throwing it on the table with the *Swallow Manor* paperwork. My vision blurring, I stare at the objects representing the two possessions I hold closest.

Drew completely ravaged both.

Chapter 47

Andrew Edward Coyne
Fool

A simple "fuck off" would have sufficed. But no, I had to go and have a conversation with her.

"Drew, oh my God, hey. Hey!"

I went through a long list of A-names, before finally remembering who the blond barreling down the sidewalk waving her arms was.

My gut reaction was to pretend I didn't see her and start walking the other way. Or to simply grunt a string of obscenities and ignore her. But then, I thought of Mary-Beth. She wouldn't approve of me being rude. Especially not to someone I'd previously slept with. I can just hear her voice now: *"You are the type..."*

So, I stopped. Turned.

"Britta." The name came out sounding like an annoyed sigh.

"Drew!" She tried to hug me. I stepped away. "How crazy! I didn't know you were in Vegas."

"Yep. In town with my girlfriend."

"Aww, Drew." She stuck out her bottom lip. It made her look like a fish. "So, it's true you're dating someone. That's cute."

"Yep." I moved to the side to try and pass. I did the obligatory polite small talk shit. Now I can leave.

"Mary-Beth was so sweet when we met. Though..." Britta laughed, and my blood turned cold. "I have to admit she's not your usual type."

I shouldn't have taken the fucking bait. I should have known better. Fool.

"You've met Mary-Beth?"

"A couple days ago. At your apartment. I came by for our weekly, well...you know." Her voice trailed off, and she laughed.

Fuck pleasantries.

"We have no weekly *thing*, Britta," I practically snarled. "Don't kid yourself. I can hardly remember your fucking name."

"Doesn't mean you've never screamed it."

My hands clenched into fists like I was about to attack. The idea of fucking anyone other than Mary-Beth felt so wrong, especially someone like the desperate bitch across from me, especially after last night.

A couple days ago.

My insides twisted. The day Mary-Beth almost burned down my kitchen. No wonder she was acting so weird.

My voice turned murderous. "What did you say to her?"

"Just the obvious. That she would never be anything more than a hookup. Poor thing looked heartbroken. She obviously doesn't understand how you operate. When are you going to tell her you're only sleeping with her for the book?"

"Mary-Beth is my girlfriend," I bit off. "Stop being such a jealous bitch."

Britta shrugged. "Jealous bitch or not, I'm not stupid. I know exactly who Mary-Beth is, Drew. You're not fooling anyone."

My eyes narrowed. My nostrils flared. I tried to remember to fucking breathe.

"You have no idea what you're saying. *I* don't even know who the author is."

CHAPTER 47

Britta pulled something from her purse, flashing it at me. I recognized it instantly.

MB-

I have a business meeting with Darcy this morning. I'll be home around five. Gonna write another book about me? If not, feel free to buy a new plant or lamp at your discretion. The photogs camped outside will love it.

And so will I.

-D

"Where did you get that?" My words are gravel under tire tracks. Where panic meets rage.

"Like I said..." She shrugged. "I spent a lovely afternoon with Minnie Maple."

I took an intentional step toward Britta, lowering my voice. "What do you want?" I growled. "What do I have to do to get you out of my fucking life?"

"Simple." Her eyes shimmered astutely. "I want to play Susan."

"Fuck off. That's not happening."

"Let me rephrase that." Britta stepped closer, lowering her voice. "I want to play Susan, or that note goes public."

Britta's nasty-ass perfume hit me, and I took a few steps back.

"Okay, so Mary-Beth is the author." I threw my hands up in defeat. "I guess it's obvious at this point. But you're fucking insane if you think I'm going to cast you as Susan."

I thought back to my conversation with Mary-Beth that morning. She's trusting me to not fuck this up. And anything involving Britta definitely classifies as a fuck-up. I should know.

"Well...maybe I should ask Mary-Beth. I'm sure she wouldn't want that note to go public. Maybe I could convince *her* I'd make a good Susan."

"*I'm* going to be the one to adapt *Swallow Manor*, so *I'll* be making those decisions. Mary-Beth signed this morning."

Five sentences.

Just when I thought I'd finally figured out my life, it only took five simple sentences to fuck it all up.

Because Britta hadn't ever intended on releasing my note. Hell, I don't even think she wanted to play Susan. She wanted money. And some asshat was filming our entire exchange, planning to sell it to the highest bidder.

Two hours later, she'd done just that.

I hadn't known exactly what Britta was planning to do, but Will and I tried to stop her anyway. Unfortunately, by the time we made it to the police department to file an official blackmail report, it was too late—the damage was done.

The video of me telling the world Mary-Beth was Minnie Maple was everywhere.

☙ ❧ ☙

I've got Darcy on the phone as I rush through the Bellagio. She wants to talk social media strategy and work on our official statement, but my only goal in life right now is getting back to Mary-Beth. I've been gone four hours. And my gut – and unreturned calls and texts – tells me that's four hours too long.

"We should take this to the court of public opinion," Darcy says. "Let's make a TikTok exposing that dumb bitch. Once the trolls get done with her, there will be nothing left."

I make it to the hallway and sprint, throwing open the door to our room. I think, before I even looked inside, I knew.

Mary-Beth is gone.

And she only left two things behind.

The pawn shop ring and the *Swallow Manor* paperwork.

Scribbled on the bottom are the words: *The only things you ever really wanted*

Chapter 48

Mary-Beth Caroline Abernathy
Sinner
Again
Always

I turned off my phone and took the red-eye back to Indiana that night. I spent the next two days in bed.

I hated Drew even more when I couldn't find anything good to watch on TV. Add *ruining my favorite television programming* to the list of things he's done.

And still more when I couldn't even bring myself to open my computer. Who knows if I'll ever be able to write again.

And when I washed my hair five times in a row and still couldn't get out all the glitter, my hatred had reached unfathomable levels.

By Sunday morning, I don't know what else to do. I end up at church.

The whispers start before I've even entered the building. Snickers from a wife to her husband. A friend to a neighbor. From a pack of teenagers I've known since before they were born. I pretend like I don't hear them, but I do.

"What's she doing here?"

"Wrote that obscene book."

"That dirty book."

"That *pornographic* book."
"Ran away with that actor."
"Did you *see* the TikTok?"
"Stayed at his house."
"Not surprised that didn't last."
"Sleeping around."
"Whore."
"Disgrace."
"Pastor Abernathy's daughter."
"*So* ashamed."

People I've known for years won't look at me. Those who will look like they're praying for my soul. They shield their kids' eyes as if looking at me will make my sinfulness rub off.

Finally, I make it to my pew. Second row, clear view of the pulpit. Nana isn't here today, but Mama is. She doesn't even flinch when I slide in next to her.

"Hey, Mama." My voice is small.

"Mary-Beth."

The service starts. My dad stands at the pulpit, glancing, out of habit, at our row. His gaze meets mine, and he smiles, his eyes crinkling at the sides. It's enough to keep me from sobbing through his sermon.

Afterward, Mama is gone before the organ even starts playing. Feeling utterly dejected and not knowing what else to do, I find Pamela Allen, the woman in charge of youth Sunday School.

"Hey, Pam!" I greet her as warmly as I can, forcing a smile. "Need any help with Sunday School today?"

"Mary-Beth, hi." Her eyes don't meet mine, and she shifts her weight away. "I, uh, I think we've got it covered today. Thanks."

"Are you sure? You guys always need help," I press with an awkward chuckle.

"Yeah...um, I think it's better if you don't." Without another word,

CHAPTER 48

she's gone. I hear her grab someone in the hallway, asking if they would be able to fill in for the twelve-year-old class.

Tears threatening, I make my way back to the chapel, empty now. I slump into my pew and can't help but sob.

Add another thing to the list: my church family. I've never felt so unwanted in my entire life.

I look up at the cross above the pulpit through blurry eyes. "If I was expected to be perfect," I sputter, "then what's the point?"

A half hour later, chatter erupts outside as Sunday School lets out. Luckily, no one comes back inside. I hide further down in the pew in case they do.

I wait another half hour, wanting to make sure everyone is gone before I slink back to my car. I'm just about to pop my head up to assess when a gentle hand on my shoulder startles me.

"Bethie."

"Daddy." I burst into tears again, diving into his arms, his comforting scent enveloping me.

"It's okay, Bethie. I'm here." He rubs my hair gently as I cry into his jacket.

I feel like I'm seven years old again, my dad coming to my rescue after Crew Carter pulled my hair the first day of second grade. Or thirteen, the first and only time I flunked a math test. Or seventeen, when I got back from that dreadful date with Sutton.

"Thank God, you're home, Bethie. We've been so worried." My dad pulls away, wiping my stray tears. His blue eyes shine down on me. "I'm so glad you came today."

I take a cleansing breath. "Well..." I laugh a little. "I think you're the only one. Mama won't even look at me. Everyone else thinks I'm...I'm—"

I can't finish that sentence.

"No one thinks that, Bethie." His warm smile doesn't have a hint of judgment. "They just love a scandal."

"This is definitely a scandal." I slump back into my seat, hanging my head.

"And there will be a new one next week. This will all blow over, you'll see."

My dad sits down and puts his arm around me.

I rest my head on his shoulder. "Daddy, do you think I'm a horrible person?" My bottom lip quivers as I look up at him.

His clear blue eyes shine. "Of course not."

"But the book—"

"I've heard it's really popular. And really, really good."

I sit up a little bit. "What?"

"That's why Nana isn't here today, you know. She got her hands on a copy and stayed up all night reading. She's really proud of you, Mary-Beth."

My heart swells. "Really?"

"Really." My dad pulls me against his chest and kisses my hair. "Now she's trying to get me to read it."

"Lord, please no." I laugh. Please, *please* no.

"Don't worry." He laughs too and ruffles my hair. "Unlike my mother, romance isn't my usual genre."

We are silent for a few moments, some of the anxiety easing from my system.

"What happened with Drew, Bethie?"

The anxiety returns. Tenfold. As do the tears. "Mama was right about him. He only wanted one thing. And now that he's gotten it…"

Again, I can't finish the sentence.

"I'm sorry, Bethie. I'm sure that really hurts." He pauses, the arm around me constricting. "Want me to kick his ass?"

My eyes dart up. "Did you just cuss?" I hush my voice and look at the cross. "In *church*?"

CHAPTER 48

"Mary-Beth, no one is perfect. Not me. Not you. Not anyone."

"Definitely not me."

My dad runs his fingers along the pew in front of us. "These seats are full of imperfect people. Every single week. But there's always a place for them here. And for me. And there will *always* be a place for you too."

"But after the book and Drew and –"

"I'm not saying that whatever happened with the book or with Drew or anything else is a sin or it isn't, Mary-Beth. That isn't up to me. But you should know that we are all sinners. We all have good and bad inside us. But that doesn't make us any less worthy. Any less deserving of love."

"Then, what about the school? They fired me. And Mama?" I bite the inside of my cheek as my voice chokes again.

"Forget the school. If they fire you over this stupid thing, they don't deserve you. You're an excellent teacher. You'll find another job easily. And your mother..." My dad sighs. "Well...she loves you, Bethie. More than you'll ever know."

"I feel like I've let her down." I smooth down the fabric of my dress. "Like I've let everyone down."

"You never let me down, Bethie. My baby girl. A bestselling author. I'm so proud."

I peek up at him through my eyelashes. "Even if it's a smutty romance novel?"

"Even then. If you wrote it, then I'm proud."

I throw my arms around my dad's neck, holding tight. "Thanks, Daddy. I love you."

"Love you too, Bethie."

We stand to leave, but my dad turns back. "Give your Mama a little grace, Bethie. And some time. She's fighting a few demons of her own."

That night, I go to my parents' house. It's Sunday night, and it's tradition. And even if Mama isn't speaking to me, tradition is tradition, damn it.

She's had eight hours. Plenty of time.

I creak open the door and take a tentative step inside. The house is quiet and isn't filled with its usual yummy Sunday-night smells. The floorboard by the coat closet that has squeaked since I was a little girl sings out when I step on it, and Mama peeks her head up from the living room.

"Mary-Beth," she says coldly from her big rocking chair in the corner. "I wasn't expecting you."

"Well…" I shrug. "It *is* Sunday."

"Yes, I guess it is." She looks up from a book. "Your father isn't home yet. He had to stay late at the church for some meetings. I haven't even started on dinner yet."

"That's okay, we don't have to eat." I take a deep breath. "Really, I just wanted to talk."

Something flashes in my mother's eyes. Dread? Betrayal? Panic? It's too hard to place and is gone in an instant. She sets down her book and motions me inside.

I slink into the big armchair next to her. The bedtime story chair when I was a child. The chair I used to take naps in between school and cheerleading practice when I was a teenager. I crack my knuckles, take a deep breath, and launch into the speech I prepared on the drive over.

"Mama, I should have listened to you about Drew. You were right about him. You were right about everything. And I'm sorry that I did it anyway. I was stupid. And I'm sorry that I said you didn't know—"

"I do know, darling." Mama sighs. "That's why I was trying to warn you."

CHAPTER 48

"What do you mean?"

"Mary-Beth, before I met your father, there was another man. Tucker Ridgeway." Mama looks past me, her eyes on the wall next to my face. "And he was tall and handsome and everything a teenage girl thinks she wants. Rebellious and dangerous and exhilarating. And oh, how I loved him. Or at least, I thought I did. And well...when we were together, I crossed the line. You know what I mean."

I nod. *Oh yes, I do.*

"Does Daddy know?"

"He does."

"And he didn't care. He doesn't care." It's not a question. I know my dad.

"No, of course not." Mama smiles, but it doesn't meet her eyes. "But...it affected our relationship in other ways."

"What do you mean?"

"Mary-Beth, when I was dating Tucker, I got pregnant."

Without meaning to, my mouth falls open.

"And when I told him...he left."

I can feel Mama's heart breaking from here. I reach over and take her hand, and she offers me a sad smile.

"And then...then I didn't know what to do." Mama's voice is so quiet and raspy with emotion, I can barely hear her. I lean closer. "So, I ended the pregnancy."

"Oh, Mama." I hop out of my chair and go sit on her lap, throwing my arms around her neck. She starts to sob, her tears wetting my cheeks.

"I was only eighteen," she whispers. "I'm sorry."

We sit in our tears for a few minutes, rocking together in my mother's big rocking chair. I rub her hair and tell her I love her and I won't judge her and this doesn't change how I feel about her. How she is the best mother and person and nothing could ever change that.

"I've always wondered," she says through a murk of emotion. "If that's why I couldn't have children. If it was God punishing me."

"No, Mama." I smooth down her hair. I've never seen it out of place like this. "Of course not. Of course, God wouldn't do that."

"I'm just so grateful..." She looks at me and smiles, her eyes shining with tears. "So grateful that whatever the reason, I was able to have you."

"I'm so grateful too. That you're my mom."

When Mama regains her composure, she looks at me with eyes that could melt steel. "And this is why I was so strict with you." Her voice switches from motherly love to tough love in an instant. "Because I didn't want this for you. I didn't want you to go through what I went through."

I nod, feeling the gravity of those words. "I understand."

"I'm sorry I didn't do my job." Her voice warbles again. "I'm sorry I failed you."

"You didn't fail me. There are just some things..." I look away, picking at my fingernails. My left ring finger is still green. "That I needed to figure out for myself, I guess."

"I hope you were careful, at least."

I laugh a little. "With the sex, yes." My mother winces but doesn't interrupt. "With my heart, not so much."

"Please tell me you didn't actually marry him."

"Lord, no. Thank goodness."

"I'm so sorry, darling." Mama lets out a relieved sigh as she smooths a lock of my hair. "Your first heartbreak hurts no matter how it happens."

I shrug. "You warned me he was the type."

Uncomfortable silence settles over us.

"So tell me about this book," Mama finally says.

Lord, here we go. "It's a romance novel. With...all the things that

CHAPTER 48

usually come with a romance novel." I laugh awkwardly. "And then some."

"What made you want to write a romance novel?"

"I honestly don't know. I'm really questioning my sanity at this point."

"Nana says it's amazing."

"So I've heard."

Mama reaches down and picks up the book she was reading. I nearly fall out of her lap when I see what it is.

"She brought over book one after church today." She runs her fingers across the cover. "And talked a little bit of sense into me. I haven't been able to put it down since she left. I'm about halfway through."

I lean back so I can look my mother in the eyes. Expecting disappointment, I only find love.

"Wait, what?"

"You're an amazing writer, darling. How did I never know?"

"So you're not—" I cock my head to the side, still convinced this is some sort of cruel joke. "You're not disappointed in me? You're not mad?"

Mama laughs and fans the book pages. "I'm not going to pretend like it isn't a shock, because it is. And I was hurt that you kept it from me, but I see why you did. I was surprised you chose such an...*arousing* topic. There are definitely some scenes I've had to skim. But, darling, you're a storyteller. A really, really good one. And it's not as bad as everyone says. I'd say it's very tasteful, honestly."

I throw my arms around Mama's neck again, squeezing her with all the energy I have left.

"I thought we'd lost you, darling. When I saw the news about..." Mama shakes her head. "After our fight, I wasn't sure you would come home. I'm sorry I didn't give you the welcome you needed. I was still hurt."

"Home is literally the only thing I want right now." I curl up in her lap, just like I did when I was a little girl. "No matter what happens, you'll never lose me."

"Having you as my daughter is the best thing in my life. I hope you know that, Mary-Beth."

"I do, Mama. I love you so much."

"I love you too, darling."

The front door opens.

"Are those my two favorite girls?"

Daddy drops his bags by the door and comes over to the rocking chair. He gathers Mama and me into his arms, where we all start crying again.

And I know at that moment, no matter what happens with my book or Drew or anything else, I'm going to be okay.

🐦🐦🐦

Driving home, I feel lighter than I have in months. Maybe years. I don't think you realize how much secrets weigh you down until you're free from them.

I turn up the Beastie Boys and crank down my window, letting the wind rustle my hair.

It seems we really are all sinners. All under construction. All just doing our best and failing a lot of the time.

But that's not a bad thing.

Actually, I couldn't think of anything better.

Chapter 49

Mary-Beth Caroline Abernathy
Mary

When I get home, Harper is at my apartment.

"MB," she says in her Mother-Goose, best-friend sort of way, squeezing me tight. Then she pushes me away. "What the hell?"

I put a hand to my heart. Lord knows it's been through enough the past few days. "What?"

"What happened to your phone? Some of us have been worried."

"Oh."

"I wasn't even sure you left Las Vegas until Kinsley Reeder tweeted that you were causing a scene at church this morning. Do you know how many hotel casinos I've looked through the past two days?"

I run a hand down my face. "I'm sorry, Harp. I turned my phone off. It was too much."

Harper pulls me back into a hug, her rainbow hair flinging into my face. "I get that, MB. I'm just glad we found you."

I snuggle in and take a deep breath. "Same, Harp."

When we finally part, Harper reveals a bottle of vodka hiding in her purse. "Wanna have a drink and debrief?"

"The purse vodka again? Really?" I laugh and lead her inside. "Isn't that how this whole mess started?"

"If you ask me, I think purse vodka is good luck."

Harper leads me into the kitchen and lovingly pours me a drink while I grab the ice cream. *Cooking for One* is still on the counter along with the plants that are now officially dead, and the empty Merlot bottle Drew and I shared. I swallow the emotion building in the back of my throat and give her a weak smile.

"Shall we?" I crook my head toward the living room. With bay breezes and spoons in hand, Harper and I snuggle onto the couch.

She tucks a foot beneath her and turns to me. "Before you say anything, MB, I think you should watch something."

She hands me her phone. I take a sip.

When I see Drew's face, I take a gulp.

"I don't want to talk to Drew." My lips pucker as the alcohol slips down the back of my throat.

"Lord, Mary-Beth. Just watch the damn video." Harper sighs and takes her own swallow. "Then you can decide if you do or don't want to talk to him."

I huff and set down my drink.

Drew's frowning face is frozen on the screen. The video, posted Thursday night, is the only thing on his Instagram page. The ads and pictures of Maggie and gym selfies—gone. The video searching for Minnie Maple—gone. Just this one lonely video that already has 81.7 million views. I hold the phone with shaking hands.

Drew is wearing a gray hoodie and sitting in our hotel room at the Bellagio. Behind him, the bed is still unmade. My ring and the *Swallow Manor* papers are on the table where I left them. The all-too-familiar feeling of anxiety settles over me as I click.

"Hey, Drew here."

My eyes sting at just the sound of his voice.

He sounds tired. And sad.

CHAPTER 49

Same.

"As many of you know, I've been searching for someone the past few weeks. And no, it hasn't been Minnie Maple. Well, maybe it started that way, but while looking for Minnie Maple, I realized I was actually looking for someone else."

Drew closes his eyes and takes a long, slow breath. When he opens them, he looks directly at the camera. "The person I was looking for doesn't have a dog named Maggie. In fact, this person is highly allergic to dogs and can't be in the same room as one for more than thirty minutes without breaking into hives. Also, this person doesn't prefer one brand of hiking boot or granola bar or face cream over another, and he actually hates sleeping in hammocks under the stars. He prefers a bed.

"This person despises kiwi-blueberry smoothies with turmeric and pumpkin seeds. He's known all along they make people puke. And taste like shit. This person tries to recycle but doesn't always. He should try harder. He hates talking about his feelings. And really hates pretending to be something he's not, though he tricked himself into thinking that's how he had to be for way too long. And he isn't the perfect Hallmark boyfriend. Turns out, he's actually a pretty shitty boyfriend. And...he doesn't enjoy starring in made-for-TV movies either. Or even acting at all anymore, really.

"Along the way, I discovered this person also has a very strong preference for how to make a peanut butter and jelly sandwich. For which *Harry Potter* book is their favorite. For In-N-Out Burger over Shake Shack. That this person would rather stay in and read a book or do a puzzle than go to a nightclub or party. That they would rather go to Disneyland and babysit and get thrown up on riding the teacups than..."—He smiles. Butterflies and tears betray me. "Just about anything else."

I open and close my hands, trying to keep them from trembling as I steady the phone. The air in the room feels like it's laced with intensity.

"In his personal life, the person I was looking for was known for sleeping with and using women. For hiding demons from his past and using them as excuses to keep people out. But when I finally found this person, I realized he wasn't like that anymore. Because when I found this person, he was different.

"All his life, this person's favorite color had been red. But—" Drew smiles. It leaks into his voice. "After meeting a girl with brown, emerald-speckled eyes wearing a green dress, he realized it had actually been green all along. He realized that reading for twelve hours straight in a library in the middle-of-nowhere Indiana is heaven, when you're sitting next to the right person. That with that person, arguing and dancing and kissing just to kiss is fun. It's everything. That opening up and letting someone in and being vulnerable and genuine is safe. That if it's the right person, it's okay to let them change you. To make you better. To let yourself fall.

"I realized that while I thought I was looking for Minnie Maple, the person I was actually looking for was myself. But not the version of myself I always thought I was, the version I thought I was stuck being forever. Because the person I found...is a person I actually want to be."

Drew stops. Rubs the back of his neck. Looks straight at the camera. His eyes are so disarmingly blue, I hold my breath.

"Please, Mary." His voice catches on my name as he blinks away tears. My own tears finally spill. "I've realized the only version of myself I want is the version when I'm with you. You make me better. Braver. More genuine. More opinionated too, but in a good way. You make me into the person I want to be. God, and *happy*. So freaking happy, Mary.

"And I know I screwed up. And I broke your trust and hurt you. Mary, you have no idea how sorry I am. I hope you'll give me the chance to explain. Because I think when I was trying to find myself, I found you

CHAPTER 49

too." Drew shifts his weight toward the camera. " Mary, you're braver than you think. Louder. Stronger. Cooler. And feistier, too. In all the good ways." He laughs. I can't help it; I laugh too. "So, please, I'm begging you, Mary-Beth. Please. Please, let me find you again."

The video ends. I don't even blink. It starts to play again, and I watch it two more times.

When I finally look away, Harper is gone.

"Mary."

I turn to find Drew standing in the doorway. He's still wearing the gray hoodie and looks like he hasn't slept in three days. He's also still wearing his pawn shop wedding band.

My heart stops as I scamper to my feet. "Drew, what are you doing here?"

"Well, when I finally found out where you were, I came as soon as I could. I wanted to come to Indiana on Friday, but Harper thought you wouldn't come home, and I don't know, I thought she might know you better than I d—"

"I mean... Drew, what *the hell* are you doing here?"

Drew rubs a tired hand across the back of his neck. "Mary, I'm sorry. It was Britta. She orchestrated the whole thing. Tried to blackmail me into letting her play Susan. And I shouldn't have talked to her. And I really shouldn't have admitted you were the author. Shit, I did it all wrong."

"You knew what this would do to me, Drew. And after everything..." My voice trails off as I swipe at a tear streaming down my cheek. "How could you?"

"God, Mary. I'm an idiot. I'm so, so sorry I'm such a fucking idiot. I *love you*, Mary. I didn't mean to hurt you. I didn't mean any of this."

"I lost my job, Drew."

"Your job?" Drew's eyes go wide with shock. "Shit, Mary. I didn't—"

"No one in town will look at me. If it wasn't for Nana, my mother would have disowned me. I can't watch my favorite TV shows anymore. I'm pretty sure I'll never write again. Everyone in the country knows my most intimate secrets. I'm still..." My voice chokes and grows quiet. "I'm still *sore*, Drew. You took everything from me. *Everything.*" My voice drops to nothing more than a whimper. "Just leave. Please."

Drew wipes away tears as he nods in acceptance, turning toward the door. "I just hope you know"—his eyes jump to mine—"I'm a better person because of you, Mary-Beth. You've changed my life. You've changed *me*. And I'm so, so sorry I couldn't do the same for you. You deserve so much more."

He grips the doorknob and stalks into the hall. When the door slams, my heart breaks into a million pieces.

I'm on my feet a split second later.

"I could sue you," I call down the hall.

Drew stops and turns back.

"I *should* sue you."

"You should," he says, shrugging. His face is stained with tears. "I would."

"I shouldn't let you have my book."

"Of course, Mary. I'll have Will send over the paperwork."

I take a few steps into the hallway.

"What am I supposed to say to this?" I motion to the phone, trying not to let my voice tremble.

"God, Mary. I don't know." Drew rubs the back of his neck and takes a step toward me. "I just thought... I thought it was a good idea. Since I didn't know where you were. And since, I don't know, since that's how I found you before. When I didn't know who you wer—"

I cut him off and stick up my chin. "Did you mean this?" I wave the phone in his face. "Did you mean this, or was it just another publicity stunt? Something to get likes and follows and movie deals and money.

CHAPTER 49

Or did you—" My voice sputters. "Did you really mean it?"

"I meant every word, Mary. Damn it, of course I did. I don't care if anyone else sees it, as long as you see it. As long as you know the truth."

"Well, I think it was a horrible idea."

Drew shakes his head. "I'm sor—"

"Because you should have just come." I'm choking on emotion as I close the rest of the distance between us. I poke his chest and glare up at him as I chastise him through my tears. "The second I left, you should have followed me. You knew where I'd be. You know me better than anyone. Even Harper.

"The past two days have been hell, Drew. With the school and my mom and everything else. But mostly because I thought... I thought you didn't care. I thought it wasn't real. I thought you didn't love m—"

Before I can finish, I'm in his arms, his lips pressed to mine. We kiss with the ferocity of starving people who don't know if they'll ever eat again.

We're both crying when he pulls away.

"Of course I love you, Mary-Beth." He strokes my cheeks, his blue eyes shining down at me. "God, I missed you. I missed you and your smart mouth so much. It's all real. It's always been real for me. And I'm so sorry. I'm sorry I'm an idiot and almost lost you."

"I love you too, Drew."

I push onto my tiptoes to kiss him again, but he drops to one knee and pulls out the pawn shop ring, holding it up. My heart feels too big for my body.

"I haven't had a chance to upgrade the ring yet. But please. Marry me, Mary-Beth Caroline Abernathy. I want to argue with you. Every day. I want you to tell me I'm wrong and piss me off. I want to push your buttons and make you roll your eyes. I want to make you louder.

Empowered. I want you to make me better. Genuine.

"The past few weeks have been the best of my life, Mary. The most fun. The happiest. The scariest, too. Because I'd never had anything real before. And once I had you, I was so freaking scared to lose you. And when I did..."

Drew's voice cuts off with emotion. He clears his throat and shakes his head, wiping away tears. "The last two days have been hell for me too. From unhappy to the happiest I've ever been to freaking wrecked. The change you made in my life, *in me*, was impossible to ignore. Or forget. I can't imagine my life without you in it anymore, Mary. In just a few weeks, you've become everything to me. So please, please marry me. I don't beg. I hate to beg. But I'm begging you. Be mine. Forever. I promise I'll spend the rest of my life trying to convince you it's a good idea, even though we both know it's probably not."

I pull Drew to his feet and push my body against him.

"I've never hated someone as much as I hate you." I put my hands on his neck. "Truly."

He grabs the fabric at my waist. "God, same."

"But I've never loved anyone more, either."

Drew wipes away tears. Laughs. Nods.

"So what do you say?" He moves a stray piece of hair from my eyes, and I lean into his touch. "Will you spend the rest of your life arguing and kissing and fighting and dancing and eating and exploring and telling stories and making love with me? Because God, I couldn't do it with anyone else. Life. Love. Hate. Any of it."

"Yes," I croak out. I can barely manage the word through my tears. "Yes, I'll marry you."

Drew squeezes my waist and kisses me. My giggles trip into his mouth.

"I knew you were the type." Drew rests his forehead against mine.

"And what type is that?"

CHAPTER 49

"My type."

THE END

Epilogue

3 Months Later

Mary-Beth Caroline Abernathy
Lion-Hearted

"And Christine knew, at that precise moment, that everything she thought she knew about life was wrong. She wasn't a forgotten plaything or novelty left on the shelf, collecting dust, never to be chosen or cherished. For life, she realized, wasn't meant to be waited upon–it was meant to be lived. Every moment. With every breath. Life was meant to be whatever she made of it. Whatever she wanted it to be. She was meant to be daring and dauntless.

"And she realized, she was. She was lion-hearted. Because, even when she felt like she couldn't, she did."

I close the book and tentatively look up at the audience. It's night one of the press tour for my new book series, and the bookstore is standing-room-only with a line stretching for blocks outside. Darcy is a marketing genius, after all.

Everyone takes a collective breath as I exhale, and then bursts into applause.

"Thank you. Thank you guys so much." I smile down at my book,

EPILOGUE

turning it over in my hands. My new Tiffany engagement ring twinkles up at me. My finger is still slightly green beneath it.

The crowd grows quiet when I look up. "You know, I really wanted to share this section because it's very poignant for me. I wrote this section of the book before my identity as Minnie Maple was so infamously revealed." I glance at Drew, and he smirks, his blue eyes shining. "But I did write it after I'd met someone who brought out my voice. My opinions. My fierceness. And being with him gave me a glimpse of what could be. What I wanted to be.

"I always knew that I *wanted* to be brave. But after meeting him, I also found myself wishing I could be open and vulnerable. I wanted to be an active participant in the life I felt was happening all around me, and to me, but that didn't really include me. I wanted to be free of my secret, but I didn't know how.

"Fear and judgment kept me on the sidelines. Kept me from reaching my true potential. I made incorrect assumptions about the people around me. I assumed people wouldn't accept me. That they would judge me. Shun me. And when I was pushed off the cliff of self-discovery, some might say a bit prematurely..." I cock an eyebrow as my voice trails off, and the crowd bursts into laughter. Drew only shrugs and keeps smirking. "Unfortunately, when my truth came out, some of those assumptions turned out to be true. And that was hard. Really hard.

"But in the end, those rejections made me stronger. More empathetic. More accepting of others. And I discovered that the people who really matter to me, love me regardless." I look at Mama and Daddy, sitting in the front row, beaming with pride. At Harper, wiping away tears. At Nana, clutching all ten of my published books. "Regardless of past prejudices, of past hurt, of past trauma, of past experience. Because when you love someone, you accept them as is. You accept the work in progress. Because, aren't we all?

"So, my advice to you tonight is: be daring. Be dauntless. Be lion-hearted. Don't let fear and judgment keep you from telling your story. Be true to who you are and remember there is no right way. Only your way. If Christine has taught us anything, it's that."

🐑🐑🐑

I sign books for over four hours. It's almost midnight when the last person finally steps forward. It's a woman about my age and height, and when I look into her eyes, I can't help but see myself. I grab a book from the nearly depleted pile.

"Hi! I'm Mary-Beth! What's your name?"

"Marley Ann," she says in a quiet voice.

"It's nice to meet you, Marley Ann. Thank you so much for coming out tonight. I'm sorry the wait was so long. Who would you like me to make the book out to?"

"Oh, just me is fine."

"Awesome."

I scribble my generic message and sign. I close the book and hand it to the girl.

She clutches the book but doesn't say anything. She doesn't turn to leave either.

"Would you like to take a selfie?" I offer.

"Yes, please." The girl chuckles and fumbles to free her cell phone.

We pose and smile, and then I sit and fold my arms across the table. I thank her again for coming.

She still doesn't leave. From the corner of my eye, I see Drew, leaning on a bookshelf, waiting for me.

The girl catches me looking past her. "Sorry, I should let you go. I'm just so nervous. You're, like, my favorite author. And I've never met someone famous before."

I nearly snort. I'll never get used to being considered famous. "Believe me, I'm just a normal person. Nothing special."

"Actually, that was what drew me to your story."

"I'm so glad you connected with the books."

"No." The girls swallows. "I mean your, um, *your* story."

"Oh." In the hundreds of people I'd talked to tonight, about half had asked about Drew and my's story. But no one had asked about *mine*.

"I, um, I was in an abusive relationship. I mean, it didn't start out like that. It never does, right?" The girl laughs softly. "But yeah, we met at church. And we both knew better, but we, you know, went too far. And then he used to use that against me to make me stay."

My throat constricts, and tears prick behind my eyes.

Marley Ann shifts her weight from side to side, her gaze studying her shoes. "He used to say no one else would want me. That I was damaged. That I should just be glad *he* still wanted me."

"I'm so sorry, Marley Ann." I shake my head. "That's horrible. You don't deserve that."

Marley Ann nods. "When I heard your story...a pastor's daughter from a small town who writes spicy romance novels.... Well, I knew I had to read them." She laughs and meets my eyes. "Mary-Beth, they were amazing. And, well...it was the first time I'd ever seen sex as a positive thing and not as a weapon. And I realized it didn't have to be like this. And I just really wanted to thank you. For giving me the courage to leave."

I stumble out of my chair and throw my arms around Marley Ann's neck. I squeeze tight, and we both shake with tears.

I pull away first but keep my hands on her shoulders. "This makes it all worth it," I rasp, tears streaming down my face. "All of it. Thank you so much for being here."

We exchange phone numbers, and Marley Ann finally leaves.

Drew emerges from behind a bookshelf. He grabs my green dress and uses the fabric to reel me in, until his hands rest on the dimples of my back.

"Well, well, well, would you look at that. Virgin Mary out here changing lives," Drew teases, his eyes gleaming. "I feel like someone predicted that..."

"Seriously, just to help that one girl." I bring my hands to my heart. "It makes it all worth it."

Drew turns serious, connecting his eyes with mine. "For every person you meet, there are a hundred others, Mary. Probably more."

"I never realized how much of an impact I could have, just by...by being myself."

"I did."

I bite my bottom lip. "You are the type."

"What type is that?"

"To believe in me...even when I don't believe in myself."

"This is just the beginning, Mary. Just wait..."

The past few months truly have felt like a new beginning. Since officially getting engaged, I moved in with Drew and got hired at one of his old elementary schools a few weeks later. In the fall, I'll be teaching kindergarten while Drew is producing *Swallow Manor*. Next spring, we're getting married in Daisy Bluff.

It's like my life has officially become a Hallmark movie.

An X-rated Hallmark movie with lots of passionate, life-changing sex starring an erotic romance writer. But a Hallmark movie, with its happily ever after, adorable everyday moments, and smoking hot, perfectly imperfect leading man, nonetheless.

I guess reformed rakes really do make the best husbands after all.

"Life is gonna be so different," I say.

Drew laughs, and his head falls back. "So different." He snaps back and smiles down at me. "But you're the type. The change-the-freaking-world type. So you'll be fine."

I rise onto my tiptoes, and his mouth covers mine as he meets me halfway.

EPILOGUE

"I love you, Mary-Beth soon-to-be-Coyne. God, you're amazing."

"I love you too."

Drew's eyes stray from my face to a door in the distance. His head cocks in that direction.

"I think I spy a closet." He runs his fingers across my breasts, and my nipples perk with instant need. "And I think the bookstore owner already locked up and went home."

Giggling, Drew leads me across the room and flings open the door.

Inside, a cry rings out, and two semi-dressed bodies jump out of view, their heads peeking out from behind various cleaning supplies.

My eyes widen. "Harper?"

"*Will?*" Drew gapes.

Harper blushes, covered waist-up with a broom. "Umm...surprise?"

Made in United States
Troutdale, OR
07/03/2023